OTHER BOOKS

DEREK ALMER SERIES

Flight of the Pawnee

Failure to Fire

JOSH HAMAN SERIES

Cherubs 2

Big Mother 40

Render Harmless

Forgotten

Inner Look

Moscow Airlift

The Simushir Island Incident

AGE OF SAIL SERIES

Raider of the Scottish Coast

Carronade

Death of A Lady

FAILURE TO FIRE

A DEREK ALMER NOVEL

Revised Second Edition

MARC LIEBMAN

Publisher:
Rotorhead Media, LLC
Savannah, TX

First edition copyright © February 2022 Marc Liebman
Second edition copyright © June 2023 Marc Liebman

ISBN Paperback —979-8-9883127-9-6

Cover images from Shutterstock and Pixabay.
Proofreader: Diane Blythe
Book interior design by – Deena Rae; E-BookBuilders, adaptation for ebook

BISAC Subject Headings:
    FIC 032000 – War / Military
    FIC 0331090 – Thriller /Terrorism
    FIC 031050 – Thriller /Military

File version: 202304025-02.027

CONTENTS

DISCOVER ROTORHEAD MEDIA

Visit Marc Liebman's website – *https://marcliebman.com* - for information about Marc, his books, blog, and podcasts.

Check out Marc's blog on the period of approximately 1770 to 1816 which is the end of the War of 1812. Through his blog, you'll learn about events in American history that do not appear in American history textbooks.

You can also subscribe to Marc's newsletter by clicking on Contact Marc on the link *https://marcliebman.com/contact/*. His monthly newsletter contains information on what books he is working on, speaking events, podcasts, and other information.

You can also find Marc on Facebook at *https://www.facebook.com/marcliebmanauthor/* and you can watch his history and aviation podcasts on his YouTube channel at *https://www.youtube.com/channel/UC_sDoFQM5wupNaCeGIvKL1g*.

Marc hopes you enjoy this book. If you spot any problems, please contact him via the Contact Marc tab on his website and describe what you found.

If you have a moment, the author would appreciate you taking the time to leave a review for this book at the retailer's site where you purchased it.

Thank you for your support

DEDICATION

Failure to Fire is dedicated to the men and women of the U.S. Armed Forces, intelligence, and law enforcement agencies that have, at least at the time of publication, managed to prevent a terrorist attack like 9/11 from happening again. Many of these men and women have made the ultimate sacrifice. Others have been maimed physically or mentally or both.

This may come as a surprise, but the United States of America is under attack. The attacks are coming from countries – notably the People's Republic of China and Iran (the largest state sponsor of terrorism in the world - who want to destroy our way of life. Why? They see a free and functioning democracy as a threat to their agendas. Both countries are using overt and covert means to challenge the United States.

Preventing terrorist attacks is a dirty, ugly business that takes place in the shadows. Not all their sacrifices were in Iraq and Afghanistan. Instead, these individuals operate worldwide as they identify and snuff out terrorist attacks before they happen. Their failures make front-page news. Their successes are buried if they make news at all.

Yet, every day, these men and women do their job because they know that *freedom is not free* and are willing to pay the price so that others don't. Thank you, and God bless you all.

A DEREK ALMER NOVEL

FAILURE TO FIRE

THE THREAT

When Na'il Miraj arrives at an al Qaeda recruiting station in Paris, he is seen by the organization's leaders as a gift from Allah. Their hope is that the former U.S. Army missile repair technician could turn their horde of out-of-date Stinger missiles into functioning weapons.

The discovery of Stinger missiles that failed to fire in a farmer's field in North Texas in the fall of 2016 should have set off alarm bells within the last few months of a lame duck administration. But they didn't.

There were those in the CIA who thought differently. Derek Almer is encouraged to start a small think tank by a friend in the CIA to research the threat of man portable, shoulder mounted surface-to-air missiles known by the acronym MANPADS. Helped by a little luck and intelligence from his contacts within the Mossad, Derek's firm learns that the terrorist group has smuggled Russian-made Igla-S's, as well as Stingers, into the U.S. Miraj's plan—shoot down enough airliners to kill thousands and shut down the world's air transportation system.

The question Derek Almer has to answer is when and where will the missiles be used?

THE THREAT NO ONE LIKES TO DISCUSS

R PGs, cyber warfare, dirty nukes, chemical weapons, and IEDS in the hands of terrorists get all the publicity. Few, if anyone, in the Federal government, the media, or the intelligence community speak about the one weapon that will, for a short time, bring commercial air travel in any country to a screeching halt.

The weapon is not a virus in the nation's or the global air traffic control system, nor a hacker who gains control of the airplane from his laptop in the passenger compartment. The weapon is relatively simple to manufacture and costs less than $50,000 (in 2008 dollars) to manufacture. Hundreds of thousands of them sitting in arsenals all over the world.

The weapon is known by the acronym MANPADS which stands for Man Portable Air Defense System. MANPADS are shoulder-fired surface-to-air missiles, and their portability and lethality make them a significant threat to anything that flies.

MANPADS are already in the hands of terrorists. In 2002, two missiles were fired at an Israeli airliner.

In 2003, one of these missiles hit a DHL cargo plane approaching Baghdad International Airport. The pilots managed to land the cargo plane safely, but it was a total loss.

On March 23rd, 2007, a Transaviaexport Ilyushin 76D was shot down. Everyone on board was killed.

In January 2013, the U.S. Navy boarded a dhow that left a Yemeni port controlled by Iranian-backed Houthi rebels. They found 10 Chinese versions of the SA-16 and 10 Russian-made SA-7s, plus tons of other weapons.

Between 1975 and January 2021, when *Failure to Fire* was initially published, there are 40 documented cases of MANPADS being fired at civilian aircraft. See https://2009-2017.state.gov/t/pm/wra/c62623.htm for more details.

MANPADS come in a variety of flavors. The U.S.-made Stinger was used by Fedayeen against the Soviets in the '80s in Afghanistan to bring down 269 aircraft. The Soviets/Russians build the Strela (known by their NATO names SA-7 Grail, SA-14 Gremlin), and the Igla series (SA-16 Gimlet, SA-18 Grouse, and SA-24 Grinch) have also had success on the battlefield.

The United Kingdom makes the Starburst and the Starstreak. France makes the Mistral. Many other countries have designed their own by combining elements of French, Russian/Soviet, U.K., and U.S. missiles to protect their ground troops against low-flying aircraft and helicopters.

The U.S. Department of Homeland Security formed the Counter-MANPADs Program Office to evaluate the threat and develop countermeasures. On March 30th, 2010, the office reported to Congress on the threat, viable countermeasure systems that could be installed on commercial aircraft, and the cost and timeline to deploy them on the U.S. airline and air cargo fleet. A redacted version of the DHS Science and Technology Directorate report is available through this link—https://fas.org/programs/ssp/asmp/documents/DHSMANPADSReport.pdf.

Before this report was issued, the Department of Homeland Security's Science and Technology division announced on January 6th, 2004, that teams led by BAE Systems, Northrop Grumman, and United Technologies were selected to develop a plan and test prototypes to help determine whether a viable technology exists that could be deployed to address the potential threat that MAN-Portable Air Defense Systems (MANPADS) pose to commercial aircraft.

The threat is so significant that later in 2004, the U.S. Department of Homeland stated some nations do a better job than others in protecting their inventory of MANPADS. How many MANPADS are in the hands of terrorist organizations is not available through open sources.

The CIA, Mi-5, Chinese Intelligence, and the Russian FSB may know, but the public does not. Nor does the flying public understand the serious threat they pose.

MANPADS are available on the black market and are cheap. Depending on the age of the weapon and its condition, some public sources say they can be bought for less than $10,000.

A typical MANPADS team consists of a spotter and a shooter. The spotter searches for and identifies the target. The shooter lifts the MANPADS that, depending on the make and model, weighs between 39 and 40 pounds onto his shoulder and points the launching tube at the target. A built-in detection system locks onto an airborne heat source within a bubble that could be up to five miles away and up to about eight to 10,000 feet.

Once the missile inside the launcher tube is "told where to go" by its seeker, the user pulls the trigger. Compressed gas pushes the rocket out of the launch tube, and the missile's motor ignites, propelling the rocket toward the target. At this point, the shooter's role is done.

In the air, the missile's seeker stays locked onto the heat source—either the airplane's structure warmed by the friction created by passing through the air or the engine's exhaust plume. MANPADS are fast and close in on their targets at between 1,300 miles per hour (Strela and Igla series), 1,600 miles per hour (Stinger), or 2,700 miles per hour (Starstreak).

The missiles have two types of warheads—blast fragmentation (think of a shotgun) and a contact or impact fuse. The blast fragmentation warhead is set off when the missile's proximity fuse says the weapon is close to the target. The shrapnel shreds the target causing an engine to fail catastrophically or a structural failure of the wing or fuselage.

Or, if the missile has an impact or contact fuse, when the missile slams into the airplane, its three to six pounds of explosive is enough to bring down or severely damage an airplane or a helicopter.

To counter the MANPADS threat, most military aircraft have countermeasure systems that automatically detect and decoy infrared missiles. Some systems use a combination of flares and/or sophisticated sets of mirrors to confuse the missile seeker and cause the weapon to miss. Other systems include lasers that confuse or disable the seeker and/or destroy the on-rushing weapon.

Several companies—BAE, Elbit, ITT, Northrop Grumman, and Selex E.S.—offer proven systems designed to counter the MANPADS threat. Several manufacturers have demonstrated that these systems can be economically installed on business jets, cargo planes, and airliners of all sizes. A U.S. government-supported program in March of 2007 installed DIRCM systems on 11 FedEx cargo planes.

At the time (2007), Northrop Grumman told the U.S. Department of Homeland Security that to install and test a directed infrared countermeasures system on an airliner would cost about $1.9M/airplane based on a fleet of 300 aircraft. Costs would drop to $1.0 million/plane for a fleet of 1,000!

Operation and maintenance costs, according to the Northrop Grumman study, would be approximately $26.50 per flight hour for 300 aircraft. For a typical three-hour flight carrying 150 passengers, this comes to $.53/per passenger. Installation on the larger airplanes used for transoceanic flights would cost even less per passenger.

If 1,000 airplanes were equipped, the cost/flight hour would drop below $13, or $.26 per passenger, on a 150-passenger airliner that needed three hours to go from airport to airport.

Northrop Grumman based its installation on the configuration now used on Boeing's C-17 aircraft. The C-17 configuration is a conformal "canoe" mounted on the belly of the aircraft. At the time of the report, Northrop Grumman stated the system could be ready for deployment in as little as 28 months. This assumes nine months to get FAA certification and the remaining time for installation and testing.

The cost of the hardware and the design of the installation is only one part of the issue. Admittedly, there are legal, labor (union contracts), and training issues that must be resolved as well.

In 2019, American Airlines had almost 900 plus airplanes in its fleet, and if Delta's, United's, and Southwest's are included, the potential number of aircraft that could be fitted with a countermeasures system is more than 3,000. Installation, system, and maintenance costs would also drop dramatically if these four airlines started installing DIRCM systems on all their planes.

As noted above, on a per-flight basis, the cost is minimal.

Weight? You've got to be kidding. DIRCM systems weigh less than 500 pounds, including the wiring, sensor, and cockpit display. This is the equivalent of two and a half 170-pound passengers plus a 30-pound bag. On a Boeing 737-800 with a maximum takeoff weight of 174,200 pounds, a 500-pound DIRCM system would have minimal impact on the aircraft's weight and balance.

The payouts to families and crew members that would result if an airliner were shot down by a MANPADS with 150 people on board would be far more than the cost of the DIRCM system. The money would have been better served by equipping some or all the airline's fleet. From a risk perspective, not equipping the commercial airline fleet just doesn't make commercial sense.

The truth is that the systems are practical, feasible, and can be installed on airliners. El Al has installed Elbit's Music system on all its planes. As a firm, they didn't want to take the risk of not having them installed on their planes.

Yet, the Counter-MANPADs Program Office study concluded that DIRCM systems weren't economically viable to install systems on U.S. airliners. Their rationale was that the systems didn't meet the study's standards for reliability. Where was the funding to determine what needed to be done to meet the reliability standards, whatever they were at the time?

This determination by the Counter-MANPADS program office flies in the face of reality. DIRCM Systems are widely deployed on military aircraft all over the world, and they are reliable. More important, they are effective.

No matter what the study found, the MANPADS threat to airliners, air cargo aircraft, and corporate jets is real.

The reality is that no government or airline wants to state publicly that MANPADs are a serious threat to civil aviation. They are afraid the danger will scare away potential passengers.

This approach will continue until an airliner drops from the sky and the handwringing and recriminations begin. The spin-meisters will try to convince us that no countermeasure system is perfect or that the attack is an isolated instance. Not true. MANPADS are out there, and it is only a matter of time before one brings down an airliner.

As this second, revised edition of *Failure to Fire* is being prepared, we've seen the lethality of MANPADS in the skies over Ukraine. Both helicopter and tactical jets that did not have a working DIRCM system have been shot down by MANPADS. We've seen DIRCM systems work in the skies over Syria, Iraq, and Afghanistan, so their effectiveness is not unknown or new.

In February 2021, around the time the first edition of *Failure to Fire* was published, FedEx notified the FAA that it was beginning a to install DIRCM systems on its aircraft. They would start with those that operate in the Mideast since the Russian invasion of Ukraine was still a year into the future.

So the question remains, why are U.S. airlines installing DIRCM systems their planes now rather than on some crash program after one has been shot down by a MANDPADS?

Marc Liebman
First written in December 2021
Revised in June 2023

WHAT ARE MANPADS?

ANPADS is the acronym for MAN Portable Air Defense Systems, which are small surface-to-air guided missiles. Most are fired from a standing position and with the launcher tube resting on the shooter's shoulder. MANPADS are infrared-guided and home in on a heat source created by a low-flying aircraft or helicopter.

Thousands of these missiles have been manufactured by defense contractors in the U.S., the Soviet Union, the United Kingdom, the People's Republic of China, and other countries under license and sold to almost every military organization in the world. Some, unfortunately, have fallen into the wrong hands.

FAILURE TO FIRE

CHAPTER 1

CHILDREN'S CHOICES

FRIDAY, MARCH 31ST, 1989, 8:16 P.M. LOCAL TIME, RIYADH, SAUDI ARABIA

Kazim Serraf's demeanor befitted his first name—calm, serene, even-tempered—and it served him well. In the kingdom's finance ministry, he had risen as far as he could go without being a member of the Saudi royal family. In return for his accurate and often candid advice, he had become a trusted advisor to the finance minister, who rewarded him with what an American friend called "generational wealth." Invested wisely, Serraf's family fortune of thirty million U.S. dollars would grow, and following generations of Serrafs would enjoy the results of his labor.

All Kazim Serraf's money was invested in institutions well away from the caldron that comprised the Middle East and the Arabian Gulf. Kazim made it a point to gently correct references made by Westerners that when in the Kingdom of Saudi Arabia, the body of water separating Iran from Saudi Arabia is known as the Arabian Gulf. In Iran, on the gulf's north shore, it is known as the Persian Gulf. On the south shore in Saudi Arabia, Bahrain, Kuwait, Qatar, Oman, and the United Arab Emirates, Arabian Gulf is the preferred name and was, as Kazim was fond of pointing out, a matter of perspective, depending on where one lived.

Kazim came from modest means. By luck, his father won a contract from the Arab American Oil Company to supply food to one of its cafeterias at a production complex in Dammam. This modest beginning grew as his father added more cafeterias. It provided the money to send Kazim to an international school where he was an excellent student. He earned the grades to qualify for entry into Saudi Arabia's most prestigious university.

Children were a symbol of wealth, and his wife Ayda bore him six—four boys and two girls. As an observant Muslim and a traditional Arab who believed a woman's role was in the home, Ayda catered to her husband's every need. She bobbed her head as she placed a tray with a pot of tea and two cups on the pearl-inlaid wooden table. Before she left the room, Ayda said, "You deal with Fatimah. She's your daughter."

Kazim sat back on the comfortable chair and tried to script the conversation he was about to have with Fatimah, his oldest daughter. Fatimah entered wearing a pair of slacks and a Western-style blouse that didn't conceal nor flaunt her striking beauty. She could be, Kazim often admitted to himself, a model.

At home, Fatimah often stated that she preferred what women wore outside the Kingdom of Saudi Arabia and refused to wear the loose-fitting jilbab unless a non-family member was in the house. Even then, she wore the garment under protest. Or stayed out of sight.

Fatimah was rail thin, just like her mother, and had large, captivating black eyes and jet-black, shoulder-blade-length hair. Chronologically, Fatimah was Kazim's third-oldest child.

When she was six years old, it was clear to Kazim and Ayda that Fatimah was not afraid to speak her mind. When she did, Fatimah's eyes shone with determination to get her way. Their daughter was, they learned, the leader of their six children.

According to her teachers, Fatimah was an outstanding student but difficult to keep challenged. Her inquiring mind, leadership, and top-of-the-class grades set her apart.

Fatimah stopped in the doorway, waiting for her father to notice her presence. Kazim waved to the chair next to his. "Fatimah, please sit down." He waited until she was seated, knees together and hands in her lap. Kazim noticed that his 18-year-old daughter was wearing nail polish, a Western fashion he frowned upon.

"Tea?"

"No thanks, Father." Fatimah used one hand to toss back her long black hair that had cascaded down onto her chest.

Kazim pursed his lips. "Fatimah, your mother and I have found a suitable man for you to marry, and we want to schedule the wedding sometime this summer."

Fatimah held up her hand. She knew the gesture was rude, but she wanted to stop the discussion before it went any further. "Father, I am not marrying Abdul. I am sure he is a fine man, but I am not ready for marriage. I want to attend a university, earn a degree, and make something of myself." *In other words, I want a career.*

"This is Saudi Arabia. A women's place is in the home."

Fatimah didn't want to insult her father, but she was not going to be married off to some man to increase the family's wealth. She would run away first and had so informed her mother. Fatimah believed she was not some prize cow to be sold to the highest bidder to improve the family portfolio.

"Father, I want to go to a university in either the United Kingdom or the United States. There, I can study for a degree and find a job to support myself. When I am ready, I will find a man. Not before."

Kazim's head snapped back at her last words. "You do realize what you are saying."

"I do, Father." Fatimah bit her lip slightly. "This is what I want, and I am asking for your support only until I graduate and have a job."

"You don't know that a British or American school will accept you. So how can you say this?"

"Father, I do know. I have been accepted at the University of London and at Brown University in the United States."

"When and how did you apply?"

"Last fall. I wrote the letters to six schools and mailed them myself. The acceptances were sent to the school and the letters in my room."

"And you think you are ready for this?"

"I do."

"And what if I say no?"

"Then I will do anything I can to follow my dream, even if I have to leave Saudi Arabia forever. This is my home, but …"

Kazim cut her off, trying not to sound angry at her defiance. He tried being conciliatory. "You are just a child. What do you know about the world?"

With the confidence of an 18-year-old who is sure she knew everything important there is to know, Fatimah replied, "I know enough to know what I want and what I don't want. I don't want to become a wife to a man picked for me that I do not know or love. Trust me, Father, I know the punishment, but I will run away."

Kazim saw the defiance and determination shining in his oldest daughter's eyes. Before the conversation began, he had three options: one - force her into a marriage that might be a disaster and reflect poorly on him; two - let her go off to a university in a strange country; or three - force her to stay at home and live with the consequences, whatever they might be. Logic told him that choice two was the only answer. He took solace in that Saudi princes sent their sons abroad to be educated and they all came back as better men. So, why couldn't he send his daughter?

"Fatimah, here's what I will agree to do. I will allow you to go to school in London because it is closer and I often go there on business. Plus, I will pay your school fees and provide a modest stipend until you earn your degree. If you cannot handle the academics, you will come home. Once you graduate, you will have three months to find a job. Once you do, you will be on your own. Do I make myself clear?"

Fatimah stood up and fell to her knees at her father's feet. There, she took his hands in hers. "Thank you, Father.... I will not disappoint you."

SATURDAY, DECEMBER 11TH, 2005, 6:49 P.M. LOCAL TIME, WASHINGTON, D.C

Adnan Maalouf couldn't wait for his guest to arrive at his apartment in Georgetown. He'd rented the flat less than a month before because the building was not in the Muslim neighborhood northwest of Florida Avenue NW and east of Massachusetts Avenue NW in Washington, D.C., where his parents lived.

He was 10 and his sister, Sabah, was four when his parents came from Lebanon to the U.S. right after the Israeli invasion in 1978. His father became a successful realtor, and his mother had become a licensed pharmacist. Both were proud that they had become American citizens.

While not wealthy, the Maaloufs were well-off and ensured their two children earned college degrees. Sabah was an account executive with a large advertising firm in New York City and Adnan worked for the U.S. State Department.

After graduating from American University with a bachelor's degree in international relations, Adnan was accepted by the Fletcher School at Tufts University. He looked like an Arab with dark-olive skin, black hair, and eyes. He was 5' 8" and 150 pounds, putting him in the center of the height chart for Middle Easterners. Right after he graduated with a Master of Arts degree in Law and Diplomacy, he went to work for the U.S. State Department. Like his parents and sister, Adnan was fluent in French, Arabic, and English.

During the interview process, the interviewers were more interested in testing his language skills than what he did during his junior year abroad at American University in Beirut or hearing how he spent the summer between his first and second year at Fletcher traveling in Lebanon, Syria, and Egypt.

After analysis of the intelligence failures that led to 9/11, President George W. Bush ordered the creation of the Terrorist Threat Integration Center, which opened in 2003. At the time, Maalouf was creating classified profiles of country leaders in the State Department's Office of Analysis for the Near East and North Africa.

The assistant secretary of state responsible for intelligence and research, who was two levels above him, encouraged Adnan to apply for one of the intelligence analyst positions in the newly formed agency. By the time Adnan was vetted and offered a job, the Intelligence Reform and Terrorism Prevention Act of 2004 changed the organization's name to the National Counterterrorism Center and placed the organization under the United States Director of National Intelligence.

Adnan's clearance was upgraded to Top Secret, and he was cleared for specially compartmented information and programs known by their code words. During his background check, Adnan passed a lie detector test. He was surprised that the interviewer asked only three questions about his trips to Lebanon in the summer of 2000 and again in 2005.

Question 1—Why did he go? Answer—To see family members and attend a wedding.

Question 2—Where did he go? Answer—Cairo, because of the flight connections. Beirut, Tyre, and Tripoli in Lebanon. He did not mention he went to Damascus, Syria.

Question 3—Who did he see? Answer—Family members at the wedding and friends from his year at the American University in Beirut.

Within months of reporting to the National Counterterrorism Center, Adnan was creating biographies of the leaders of terrorist organizations based in the Middle East. Maalouf either knew of or met some of those he was researching. Some he considered close friends and none were listed in his report of foreign contacts from his most recent trip to Lebanon. And, unknown to American law enforcement agencies, one was about to knock on his door.

SATURDAY, FEBRUARY 27ᵀᴴ, 2011, 9:48 A.M. LOCAL TIME, DALLAS, TEXAS

When Neil Mirage bought a ticket for American Flight 48 to Paris online, the instructions said he needed to check in at least two hours before departure. From his experience flying all over the world during his eight years in the Army, Mirage thought the requirement was rubbish. Still, now that he was out of the Army and unemployed, he had time to kill.

Check-in and security took 20 minutes. Neil put his backpack, which was also his carry-on, on the seat next to him in DFW's Terminal D. The desert-tan pack had all his clothes and toiletries. His laptop and the two books he brought were at the top, for easy access. Both novels were in English.

In Neil's left pants pocket, other than the change from his lunch at McDonald's was a thumb drive with a complete copy of his military service record. Most important were scanned copies of the certificates showing his military occupational specialties: 94T— Short Range Air Missile Defense Missile Repairer and 14S—Missile Defense Crewmember.

Also on the removable drive were files containing his orders to Army aviation units in Afghanistan, where he checked out and performed field repair on Hellfire missiles. There was another file with details from an assignment to examine captured disabled Taliban IEDs and Soviet ordnance.

Mirage picked seat 34C on board the Boeing 777 because only a few seats around 34C were taken when he checked in. When the cabin door was closed, no one sat in 34A or 34B. Once his dinner tray was taken, Neil raised the armrests, folded his jacket into a bundle for a pillow, and laid on his side. Mirage reviewed what he would do in Paris and drifted off to sleep.

From Charles de Gaulle Airport, he wanted to take the RER train to the Paris metro. He'd already made a reservation at a small hotel in St. Denis. Once there, he planned to log onto several websites in an internet café and send an email to an address he'd memorized shortly after he received his honorable discharge.

Born in Aleppo, Syria, as Na'il Miraj, he became a U.S. citizen when his parents were naturalized and changed his name to Neil Mirage. He wasn't being recruited; he was a volunteer with special skills he thought al-Qaeda might find valuable. If his parents knew what he was about to do as Na'il Miraj, they would have been horrified.

CHAPTER 2

MISFIRES

THURSDAY, MAY 12TH, 2011, 6:48 P.M. LOCAL TIME, JALALABAD, AFGHANISTAN

On the day after Bin Laden was killed, the news media focused on the raid and Bin Laden's burial at sea. In the U.S., pundits celebrated that the world's most-wanted man had finally met his maker, and many said the war against terror was over.

Others on both sides thought that Bin Laden was simply a high-profile casualty in a more prolonged war and knew better. Once the raid returned with sacks of computer hard drives, removable drives and diskettes, Bill Virdon, Yale class of 1974, the head of the exploitation team, had his experts focused on three tasks:

First, cataloging the information from the computers, phones, and storage devices into a searchable database that could be exploited.

Second, transmitting the encrypted information to CIA headquarters in Langley, Virginia, and NSA offices in Fort Meade, as well as FBI labs in Quantico, Virginia, and the National Counterterrorism Center in Tysons Corner, Virginia.

Lastly, determining what information could be acted on immediately.

When he was at Yale, Virdon's fellow students and professors ridiculed him when they learned about his choice of employers. Their criticism made his desire to go into the agency that much stronger.

During the Soviet occupation of Afghanistan, Virdon was a case officer in Afghanistan helping the mujahideen fight the Red Army. When that war was over, Virdon came back to the U.S. as one of the CIA's experts on the country. He knew the tribal customs and spoke Pashto, Dari (Farsi in Iran), and Arabic fluently. His squat, slightly overweight body, dark hair, and full gray-black beard allowed him, if dressed appropriately, to pass as a local.

Virdon warned agency directors of the growing threat of the Taliban and al-Qaeda. He was contemplating retiring at the end of the fiscal year that ended September 30th, 2001. 9/11 happened and at age 59, volunteered to go back into the field, figuring he had a few good years left.

Since the attack, he'd been "commuting" between Langley, Kabul, and Karachi with stops at places he would call interesting. Now 69 and well past mandatory retirement age, Virdon was kept on as a "contractor." He turned to Lieutenant Commander Jacob Sobrano, who was assigned to help him and sitting next to him. Sobrano was a SEAL and a veteran of many missions, some successful, some not against the Taliban and al-Qaeda.

Virdon waved his hand over the material on the conference room table. "The next battle I must fight is to ensure the guys in the field have access to this material. The bureaucrats in the intelligence community will want to analyze the data and debate its implications until the cows come home. Having this info is both power and control. What blows my mind is that some of these bozos don't seem to care if the trigger-pullers get what is usable as fast as they can so we can kill and capture as many of the bastards as possible. I'm going back to Langley with the material and will try to get as much as I can out to the operators as fast as I can."

"Will the intel guys at SOCOM get access?" Jacob pronounced the acronym SOCOM for Special Operations Command as "so comm."

"That's one of the goals. My job is to speed up the process because the original plan was to analyze the material here in Kabul first."

THURSDAY, SEPTEMBER 8TH, 2016, 10:00 A.M. LOCAL TIME, DALLAS, TX

The Evans Group was one of the largest independent advertising and marketing communications companies in the U.S. Its standard practice was to review each major account annually within two weeks of the anniversary date of the contract. For the Freedom Group, which signed on August 28th, 2015, today was the scheduled date of the review.

Eileen Tanner Almer, vice president and client director, led the effort to win the account, which at contract signing was forecast to generate $24.8 million in billings and $5 million or 20.2% in profit.

The reviews were conducted by April McClellan, Partner and Chief Operating Officer and President Stan Evans, President, and CEO. When Eileen walked into the room, she planned to share the introductions that The Freedom Group's Senior Vice President of Marketing had made that Eileen was sure would turn into new clients.

Eileen was a freelance illustrator when April recruited her as a creative director. Her work won awards for the agency and made her client's cash registers ring. And Eileen was adept at winning new business.

At the last quarterly review of her client portfolio, Eileen's clients generated roughly over $135 million or approximately 18 percent of the agency's $750 million in billings and 24 percent of the firm's profits. Her portfolio was the fourth largest but number one in profits and had the highest client satisfaction scores in the agency.

However, since the original pitch to Freedom Group, Eileen married Derek Almer and moved out to his ranch in Ivanhoe. Driving the 80 miles from Ivanhoe to the Evans Group's offices off Central Expressway every day was a beating so Eileen came in two days a week for meetings and worked from the Derek's ranch where she found herself much more productive.

In the fall of 2015, Eileen helped her then fiancé Derek defend the ranch against an attack by Sinaloa soldiers and stop al-Qaeda's top bomb maker from spraying sarin nerve gas on the fans at Texas-OU football game and Texas State Fair goers. For her role, Eileen was awarded the Presidential Medal of Freedom.

Stan walked in followed by April and he took his customary place at the head of the table. He wasn't smiling when he looked at Eileen. "OK, you know the drill. Give me the recap of the numbers and a forecast. Then, we'll talk about any issues the firm may be facing."

"Sure, Stan. Here's the bottom line. When we signed the Freedom Group contract, we thought we would generate twenty-four point eight million. As of the end of last month, we billed thirty-point one million. Gross profit on the account is eight-point-two million or twenty-seven-point-three percent of billed revenue. The profit includes the ten percent we make in media commissions. For the next twelve months, my billings forecast for the Freedom Group is that we should gross in the thirty-three million range."

Stan, who was approaching 60, put his hand on his chin. "All this from a gun manufacturer who may be out of business in a few years."

"What do you mean by that?"

"I mean, I don't think we will have an account in three years because the lawsuits over the Sandy Hook shooting will bankrupt them."

"Stan, I disagree. The Connecticut State Supreme Court said the Freedom Group had immunity from lawsuits based on the Federal Protection of Lawful Commerce in Arms Act of 2005. Based on the that law, they tossed out the lawsuit."

"Trust me, the anti-gun lobby will try again. Make sure our billings are protected and ensure none go over thirty days. If needed, give them a five percent discount if they will pay within ten days."

With that said, Stan Evans walked out of the room. April quickly followed, leaving Eileen stunned, annoyed, and angry.

SUNDAY, SEPTEMBER 11TH, 2016, 8:36 P.M. LOCAL TIME, IVANHOE, TX

Dawuud Ghanem looked to the east where he saw the white landing lights on the airliners headed to Dallas Love Field and DFW Airport. They looked like a string of pearls hung in the black sky as they descended to 8,000 feet and headed for the navigational aid on Jones Field in Bonham, Texas, 17 miles to the west.

Four days earlier, Ghanem sat in the parking lot of an abandoned store a few miles from where he was standing with a radio tuned to the air traffic control frequency. While the slow-flying airliners were a bit higher and farther away than he'd have liked. He rationalized, after listening to Dallas Approach, that most would be descending and coming toward the missiles. This would put the targeted airliners in the missile's performance envelope.

That led him to use Google Maps to search for a field roughly 500 yards on each side, with the nearest house at least half a mile away. The imagery showed a dirt road to a perfect field surrounded by trees.

To the west, lightning backlit the clouds that would bring heavy rain to the Dallas area that Texans would say, "was like a cow pissing on a flat rock." Ghanem was sure the rain would obliterate any trace of his presence as he and three others unloaded crates from the back of the stolen Ford pickup. One by one, the contents were checked. It was time.

Ghanem, along with the other three men with him, were from the third generation who grew up in Palestinian refugee camps in Lebanon. His father moved his family out of the camp to Baalbek because he was hired to repair trucks for the Syrian Army.

Even though he was only 5'6" and 140 pounds, Ghanem had no trouble lifting the long 59.8-inch, 33.5-pound tube and pointing the end in the general direction of the lights in the sky. In daylight, they could read the yellow lettering on the olive-drab tubes. In the darkness, the tubes were black, and the lettering was invisible.

The man standing next to him whispered. "System is on."

Dawuud swung the launcher back and forth so that the seeker could see the heat plumes of the approaching aircraft. "No lock. No indication of a target."

His assistant asked. "Do you have a light?"

"Oh yes, when I turned the system on, the software went through all the tests so I know we have battery power. But the sensor is not picking up any targets."

Dawuud lowered the launcher and looked at the other man with a launcher. "Are you getting a lock?"

The man shook his head. Dawuud had fired many Stinger missiles at Soviet and U.S. aircraft in Afghanistan. Each time, the weapon worked perfectly. They were simple to use. Point at the target, get a tone or a light saying the missile seeker had a target, and pull the trigger. Almost instantly, there was a whoosh, and the missile was on its way, snaking toward the airplane or helicopter. He would see a puff of smoke in seconds, followed by a fireball plunging to Earth.

This should be no different. The airliners were well within the missile's engagement envelope. He opened another case and took out another Stinger. After turning it on and waiting for the missile launcher to boot up, he aimed at an approaching landing light. No lock.

Ghanem turned to a man he only knew by his first name, Zahir. His tone was curt, colored by frustration. All this work to get the Stingers into the U.S. and into a perfect firing position was for naught because the missiles didn't work. "I thought you had checked these weapons out. You told me that they were perfect."

"I did. The batteries were new, and the nitrogen coolant tanks were charged."

Without the nitrogen, the seeker would not be cooled and could not differentiate the exhaust plume from the sky. Without a battery, none of the launcher's electronics would work.

"I know that. Let me have one of the other missiles."

Dawuud hoisted each of the Stinger launchers onto his shoulder one after another after he made sure they were turned on. Pointed at an aircraft passing overhead, he could not hear the tone that said the missile seeker had locked onto a target. Nor was there the light in the sight that said the seeker had found a plane. In frustration, he threw the last one on the ground.

"Let's get out of here. Our work is done. We cannot kill any infidels tonight, but we must live to fight another day."

"Do you want to load the missiles back onto the truck."

"No, leave them here. They are all junk. They will send a message to the Americans that we can kill many of them at any time. The attack 15 years ago that brought down that infidel's World Trade Center was just the beginning."

MONDAY, SEPTEMBER 12TH, 2016, 11:58 A.M. LOCAL TIME, PESHAWAR, PAKISTAN

When Fatimah bought the airline ticket to Peshawar, she listed the reason on the Samba Bank's internal travel request form as "business development meeting with al-Kanz." It was not a lie. The words kept running through Fatimah Serraf's mind as she sat in a pale green side chair in the lobby of the Emaraat Hotel in the heart of one of the oldest cities in the world. She was both confident and determined to win the al-Kanz account.

Serraf's rise in the private banking world started in 1998 when Citibank UK hired her as an intern while she was working on her doctorate at the London School of Economics. Once she had her doctorate in economics, the bank hired her full-time as an account manager. Three years later, an up-and-coming woman she met while at Citibank and who would later become the CEO of Samba—one of the Middle East's largest and safest banks—recruited Fatimah. She was offered a position as a senior vice president of wealth management in Samba's private bank.

Initially, the assignment met stiff resistance from the traditional Saudis who didn't like working with a woman but who caved when they learned Fatimah was the brains behind the very high ROIs (return on investment) they earned. Her concession to working in Saudi Arabia was that when in the presence of Saudi clients, she had to wear a niqab so that only her eyes were visible.

The rest of the time, instead of the Western clothes she preferred, she hid her attractive looks in a black or dark gray niqab. This, Fatimah thought, was a small price to pay for working in her native land. The job at Samba offered her a promotion, a higher salary, a larger bonus, and generous stock options.

The sheikhs who benefited from her work recommended their friends, and Fatimah's personal client list flourished. One lead came from a boyhood friend of her father who represented Green Crescent Holdings. This led to working with the founder of the Saudi Binladin Group.

For Fatimah, the position in Saudi Arabia was a triumphant return and vindication of going to the University of London and then to the London School of Economics. In early 2016, Fatimah was promoted again and was now the head of international operations for Samba's private bank.

Fatimah told Samba Private Bank's chief operating officer that she was headed to Peshawar to meet a senior executive of the al-Kanz Real Estate Group who owned the four-star Emaraat and other hotels and real estate in Pakistan, Oman, and the UAE. She was encouraged because the man wanted to finalize an arrangement in which the bank would manage a part of his personal portfolio. In return for the bank providing credit instruments for more real estate investments, Samba would have the option to participate as an equity partner.

The meeting that was the official reason for Fatimah's visit to Peshawar took place at nine in the morning. She was now waiting for another client whom she'd never met, but for whom she had been managing a portion of his investment portfolio since her first days at Citibank. The client moved with her when she joined Samba in 2001.

For the first time since Fatimah started working with Green Crescent's founders, she was about to meet the man who managed Osama bin Laden's personal fortune. At first, she was repelled by the idea, but rationalized that as a banker, she shouldn't be judgmental about her client's politics. Her job was to make them lots of money.

Fatimah sank further into the rationalization quicksand when she started suggesting ways Osama could move money surreptitiously to avoid the taxman in countries where the profits were earned. It wasn't money laundering, but the age-old game of avoiding taxes on the 15 to 20 percent return she helped them generate. Some of her recommendations were accepted; some were rejected. To her, the choices were random.

"Miss Fatimah Serraf?" It sounded like a question, but it was more of a statement. The man standing before her was of medium height and had a neatly trimmed beard.

"Yes."

"Please come with me."

After she stood, Fatimah pulled the cloth around her neck up to convert the hijab into a niqab so that only her eyes were showing. The man gently but firmly held her bicep and led her to a car parked in front of the hotel. When the Mercedes pulled away from the curb, the man held out a hood. "If you don't mind. This will be only for a few minutes."

Fatimah sat in the darkness, listening to the sounds of the car being driven. She kept reminding herself that al-Qaeda wouldn't kill the woman who handled their money. She wasn't sure if she was being arrogant, stupid, or naïve.

The car stopped, and the man sitting next to Fatimah removed the hood before he got out and held the door open for her. She looked around and the apartment building looked like any other in Peshawar—run down, needing repairs with telephone and power lines running all over the structure to the power poles.

Fatimah was ushered into what she figured was a small flat's living and dining room. The only furniture was a table and three chairs. Cushions were piled in a corner next to a row of weapons she recognized as AK-47s leaning against the wall.

"Please sit." It was more of a command than a request. The man moved to a corner and stood with his hands clasped in front of his stomach.

"Thank you for coming."

Fatimah turned in the direction of the soft, lilting voice speaking Arabic. The man looked more like an Iman from a mosque than a successful surgeon. Anxiety washed over Fatimah when she realized she was in the same room with one of the most wanted men in the world—Ayman al Zawahiri.

The former doctor eased him himself into the chair opposite Fatimah. "I thought we should meet. We have more work for you to do that we should discuss in person. Then, when we agree to a plan, you can do your part."

Fatimah nodded, knowing that whatever they asked had to be made to look legal.

CHAPTER 3

HEADS IN THE SAND

The rain gauge on the post behind his house told Andrew Sullivan that over the past two days, over two and a half inches of rain had fallen. The soaking would give him another good cutting of eight rolls per acre of the coastal Bermuda grass he grew as cattle feed.

Shafts of light from sunlight streaking through gaps in the clouds created shadows on the fields behind the house when he put his empty coffee mug down and headed out the door. His most immediate task was to round up any cows that sought shelter in the woods and check for any damage from the lightning.

Sullivan's six-wheeled John Deere Gator fired right up at the push of a button, and before he could turn around to call his dogs, the older of his Labradors jumped onto the seat next to him. His younger brother, a chocolate-coated member of the same breed, made himself comfortable in the Gator's bed.

The most likely area of his 10,000-acre ranch where some of his herd would go into the woods to get out of the pelting rain was down near the lake. Finding no cows in the woods, he checked the fencing that separated his fields. On almost every trip, he'd find a break in the wire, and keeping it in good repair was a never-ending task.

Entering the field where the six horses his daughter owned usually grazed, Andrew sensed something wasn't right. None were there.

Sullivan ensured the .45-caliber pistol remained in the holster under the bench seat. The Colt Model 1911 had a round in the chamber. To fire the pistol, he had to click off the safety and pull the trigger. In the scabbard holster on the right side of the Gator, there was a 12-gauge, semi-automatic shotgun loaded with bird shot. The primary purpose of the Remington A-5 that his great-grandfather had bought new in 1905 was to end the life of any poisonous snakes he found. Friends often suggested he put the Remington on the mantel to preserve it for posterity. Its low serial number, provenance—the family had a bill of sale signed by the gun's designer, John Browning—and great condition made it extremely valuable. Someday, he thought, he would buy another one, but this one had sentimental value. It was like a trusted old friend.

The other scabbard on the Gator had a lever-action Model 1894 Winchester 30-30 he used to kill coyotes who tried to cut a calf out of his herd. Donkeys mixed in with the cattle usually did this work for him, but every so often the 30-30 was be needed.

About halfway across the field, Andrew lifted his foot off the accelerator and let the Gator slow. The ATV hadn't come to a stop when the low growl and curled lip from Rory, the older lab, reinforced Andrew's feeling that something, as his Naval Aviator friend and neighbor Derek Almer often said, was not "cricket." That was when he spotted a pile of crates that took him back to his days in Iraq after Desert Storm where he was a paratroop company commander. Andrew left the Army to run the ranch after his father had a near-fatal heart attack.

Andrew felt naked and exposed sitting in the middle of his field with no cover or concealment. Anyone who was a decent shot could take him out, and he'd never know what hit him.

He was scared and mashed down on the accelerator, rationalizing that a moving target was difficult to hit than a stationary one. Twenty yards from the pile, Andrew spun the steering wheel and lifted his foot off the gas. The Gator slid to a stop on the wet grass 10 feet from the four crates someone had attempted to camouflage with loose grass and branches cut from a nearby tree.

Cell phone coverage was intermittent to non-existent off FM273 northeast of Bonham, a town of just over 10,000 about 120 miles northeast of Dallas, Texas. The local ranchers wanted to keep it that way so there were no cell phone towers in the area between Bonham, Ivanhoe, and Telephone. In fact, there were none until one got close to Paris, Texas, which was 35 miles to the east, or Dennison, Texas, which was about the same distance to the west.

The way to communicate from the fields was via small handheld radios. Andrew keyed the one he always carried that had a range of six miles and was good anywhere on the ranch.

"Nancy, its Andrew. Pick up. It is important." Nancy was his wife and ran a small veterinary practice for the local ranchers.

"What's up, sweetie?"

"Call Derek and tell him I just found four Stinger FIM-92E missiles in the center of the field where Heather practices. He and Eileen are in Florida, so call his cell phone."

"Are you in any danger?"

"No. I don't think so."

In the time needed for an FBI agent from the Dallas field office to fly out on a Dallas Police Department Bell 206 helicopter, Andrew had time to explore the area around the four olive drab cases. He took pictures with his cell phone, more as a keepsake, than for evidence. From the footprints in the black soil, he was sure there were four men and a pickup truck.

The agent waited until the noise from the helicopter subsided and then stuck out his hand. "Jeffrey Anderson, Special Agent, FBI."

"Andrew Sullivan." Noting that he was a member of the 101st Airborne Division, a Desert Storm vet who retired as a full colonel from the Texas National Guard didn't seem appropriate. His ball cap with the Screaming Eagle patch and the wreaths on the bill, a.k.a. "scrambled eggs", said enough.

"Did you touch anything?"

"No. Everything is as I found them. I walked around the containers and traced their footsteps to where the truck was parked.

My boot prints are off to one side. The rain made it pretty muddy, making their tracks easy to find."

The special agent stared at the four boxes about five feet long and 20 inches square. He then took a few steps to examine the missiles more closely. "Do you know what they are?"

"Yup. They're E-model Stingers. Whoever was here tried to fire them, and they didn't work for some reason."

"Why here?"

"That's easy. We're right under the Standard Terminal Arrival Route for DFW Airport. All the airliners arriving from the northeast quadrant pass over or near the Bonham VORTAC." Andrew pronounced the abbreviation for the navigational aid as "vor-tack." "They're descending through eight thousand feet and are below two hundred and fifty knots. At night, it looks like a string of pearls because the airliners are about three to five miles apart. To a guy with a Stinger, this is a target-rich environment."

Anderson looked up at an airliner passing overhead. "Why didn't they shoot?"

"Good question. My guess is that they didn't anticipate the heavy rain and clouds that would have obscured their targets and made it difficult for the missile seeker to acquire a target. Or, they had problems with the missiles."

"And you know this how?"

"One, we were equipped with Stingers during Desert Storm and taught how to use them."

Andrew pointed with his right hand; fingers extended. "Two, Stingers have batteries and coolants to help the seeker find its target. If the batteries are low or the coolant leaks out, they won't work."

"Oh." Special Agent Anderson took a few steps to get a different view. "I'm assuming that this is your land. I'm informing you that this is now a crime scene, and we need to keep everyone, including animals, away from this area."

"No problem. The only other person who knows about them is my wife, who called your office." Andrew deliberately didn't mention that Nancy talked to Derek Almer who said he'd be landing in about an hour and would stop by.

"Good. Let's keep it that way."

THE SAME DAY, 10:09 A.M. LOCAL TIME, DALLAS

The jogging paths around Bachman Lake were an ideal place to take a walk. They were never crowded except on Saturdays and Sundays, which gave the four men a place to talk privately. Their conversation was interrupted by noise from the arriving Southwest Airlines 737s that passed just 200 feet over their heads as they approached the Dallas Love Field's Runway 13 Right.

Ghanem set the leisurely pace. "Zahir, you are the cell leader. We rented an apartment for you near the small, but active Muslim community in Plano. Join the local mosque, but do not try to recruit anyone. Do not draw attention to yourselves, and you will receive a stipend from Holy Land Foundation. Maintain contact the way you were trained. When we need you to do the work of Allah, we will let you know."

Zahir nodded. "Allah be praised. I will do this." The Jordanian spoke in English which he learned in a school in Amman. He was one of the first to build what the Americans called improvised explosive devices powerful enough to destroy mine-resistant vehicles in Afghanistan.

"Good. We will give you money to buy three used sport utility vehicles with low mileage. We will need them for future operations."

Again, Zahir nodded. He was here to help destroy the country that built planes for the hated Israelis.

THE SAME DAY, 10:17 A.M. LOCAL TIME, DALLAS

The real reason that Eileen came into the office was that Madge, The Evans Group's receptionist, called and said FedEx tried to deliver a package yesterday that required her signature and ID. The driver said he would be back around 10 in the morning.

Eileen walked through the door right behind the FedEx driver, signed for the package, and brought the box to her office. Based on its weight and the return address, she was confident she knew what might be in the box.

She was plugging her 16" MacBook Pro into her docking station when April McClellan appeared in the doorway. After Stan Evans's abrupt departure from the Freedom Group review meeting, Eileen felt betrayed by the woman who was her mentor. She was still annoyed at April, and her voice reflected her feelings she didn't feel like hiding. "What do you want?"

"May I come in?"

"Sure." Eileen's voice was terse as she fought back the urge to say what was really on her mind.

"Are you still stewing over Stan's comments?"

"Comments, no. Behavior, yes. He was condescending and rude, considering that I am ranked number one in all the categories used to rate client partners."

"He's been getting an earful from others in the firm about you. Many of your peers are upset because your clients are more profitable and the supporting staff get bigger bonuses and hence want to work for you rather than them."

"Not my problem. My ..." Eileen hesitated and then decided to use April's word. "... peers manage their own portfolios and make their own decisions on how they sell and price their work."

"That's not all. Many are nervous about your..." April's voice tailed off.

"Notoriety that came with the Medal of Freedom. Or that that I've been interviewed on national TV. Or that I have a potential new client pipeline that is the healthiest in the firm." She wanted to add but didn't — *how about they may be feeling guilty in that I did something to defend our country and they haven't.*

"That and many have expressed fear that the Sinaloas may come into this office to try to kill you."

Eileen laughed. "Yes, Derek and his friends, along with my father and I gave the Sinaloas a bloody nose, but they're back at doing what they do, which is selling drugs. We're no longer a threat to them. This tells me that there are many fertile minds around here with nothing better to do than fantasize about something they know nothing about. I can imagine what the rumors are... Well, I take that back. No, I can't."

"I need to ask, and please don't get angry. Are you carrying?"

"Carrying what?"

"A gun."

Eileen banged her briefcase on the table. The anger bubbling below the surface now came out into the open. "April, number one, don't ever ask me that question again! Number two, whether I am carrying is none of your fucking business nor the agency's. Now, will you please leave? I have a conference call to prepare for with one of the many highly profitable accounts I manage."

"Stan wants to know."

"Fuck Stan. If he had any ..." Eileen stopped. She pulled her laptop out of her docking station and slid the 16" MacBook Pro back into her briefcase. "I'm going to take the call someplace else. The air here reeks of bullshit and hypocrisy."

THURSDAY, SEPTEMBER 15TH, 2016, 7:28 P.M. LOCAL TIME, CAMELOT, (DEREK ALMER'S RANCH)

Derek was cutting up chunks of steak to put in each of the five dog dishes lined up on the island in the kitchen. All five Standard Poodles— Derek's four, Zeus, Athena, Rocky and Tux, and Eileen's Lucie—were sitting somewhat impatiently in a row. They smelled what was coming and looked at Derek with the "human, hurry up and feed us" look.

He'd just returned from San Diego after spending the day with the Navy Criminal Investigative Service and the FBI. One of the enlisted men in HSC-85, an E-5, and a jet engine mechanic, was stopped at the gate of Naval Air Station North Island on a routine stop and search. Dogs found two one-kilogram bricks of cocaine in the car.

With the unit's CO deployed in Columbia as one of the pilots in a two-helicopter detachment and unavailable, as the XO, Derek had to meet with the Naval Criminal Investigative Service so he flew his Aerostar to the Naval Air Station. Derek had an approved DD Form 2401 that allowed him to land on any U.S. military facility in the Aerostar.

He could see something was bugging Eileen as she banged the knife on the cutting board while she chopped vegetables for the stir fry they were making for dinner. With the dog dishes on the floor, he slipped his arms around her from behind and rested his chin on her shoulder. "Lover, what's eating at you?"

"Nothing."

"When you say nothing, you mean something. So, what is going on?"

"I don't want to bug you."

Derek gently turned her around. "Bug me. Something serious is happening at work, or you are really pissed at me."

"Work. Stan and April are being assholes."

"About what?"

By the time Eileen was finished, she was crying and finished by saying, "I've poured my heart and soul into that goddamn agency, and this is what I get."

"So, tell Stan and April to take the agency and shove it up their ass. You don't need the money. We don't need the money. You can stay here and paint. The gallery in Dallas has been asking for more of your paintings, so create them."

"Today, I almost quit."

"Well, talk to Avery so you are prepared legally, and then, the next time they piss you off, quit."

"Are you sure you don't mind?"

"Look, ultimately, Stan will want to find a way to replace you with someone cheaper who is beholden to him, not an independent soul like you. As the number one client executive, April and he may see you as a threat. Most likely, they fear that you may take some of the clients and start an agency, or worse, go to a competitor. Just be prepared so you have staked out the legal, ethical, and moral high ground when you say good-bye."

FRIDAY, SEPTEMBER 16ᵀᴴ, 2016, 7:48 A.M. LOCAL TIME, WASHINGTON, D.C.

Only five men were sitting on the couches and easy chairs in the Oval Office. The president sat in a separate chair facing his Director of

National Intelligence, the head of the CIA, his chief of staff, and his National Security Advisor.

The president sat with his feet crossed as he flipped through the dark-blue notebook after the CIA director provided a summary. "Is there something I missed? There is nothing new here."

The National Security Advisor spoke up. "Yes, Mr. President, there is. The fact that four Stinger missiles found their way into a farmer's field in Texas is very significant. These missiles were left in Saudi Arabia after Desert Storm. We are investigating how they were smuggled into the U.S."

"These are old missiles and are not a threat, correct?"

"Yes, Mr. President. However, we need to determine if more missiles are headed our way, and we can't count on them all failing to fire."

"Is the FBI involved?"

"Yes, Mr. President."

"Good. Then, we need to let them do their job."

The National Security Advisor saw the Director of the CIA nod slightly as if to say, I would like to speak. "Mr. President. This is more than a law enforcement problem. If al-Qaeda or the Taliban have Stingers, then with a few missiles, they can bring our entire air transportation system to a halt by shooting down one or two airliners. If they have them in the U.S., we must look for potential launch sites around our commercial airports. I must emphasize, sir, that this is a very, very real threat."

The president looked at the Director of the CIA and his National Security Advisor. "If the word gets out that we are looking for these, these... MANPADS, as you call them, the press will stir up the flying public, and Fox News will attack this administration as further proof that we are weak on national security. That cannot happen."

The president took a deep breath, and the two others in the room waited for him to continue. "If we find the source of missiles, we're not going to threaten or invade some country over a couple of Stinger missiles. Look, I was elected to end wars, not start new ones. We need to change our image in the world from being the local bully to being much more of a partner who will consider the needs of our neighbors. Therefore, we will treat this as a law enforcement problem, and I will instruct the attorney general accordingly. Plus, I will emphasize that the FBI must keep a lid on this. We're not going to set off a nationwide panic over a couple of missiles. Understood?"

Hiding his disappointment, the head of the CIA nodded as he spoke. "Yes, sir."

SATURDAY, SEPTEMBER 17ᵀᴴ, 2016, 11:36 A.M. LOCAL TIME, DFW AIRPORT

A clean-shaven Dawuud Ghanem stood patiently in line at the security checkpoint in Terminal A, holding his boarding pass to JFK. To reach Karachi, Pakistan, he was booked on a British Airways flight to London Heathrow and a connecting flight on a Pakistani International Airlines to Karachi. Assuming the planes were on time, the trip would take almost 24 hours.

Along with his boarding pass, Dawuud had his U.S. Citizenship and Immigration Services "green card" ready to show the TSA agent along with his Qatari passport. The green card was issued when he was a student at American University in Washington, D.C., was still valid. After 9/11, the laminated card raised fewer questions than his Pakistani passport.

Dawuud wasn't afraid that some in al-Qaeda would label his mission a failure because they failed to shoot down the airliners. The man who prepared the missiles was supposedly an expert. So, there were only two possible explanations: either the missiles were truly faulty or Na'il Miraj sabotaged them.

So, what happened?

He would have to find out before they tried another attack. Everything else—logistics, location—worked as planned. Only the missiles failed to fire.

THE SAME DAY, 5:30 P.M. LOCAL TIME, MACDILL AFB, FL

At 10-minute intervals, a stolen three-year-old Honda Accord and a 2009 Chevrolet Impala drove through the Air Force base's gate on Bayshore Boulevard. The thieves figured that, since they were stolen less than an hour ago from the University Mall parking lot, they would be through the gate by the time the owners had reported the thefts to the police who, they assumed, would notify the Air Force base's security detachment.

The two visible occupants in each car were in their twenties with close-cropped hair that screamed military. Each had a forged military ID card and access badge identifying them as officers assigned to the 6th Operations Support Squadron of the 6th Air Mobility Wing. Both cars were waved through the gate.

The cars kept to the posted speed limit down Bayshore Drive on MacDill before pulling into a parking lot off Hillsborough Bay. The trunks were opened, and the number of men doubled from four to eight. From the footwell behind the front seat of each car, each man pulled on a vest with 12, 30-round magazines, two fragmentation grenades, and short-barreled AK-74U assault rifles.

The AK-74Us were first introduced into the Russian military in 1974 as an answer to the U.S. Army's very successful M16 carbine. Instead of the NATO 5.56mmx45 round, the AK-74U fired a slightly smaller 5.45mmx39 cartridge at a slightly higher muzzle velocity. The U's folding stock and the shorter barrel made it easier to point and shoot, but beyond 200 meters, it was not as accurate as an M16.

Before they entered MacDill, the men had been given a map of the base, a detailed layout of the building, and an event timeline. With this information, they planned their attack.

The Bayshore Club was built while the runways were being constructed just before World War II. Named after a World War I Army aviator who was killed in a 1938 airplane crash, MacDill Air Force Base was completed and officially dedicated on April 16th, 1941. The base had been home to Air Force strategic bomber units until 1960. Then, it became a fighter base until U.S. Central Command and U.S. Special Operations Command took up residence.

Located right on Tampa Bay, the Bayshore Club was an ideal facility to host a U.S. Special Operations Command dining-in for officers above the rank of major or lieutenant commander. After 9/11, the dining-in was held on the weekend after the anniversary date.

Derek Almer, who knew many of the officers, was on active duty at Special Operations Command for two weeks and was invited. He'd heard about but had never met the evening's keynote speaker, a retired rear admiral and fellow helicopter pilot named Josh Haman.

In the dining room, the table was arranged in an upside-down U with a short table for the junior officer known as Mr. Vice, in the gap. All the other officers were seated according to rank and seniority with those most senior at the base of the U with the Commander, U.S. Special Operations Command in the center, and the honored guest and speaker next to him.

On Mr. Vice's table, a large sterling silver bowl was next to a bottle of wine and China with the command's logo, silverware, and glasses. Alongside Mr. Vice's plate was a steno pad and a pen. Although not required, Mr. Vice could record the fines doled out by the president of the mess who was the four-star general and commander of Special Operations Command. The cash from the fines would be deposited in the bowl.

Mr. Vice, a recently promoted major named Nathan Grayson, signaled the sommelier, who, with a great deal of flair, opened a bottle of wine and poured about half an inch into his glass. Grayson swirled the claret-colored liquid around in the glass, held it up for all to see, and took a sip. He already knew the taste because he'd sampled the burgundy when he selected it. But ceremony and tradition rules at a dining-in.

Satisfied, Major Grayson stood up and rang the silver bell on the right corner of his table as a signal for conversation to stop. A quiet took over the room and he spoke in a loud, clear voice, "General, the wine is fit for toasting and drinking."

Dining-in etiquette gave Major Grayson the option of referring to the commander of the Special Operations Command as either General or, because he was the president of the mess, Mr. President. Anyone else sitting at the tables had to be addressed by their rank and last name. Getting a name and a rank wrong was a finable offense. Fines were either set by the president of the mess.

"Mr. Vice, I am glad you covered both areas. However, as a major in the United States Army, I would have assumed that you would have thoroughly checked out the choices and only picked the best for our consumption. However, since you did not graduate from the United States Military Academy, I will take that into consideration. Fine is one dollar. You may proceed."

Ceremoniously, Grayson took a dollar bill out of the wad stuffed in the left front pocket of his pants where he now had 49 one-dollar bills left. In his right front pocket, 20 bills with Lincoln's portrait were neatly folded. He anticipated this was going to be an expensive night.

The four-star general waited until he was sure each officer's wine glass was filled, not to the top, but about an inch from the bottom. He stood and held up his glass, "To the president of the United States…"

Each member stood and held up his glass and spoke… "The president…" and drained his or her glass. This toast and the next one was the hardest to swallow. Few, if any of the members of the mess had any respect for the president of the United States, who they viewed as indecisive and whose view of the world was not aligned with reality. Unfortunately, as members of the U.S. military, they had no choice but to execute his orders.

Waiting stewards quickly refilled their glasses, Nathan Grayson nodded in the direction of the head table. The president of the mess nodded slightly in return. "To the vice president of the United States…"

"The vice president." The drinking and refilling process was repeated. Four other mandatory toasts—to the Secretary of Defense, the Chairman of the Joint Chiefs, the Special Operations Command, and to those who gave their lives in battle for the United States—followed. When the last one was completed, Nathan Grayson looked at the senior member of the foreign officers present, an Australian colonel. He along with, as the Canadian and British officers had agreed to reduce the mandatory toasts to one for each of their respective countries, their armed services, and one to the queen. All agreed.

After the toast to Her Majesty's Forces from Australia, Canada, and Britain was finished, Grayson again looked around the room. "Do any members of the mess want to propose a toast?"

"I do." The voice was feminine and loud and clear and from one of the back tables where the most junior officers were sitting. "I would like to propose a toast to our distinguished guest, the holder of not one, but two Navy Crosses and fellow rotorhead, Rear Admiral Joshua Haman."

The president of the mess leaned forward. "Lieutenant Commander Cassidy, you may propose such a toast. However, it is rude to mention one's decorations. Our guest's decorations are on his uniform, and the navy-blue ribbon with the white stripe and gold star is in plain sight for all of us to see. Fine is five dollars."

"Yes, sir." Before she spoke again, Kathleen Cassidy, call sign "Hopalong", took a five-dollar bill out of the black leather purse that was part of Mess Dress White for female officers and held it up. A steward brought over the silver bowl into which she dropped the bill. She earned the call sign because when Kathleen became excited, she hopped sideways like a puppy wanting to play.

"To Rear Admiral Haman, a fellow special operations warrior and helicopter pilot who helped pave the way for the rest of us...."

"Hear, hear. Rear Admiral Haman." More wine was drunk.

A Navy captain who was going to retire on September 30th and begin a second career with a defense contractor stood up. "Mr. President, I would like to toast the defense contractors who make the fine weapons we use to destroy our enemies."

"Captain Hollingsworth, sit down and shut the ... hell up." The general almost used the "f" word and would automatically incur a 20-dollar fine but managed to catch himself. "They should be toasting us for putting up with the crap they sometimes build. They make millions while we go off to do and to die. Your fine is fifty dollars for an inappropriate toast. You should be able to afford this because next month, you'll have a nice civilian salary to go with your retirement check."

A green beret known for being a ladies' man stood up. "Mr. President, I would like to toast our fellow officers who ..." The major paused for a few seconds as his brain fished for the right word. "... are of the fairer sex."

"Major Sequin. Your fine is twenty dollars for a politically incorrect toast. Sit down. We don't differentiate between male and female officers. Anyone assigned to a role in this command has met our stringent performance standards. If they can't, they don't get in the door."

After several more toasts, Major Grayson stood up. "Mr. President, the time has come for our evening meal." He waited for the general to nod to the chaplain, an army lieutenant colonel sitting where he should be based on his date of rank. The chaplain had instructions from Grayson to be brief and non-denominational.

The chaplain who was an ordained Catholic priest began with the words "Our Heavenly Father...." A hundred words later, he finished, and the members of the mess said, "Amen."

Grayson waited what he hoped was an appropriate amount of time before he rang the silver bell. On cue, two stewards entered carrying a steamship round of beef on a very large cutting board. "Mr. President, may I parade the beef so that all can see what will be our dinner? I will, of course, test it to make sure the beef is fit for human consumption."

"Proceed." The general's silence was a cue to all the other members of the mess as Grayson and the two stewards followed by a man in a chef's hat walked around the C-shaped table. When they finished, the cutting board was placed on a table brought in for the purpose of carving and serving. The table with the steamship round of roast beef was next to another table with side dishes. A chunk was sliced off and placed on Grayson's plate. He was served a salad and another plate with a small selection of side dishes. His first bite was a small forkful of the salad, which was followed by a bite of the roll and each side dish. Finally, as all the members of the mess watched, he cut off a small piece of the roast beef and chewed for a few seconds, savoring the texture and meaty taste.

Satisfied what he tasted was what he'd ordered, Major Grayson stood up. "Mr. President, I have the pleasure to inform the mess that the beef is excellent and all the other dishes are fit to eat."

"Mr. Vice, I would expect nothing else. Fine is five dollars for stating the obvious."

The most senior officers were served first, but no one touched his food until the president of the mess picked up his knife and fork after he looked around the table to make sure each officer was served. The movement was his signal to begin eating.

Outside the club in the parking lot, Captain Vicki Stratton, West Point Class of 2004, stood under a small group of palm trees. A veteran of three tours to Afghanistan as a member of the 10th Mountain Division, she was the commander of the dining-in's security detail. She was wearing full battle dress and leaned back against the hood of the armored Humvee that the base's Air Police security force gave the team to use as a command post.

With essentially the entire leadership of the Special Operations Command in one room, the general insisted that the command provide their own quick reaction force. Her assignment came directly from the commander of the Special Operations Command who also used the call to congratulate her on her selection for promotion to major.

In Vicki's first tour in Afghanistan, she was a platoon leader. On her second, she was a company commander who built a solid reputation for being cool under fire and tactically smart. On her third, she was supposed to be on the division's 2nd battalion, 4th Infantry Regiment operations staff, but when Charlie Company's commander was killed early in her tour, Vicki volunteered to take over his company. If she was wearing her uniform, besides the campaign ribbons, one would see that she'd been awarded a Silver Star and two Bronze Stars, both with Combat Vs so no one was surprised that she'd was selected for promotion to major.

At any one time, she had 14 of her 18 men and women in two-soldier teams, patrolling the club grounds, trying to stay out of sight. Two more two-man fire teams loitered in the shadows near the Humvee where Vicki was standing. She had the vehicle parked 100 yards from the club's portico so she had a clear view of the front and one side of the building.

Inside the Humvee, the driver slowly swung the M-249 machine gun as he looked through the night vision devices, and the team's radio operator had his M4 carbine handy. Every soldier in the security detail was connected to each other via short-range radios.

The two cars that stopped under the portico caught Vicki's attention. She saw the recognizable silhouette of an AK-74 despite the attempt of the man getting out of the driver's seat attempt to hide it.

Bastards!!! Vicki ran toward the cars, unslinging her M4 carbine at the same time she keyed her mike. "Bad guys, bad guys... At least four at the front door. Seal the entrances. Meet Team Actual at the club entrance. Condition Red, repeat CONDITION RED!!!"

She heard the acknowledgments on the radio. The rally point was a nook in the foyer from where they could control access to the room where the dining-in was being held.

Vicki didn't have to turn around to see if her fire teammate, a Green Beret sergeant, was next to her. Over her pounding heart, she heard the clumping of his boots on the asphalt.

The third man out of the second car turned toward the two charging soldiers and opened fire. Vicki zigged and zagged. The first burst chewed up asphalt where she'd been. As she ran, she squeezed off short bursts at the two targets she could see. Both men sprawled to the ground.

A third appeared from around the edge of the building and let loose a long burst. Vicki felt a burning sensation followed by eye watering pain as the three rounds hit her just below her Kevlar vest. Suddenly, her legs stopped working and she went sprawling to the ground. As she grabbed for her carbine, she saw the Green Beret's lifeless eyes looking at her.

Over her head, tracers from the M-249 streaked by and stitched both cars. The windows shattered and two more of the attackers were lying on the ground, either dead or dying.

Inside the room where the dining-in was being held, distinctive rattling of an AK being fired and sharp report of an M4 along with the rattle of an M-249 being fired stopped all conversation. The commander of the Special Operations Command took charge immediately and yelled to turn the tables on their side and dump the food on the floor.

Derek was astounded as to how many of the attendees were carrying weapons under their mess dress. He pulled out his Smith & Wesson M&P 9mm Compact that had one in the firing chamber and 12 in the magazine. In his coat pocket, he had a spare magazine with 12 rounds. Not very much for a firefight.

With a fort set up in the center of the room, the general directed additional tables to be placed around the edge separated by chairs to create an extra level of protection. With that done, the general ordered men and women with weapons to the front and those unarmed to get down in the floor in the middle. Smiling, he looked around and said,

"Ladies and gentlemen, welcome to the Alamo! Do not fire until you are sure your target is a terrorist. We need to conserve ammunition because we could be here a while."

As each attacker ran toward the dining-in, they fired bursts at anyone they saw. Their primary goal was the staff of the hated Special Operations Command. Killing anyone else was of secondary importance.

Gamal, the leader, shouted "*Allah Akbar*" several times as he emptied a full magazine into the crowded bar where he could hear women screaming and men yelling. He tossed in a grenade and didn't wait for the explosion. They weren't his targets and charged down the hall, followed by his three accomplices.

While two of his men trained their weapons up and down the hallway, Gamal held up a second grenade and waited until his comrade had one in his hand. He counted to three and then pulled the pin and tried to kick open the door.

The solid-wood door gave a few inches but didn't give way. The chairs wedged under the door stopped any movement. Gamal pointed to the two door handles. "Put your grenade on the handles, then we'll move away and get down on the floor. After it goes off, we'll toss another grenade . After it explodes, go in and kill the infidels."

The man opposite Gamal nodded and did as he was told. The blast shattered the door. Gamal tossed his second grenade into the room and heard the shout, "Grenade!" A second later, the olive drab globe flew out the door, banged into the wall on the other side of the hall, and fell to the floor.

All four attackers dropped to the floor before the grenade sent shards of hot metal up and down the hallway, peppering the four men. Gamal ignored his wounds, nodded and the four men got up and shouted "*Allah Akbar*" as they charged into the room ready to mow down American soldiers.

Gamal expected to find the Americans cowering under tables or running for their lives. Derek Almer was one of a half-dozen members of the Air Force, Army, Marine Corps, and Navy in their mess dress uniforms who stood up in unison with pistols leveled. Almost instantly, each man fired a well-aimed double tap at one of the attackers.

The last thing that Gamal and his team saw was the ripple of muzzle flashes coming from a mix of 9mm and .45-caliber pistols.

Each man crumpled as he was hit by at least six rounds in the chest and upper body before any could pull his AK-47's trigger.

Two Marines jumped over the tables and kicked the weapons away from the four men whose blood was staining the carpet. Satisfied that they couldn't pick up a weapon, they touched the neck of each inert form and confirmed that they were all dead.

In the distance, Derek could hear the sirens signaling ambulances were on the way. Over the wail, the general shouted. "Take their weapons and ammo. We sit tight and wait until the cavalry arrives."

The diners didn't have to wait long. Four men in battle dress appeared at the door. "General, all clear. We will take the department heads to the command center as soon as we can."

"Sergeant, call the duty officer and have him issue an immediate recall. We need to count noses and ensure this is not one of a series of attacks."

"Yes, sir."

"Any casualties?"

"Yes, sir. I don't have a good count, but there are at least a dozen or more dead in the bar. Sergeant Crandall who was on the security team was killed, and Captain Stratton is in bad shape. She along with some of the wounded from the bar are on the way to the hospital. Sir, these bastards came into our front yard."

"Yes, they did. Hopefully, we will be allowed to make them pay."

As Rear Admiral Haman was led out of the room with SOCOM's senior officers, Derek Almer regretted not spending more time with the man.

MONDAY, SEPTEMBER 19ᵀᴴ, 2016, 8:30 A.M. LOCAL TIME, IVANHOE

The winding half-mile drive from route FM-273 to his house allowed Andrew to walk to the porch and wait for the plain Jane Chevrolet Malibu and the Fannin County Sheriff's cars to arrive. He knew both cars were coming because Special Agent Anderson had to push the intercom button so Andrew could open the gate. The high-resolution video camera at the top of the steel frame with the S&S brand showed both cars.

Anderson didn't bother to put on his sport coat as he got out of the car leaving his gold badge and .40-caliber Glock pistol visible. Instead, he grabbed a folded piece of paper. Behind him, the sheriff's deputy reported in by radio, and, after he closed the door, he leaned back against the hood. He knew from growing up in Bonham that the Sullivan family had owned this land since the 1880s. While he didn't socialize with the Sullivans, everyone in the department respected the family and what they did for the community.

Anderson knew what he was holding and didn't like it, but orders were orders. "Mr. Sullivan, can we go inside?"

"Sure."

Before Andrew opened the screen door, he looked at the deputy. "Deputy Carruthers, do you want to come in?"

It was in the mid-70s and the forecasters said the temperature would only get into the low 80s today. Fall was just around the corner.

"No, sir. I'll just sit on the porch."

Andrew led the FBI agent to the large family room. "Special Agent Anderson, what can I do for you?"

"Sir, I need you to sign this, acknowledging its receipt and agreement to the terms in the document."

"What terms?"

"It is a Federal Northern Texas District Court order as well as a letter from the attorney general of the United States that orders you and every member of your family not to discuss the discovery of the four Stinger missiles on your property or anything else you found that day."

"Before I sign this, I will have my attorney look at it."

Anderson was afraid he would get that answer. "Sir, I have been instructed to tell you that if you do not sign this letter now, I am to arrest you for obstructing a federal investigation. You will be held in jail until you sign the document."

Andrew Sullivan gave the agent an incredulous look. "You've got to be shitting me."

"No, sir. I don't like this any better than you. However, we are dealing with national security, and my orders came directly from the director and the attorney general, who called me last night. I was told to get my ass out here as fast as possible with the court order that would be waiting for me at the office when I arrived this morning."

"What the fuck is going on?"

"Sir, I don't know. Please don't force me to arrest you."

"May I at least read the damned court order?"

"Yes, sir, of course."

As Andrew read, he became convinced his attorney would have a fit that he signed the acknowledgment stating that if he violated the restraining order, he would be accused of crimes ranging from obstruction of justice to spying and treason. "This is preposterous. Do you have a warrant for my arrest with you?"

"No, sir, but I can have one here pretty damn quick."

"I suggest you do so. In the meantime, I will fax this to my attorney and call him. If he says sign, I will; if not, you will have to arrest me."

The special agent nodded in agreement. He thought this was bullshit and told the director after the attorney general hung up that actions such as this would come back and bite the bureau in the ass. The director agreed, but he had no choice. He worked for the attorney general, and the attorney general worked for her friend, the president of the United States.

TUESDAY, SEPTEMBER 20TH, 2016, 2:26 P.M. LOCAL TIME, BONHAM, TX

Andrew put the last bag of the groceries into the back of the family Suburban at the Brookshire's at the intersection of U.S. Highway 82 and State Highway 78 in Bonham when he recognized the snarl of the two Lycoming TIO-540s in Derek Haman's Aerostar 701P. He knew his friend, pattern traffic permitting, loved to fly down the 4,000-foot runway at 500 feet at cruise power and at the end, pull up into a steep climbing turn.

According to Derek, if he flew the maneuver perfectly, he'd arrive abeam the numbers at 1,000 feet with half flaps and the gear down and locked at 110 knots. From there, he would ease the throttles back to 15 inches of manifold pressure as he descended while making 180-degree left turn. With the flaps full down, the pressurized twin slowed to 90 knots. Over the numbers on the upwind end of the runway, Derek flared the Aerostar gently to let the airplane settle on the centerline on the first 100 feet of the runway.

He'd flown with Derek many times and watched him make this approach without touching the throttles after the initial power reduction. Despite the fact he was flying a non-standard approach, no one at the airport cared if there was no other plane in the traffic pattern.

Andrew stopped his Suburban at the edge of the concrete ramp where the self-service fuel pumps were located. Derek waved to Andrew as he climbed down the lower half of the clamshell-shaped door and headed toward his neighbor.

The two friends shook hands. Derek's ice-blue eyes focused on Andrew. Some thought Derek's eyes were lasers because when he fixated on you, the intensity behind them made some uncomfortable. "This is a pleasant surprise. Are you here just to help me refuel, or do you have more bad news?"

The two men became friends when Derek was looking for some property, and a friend in the Navy suggested he call Andrew. At the time, the cattle business was in the crapper, and the Sullivan family was struggling financially and might lose the ranch without an influx of cash.

Derek remembered the conversation well. "Andrew, if you have enough land to sell, I will pay a premium and build a house on it. Someday I'll get my money back, and you get the money you need now." A few days later, they closed on 300 acres of mostly tree-covered land. Over the next six months, Derek acquired another 200 acres from another rancher also in need of money. The house was finished six months after he closed on the first parcel of land.

As they shook hands, Andrew shook his head. "This is a good place to talk because you wouldn't fucking believe what happened yesterday."

"Tell me."

Andrew gave him a synopsis of his conversation with Special Agent Anderson before adding, "My lawyer says it is legal intimidation and, if I wanted, I could fight the government. He said taking on the attorney general of the United States would be an economic battle, more than a legal one. His advice was to pretend to obey and don't do anything overt that will catch their attention such as going to the media."

"Sounds like good advice. The only winner if you told the Feds to fuck-off will be your lawyer!"

"Yeah, that's what he said too." Andrew looked at his friend. "Do you still have that secure satellite phone that gives you access to high mucky mucks at Special Operations Command and your friend at CIA?"

"I do. Do I need to call them?"

"Depends on what you learned in San Diego."

"Not much. I had lunch with two SEALs I know—Jacob Sobrano and Ed DeCosta—and they're going to do some digging. Both the DIA and CIA have teams trying to keep track of missing weapons like Stingers and the Soviet, excuse me, Russian-made SA-7 Grails, SA-18 Grouses, and the new SA-24 Grinches. They now know when and where they were stolen."

"Good. I think that when the missiles failed to fire, they were left as a message that another 9/11 is about to happen."

"Andrew, my good friend, I think you are right. Let's hope the guy in the White House is paying attention."

"I wouldn't take that bet."

"Don't be a cynic!" Derek turned and picked up the fuel nozzle.

CHAPTER 4

BIRTH OF A WEAPON

atimah was tired of working for others and wanted to own a private bank of her own. Rather than receive only a portion of the fees she generated, if she was the president or owned the bank, Fatimah would receive the fees and a large share of the profits. She wanted unfettered access to financial markets around the world and to be able to set the bank's policies, not have someone else create them.

Finding a small private bank that could be acquired was something that Fatimah had been considering for a year. She'd began researching potential acquisitions, and the pursuit didn't take long.

Her strategy was simple—overwhelm the owners with money and let greed take over. Bahar, Nazari & Touma's small size—less than 200 employees and offices in Dubai, Riyadh, London, and Karachi—made the bank an ideal target.

Fatimah assured the owners that they could stay if they wished, but once the deal was closed, their clients would remain with the bank if they left. She sweetened the deal with a new bonus plan Fatimah hoped would encourage them to stay. Or at least until she could find replacements.

In the organization charts filed with the State Bank of Pakistan which regulated banks in the country and served as the country's central bank, Fatimah was the chief executive officer. The prior holder of the position was now the chairman, but she owned 71 percent of the shares held by Fatimah's investment group, which now owned 80 percent of the Bahar, Nazari & Touma's shares. This gave her control of her investors, all of whom were clients. To a man, they all believed her pitch that investing in her group to buy the bank would increase the money she made for them.

On her desk were the layouts of the bank's new logo. Fatimah slipped off her shoes and enjoyed the cool feeling of the deep plush carpet as she walked across the room and put the artwork on the top shelf of a bookcase.

Behind her, sheer curtains softened the bright morning sunlight coming through the floor-to-ceiling windows. From the 7th floor of the 10-story building on I. I. Chundrigar Road in the heart of Karachi's financial district, Bahar, Nazari & Touma's headquarters was a couple of blocks from the country's stock exchange. On the same street, one could find the offices of Citibank, Standard Chartered, and the National Bank of Pakistan, along with Pakistan's major media companies.

She loved the new simple logo that featured a curved sword known as a scimitar in the West. The Arabic word for the weapon with a long-curved blade was saif. A saif was called a talwar in Pakistan, Northwest India, and Bangladesh. The log and the words Talwar Bank were between the hand guard and the tip of the blade. Fatimah would present the new graphics to the other executives later today. When she acquired the bank, she told them it would have a new, more aggressive look. The new logo was the start.

Fatimah was in a hurry, and this was a pleasant diversion in her efforts to remake the bank to fit her vision. She had clients to make richer and, in the process, make herself much wealthier.

WEDNESDAY, SEPTEMBER 28TH, 2016, 1:49 P.M. LOCAL TIME, KOVROV, RUSSIA

The result from taking parts from little bins and small boxes was now sitting on Gavrie Zolnerovich's test bench—an Igla-S missile. When the testing was complete, the missile would become serial number 9K-338-S-004546-VAD-16. Gavrie looked at the two components—the missile and the launcher—for a few seconds before connecting the umbilical cord to the test set. Painted light gray, the Igla-S missile contrasted with the olive-green launcher tube and the shipping crate at the end of the test bench.

Zolnerovich began working at the V.A. Degtyarev Plant in 1988 on Truda Street in the small city of Kovrov after he graduated from Novosibirsk State University. Before he entered the university, he'd spent two years in Afghanistan as an infantryman. When Zolnerovich graduated as a mechanical engineer, he was assigned to the plant in the small city due east of Moscow and almost halfway to Nizhniy Novgorod.

In the plant, Zolnerovich's primary job was as a mechanical engineer. The pistol grip assembly on the Igla-S was his design. His seniority and intimate knowledge of the missile's and launcher's inner workings were why he was made the plant's final inspector.

If a missile failed his tests—and one in five did—he could either fix the Igla-S on his table or tell the manufacturing supervisor exactly what needed repair. This way, he knew what went into the shipping cases would work as designed.

The factory began building machine guns for the czar in 1917 and was one of the few plants that wasn't moved east to avoid the onrushing Nazi armies in 1941. Today, besides machine guns and unguided rockets, the plant made the 9K-338-S known in the Red Army as the Igla-S or by the NATO designation SA-24 with the code name Grinch.

Zolnerovich pushed a toggle switch on the test set he designed to check the missile's electrical circuits. A row of green lights lit, and a needle stopped at the correct voltage and amperage, telling him the battery and circuits were operating as intended. Another gauge said the pressure in the bottle filled with liquid nitrogen was correct.

The reading's date and time were logged onto the sheet with all the missile's component serial numbers. With the paperwork finished, Gavrie unhooked the test set and inked the serial number onto the rocket and the tube. Next, he slid the 11.7-kilogram (5.73 pounds) missile into the launcher tube before attaching the small wire that connected the trigger to the missile. Igla-S 9K-338-S-

004546-VAD-16 was now fully operational. With the missile and tube nestled in the hard, black foam, Zolnerovich latched the case and performed his last task—re-inking the roller and applying the serial number to the top and both sides of the case.

Satisfied, Gavrie ran his hands through his thick gray hair that long ago lost any strands of its original brown color. As he did, he wondered for the millionth time what genius devised the numbering system.

The first two characters—9K—were the Russian designation for a missile. The digits "338" designated the model of the missile, and "S" indicated the model was the improved version. The seven digits indicated that it was the 4,546[th] one made. He often wondered what would happen if they ordered more than 99,999? He never asked because the inquiry could be considered by some in some in today's FSB as questioning the system. When Zolnerovich was in Afghanistan, one of his friends often criticized Soviet policy. He endured a brutal interrogation by the KGB before being sent home and discharged with a note in his file that he was politically unreliable. For a Soviet citizen, that was tantamount to ensuring the individual would never be given anything but a menial job.

"VAD" indicated his factory. If the letters were "KOL," the manufacturer was the creator of the Igla series of missiles, the Kolomna Design Bureau. The last two digits in the serial number were the year of manufacture (i.e., 2016).

Assuming Zolnerovich didn't have to troubleshoot a problem, it took him about 20 to 30 minutes to check each missile. The two pallets, each with 12 tested missiles now included Igla-S 9K-338-S-004546-VAD-16, represented his work over the past two days as a tester and final inspector.

THURSDAY, SEPTEMBER 29TH, 2016, 2:56 P.M. LOCAL TIME, 60 MILES SOUTHEAST OF KABUL, AFGHANISTAN

To reach the cave in the shadow of the 4,755-meter tall (15,600 foot) Mount Sikaram on the Afghani/Pakistani border, Dawuud walked for six days, and he was sure the entire trip was uphill. This was after he spent nearly 30 hours en route from Dallas to Karachi. He waited two hours after clearing customs for his flight to Peshawar, where he spent the night at a cheap hotel. The next day, he rode in a Toyota Land Cruiser over the Khyber Pass.

Once the Toyota was out of the valley, Dawuud breathed more easily because they were out of Peshawar's acrid-tasting pollution and dust that clogged one's nostrils. While the trip was only 135 kilometers (85 miles) from the airport in Peshawar to the heart of Jalalabad, the trip took almost four hours due to the slow-moving truck traffic.

From Jalalabad, Ghanem's driver headed south into the mountains of Tora Bora. His driver turned off the paved road onto one made from gravel. A few kilometers later, the driver parked in a wooded area at the base of a rock outcropping. A man with an AK-47 slung over his shoulder emerged from the trees.

Dawuud took his backpack from the Land Cruiser and, when he had it positioned comfortably on his shoulders, he nodded to the man standing patiently in front of him. Without a word, the man led him to a path where he joined a larger group of men for a hike that took six long days to reach the caves.

There, Dawuud found Na'il Miraj's workbench made from a sheet of ¾-inch thick plywood supported by empty ammo crates. Light came from a combination of electric lights and gas lanterns that hung from nails hammered into holes drilled in the rock. On the left side of the bench, Miraj had stacked oscilloscopes and other test equipment. His toolbox was on the right side of the bench. In the center, two binders were kept vertical by rusted mortar rounds sitting on their fins used as bookends.

Stacked on the opposite wall of the cave, about 100 meters from the mouth, a dozen Stinger missiles waited for Miraj's inspection along with the same number of Soviet-made SA-14 Grails. All were well past the dates when the batteries should be changed, the nitrogen bottles purged and re-charged, and the rocket motors inspected.

Miraj, who already knew about the missile failures in Texas sensed someone was in his workshop and turned around to see Dawuud Ghanem. "Welcome back to Afghanistan. How was your trip?" He spoke in English, knowing that most al-Qaeda fighters wouldn't understand the conversation. Miraj's Pashto and Dari, while passable, were far from fluent. English was his best language, followed by Arabic.

Ghanem was in a hurry to get to the cause. "Do you know why the missiles didn't fire?"

"No. Tell me exactly what you did and what happened." He had been working on the problem since he'd learned of the failed shoot and believed he knew the answer.

On his way up to the cave, Ghanem decided to be direct and watch the man's expression. That would tell him if Miraj knew they would fail when they left his shop.

"Na'il, the batteries were charged, and the system went through the test sequence, but the missiles wouldn't lock onto a target. And, when I pulled the trigger, nothing happened. The best I can figure is that the nitrogen leaked out, and without the gas, the sensors couldn't detect a heat source."

"The bottles were full and sealed when they left here."

Ghanem levered himself onto the boxes of Stingers. "So why did they fail?"

"I don't know." Miraj hung his head for a few seconds. "The Americans code into the software so that after a certain date, the missile can't be fired. I will make sure the rest of these missiles are ready to go. Then we will fire them at the Americans and see if they work."

Dawuud slid off the crates. "I have a different idea. Can you download the software that is the brains of the missile?"

"You mean onto a thumb drive?"

"I don't care onto what, but I want someone to look at the code. Is that possible?"

"Maybe. I can try, but if we can look at the code, you'd need to find some programmers familiar with missile systems who know what they are looking at. Where are you going to get them? This is not Microsoft Office."

"That's my problem. You get the code on a CD or a thumb drive as quickly as you can."

MONDAY, OCTOBER 3RD, 2016, 2:38 P.M. LOCAL TIME, POCHEP, RUSSIA

Located in the heart of a strategic land-locked peninsula of Russia that juts into two countries—Belarus to the north and Ukraine to the south—Pochep is a small city of less than 20,000. The town sits at the intersection of two of Russia's main railroads—an east-west line joins the Trans-Siberian line and another that goes southeast to the Black Sea port of Rostov-on-Don. For 25 months, from August 22nd, 1941, until September 21st, 1943, the Nazis occupied Pochep. Other than send the town's Jews off to concentration camps to be exterminated, they did little to damage the city.

Pochep is the administrative center of the Pochepsky District (the rough U.S. equivalent to a county) in the Bryansk Oblast or what Americans would call a "state" in Russia. South of town is the other item of interest—a large chemical weapons and ammunition storage facility.

At the peak of the cold war, the weapons depot stored over 7,500 tons of nerve agents along with bombs, air-to-ground and surface-to-air missiles. After the collapse of the Soviet Union in 1991, Pochep was designated as a facility where chemical weapons were to be destroyed.

In 2010, the Russian Federation notified the world that it couldn't meet the Chemical Weapons Convention's 2012 deadline to eliminate of all its chemical weapons. The Russian announcement said the delays were due to "technological problems" and a lack of funds. Destruction, the government said, would now be completed by the end of 2016. With that deadline approaching, the Russian government said they should finish the destruction by the end of 2018.

The new commander of the Pochep facility, Colonel Serik Saliemenov, knew otherwise. The delays were not a result of insufficient funds. Instead, they were the result of a lack of will. No one in the Russian military wanted to destroy them.

As a Radiation, Chemical and Biological Defense unit member, Saliemenov spent the first part of his career learning how to employ what was known in the U.S. as "special weapons." Now in 2016, he was supposed to oversee their demise. The solution was typically Soviet—make a show of complying with the treaty conventions and send reports showing progress and delays, then with each missed deadline, issue a new set of excuses and promise to do better.

Before Saliemenov arrived, almost half of the arsenal's older, mostly obsolete models in the Pochep depot had been shipped away to make space for a state-of-the-art destruction facility. Plans were made, purchase orders issued, and some equipment deliveries were made, but nothing was built. As a chemical engineer, Saliemenov knew that Russia didn't have the technology or the skill to build what was designed and needed. He also didn't see the country spending the rubles to create a functional chemical weapons destruction facility.

Saliemenov was boxed in. One wall was a job he was well qualified to do but he also knew he would never get what was needed to execute his orders. Another was money—he needed much more than his pension would provide. His career was nearing its end, and he was afraid of retirement. Saliemenov could see what the new economy was doing to his friends struggling to live on their Army pensions.

The Russian Radiation, Chemical and Biological Defense colonel wondered how long his superiors in Moscow would allow him to maintain the charade of pretending to destroy the remaining chemical weapons stored at Pochep. What the Western nations were being told and what was not being done wasn't his problem. If Moscow doesn't provide the equipment, he can't dispose of any chemical weapons.

Saliemenov saw his time in Pochep as a race between finding a source of money so he could tell his superiors he was retiring— he liked to use the term "fuck off"—and when someone decided to make him a sacrificial lamb for not making progress.

Early in his career, Saliemenov learned that one of Stalin's favorite tactics was whenever he was assigned an important task, he already had a scapegoat in mind in case he failed. The scapegoat could be the individual who gave him the job or someone else convenient to blame and eliminate.

As he sat in his office in the two-story brick administration building, Saliemenov smiled as his plan came together. The scheme had been rattling around in the back of his mind, and now knew who the scapegoat would be and where he could get money to support his retirement. In his military-and engineering-trained mind, with careful execution, he would be well off for the rest of his life.

TUESDAY, OCTOBER 4TH, 2016, 11:56 A.M. LOCAL TIME, BONHAM, TX

Over the staccato noise of the Briggs & Stratton engine on the tug he used to push the twin-engine Aerostar 601P into the hangar, Derek heard the ringtone of his cell phone. Curious, he released the handle that engaged the drive, and the tug went into neutral. The number showed that the caller was from the country code 972 and the number was a familiar.

"Yitzhak, how are you?"

"I'm fine. How is Eileen?"

"We're good."

"I heard about the shooting at MacDill."

"That was ugly but could have been a lot worse."

"I heard that too."

Before Yitzhak Aranow joined Mossad, he'd spent many years in the Israeli special reconnaissance unit Sayeret Maktal. "Yitzhak, this isn't a social call, is it?"

"No. I'd like to send someone from our embassy in D.C. to talk to you. Unofficially, of course."

"I'm a CIA contractor, and I will have to report the meeting."

"I know that, but you know how Washington works."

"I'm not sure I do anymore. I don't know anyone in this administration who would listen to me other than Don Sanderson." Before he stopped an al-Qaeda attempt to spray the Texas–Oklahoma football game with sarin nerve gas, the administration shunned Derek because his hypothesis didn't fit the narrative the president and his advisors were peddling to the American people. Had al-Qaeda managed to spray sarin as Harun al-Rashid had planned, the death toll would have been in the tens of thousands.

"That's our problem, too."

"Yitzhak, you have Jews on the president's personal staff. Someone in Israel should know them well enough to have a serious conversation. Then, hopefully, the CIA or the DNI will pay attention."

"That is the problem, Derek. The CIA will talk to us, but they are not listening, if you know what I mean. The DNI won't take my boss's call. The administration has a view of the world that won't change despite what the facts are."

"I don't know what I can do to help."

"Will you talk to my guy?"

"Sure. But, like I said, I don't know what I can do to help."

"Good…. And thanks. The man's name is Zvi Rosenthal. He'll give you a piece of info that only you and I know, so you know he's not an imposter. I'll email you a recent picture of the two of us."

"When will he get here?"

"Tomorrow."

"This must be really important."

"I wouldn't be asking if this wasn't serious."

THE SAME DAY, 5:39 P.M. LOCAL TIME, LOS ANGELES

The realtor's office was just off I-5 in the 91502 ZIP Code™, which put the building in the heart of a middle-class neighborhood in Burbank. The house Daniel Morcos just visited was perfect—three bedrooms, two baths, and most important, a two-car garage with a single door. The garage was large enough for a panel van.

The realtor was eager to rent the 1,600-square-foot house to him for six months. At first, the woman insisted on a one-year lease, but he said he'd prefer a six-month and was willing to pay a slight premium of $50 per month. With the rental price settled, Morcos signed the lease for the house near the intersection of West Alameda and South Lake Street.

This was not Daniel Morcos' first trip to the United States. He grew up in Aqaba, Jordan, where his father owned two hotels that could be considered on the beach. His older brother managed a third hotel, a very profitable, three-star property that catered to businessmen in the country's capital of Amman.

By Jordanian standards, the Morcos were wealthy. By American or European standards, they were simply well-off. Daniel graduated with honors from the State University of New York's Stony Brook campus. With his father's blessing, he accepted a job with the real estate giant Jones Lang LaSalle. After his initial training in 2002, he was assigned to the firm's Century City office in Los Angeles.

Morcos worked at Jones Lang LaSalle long enough to convert his student visa to a green card. Eight years ago, he tried to reach a childhood friend on a visit to his family in Jordan. At first, Ahmad Zayed's parents were reluctant to talk to him but would see if they could get a message to their son.

When they met two days later at a beachside café in Aqaba, Ahmad seemed nervous and kept looking around. When Daniel asked why, Ahmad said, "The secret police are all around."

"You mean the General Intelligence Directorate?" Daniel referred to the Kingdom of Jordan's intelligence agency, known for its efficiency, thoroughness, and brutal interrogation methods.

"Yes."

"Why would they be interested in you?"

"Because they are helping the Americans and the Jews. They do not want us to succeed."

"Who is us?"

"Al-Qaeda."

"What do you do for them?"

"I find people with special skills or passports and visas that make them useful to our cause."

"Like me?"

"Yes."

That conversation took place in the spring of 2008. In February 2009, after his 2008 bonus check was deposited in his account, Daniel resigned from Jones Lang LaSalle. The woman from HR wrote down his reason for leaving—Daniel was going back to Aqaba to help his father start a real estate business—and noted he was eligible for rehiring.

Daniel Morcos could travel to and from the U.S., almost at will because he had a California driver's license, a green card, and a

Jordanian passport. On each trip, he was either given a package to carry or a task to accomplish. He was sure al-Qaeda was vetting him.

His last mission before this one was to make careful notes of the security processes at two U.S. airports. The report carried back to Jordan in a file on a thumb drive was very well received.

Morcos sat for a few minutes before he started the rental car's engine. Los Angeles was the last of what amounted to a long, five-week, seven-city tour that began with renting a house in Franklin Square on Long Island. Then, he drove to Boston and rented a house in nearby Worcester. From there, Morcos flew to Atlanta and leased a home north of Hartsfield International Airport in a town called East Point.

His next stop was Chicago where he found another house in Des Plaines, Illinois. From Chicago, he flew on an American flight to DFW and rented a house in Farmers Branch, Texas. Then it was on to Phoenix, and now L.A.

The houses were all the same—three bedrooms, two baths, a two-car garage, and a floor plan of between 1,500 and 1,800 square feet. All were in middle-class neighborhoods that, while not run down, were full of rental homes.

Before he put the car in drive, Morcos called a number in Long Island City. In less than three minutes, he gave the man who answered the phone the address and received instructions on where and to whom he would deliver the keys. The signed lease was put in an envelope and mailed to the address he knew by heart.

For a Jordanian, Morcos was very light-skinned. He had light brown hair and often his father kidded him that someone in his mother's family was Scandinavian. Near Los Angeles International Airport, he checked into the Sheraton Gateway where he planned to stay for two days before he boarded the flight he had booked to Dulles and then to Jordan.

WEDNESDAY, OCTOBER 5ᵀᴴ, 2016, 4:42 P.M. LOCAL TIME, POCHEP

Missile 9K-338-S-004546-VAD-10 and 23 of its cousins—serial numbers 004547 through 004570—was strapped to a wooden pallet.

Along with a half dozen pallets of newly manufactured 57-millimeter S-5 rockets, the 24 Igla-S' were placed in the last boxcar in a munitions train that had other rail cars packed with conventional 250- and 500-kilogram Mark 62 series bombs and 25-centimeter S-24 rockets.

The train chugged into the Pochep weapons storage complex's internal train loop earlier in the morning and stopped for unloading. Missile 9K-338-S-004546-VAD-10 and the other 23 were the last to be unloaded.

The worn tires on the forklift crunched along the pebbles and rocks that accumulated on the concrete road between the train and the bunker. At the entrance, the forklift stopped. Lieutenant Colonel Gregori Tzuri checked off the serial number of each missile on the list on his clipboard and pointed to a corner of the bunker that, until a few years ago, stored bombs and artillery shells designed to be loaded with either sarin or VX nerve gases. The precursors for the nerve agents that would go into the bombs and shells had been destroyed.

Bunker 11 was one of the six that were cleaned of any residue and used to store conventional munitions. Based on what Tzuri learned, the cleaning amounted to sweeping out the 1,000-square-meter bunker before hosing down and scrubbing the floor with soap three times. There were places in the floor that still had a sticky, brownish-colored residue that no one could tell him what the material was. When Tzuri first arrived, he made the decision not to touch anything inside the bunker.

The pallet with 9K-338-S-004546-VAD-10 was one of eight in the 50-meter-long by 20-meter-wide bunker. Tzuri had already read the messages informing the complex that four more shipments of Igla-S missiles were coming in the next two weeks. Bunker 11 was an ideal place to store them.

Three meters above Tzuri, the bottom of the concrete was streaked with rust from the rods reinforcing the two meters of concrete that made up the roof which was topped by a foot of dirt covered with grass and weeds. From the air, the bunker's entrance was noticeable only by the gravel road that led to its entrance.

Satisfied that serial numbers matched the manifest and the pallets with the missiles were arranged neatly along the wall, Tzuri entered his code in the bunker's security system. Then, he pushed the button to turn on the electric motors that closed the steel-reinforced doors, which began to clank and squeak as they moved.

No matter how much sweeping of the door tracks was done, soldiers could never get all the rocks out of the tracks and Tzuri worried that stones that the steel wheels didn't crush would derail the doors. Six bunkers in the complex could no longer be used because their doors had jumped the tracks, and the facility didn't have the equipment to lift them back into position.

The two doors, made in the 50s, needed two full minutes to close. Once the doors were shut, Gregori Tzuri dropped the pins that locked them in place before looping a large padlock through the hasp. His last task was to slip strands of safety wire through the holes and squeeze a lead seal into place. Anyone who opened the locks would have to break the seal. Even then, they would need the six-digit code to allow the doors to open.

Tzuri believed anyone who really wanted to get into the bunker could. He had no idea how many people had the codes and he was forbidden to change them. The locks and safety wire made the bureaucrats in Moscow happy, so on they went.

Satisfied the missiles were safely stored, Tzuri rinsed off his rubber gloves and boots at the decontamination station even though he was told there was no danger from the residue. He didn't trust those who didn't have to live with the risk.

Back at his desk in his office, Tzuri was finishing the paperwork when Saliemenov stuck his head in the door. "All finished?"

"Yes, sir. The workers are unpacking the equipment that came today. I think we received the big mixing tanks for the weapon decontamination station that were supposed to be here a month ago."

"What about the weapons?"

"All conventional weapons. They are all stored in bunkers nine, ten, and eleven."

Saliemenov knew his deputy was referring to the row of bunkers in the best shape at the southern end of the parallelogram-shaped complex. "Good."

"I'll have the report you can send to Moscow finished in a few minutes. Then, on my way out, I will give the train engineer his travel orders, and we're done for a few days."

"Excellent." Saliemenov looked at the younger officer who had graduated from the Mikhail Kalinin Military Artillery Academy in Leningrad in 1994. Tzuri was sent to Chechnya toward the end of the First Chechen War. Then, in 2002, he was sent back to Chechnya as a mobile artillery battery commander. His leadership kept his unit from being overrun by the rebels. Tzuri was wounded in the firefight but finished his tour.

The older man, a native of Grozny, the capital of Chechnya, paused while debating whether to invite his number two to dinner. He was a bachelor, and Tzuri's wife lived in Balti, Moldava.

"Care to join me for a beer when you are done?"

Tzuri looked at the colonel thinking he'd only been here for less than a month and maybe he should get to know the man better. Saliemenov was also a veteran of both the Chechen Wars. Maybe they know some of the same people. "Sure."

CHAPTER 5

FROM WALL STREET TO TERRORIST

THURSDAY, OCTOBER 6TH, 2016, 1:29 P.M. LOCAL TIME, KARACHI,

Fatimah didn't want certain email conversations to go through Talwar Bank's computers. So, rather than login from her company computer, she went to an internet café two blocks down the street from bank's offices at the Sidco Avenue Center in the heart of downtown Karachi. She picked the café because she could have a late lunch and use a "public" computer to access her personal G-mail account.

Sitting at a computer in the back, Fatimah logged onto a secure website. She sipped her cup of coffee while she waited until the local server in Karachi "found" the server in Egypt that connected to one in the Sudan that housed the site through which she could send and receive emails.

While the messages were downloading, Fatimah was wearing a niqab over her Western-style business suit and pulled the cloth down to allow her to sip the strong coffee. On days when she was feeling lazy, she didn't spend much time on her hair because the garment hid it. She hated the niqab, but here it prevented anyone from recognizing her.

With the emails all downloaded, Fatimah typed in an address from memory. On the subject line, she simply typed two words "set up."

She figured that while the server's location may trigger interest by NSA, assuming the agency knew the hosting site existed, the words "work done" were innocuous enough. And, if an NSA analyst downloaded the email and broke the encryption, he would find a dull business note. Fatimah was confident that an NSA analyst would not be able to connect the dots between the names or a pattern of communication or what was really said.

Fatimah thought for a few seconds and then began typing.

Mustafa,

Corporations and bank accounts created in agreed upon countries and deposits made as specified to provide local funding as needed. Account numbers and passcodes now on file at my location. Ready to disburse money as needed. Please advise on amounts, subsidiaries, and timing.

Batool

Batool was her code name given to her by al Zawah and meant "a true devotee of Allah." In response to Mustafa's request, she set up accounts in countries where bank secrecy laws and attorney/client privilege would make determining the owners difficult, if not impossible. The accounts were owned by corporations, some dummy, some real, and law firms who acted as agents.

The law firms could not be compelled to divulge the names of their clients or who paid their bills unless one went to a local court and provided enough evidence for a judge to conclude the money in the account was profit from criminal activity or being laundered to hide its origin. Since the money was coming from a mix of corporate and personal accounts, the initial deposits were legitimate. Once the deposits were made, the funds disappeared into the maze Fatimah had created.

Fatimah had the only key to unlock the network documented on a flow chart on a thumb drive that contained the account numbers, usernames, and passwords. The encrypted file was stored on three encrypted flash drives. One was on her key ring, which also contained information on her finances. The second was in a safe deposit box in a bank in London. The other was in a safe in Pakistan's Northwest Territories.

Fatimah opened the sent folder to make sure the email was there. Satisfied, she finished her expresso and logged off.

FRIDAY, OCTOBER 7ᵀᴴ, 2016, 1:46 P.M. LOCAL TIME, DALLAS

When Eileen returned after taking the team on one of her accounts to lunch to celebrate strong results from a new promotional campaign, the receptionist waved her over to her desk. Eileen shrugged off her light coat and asked, "What's up Madge?"

Madge was the receptionist and whispered softly. "Stan says not to let you into the offices until you answer his question. Doesn't make sense to me. Do you know what is going on?"

Eileen's face may have given her emotions away. She tried to stay pleasant but was sure she failed. "Madge, thanks. Damned if I know. I'll go see what he wants after I drop my purse and coat in my office."

"Promise…"

Eileen said, "yeah," over her shoulder as her mind formulated her next steps. When April reported back to Stan with her answer to the question "Was she carrying?" Stan responded by banning her from the office until she told him. In her office, she did more than hang her coat and put her purse on the chair. She took a thumb drive from her purse, shoved into the USB port, found the letter she was looking for, and printed three copies.

After signing two and stuffing them in separate The Evans' Group envelopes, Eileen scribbled Stan Evans on one and April McClellan on the other. Fully armed, she strode down the hall to Stan Evan's office. Melanie, a woman who'd worked for Stan before he started The Evans Group, tried to stop Eileen, who was on a mission and was not to be denied.

"Stan is working on an ad and doesn't want to be disturbed." Melanie thought her words would stop Eileen. They had in the past, but not today.

"Too bad." Eileen opened the door, and Stan Evans looked up, surprised by the intrusion.

"Who let you in? I told Melanie I was not to be disturbed."

Eileen slapped the envelope with his name on his desk. "This is the answer to your fucking question."

She didn't wait for an answer and left Stan staring at the envelope. On the way back to her office, Eileen handed the second copy of the note to Melanie asking her to give it to April. Now the former client partner, VP and Creative Director, Eileen Almer walked out of The Evans Group much calmer than when she entered Stan's office. Her admin was taking the day off, and Eileen was too fired up to speak with anyone at The Evans Group.

In the car on the way back to Camelot, the first person she called was Derek who said, "Good girl."

Off U.S. 75 in Allen, TX, Eileen stopped at a Starbucks and connected to the Internet. She spent the next 10 minutes sending emails that her attorney had already vetted from her personal email account to her clients. Once they were "electrons," Eileen bought a Starbucks Cold Brew with milk before she got back in her BMW M3 and headed to Camelot. She felt as if a weight had been lifted off her shoulders.

Eileen was on the off-ramp from U.S. Highway 75 onto State Highway 121 when her phone buzzed. The screen on her BMW's dash said the caller was April McClellan who was on her way back from a meeting in New York. She tapped the touch screen to accept the call. "Hi, April."

"Where are you?"

"About forty minutes from home."

"I don't suppose I can talk you out of this?"

"No, you can't. I'm gone."

"The firm is going to miss you."

"That's bullshit, April. Stan apparently wanted me out, so now he's got his wish. Based on our last conversation, you said many of my peers were unhappy with me, and others were, to use your word, uncomfortable with the Freedom Account and being around me. So, I solved your problem."

"This didn't have to end this way, you know."

"Maybe, maybe not."

"What does that mean?"

"I was planning on leaving in a few years, I just hadn't figured out when. Stan just made it easy."

"Oh."

Eileen downshifted for a light and let the BMW coast to a stop. "April, my employment contract is pretty clear as to what The Evans Group owes me in terms of bonus and profit sharing. The letter sitting on your desk and the one I gave Stan has a clear accounting of what I am owed. So, I've seen Stan play around when others quit abruptly. I expect all the money owed to me to be paid on the fifteenth of October. My recommendation is don't fuck with me."

"I understand. I gather you spent some time planning this move."

"Not really. I knew I was done at The Evans Group after the Freedom Group annual review. Stan wasn't even interested in the fact that the SVP of Marketing was about to introduce me to several large accounts and strongly recommend they hire …." Eileen almost said The Evans Group but stopped. Instead, she said, "… me."

With that, Eileen floored the accelerator, enjoying the acceleration of the M3 and the growl from the exhaust. She eased the shift lever into third and lifted off because she was already 25 mph over the speed limit. "One more thing April, when you call my clients, I'm sorry, they're no longer mine; they belong to The Evans Group, don't lie to them."

"Who do I call?"

"My account teams know the names. I am sure they will help you on Monday. Look, I've got to put some gas in the car, so I will hang up. Have a great weekend, April."

The car didn't need gas, but it was an excuse to end the call with April and to take her third call from a client. Eileen didn't care if the companies left the Evans Group or stayed, and their relationship was no longer her problem.

SATURDAY, OCTOBER 8ᵀᴴ, 2016, 1:26 P.M. LOCAL TIME, MOSCOW

As Serik Saliemenov emerged from the Moscow Metro's Orange Line's Leninskiy Prospekt metro station, the crispness in the air told him that winter was coming. While he walked northwest along the Third Ring Road, the thought of another cold, Russian winter gave Serik goosebumps.

He'd had his fill of the snow, wind and long, bitter cold nights and the gloomy overcast days that seemed to go on forever. If he had a choice, he would live someplace where the sun always shined and was warm. When he retired, he would find that place.

Two weeks ago, Serik had lunch with his long-time friend, Maxim Novokov, with whom he spent many a lonely night with on a hilltop in Chechnya. Saliemenov was a Chechen only because Stalin moved his grandparents there from Minsk in the late 40s after the war in his program to 'redistribute' and 'homogenize' the Soviet population. What Stalin was feared were ethnic minorities and/or religious groups who might oppose his rule.

Novokov ran what he called an information exchange. He either had, or had access to, accurate information to sell or knew where to get what a client wanted. His was a service that was in demand particularly in a country where misinformation or disinformation by government agencies and news organizations was the norm.

If he didn't play favorites, Maxim knew he was more valuable alive than dead to the mafiya, the FSB and the oligarchs who ran most of Russia's businesses. All willingly paid the asking price for his services when they wanted to know the truth. Novokov believed he was in a race to make enough money to disappear before somebody decided he knew too much.

Of his steady customers, the FSB was cheap or greedy depending on which side of the question he was on. Everything with them was a negotiation. If an FSB officer was selling, he wanted too much. If FSB officer was buying, Novokov's price was too high. He believed dealing with anyone in the FSB was a crapshoot between acquiring the information from a source within the organization or being taken to the Lubyanka to be interrogated and tortured.

Novokov told Serik to bring a copy of Dostoevsky's *Brothers Karamazov* that had a cover readable from a few feet away. He was to sit at the end of specific bench at the south end of Gorky Park. A man would ask, "Had he'd ever been to Argun?" His answer should be, "Yes, many years ago, in 2002." The man should answer "Me too."

Saliemenov was thirty minutes early and made himself comfortable as he waited. The noise from the traffic hurrying over the bridge 200 meters away was barely audible. From his position, he could, without turning his head much in either direction, see who was coming and going. Bored, Serik watched couples and families stroll along the wide walkways along the Moscow River.

He made sure his Makarov pistol was loaded and handy in his right coat pocket. The small pistol wasn't an ideal self-defense weapon, but did have the advantage of being small, concealable, and most important, available. The semi-automatic pistol along with the three spare magazines in his back pocket came from the depot's armory.

Serik pretended to read a passage in the middle of the book when he spotted a man looking at him who turned away when he looked in his direction. His watch showed the time to be 9:50 in the morning. When the man stood sideways to the railing overlooking the Moscow River, Serik suspected he was either his contact or a scout.

The stranger took out a small phone that Serik recognized as one of those new cell phones. There wasn't any coverage in Pochep so he didn't need nor could he afford one. He could see the man, who was average height and build, had a dark, but well-trimmed beard. Fifteen years before, he saw many men with similar beards in Chechnya, most of whom were trying to kill him.

Saliemenov swallowed hard. Old feelings and emotions died hard.

"May I sit down?"

The voice caused him to turn away from the man with the cell phone.

"Please do. I need only this end." Saliemenov moved the bottle of mineral water from the bench to a place on the ground next to his leg. As he turned to the man, he stuck his hand in his pocket. The cold steel of the Makarov was reassuring.

The man who was dressed casually in jeans, walking shoes and a light windbreaker rested both elbows on the back of the bench and leaned back. "The weather is nice today. It is a lot like Argun. Have you ever been there?"

Saliemenov debated if the phraseology was close enough. He decided to answer thinking that if it turned out to be an idle fall afternoon conversation, nothing bad would come of it. "Yes, back in

2002. But the weather was not as nice as this." He too would go off the script, but not very far.

"Me too."

Now what does he say? Novokov said let the man lead the conversation, so Saliemenov kept quiet.

"I left the Army in 1985 and started what became a successful import/export business."

Saliemenov decided to let the man continue and not say anything.

"I have a customer who wants some interesting toys and I am told you know where I might be able to find them."

By toys, Saliemenov assumed that he meant weapons. "Depends on what kind of toys you are looking for. The ones I know about are very closely controlled."

"But you could release them if you had the proper paperwork, correct?"

"I could, yes."

"Excellent. I am looking for some arrows and other weapons that were taken off the market. Do you know of any?"

Saliemenov knew what the man wanted. Arrows were Igla-S's and the weapons off the market must mean the bombs that could be filled with sarin and VX. "I do. How many do you want?"

Neither paid any attention to the man walking by with one hand stuffed into the pocket of his light blue windbreaker. The other held a cell phone pressed to his ear.

The coldness in the man's eyes that was his 'partner' in this conversation made Serik feel uncomfortable. For a second, he wondered what he was doing on this bench.

The stranger stood up. "It is a nice day for a walk. Shall we?"

Saliemenov followed suspecting walking made recording their conversation harder for the FSB. The stranger waited until they were twenty meters from the bench before he spoke. "I want twenty-four Igla-S's and the same number of two hundred and fifty-kilogram chemical bombs loaded with either sarin or VX. You have the necessary chemicals, no?"

Serik swallowed hard. "We are expecting a shipment of the precursors in the next week or so to destroy. Do you have the men and equipment do transport them?"

"I do."

"Good." Serik was wondering when the business part of the transaction would come. They've established that he has control of what the man wants.

"I will pay five thousand U.S. dollars for each missile and ten for each bomb."

"I want twenty-five thousand for each missile. They are brand new. Ten for each bomb is acceptable.

"Fifteen for each missile."

"Twenty."

"Done."

"I want half by the end of this coming week and half when you let me know when they are going to be picked up."

"Half next week and half after we pick them up. All payments in U.S. dollars."

Serik thought for a few seconds. They could kill him when they take delivery of the weapons up and they would only be out half the money. He decided to take a slightly different tack.

"Are you going to want more weapons? There are other things in my store that may be of interest."

"Yes. We will arrange for their delivery when we need them. This is only the first order."

"How do I contact you if something goes wrong?"

"You don't. I expect you to have the weapons ready and solve any problems prior to delivery."

Saliemenov thought that was cold. "Will you bring the necessary paperwork with all the approvals?"

"Yes."

The commander of the weapons depot studied the man who, he guessed was near his age. He had a jagged scar on his is forehead probably made by a piece of shrapnel. "Are you going to be with the team that takes delivery? This is the only way I will know that the weapons are delivered to you."

"My men will know you."

Saliemenov wasn't sure if the stranger was telling him what he wanted to hear or if he was playing with him. Time to find out. "I want half the money by the end of next week and half within twenty-four hours after delivery."

"Done. Where do I send the money?"

Serik handed him a slip of paper. It was an account he'd just set up at the Swiss private bank Lombard Odier on Friday with his life savings. The bank was founded in 1796 and had an office in Moscow. He told the Swiss bank officer he was setting up an account because he didn't trust Russian banks and there was more to come. The bank officer didn't ask where Serik would get the money.

"I will check with my bank on next Friday to see if you have transferred the money. No money, no deal." Serik knew that the $360,000 deposit would make the Swiss banker happy and prove he was a man of his word.

"The money will be there." The man stood up and didn't offer to shake hands. He just walked away and, out of the corner of his eye, Serik saw the man with the cell phone who was standing by the railing walk in the same direction. Either he was a tail by the FSB or militsiya or an associate. If he was the latter, there was no danger. If it was the former, he decided he would try to save his skin and tell everything he knew, which was not much.

THE SAME DAY, 7:27 P.M. LOCAL TIME, MOSCOW

The flat was in a dingy part of Moscow that was, to anyone from west of the Iron Curtain, a perfect example of the inefficiencies of the Soviet economy. Rust-streaked five-story buildings known as Khrushchev Houses or in Russian as Khrushchyovka lined both sides of the street. To accommodate modern conveniences such as satellite dishes, telephone lines, and air conditioners, occupants punched holes in the concrete walls willy-nilly. Wires from satellite antennas and air conditioners went from porches and windows to power and telephone poles.

Officially known as the K-7 design, architects designed the buildings to be an easy-to-construct, quick fix to the Soviet Union's post-World War II housing shortage. Structural engineers created three standard apartment designs—30, 44, and 60 square meters, and the layouts were not optimized for living.

Inside a K-7 apartment, there were no halls. Access to any room of the apartment was from the combination living and dining room. The six square meter kitchen was what Westerners would call a nook off one end of the living room. Bathtubs in the bathrooms were shortened to 120 centimeters or less than four feet to fit into the allocated space.

Khrushchyovkas were built from prefabricated sections and assembled throughout the Soviet Union and neighboring Warsaw Pact countries. Construction of the K-7s started in the early 1960s, and by 1971 the need for more apartments on the same piece of real estate led to nine- and 12-story buildings. The buildings were supposed to be occupied only for 25 years. Still, chronic housing shortages and a growing Russian population kept them in use.

Central planning and the need to build them quickly drove assumptions, such as only two adults and two children would live in each K-7. However, when they were finally occupied, most had two and sometimes three generations in each apartment.

The 30-square-meter flat on the second floor where the four men were sitting around the table was one of the 64,000 Khrushchyovkas built in Western Moscow between 1961 and 1968. Like others in the building, the apartment had a dish clamped to the railing of the small porch. It was a dual-use satellite communications and TV antenna disguised to look like one just for satellite TV.

The apartment was once occupied by a family who left Russia for greener pastures outside the Soviet Union. Through a combination of bureaucratic inefficiency, bribes, and forged documents, the flat was now in the name of a fictitious owner so it could be used as a safe house and command center.

Two 19-inch flat panel HD TVs were connected to a laptop on the center of the table. One screen had a collage of surveillance photos. The team leader leaned over the keyboard to watch the video of two men on a bench. The voiceover was recorded by a parabolic microphone concealed in a van parked on the other side of the river.

After twice watching a replay, the team leader stood up. "So, who is Dawuud Ghanem meeting with? When we find that out, we will know why he turned up in Moscow."

MONDAY, OCTOBER 10TH, 2016, 9:16 A.M. LOCAL TIME, SAN DIEGO

The wide stretch of beach at the Naval Air Station North Island was a great place to have a meeting. To the four men who left their shoes on a bench by a picnic table near the Navy Lodge, the sand, cooled by the 65-degree Pacific Ocean water, was comfortable underfoot.

Derek Almer, who at six feet, was tallest of the four, all of whom ranged from 5'8" to 5' 10". After meeting Zvi Rosenthal, Derek called Don Sanderson, a Director in the CIA's Strategic Services and Operations organization, who said he would be in San Diego for a meeting at the Navy Special Warfare Command on the Naval Amphibious Base Coronado. Don suggested the location because North Island was well away from prying eyes in D.C. and didn't have to answer questions from his superiors on why he was in San Diego.

The third man was Lieutenant Commander Ed DeCosta who was a SEAL on the Naval Special Warfare Group One staff. During their tours in Afghanistan, he became friends with the fourth man, Jacob Sobrano. If any superior officer asked Derek, he would say he was meeting with the two SEALs to discuss potential training exercises as the executive officer of HSC-85 based at Naval Air Station North Island.

Don stopped and looked at Derek first and then at the two SEALs. "What I just asked you is off the record. You can say no."

Derek shook his head. "What you are asking sounds harmless enough. You want me to establish a business under an indefinite order, indefinite quantity government contract using an existing defense contractor as a cut-out. The work is intelligence analysis with three deliverables based on our independent judgment. Look at our intelligence and determine where the MANPADS are being acquired. Two, figure out how al-Qaeda is getting into the U.S. Three, provide a defendable hypothesis on what the bad guys are planning. The question I keep asking is why?"

"Because the CIA is hamstrung. The head of the CIA reports to the Director of National Intelligence who reports to the president. The president sees this as a law enforcement task and has delegated the task to the FBI. We try to coordinate through the National

Counterterrorism Center and other formal relationships. Still, the FBI is stonewalling us even though both CIA and NSA can help. The agency fears that if MANPADS are used in the U.S., the CIA will be blamed even if the agency has given the president briefings and he turned the matter over to the FBI. In my world, 'I told you so' doesn't cut it. Second, if our analysts find the bastards with the missiles outside the U.S., the president may not let us act."

Don took a deep breath. "An independent contractor to the CIA has more freedom of thought. I'm not going to tell you the answer. I want you to develop a fact base and recommend actionable options based on your analysis."

Derek made a face. His ice-blue eyes focused on Don. "So, what you are telling me is that you want this new organization to be prepared to act if the president doesn't authorize direct action."

Don's eyes sparkled. "If need be."

"So, what happens if we get our collective dicks caught in our zippers?"

Jacob's burst of laughter stopped the serious conversation. Don looked at him. "Jacob, what's so funny?"

"Derek's reference to getting his cock caught in a zipper reminded me of something that happened to Derek in Afghanistan that was really funny."

Sanderson looked curious. "OK, I'll play straight-man. What happened?"

"Derek was one of the four rapid reaction force helicopter pilots and is supposed to be airborne within five minutes of getting the order to launch. Well, about three in the morning one night, the order came, and we were all asleep. Derek flies off the cot, stuffs his feet into his boots, and runs to the helo."

Jacob paused for a few seconds, relishing that he was about to cause some good-natured embarrassment. Every time he's told the story, Derek's face turned red. "As we're running down the hall, I hear this painful OOOOWWWW. When I turned around, I could see Derek fumbling with the zipper of his flight suit down around his crotch as he ran down the passageway."

"The mission turns out to be a false alarm, and we were back on the ground in about thirty minutes. When we land, Derek says to his copilot and me, you do the debrief. I've got to go to sick bay."

Derek shook his head, knowing what was coming. Don was hearing this story for the first time and was paying rapt attention.

"What's wrong, I ask?" Jacob could barely control his laughter. "Derek says I got my dick caught in the zipper on the way to the helo, and it is still bleeding, so I'm going to see the medics."

"The debrief took only a few minutes, and I couldn't get down to sick bay fast enough. When I walked in, Derek was sitting on one of the beds on a bloody pad, and the corpsman was squatting in front of him. The enlisted man says, 'I need to consult with others.' Shortly, all the corpsmen on duty along with every nurse and doctor on duty were in the room studying Derek's private parts."

Don bent over from laughing.

"Wait, it gets better. In comes the surgeon on duty, putting on a show as he pulls on a pair of surgical gloves and snaps the latex. Then, he proceeds to examine Derek's dick. After about a few minutes of intense scrutiny in which he examined every millimeter of Derek's penis, he stands and says to Derek loud enough for everyone in the room to hear, you're lucky. You won't need stitches. I'm going to put some ointment that may sting."

Jacob paused in the tale to let Don stop laughing. "When he applied the ointment, Derek winced, and the doctor told Derek, if I were you, I wouldn't get a hard-on until this heals in about two weeks. If you're lucky, there won't be any scar tissue."

Each time he started speaking, Don looked at his good friend and giggled. Derek put his hands on his hips to show impatience and looked at Jacob. "Are you finished?"

Jacob had to force himself to keep from laughing. "Yeah."

"Good… Let's get back to what's behind this. Don, you're telling me that the DNI has officially washed his hands of the problem. Unofficially, the CIA hasn't because it understands the risk if we do not find the missiles and their owners."

All four in the conversation knew DNI was the abbreviation for the Director of National Intelligence.

"Yeah… Pretty much. If the FBI asks for our help, we'll give it to them, but…." Don paused for a second. "That's problem one. The second is that the current reality in the Middle East and the Arabian Gulf doesn't fit the administration's narrative. In other words, there is the reality of what's going on and the administration's perception, and they're not even close. We used to have frequent contact with the Mossad, and now we are not supposed to talk to them."

"Ouch." The word just popped out of Derek's mouth.

"Which brings me to problem three. The president, through the DNI, often asks the head of the CIA about covert operations. The current director's view is that, if asked, he will tell the president only in private to lessen the chance of a leak, limiting the number of opportunities. The White House, as you probably know, leaks like a sieve."

Derek interrupted. "Let me guess. The president doesn't ask the same question of the Chairman of the Joint Chiefs because, thanks to the posse comitatus laws, he can't use military force within the boundaries of the U.S. So, theoretically, even if his intelligence staff found the missiles, he can't use his assets. And, because of that, if a small company is hired under a broad contract, the relationship and the cost is buried in the belly of the Special Operations Command. And the deliverables have deniability because they come from a contractor whom the political hacks can dismiss."

"Derek, my friend, you are a genius."

"OK. So, part one of this exercise is to find the sources of the missiles, figure out how they are coming into the U.S. Part two is either destroying the missiles or preventing the bastards who have them from using them or both."

"That's it. Do part one first, and then we'll figure out how to take care of part two." Don looked into Derek's eyes. "I'll make sure you have all the raw intel we have. And I promise I won't let you or anyone working with you guys go into harm's way unless there is a way to get you out. No one-way missions."

Derek stuck his hand out. "Done. I'll get back to you with a plan and a company name."

"Good. Then I'll find you some competent help. The reason Ed and Jacob are here is because they can give us some names and because, initially, you report to Ed. On this, we communicate only face-to-face or on a secure phone."

TUESDAY, OCTOBER 11ᵀᴴ, 2016, 10:46 A.M. LOCAL TIME, CHITRAL, PAKISTAN

Chitral was an ideal location for a base of operations because it was 1,100 meters (3,608 feet) above sea level and surrounded by mountains. The city sits at the base of the highest peak in the Hindu Kush - the 7,808-meter-tall (25,289 feet) Tirich Mir. It's remoteness and large population, estimated at 600,000 souls, made Chitral the perfect place for Sameer Rahal to set up shop.

Land access to the rest of Pakistan from Chitral depends on a single road—N45—that goes south over the Lowari Pass. Snow blocks the two-lane highway from the rest of Pakistan for six months of the year. Once winter sets in, the only other access is via Pakistani International Airlines flights to and from Islamabad and Peshawar.

Rahal bought a whitewashed, three-story concrete and cinder block building a short walk down Shahli Bazar from the town's post office. A large square canvas cover on the roof hid a satellite antenna from U.S. satellites and UAVs.

The building was ideal, with a garage that could be converted to a store or workshop and separate apartments on each floor. The 100-square-meter second-floor apartment (1,076 square feet) housed Rahal's security team, and he lived in a similar size flat on the top floor.

The house had other attractive conveniences, i.e., a generator that could power both apartments, a freshwater well, a pump to provide running water, and an underground connection to the city's sewage system.

Rahal's and al-Qaeda's contacts inside the Pakistani secret intelligence service—ISI—said the intelligence agency was not interested in Sameer's comings and goings if al-Qaeda didn't threaten the Pakistani government. Despite heavy American pressure, ISI pursued a live-and-let-live philosophy. They only passed on to the Americans information that achieved one of ISI's goals.

Sameer wasn't naïve enough to think that ISI didn't know who he was. For the moment, they weren't interested in him. That could change in a heartbeat, but for now, this was the world in which he operated.

Chitral had another advantage. It was a short walk from the beginning of the trails into Afghanistan that could be traversed almost all year round.

A discrete knock on the apartment door signaled the arrival of Rahal's guest. Entrance to the upper floors required both a key and getting past an armed guard. Sameer opened the door, knowing who would be there, and embraced the man who epitomized Western news media's portrayal of the "typical" Afghan—dark beard, black eyes, long flowing clothes, and a turban known in Afghanistan as a lungee. "Abdul, how was your trip?"

His visitor's name was Abdul-Mu'izz Hakimi. His first name implied he was a "servant of the giver of might and glory.

"This time of year, the trip is easy, and by following the Drosh-Jalalabad Road, we only needed three days. The Pakistani police at the border station spent two minutes looking at our papers and waved us through!"

"Excellent. Please sit down… Tea?"

While Arabic was their native tongue, for security reasons, Sameer spoke in English, knowing his fellow Yemeni citizen also grew up in Aden. Both learned English, first in a school run by British ex-pats and then at Cambridge University. Speaking English was done as a matter of security since none of the guards in the building spoke it.

"What was so important that I came so quickly?"

"We are planning a new operation that will rock America and hurt the West. The Doctor has approved our plan."

"What are you going to do?"

"I can't tell you, but I need you to assemble eight teams, each with four men. All of them must speak passable English."

"That's thirty-two men for an operation in America?"

"Yes."

"Will they be martyred?"

"Probably. We expect most to be killed, but we are not sending them as suicide bombers."

"Good." Abdul didn't like spending the time and money to train men and women only to have them blow themselves up and kill only a few of the enemy. If they could, by their death kill hundreds as Hezbollah did in the Beirut bombing of the Marine barracks, then the sacrifice was justified.

"Any other special needs?"

"Yes, we will train them on weapons like the Stinger."

"All of al-Qaeda's Stingers are old and, from what I heard, do not work. Are you getting new ones from the Taliban?"

"No. Trust me, new ones that will work will be provided."

"When?"

"I can't tell you."

"When will this operation take place?"

"Just have the men ready to travel before the winter snows come. Do we have enough?"

Abdul nodded and took a sip of his tea. "Yes. Our recruiting is doing well. We have many true believers from England, Canada, and America. I will make sure one American is on each team."

"Excellent. Once they are selected, seclude and cut off their communications."

"I will. What about travel?"

"Arrangements will be made. Just get them ready."

Abdul made a face that was visible despite his long, black beard. He knew what he was being asked. Finding 32 men who could operate independently in eight, four-man teams would not be a trivial task. He will have to select many of their best recruits. "*Insha Allah.* I will make sure they are well trained."

"Both 'The Doctor' and I have faith in you."

THE SAME DAY, 1:09 PM. LOCAL TIME, CAMELOT

Right after Derek and Eileen were married, he had a contractor build a studio between the house and the barn. Oriented roughly north and south, one end was all glass, and the air-conditioned building was connected to the house via a glassed-in walkway. Shutters and blinds on the floor-to-ceiling windows let her control the light on her easel. The other end of the 15' X 20' long structure was set up as an office. Outside, a steady rain from dark clouds beat on the glass, making the world grayer and darker than it seemed.

When Derek walked into the studio, Eileen was sketching the outline of a painting on an easel. Seeing him, Eileen put down her pencil and gave him a hug. "I didn't expect you until this afternoon after the rain stops."

"The GPS approach to Runway 35 wasn't all that bad. I broke out at about a thousand feet and was more worried about airframe ice than how low the ceiling was. I'm glad to see you've started painting again."

"Me too. Glad you're back. How was the trip?"

The distance from North Island Naval Air Station to Jones Field, outside Bonham, is roughly 1,100 nautical miles. Derek pushed the throttles on his Aerostar 701P forward at North Island just at 6:02 a.m., which was 8:02 a.m. in Bonham. At Flight Level 220 (roughly 22,000 feet), the piston twin cruised at 250 knots and, with a 40-knot tailwind, made 290 knots almost the whole way.

The plane touched down three hours and 48 minutes later at 1150. By the time Derek filled the tanks in each wing and used the tug to back the plane into the hangar, it was close to 12:30 p.m. When he wasn't talking to controllers or navigating, the trip gave Derek time to figure out how to execute the plan discussed on the beach in San Diego the night before.

"So, I've got a deal for you to use your business skills if you're interested."

"Doing what?"

"Helping me start a company that does research and analysis for the Special Operations Command and the CIA."

"Sounds like fun. I'm in."

"Don't you want to know the particulars?"

"I do, so what's the deal?"

"You're going to be the CEO and own fifty-one percent of the stock. Here's why…" Derek explained that this structure made the firm a small, disadvantaged, woman-owned business which in the government contracting world are given favorable treatment in competitive procurements. Eileen would handle HR, legal, contracts, marketing, and finance. As the COO, Derek would focus on the analyses being produced and customer contact.

"Derek, are you sure you want to do this? The last time you wound up fighting the FBI as well as the CIA because nobody would believe you. It led you to being arrested and charged with heinous crimes because you trashed some bureaucrat's cherished hypothesis."

"Trust me, I've thought about just that scenario, and Don and I hashed this out so it will be different this time. We'll have a government contract and a statement of work to say nothing of official clearances."

"OK, I just don't want you sticking your neck out without an official government sanction, if you know what I mean."

"I do." Derek paused and held Eileen's hands. "You're going to need a clearance. I've already called Avery to set up the company. We need to go sign the certificates and write a check for $1,000 for the initial stock."

THURSDAY, OCTOBER 13TH, 2016, 1:36 P.M. LOCAL TIME, LONDON

From her small suite on the seventh floor of the Dorchester Hotel, Fatimah could see the rows of lights along the paths in Hyde Park. Other than that, the park was a black void surrounded by a city of light.

Fatimah raised her glass of a Cote de Nuit red burgundy that was, as the hotel's head sommelier said, excellent. When Fatimah checked in, the clerk handed her an envelope with a handwritten note from the sommelier saying that the wine scored 98T. The bottle came from what was considered an outstanding vintage. The T in the rating system suggested that the wine was still a bit tannic, youthful, and immature. The glass she was sipping was the remnants of the bottle that had warmed up to room temperature by now.

Once she decided to visit Talwar Bank's London office for the first time, she had her secretary make the flight arrangements. In Talwar's offices in Egypt, the U.A.E., and Pakistan, the bank followed the Muslim work week of Sunday through Thursday. Fridays and Saturdays were holidays.

The London office was the exception, open Monday through Friday and closed on weekends. The Thursday visit gave Fatimah what was, in effect, a long weekend in London before returning to Karachi on Monday.

Once she knew her arrival time in London, Fatimah dialed a number from memory. A woman answered and asked for her customer code. She responded with the letters F and S followed by her customer 6984 and then the letters HBD. Fatimah recognized the woman's voice as the escort service's proprietor. The conversation to describe what she wanted took less than two minutes. There was no need to exchange financial information. Fatimah's credit card information was already on file, and she knew the charges.

The young man did his job well. Fatimah was still totally naked as she took in the city from the suite's picture window. For the first time in weeks, she was sexually satisfied, and her mind wandered as she remembered her first thought when the papers to buy the bank were signed. Now she will make money two ways, one from her efforts and one from the work of others. Fatimah planned to buy out her investors as soon as she had the funds, and Talwar will be all hers.

In the male-dominated Arab world and, to some extent, international banking, Fatimah was a rarity—a single woman with money and power. She had the two legs of the triad that gave her an edge over men and refused to use the third - sex. When Fatimah wanted, she could ooze sexuality, but doing so was, in her mind, unprofessional. She wanted the results of her work to stand for itself.

To Fatimah, power was less intoxicating than money. In London, where she could wear Western clothes, her wardrobe was stylish and expensive, and with her looks, she could have been a model if she so chose. In the Muslim world, the niqab hid her face, and an abaya or chador hid her figure.

Fatimah's virginity vanished years ago in a London flat while she was a University of London student. She believed men were willing to "pay" for sex, so dating was simply a way to create the transaction. Most men found Fatimah intimidating—sexually and intellectually— which made sustaining a long-term relationship difficult.

That was, she thought, God's will. Someday, Fatimah believed she would find the man who could satisfy all her sexual needs. In the meantime, she wanted to make enough money to be considered very wealthy.

CHAPTER 6

NEW GENERATION OF WARRIORS

When 16-year-old Aazar Rahim arrived at the cave complex, he was soaking wet and shivering. For the last kilometer, he and the donkey led walked in a steady, cold rain. After he unloaded the two cans of goat milk and six rounds of kadchgall, a hard cheese made from a combination of goat's milk and yogurt, Aazar was invited into the cave to get out of the rain.

A guard pointed to a fire and told him he could stay there until the rain stopped and he dried out. Aazar thanked the man for the offer and tied the rope around the neck of the donkey he used to lead the pack animal to a nearby tree. An hour later, a man who spoke Pashto with a funny accent led Aazar farther into the cave to give him water and food. Along the way, they stopped in a widened area. There he saw two stacks of olive drab crates, and Aazar, who had what Americans would call a photographic memory, needed only a few seconds to memorize the writing on the sides.

SATURDAY, OCTOBER 15TH, 2016M 11:07 A.M. LOCAL TIME, MOSCOW

Today was the day. Serik tried to read a book on the train from Pochep to Moscow but couldn't. For much of the week, he wondered who the mystery man was. He spoke Russian with an accent, and Serik was sure the stranger was not Afghani but an Arab or an Iranian. Who cares, he was about to find out if the stranger was a man of his word.

Serik was on the train because there were no Internet cafés in Pochep, a town Serik thought was locked in a time warp. Surrounded by small collective farms, the city had not progressed much past the 1950s, and most apartments still didn't have phones.

The Internet? Some in Pochep knew about the world wide web but to most, the Internet was either an unknown or beyond comprehension. Even if a resident of Pochep had a computer—an expensive luxury for most Russians in rural areas—to connect to the Internet, the individual needed access via a wireless network or an apartment with a dedicated telephone line. Neither existed; therefore, connectivity to the outside world didn't exist in Pochep.

Optimistic predictions by Rostelcom, the state-owned telephone monopoly, and the Ministry of Communications and Mass Media that rural Russia would soon have a modern telecommunications network weren't believed. Rostelcom network didn't have the capacity or the budget to provide individual apartments with its own phone line. Even if it did, the data rates would be so slow that a modern laptop would get "frustrated" and time out.

Serik's plan for the day was simple. Take an early train to Moscow. Find an internet café near the Kursky train station to check his account at Lombard Odier and his email. For security purposes, Serik wanted to contact the buyer only through an intermediary, and that was Maxim with whom he was about to have lunch.

The Kursky station, originally built in 1896, is Moscow's busiest. Trains from Ukraine and southeast Russia connected to those going to St. Petersburg, Rostov-on-Don, and Kiev to the south, Minsk to the west, and to Nizhniy-Novgorod, the first large city to the east on the way to Siberia. From Kursky, Serik also could catch a train on three Moscow Metro lines, the Number 3—Arbatsko-Pokrovskay, number 5—Koltsevaya, and the number 10—Kakhovskaya.

Saliemenov crossed Kurskogo Voksala and entered the indoor mall where he knew, amongst all the stores, there were several cafés where he hoped to find an open seat in front of a computer. He had time to wait because, from where he was, it was only about a 15- to 20-minute walk from the restaurant where he would meet Maxim.

The size of the pre-lunch crowd in the mall surprised Serik, who wished his salary as a colonel give him the income to buy more consumer goods. He rationalized that many were useless in Pochep unless one had a satellite dish to receive Western TV stations. Russian TV programming was boring.

The first café he entered had a computer workstation open in the back. As he lowered himself into the seat next to a young couple in their twenties, his nervousness about using the computer returned. He was afraid of two things. One, he would make a mistake and, as a novice, need to ask for help. Two, he wondered if someone from the FSB was watching?

Growing up in the Soviet Union, the government wanted you to think that someone in the government was always watching, and a negative word from a watcher could lead to an unpleasant session with the KGB, now known as the FSB. While their name had changed, their power and methods hadn't.

Serik took a deep breath and logged onto his email account, and there was nothing new. From there, he entered www.lombardodier.com. To ensure he would not tap the wrong keys, he used his forefingers to enter the letters and characters of his 16-digit password, one at a time. When he was done, the summary sheet said his account balance was $401,062. He couldn't help but smile when he saw the deposit of $360,000 had been made!

Serik glanced to the side, and the young couple was engrossed in reading the text of a site that he thought was, from the typeface, in English. Emboldened, he studied the transaction summary telling him the money was deposited on Wednesday. Under the deposit, there was a series of numbers that he didn't understand that provided confirmation of the money transfer.

Serik looked again at the amount to ensure his eyes were not playing tricks on him. They weren't, and he logged off, and then, as

Maxim insisted, he deleted the browsing history. Done. His watch said the time was 1115, and he needed to meet his friend.

TUESDAY, OCTOBER 18TH, 2016, 7:26 P.M. LOCAL TIME, KARACHI

The concierge waved at Fatimah as she walked across the lobby's marble floors to the 10-story condo complex. Her heels clicked on the stone as she closed on the semi-circular desk that, at one end, was manned by the concierge and the other by the building's security guards.

No one reached the elevator bank without being challenged unless the guards knew you. Once in an elevator, residents inserted their access cards into a slot before selecting a floor. There was a separate access card for the underground garage for those who owned cars.

The concierge placed a logbook on the counter as Fatimah approached the desk. "Madame Serraf, you have an envelope that was dropped off late this afternoon." He spun the logbook around and held out a pen so Fatimah could sign for the envelope.

It wasn't the first time something was delivered to the building for her. Like the others, the sender wrote her name in English in a precise, neat hand.

Fatimah slit open the letter in her apartment using an opener shaped like a miniature saif. Inside, on a single sheet of paper, there were handwritten figures without headings in four columns. The first column was the bank account number, and the second was the amount needed to be moved. The third had the bank routing number, and the fourth was the account number into which the deposit was to be made.

Since the letter was delivered today, the sender wanted the money in the recipient's account tomorrow. That meant she had to log on now so the transfers could occur before midnight.

Moving the money also meant that she had a decision to make. Do the work in her condo? Or go to one of the many internet cafes a short walk away? Eat first, then work? Or vice versa?

Fatimah suspected the American NSA monitored emails and mobile phones. She assumed the agency looked for patterns and keywords and might not download a series of small banking transactions initiated from a small Pakistani private bank. Tired from a long day, Fatimah changed clothes before taking hummus and pre-cut vegetables from her refrigerator and putting them on her desk beside her computer.

Her home office was set up just like her office at the bank. Three 36-inch flat panel monitors were arranged in an arc. In the center, she had a docking station for a laptop or, as she preferred now, to use the computer on the floor.

First, she entered a password allowing the computer to start booting up. Next, she had to enter a series of passwords that convinced the software that encrypted the data on the hard drive that she was the proper user. Last, she typed in the encryption key that unlocked the files on the computer. Every day, an email arrived that gave her a link to a website that provided the daily key.

As she pressed the single sheet of paper flat, Fatimah noticed that there were more and more rows each time. The only record would be the electronic fund transfer between banks and accounts, along with the transfer fees. No paper trail could exist. When she was done, Fatimah shredded the sheet of paper and then dumped a portion of the little squares into the trash can under her sink. The rest went into a plastic bag that would go in a trashcan someplace along the street on her way to work tomorrow.

Satisfied that her work was done, Fatimah checked her email and found nothing that couldn't wait until the morning. It was time for a glass of wine.

WEDNESDAY, OCTOBER 19TH, 2016, 9:47 P.M. LOCAL TIME, HINDU KUSH

The cold, clear mountain air made Ghanem shiver. He'd forgotten that in October, at 3,100 meters (10,170 feet) above sea level, the air was dry and cold, and winter was not far off.

Ghanem sat on a stack of four olive-drab crates with yellow U.S. Army markings. Behind him, four Stinger missiles in their launchers were leaning against the rock wall. Their location on a small cliff gave Dawuud and Na'il a perfect view of the valley where U.S. helicopters transited to the base of a provincial reconstruction team in the Kunar district of Afghanistan.

Scattered around him was a security team of two dozen men who carried the missiles to this spot that had a special meaning to Ghanem. Three years ago, he fired a Stinger for the first time at an Afghan Army Mi-8 helicopter. His victim, packed with a dozen soldiers and three crew members, plummeted in flames. There were no survivors.

Ghanem looked at the other man standing next to him. "So Na'il, do you think Americans are flying tonight. This is, after all, their Sunday and is supposed to be a day off."

Na'il looked at the black sky. They would hear the helicopter long before they saw one. "This is a war zone, so there aren't days off. The U.S. Army likes to operate at night, so we might get lucky." He paused to drink from a bottle of water that had gotten cold in the minus five, Celsius (23° Fahrenheit) air. "I'm sure we will see some helicopters soon."

THE SAME DAY, 10:02 P.M. LOCAL TIME, HINDU KUSH, AFGHANISTAN

Twenty miles to the west of where Ghanem sat, Jacob Sobrano rode in an Army UH-60L Blackhawk on the way to see an old friend from an earlier tour in Afghanistan. Right after takeoff, the helicopter climbed so it was flying 3,000 feet above the terrain to get out of small arms range and accelerated to 130 knots. From his seat behind the aircraft commander, Jacob Sobrano could see the second Blackhawk flying what was known as a "loose deuce." From the soft glow of the formation lights, he guessed the other helicopter was about 200 feet above and 1,000 feet to the right.

Listening to the chatter on the intercom, he learned the pilots were changing tactics as they entered the narrow Pech Valley that led to Asadabad. The helicopters flew close to the steep slopes on the north side of the valley to reduce their noise footprint and make them harder to see because they weren't silhouetted against the sky. Below them, the Kunar River was a shiny black ribbon flowing toward Kabul.

Sobrano was on the helicopter because an intelligence report said a tribal leader told the provincial reconstruction team commander that a member of his tribe knew where al-Qaeda stored at least a dozen Stinger missiles. As proof, he brought a piece of paper with the serial numbers of three missiles given to the Mujahideen in late 1988 by the CIA and were known not to have been fired.

The trip was an excuse for Jacob to see the tribal elder with whom he had worked. Before he left, Sobrano was told by the head of the special operations command that if he thought a raid was needed, the general would sell the attack to the head of the International Security Assistance Force.

THE SAME DAY, 10:05 P.M. LOCAL TIME, HINDU KUSH

The noise was faint, but the beat of rotors from approaching helicopters was distinctive. Hear the sound once, and you'll remember the noise forever. Na'il reached out and touched Ghanem's arm and whispered. "Listen."

Ghanem hoisted one of the Stingers onto his shoulder, as did Na'il. With the missile launcher on his shoulder, Na'il pointed his toward the valley and switched the missile to the 'on' position. "Remember, wait until the helicopters have passed, and then we'll shoot them in the ass."

The noise got louder, but neither Ghanem nor Na'il couldn't see the helicopters. One of the men rose out of the scrub bushes and pointed to the sky. "There."

Ghanem gently swung his missile. The closely spaced beeps were replaced by a loud tone telling him the missile seeker had acquired an exhaust plume. "I got a target."

Na'il found his seconds later and pointed his missile at the blacked-out shape at about the same altitude. The missile seeker responded with a growling tone.

"Shoot right after I do." Ghanem didn't wait for an answer and squeezed the trigger that un-caged the missile's gyro system. He couldn't see the target in the range ring but was sure he was close enough to get a hit.

The recoil from the gas that ejected the Stinger missile from the tube shoved Ghanem back despite leaning forward and anticipating the push to his body. The snake-like glow disappearing in the distance told him that the missile was on the way. A second later, the one from Na'il followed.

On board the helicopter, Jacob heard the door gunner scream, "Missile, eight o'clock low." The pilot pushed the cyclic to the left and forward to roll the helicopter and dive toward the valley floor. Jacob grabbed the seat rail and heard six bangs as the pilot fired flares.

Through the open door, Jacob was horrified as he watched the missile slam into the other UH-60 which erupted in a ball of fire. It slowly arced downward like a burning match that was dropped. The Stinger headed toward their helicopter waffled, and lost contact before regaining a target lock. The helicopter had almost passed out of the Stinger's maneuverability cone when the proximity fuse set off the warhead. An expanding cone of square tungsten steel fragments fanned out like a shotgun, shredding the right side of the fuselage and the door gunner.

Shielded by the gunner, neither Jacob nor the other SEAL in the cabin or the other door gunner was hit. The instrument panel in front of the pilots lit up like a Christmas tree telling Jacob the helicopter was mortally wounded. He didn't know what the lights meant, but when he heard an engine unwind and the UH-60 slow, Jacob's instinct told him they were in deep trouble.

The co-pilot yelled as he keyed the intercom, "Brace yourself. We're going in."

Jacob felt the nose pitch up and heard a grinding sound before the world went dark.

He wasn't sure how long he'd been out, or what woke him, the crackling of cooling metal or the groan of a wounded man, but the one thing Jacob knew was that his head was throbbing. He also knew that he had to get everyone out of the helicopter and ensure help was on the way.

From what Jacob could tell, the fuselage was close to level. Gingerly, he climbed out of the helicopter, took a few steps into the woods, squatted down, and listened. Other than noises from the dead helicopter, he heard nothing, and his senses told him that they were alone, at least for now.

Back at the helicopter, he found the other SEAL, Chief Petty Officer Henry Tomkins, administering first aid to the wounded gunner. The other gunner pulled the emergency release on the pilot's door and was helping the Army Aviator out of the cockpit.

Jacob pulled one of the M4 carbines from the rack and shoved a magazine into the well. He pulled the bolt back and let it slam forward to insert a cartridge. "I'm going to scout around. I'll be back in ten minutes."

The pilot, a Chief Warrant Officer Chris Ellsbury took his AN/ARC-112 radio out of his survival vest. "Sir, I'll call the cavalry."

After nodding in agreement, Jacob paused, and instinct suggested he head up the mountain. When he returned, Chief Zachary Tompkins emerged from the trees. "Sir, I've got everyone about twenty yards from here. There's a group of rocks where we've set up a perimeter that protects us from all sides. We got four M4s with six magazines per man, plus the M-240 machine guns with four belts out of the helicopter for the door gunners to use. We all have our M-9 pistols with three magazines if they get very close. It's not much, but we'll bloody their nose if they come at us."

Jacob nodded. "If we conserve ammunition, we can hold out until we're rescued. How is everyone?"

"Sir, we've got one with puncture wounds on his arms and legs, but if we can get him to a hospital in a couple of hours, he should live. His vest stopped the fragments from hitting anything vital. The co-pilot has a broken leg, and the pilot is like us, banged up."

"Ellsbury reach anyone?"

"Yes, sir. They're supposedly sending out a rescue party escorted by gunships. We'll get an update at the top of the hour. They've got our location via the secure GPS link in the radio. My guess is that they'll get here right after dawn. Ellsbury told them that at least two Stingers were shot at us, which will make the rescue helicopter pilots cautious."

"Understood."

"Sir, do you want to destroy the helicopter?"

"No, not yet. A fire will attract flies just like a pile of fresh shit!"

The chief petty officer smiled and stuck out his hand. "Sir, this way to the Alamo."

"Let's hope this doesn't turn into the Alamo. If I remember, Chief, your Texan ancestors died there."

When Jacob first got to the little fort, there were, as Chief Tomkins instructed, improving their position. Jacob asked them to face him so he could learn their names, give them their assignments, and outline the plan to enable them to survive.

Jacob pointed to the wounded gunner first. "I'm Sergeant Chris Jones, and I damn sure don't plan to die in this fucking shit hole. I may be full of holes, but I can still fire my M-240 or an M4."

"I like your spirit, Sergeant Jones."

"I'm Sergeant Hector Jiminez and the crew chief."

"I'm CWO-2 Gale Beauregard. And its Gee Aaaa El Eee." He spelled out the letters in a drawl that told Sobrano he was from someplace in the deep south.

"Any relation to the Confederate general?"

"Yes, sir, a direct descendant."

"Can you walk?"

"Yes, sir. It'd be easier if my leg was splinted."

"We'll worry about that once we have our little fort built. Right now, here's how we will survive the night."

THE SAME DAY, 10:12 P.M. LOCAL LIME, AFGHANISTAN

Ghanem stared at the funeral pyre that was one of the Blackhawk helicopters and turned to Na'il. He was obviously pleased. "The missiles work, which means we fixed the software. Our test is done. Tell the men to pack up, and we return to Pakistan in the morning."

"Ghanem, the Americans will mount a rescue effort tomorrow. We have four missiles and will be able to shoot down more helicopters. That will teach the Americans an important lesson."

"No, we will leave at first light."

"Like cowards."

"No, Na'il, not cowards, but smart warriors. Leaving is a strategic move because if we stay, the Americans will come with Apache helicopters and chew us up. We came to test the new software in the missiles, and now that we know they work, you will fix the rest of them. And then, we have another mission for the Stingers that is far more important than shooting down another helicopter or two."

Na'il stood with his hands on his hips and didn't say anything. He came to Pakistan and Afghanistan to kill Americans, and now Ghanem was running like a scared dog. Why?

THURSDAY, OCTOBER 20TH, 2016, 5:01 A.M. LOCAL TIME, AFGHANISTAN

A snap of a piece of dried wood caused Jacob's head to snap around toward the sound wishing he had a set of night vision goggles. Ellsbury and Beauregard, who still had their AN/AVS-9 goggles on their helmets, pointed up the slope and held up five fingers three times.

Fully alert, Jacob pushed on Chief Tomkins boot. "We've got company."

"Yeah. I heard."

The darkness lit up with a large whoosh. Jacob yelled. "RPG." The words had just come out of his mouth when the 750-gram warhead exploded. Dirt and shards of rock flew everywhere. Before he could look up, another RPG streaked overhead and slammed into a tree 100 yards farther down the mountain. The din from the branches straining and snapping as the top of the tree crashed down drowned out the next two RPGs that flew by their position. The fifth hit two feet to the left of the first one. Lots of dirt and bits of rock landed on the six Americans but didn't cause any casualties.

Without prompting, Ellsbury was already on the survival radio and spoke up. "Sir, we should have some Apaches overhead in about fifteen minutes."

Jacob didn't have time to answer. Rounds from a Soviet-made PKM machine gun started knocking chips off the rocks. He peered around, looking for the stream of green tracers, and was about to say something when the M240 about two feet away responded with two short bursts. The firing stopped for about 30 seconds.

Behind him, Jacob heard Chief Tomkins, who was on his fifth deployment to Afghanistan and spoke fluent Pashto and Arabic as well as Spanish and English, quietly remind the two pilots to check to make sure that their fire selectors on their M4 Carbines were on single shot and to fire only when they see targets. The wounded door gunner was on his back, propped up in the center of their little circle. He had his survival radio on to talk to the arriving Apaches and his 9mm Beretta pistol in his lap.

The red dot in the reticle of the scope of Jacob's M4 filled with a human shape, and he squeezed the trigger. The man staggered, and he squeezed again. The target went down.

He moved the rifle barrel slowly, searching from his spot between two large rocks. Another shape. Center the reticle and squeeze the trigger. The shape slumped over. Jacob kept finding targets and firing this until the rifle clicked empty.

Reload and search for targets. Squeeze the trigger. Fire again if needed. The shooting suddenly stopped when Jacob figured he was halfway through the second magazine. He rolled on his side to survey the little group. The silence was interrupted by a loud twang. Both he and Chief Tomkins knew the sound meant a grenade was coming.

The little ball banged off a rock and rolled to a hissing stop right by his stomach. In one smooth move, Jacob scooped up the round grenade and tossed it out, hoping there was enough time left on the fuse so it would explode outside their rocky bastion. The grenade exploded with a bang 15 feet away, and he felt like someone stabbed his legs and upper arm in several places.

Chief Tomkins lunged across the little pit, caught a second grenade in midair, and threw it back in the direction from whence it came. His efforts were met with a burst of gunfire that the M-240 gunner responded to with a three-second burst that lasted through the explosion. There was a scream and no more firing.

Jones spoke loud enough just so those in the hole could hear. "Sir, the Apaches are about three minutes out. We need to show them where we are. What should I tell them?"

Jacob looked around. "Tell them to look for the red tracers in two to three-second bursts, starting in about a minute."

"Yes, sir."

Both gunners spoke at the same time. "Tell us when sir."

Jacob looked at his watch and ignored the AK-47 rounds pinging off the rock behind him. It was 5;20 in the morning, and daylight would soon be upon them. "Jones, tell them to stand by." Jacob held up five fingers, then four, then three, then two, then one and said, "Now."

The co-pilot and the unhurt gunner fired three, three-second bursts from each M240. "Sir, they spotted us and will look around us with their thermal sights to find any bad guys."

One of the AH-64s flew low over their position and then continued about half a mile before pulling up in a 90°-right climbing turn. The other one fired several bursts before reporting that they saw many men moving back up the hill.

Sergeant Jones, who Jacob guessed was in his early thirties, spoke up. "Sir, the Apache flight leader wants to know if we can move. He says there's a clearing about 100 yards downhill to our north where they can get a Blackhawk in to pick us up."

Jacob looked at the young man who was lying on his back. "Can you walk?"

The young pilot thought for a few seconds. "Damn straight, sir."

"Good. Get an ETA for the Blackhawk, so we know when to move."

Daylight was beginning to filter down through the trees. From his position, Jacob could see at least 300 feet and the wreck of their crashed Blackhawk. Seeing the hulk, he realized their attackers were using the downed helicopter for cover.

"Ten minutes, sir."

"Good, tell them that the bad guys are using the wrecked helicopter for cover." The SEAL officer waited until Ellsbury received an acknowledgment of his instruction. "Gentlemen, I guess we better be going. Chief Tomkins, you take security and make sure no one gets behind. You…" Jacob pointed to the pilot, "help out your co-pilot and…." Jacob pointed at both gunners, "you two help each other and follow me at ten-foot intervals."

When he emerged from the trees, a low rock wall bordered the field. Jacob headed for the corner that would give them some cover in case things went wrong.

When he saw the two Blackhawks closing in on the small field, he turned to Chief Warrant Officer Ellsbury and held out his hand. "Give me the radio."

The warrant officer gave him a quizzical look. "I'm going to change their mission. I'm going to have the Apaches destroy our helicopter. The first Blackhawk will take the four of you back to Bagram and a hospital. The second one will take Chief Tomkins and me to Asadabad so we can make our morning meeting. If the mission commander gives me any grief, I'll have a four-star asking him why he didn't take me there within seconds after I touched down."

THE SAME DAY, 9:36 A.M. LOCAL TIME, ASADABAD

When Jacob walked into the meeting area in the provincial reconstruction team compound at 9:15 a.m., he suspected the new eight-foot wall was constructed from cinder blocks and covered with mud to give them some ballistic protection and privacy. The wooden benches arranged in a circle roughly 12 feet across were for the tribal leaders and the two Americans.

Even though he was dog-tired, Jacob stood, waiting for the tribal leader as a matter of respect to the older man. On the bench next to him was a pouch with 10 South African one-ounce gold Krugerrands and the other was a box with a brand new, Beretta 92F, four spare magazines, and a box of 50 rounds.

Jacob planned to give the tribal elder the pistol as a thank-you for coming in. If the information was valuable, he would give him the coins. Before coming, the two Americans decided to rely on their Pashto and not invite an Afghan Army interpreter.

Army Lieutenant Colonel Gomez, a small, wiry Hispanic, followed Qaedar Rahim, the elder and leader of the Nasar tribe, into the center of the circle of benches where Sobrano and Chief Tomkins waited. Also, with Gomez was an Afghan army interpreter.

Rahim's gray-black beard appeared to be matched by a fashion designer to the charcoal vest, light gray linen sheath, and pants of his traditional perahan tunban. Like many Afghans, he wore a pair of leather sandals and a linen turban with an extra length hanging down his back.

What struck Jacob most of all as he looked at the Afghani were his coal-black eyes. They were at once inquisitive and soft, and Sobrano had seen them when they became hard.

Jacob put his hand over his heart in a traditional Afghan greeting. "Sheikh Rahim, may peace be with you." Jacob was careful to pronounce the words carefully in Pashto.

The older man replied, "Peace to you." The older man paused for a second, fixed his eyes on Jacob's face, and spoke in Pashto. "Thank you for coming. I hope life is treating you well."

While he never asked, Jacob believed the man to be in his late forties. Given what the man has been through, he was lucky to have lived this long. Jacob responded in Pashto. "I have been blessed, but God has not yet blessed me with a wife and sons."

"He will in time. You are still young and strong. My sons have given me grandchildren, so I know my line will continue."

Jacob smiled and took the man's offered hand in both his. He wasn't sure if he uncovered something about the man standing before him.

The Afghani spoke in Pashto, "Welcome back to my country. I am glad we can converse in my language without an interpreter or anyone else."

The Afghani elder turned to the interpreter and spoke slowly. Jacob was sure he was doing that to ensure he understood Rahim's words. The interpreter turned to Lieutenant Colonel Gomez, who gave Jacob a harsh look after he heard the translation and left.

Qaeder gave him a quizzical look when he saw Gomez's face. Chief Tomkins stood silently by Jacob's side, and he rescued him.

"You remember Chief Tomkins, and he still works for me, and his Pashto is better than mine."

Rahim smiled. "Good, he can stay." He made a sweeping gesture toward the bench next to him. "Let us sit."

Jacob forced himself to keep himself from exhaling noticeably as he sat. As he sat down, Rahim looked at the box containing the Beretta 92F and probably was wondering what was in the pouch on top of the box. Chief Tomkins sat on his left and leaned forward to face the Nasar tribal elder.

Qaeder looked at both men and spoke softly so that only Jacob and Chief Tomkins could hear him even though there wasn't a human being within five meters. "You are here because of what my son saw?"

"Assuming that you are talking about the missiles, yes."

"You cannot put him in danger. He is one of the two sons I have left, and the rest have been killed by the Russians and the Taliban, both of whom are bad for my people and my country."

Jacob nodded, not wanting to interrupt.

The old man reached into his pocket and pulled out a wrinkled piece of paper. "My son has a very good mind. He memorized these serial numbers and wrote them down for me. He said the cave has at least twelve missiles."

Jacob did nothing until Qaeder handed him the sheet, and the numbers looked familiar. After a few seconds, he handed the piece of paper to Chief Tomkins, who took out a small spiral-bound notebook with a list of missing Stingers and found four on the list of missing Stingers.

"I don't want to put your family or any members of your tribe in danger. I know you took a risk coming here. The Taliban does not like you talking to us."

The Afghani looked at Jacob as a signal to continue.

"My point is that we are helping you create a better life for you, your family, and all those you lead. That alone allows you to truly serve Allah. The Taliban wants to rule in accordance with a strict interpretation of Sharia law. That denies you access to modern medicine and means your people will continue to die at an early age. Taliban rule also condemns you to be farmers who cannot use new techniques to produce more and better food. Their policies make you slaves to them. Allah did not want his people to be slaves to al-Qaeda or the Taliban."

"You know my problem well."

"I do. That is why we are here." Jacob wanted to ask his second question but waited to see if Rahim knew.

"The missiles are in a cave, not far from here, east of Asmar, just this side of the Pakistani border. My son Aazar says the cave is more like a repair shop than a storehouse, and there are many, many missiles there."

"How many times has he been there?"

"He takes them milk and cheese twice a week. They promise to pay, but we never receive any money. Only promises. Aazar can take you there."

"That would put him in danger. I do not want to do that."

The Afghani's face hardened. "That is Aazar's decision, not yours."

"When can I meet him?"

"Whenever you want. He comes with me to discuss projects with Colonel Gomez every week."

"Good." Jacob went outside and asked Colonel Gomez for a map of the area around Asmar.

Colonel Gomez appeared with a rolled-up map a few minutes later. "Thank you, Colonel." Jacob was trying to be polite and not ask him to leave again, and he took the hint. Once Gomez was gone, Chief Tompkins rolled out the map on the bench and used scoops of loose dirt to hold it down.

Qaeder studied the document for a few seconds. He then traced his finger along a ridge line. "The cave is in this area." He pointed to an oblong, kidney-shaped ridge line northeast of Asmar.

"Are you sure?"

"Jacob, your CIA taught me to read a map, and I fought the Russians for ten years in these mountains. So, yes, I am sure."

Jacob smiled. "Good, I will be back one week from today. Then, we can meet your son."

Qaeder started to say something and then stopped. Jacob knew what he was asking but was too polite to put the request in words. Jacob stood as he picked up the box and the pouch.

"Sheikh...." He used the term as one of deference and respect knowing that it was not the man's proper title. "These are for you. There are four magazines for the pistol."

Jacob held the pouch while the man looked at the brand-new pistol and then closed to lid. He was prepared to ask the man not to load the gun because it would have put Chief Tomkins and him in danger if the old man wanted to become a martyr.

"And these are to add to your tribe's wealth."

Qaeder hefted the pouch noticing the weight, and the gold coins clinked softly. He peered into the bag and pulled out one of the Krugerrands.

"There are ten gold coins in there."

The tribal leader smiled and nodded. "I thank you. Allah thanks you. Aazar and I will meet you here in one week. No need to tell anyone else."

THE SAME DAY, 3:36 P.M. LOCAL TIME, NEW YORK CITY

When he walked into his apartment building on Manhattan's upper east side, carrying several bags of groceries, Qusay Jabbor stopped by the bank of mailboxes. Putting the plastic bags down, he opened his mailbox, which was stuffed full. He suspected some of the items were important but most were junk.

The mail went into one of the grocery bags. In his apartment, Jabbor put his purchases away before laying out the envelopes on the table in what he thought would be the order of importance. There were two 9" X 12" Manila envelopes. One had familiar handwriting and was sure it contained the lease to the last home Daniel Morcos rented.

Qusay had never met the Jordanian. Their only contact was a series of short phone calls just before and after Morcos signed each lease. In the first conversation, he'd tell Morcos which account to use to make the deposit. The second was what to do with the keys. Now that the lease was in-house, so to speak, he had to decide from which bank accounts he would send the money to the realtor per the rental contract.

The six-month terms of the leases were too short for the banks to bother with electronic payments, so he had to write the checks manually. Or, as he preferred, go to the bank, get a cashier's check, and mail them.

Since arriving back in the United States from his native Oman, Qusay had been building al-Qaeda's financial support infrastructure for future attacks. He had a network of domestic and international bank accounts where money could be received, transferred, bills paid, and cash dispensed by dummy corporations that leased vehicles and rented properties.

The second Manila envelope came from Delaware's Secretary of State's Office with the incorporation papers for the fifth and last corporation he decided to establish. All, like S.A. Services, which he used to pay the leases, had non-descript names.

Qusay came to the U.S. to study accounting at the University of Arizona. After graduation, he joined KPMG as a consultant in the firm's oil and gas audit practice, staying for almost 10 years. KPMG helped him convert his student visa into a green card, so now he could travel to and from his native country and the U.S.

After working in Houston on KPMG audit clients, Qusay passed the CPA exam in Texas. With that certification in hand, he waited three years before asking KPMG to find him an assignment in the U.A.E. The accounting firm transferred Jabbor to Dubai, a city only 40 miles from his family in the seaside town of Fujairah.

Qusay found the work in Dubai much less interesting than he experienced in Houston. Opportunities to advance were limited; to do so, he would have to move back to the U.S. since work permits in Europe were very difficult to acquire. Working in Dubai was, however, comforting, and Jabbor was happy to be back in the Arab world.

When he needed a car to drive across the peninsula that separated the Arabian Gulf from the Gulf of Oman to Fujairah, Qusay rented one even though he could afford a vehicle. His father was a successful businessman whose restaurants catered to Oman's growing middle class.

He believed that paying for his four years at the University of Arizona was his father's way of saying, 'Here's your inheritance.' Qusay grew up listening to his father's mantra, "Get a good education because it is the key to earning your way in the world." It was a challenge that Qusay readily accepted.

Qusay was still restless. The growing Western influence in his native country made him uncomfortable. Throughout his life, he had been an observant Muslim. Soon after arriving in Dubai in 2012, he began to attend adult classes at a local mosque. Qusay had seen the West in Houston and preferred a more traditional world. He concluded the West was draining the Emirates and Oman of their natural resources. The flow of oil had to stop, so the messages from the mullahs resonated in his brain.

THE SAME DAY, 7:48 P.M. LOCAL TIME, WASHINGTON, D.C.

Adnan first met Dawuud when they sat in a small restaurant in Tyre, talking about the future in late October 2001. By then, the U.S. government had released information on the U.S. Special Forces on the ground and coordinating air strikes in Afghanistan. What Adnan didn't know was that Dawuud was sent by al-Qaeda to cultivate Maalouf as a source of intelligence.

Adnan didn't need much convincing because he visited friends in Hezbollah. In the halls of the State Department and now at the National Counterterrorism Center, he never notified either agency of his contacts, as Adnan was required to do.

Now, Adnan had to be even more careful, not so much with what he passed, but how he transmitted who was on the target list and where they were in the pecking order. Nothing was in his apartment.

The list could be passed quickly in various ways to make it more difficult to detect his treason. Today's meeting was like any other. Meet a friend from school, have dinner, and pass the names verbally.

Adnan's only worry was that if his contact was being watched, he could become a target of an investigation. If he was arrested, Adnan would claim he is innocent, and what they talked about was hearsay.

The location for the meeting was a small Mexican restaurant near his apartment. Both liked the spicy food, and Adnan figured the hole-in-the-wall taqueria was not a location where the FBI would look for two Arab men.

As a security precaution, Adnan waited until their meal was served before listing the top five new targets for drone strikes. His contact, whom Adnan knew as Hamin Sabbag, listened intently. He asked a few questions on why and then, one more time, asked Adnan to repeat the names as he memorized them.

Sabbag started to pull out a pen and write on a napkin, and Adnan put his hand on the man's wrist. "No written record."

Hamin nodded. "I'm sorry. I forgot."

This was the third time Adnan had met Hamin and he suspected Hamin was having trouble remembering the target's names in order of their priority. Worse, he may have mixed them up, resulting in a senior al-Qaeda leader being killed.

Maalouf rationalized that giving al-Qaeda names was a crapshoot. Any day, the ones on the list could be on the receiving end of a bomb or Hellfire missile. At their first meeting, Adnan repeated his assertion that he had no control over the means or when an attack would happen. If some targets were suddenly hard to locate after he passed on their names, he suspected someone in al-Qaeda was playing God by deciding who would be warned and who would die.

Hamin put a hand on Adnan's shoulder on the sidewalk outside the restaurant. "Next time, you may have a new contact. I am not good at this and have asked to return and take my place with my brothers fighting the infidels."

Adnan held out his hand. Suspicions confirmed!!! "May Allah be with you."

"*Insha Allah...* God willing, we will succeed and kill many infidels."

CHAPTER 7

PICK-UP AND DELIVERY

One of his perks as the depot commander was that every morning, a driver picked Saliemenov up at his quarters. Each day, he climbed into the passenger seat of the GAZ-69 four-wheel drive truck built in the '70s. Tzuri, who preferred to live in Pochep walked to the base every morning. Saliemenov thought the winter may change Tzuri's decision to make the two-kilometer-long walk to the headquarters building and move into the barracks. Unknown to his commanding officer, when Tzuri arrived at the front gate, one of the guards drove him to the headquarters building.

The duty officer saluted Saliemenov, who returned the gesture. He then scanned the log to see what had occurred during the night. When he finished, the young officer spoke up.

"Sir, we just received a phone call notifying the depot that a convoy will arrive today around 1100 hours to take delivery of weapons stored here. I checked the logs, and this is the first time the depot has been informed of this transfer."

Saliemenov grunted. "Does the notification tell you what they are supposed to pick up or deliver?"

"No, sir."

"When they arrive, have the guards bring the convoy commander to my office with his paperwork before the vehicles are allowed to load any weapons."

Saliemenov nodded to dismiss the lieutenant and headed to his office, thinking he may have a message from Maxim's friend telling *me they were arriving today. If their paperwork does not list what was purchased, I will call Moscow and see what I can learn. If they want the SA-24s and chemical bombs, I will have Tzuri sign the papers. This way, his neck is in the noose, not mine. By the time Moscow figures out I was involved, I should be living on some tropical island.*

THE SAME DAY, 2:57 P.M. LOCAL TIME, POCHEP

The grey clouds had begun to spit their heavy, cold rain. From Gregori Tzuri's office window, the wet shiny red, brown, and orange leaves of the deciduous trees around the compound meant only one thing—the Goddamn Russian winter was only a few weeks, or, at best, a couple of months away.

In front of him were the documents Saliemenov handed him authorizing the release of the weapons. While they appeared in order, two facts kept rattling around his brain. Neither had to do with the list of Igla-S serial numbers that included 9K-338-S-004546-VAD-10 and 23 others. Nor was the loading the trucks with 24 empty 500-kilogram chemical bombs or the drums of chemicals that would create Sarin gas if mixed and loaded properly into the bombs.

Fact one was the man. Gregori sensed he wasn't a native Russian even though his Russian was excellent. So, where was he from?

Fact two was the destination—the 195th Arms Storage Facility near the port city of Rostov-on-Don. The address was outside the city where the Don River empties into the northeast corner of the Black Sea.

The documents were written as a routine transfer of weapons from one storage depot to another. The fact that the 195th was unknown to Tzuri and not on his list of arms depots and by an international port made Tzuri suspicious. He was aware the Soviet Union and now Russia surreptitiously shipped weapons to shady organizations, hoping they would cause problems for Mother Russia's enemies.

Calling Moscow and asking questions would start a process over which he had no control. Talk to the wrong person, and he would be the target of the investigation and not what happened to the weapons or who authorized their transfer.

As soon as an investigator saw "of Jewish origin" in his file, the latent anti-Semitism that bubbled just beneath the surface of Russian society would come into play. In the files of the Ministry of the Interior (MVD), which controls all the police forces, and the FSB (Federal Security Service, formerly known as the KGB), they would find copies of the emigration visas that let his parents go to Israel.

On Tzuri's desk were five copies of the original order, all with the necessary stamps and signatures. The original would go into a file in Pochep. The second stayed with the shipment, and when the weapons arrived at their destination, the receiving facility would put a copy in its files and send Pochep the third copy documenting the shipment had arrived. The fourth was sent back to the organization that originated the orders with the necessary stamps certifying their arrival and transfer of control. None of the instructions said what to do with the fifth copy.

Tzuri typed a memo stating that he did not believe that the 195th Weapons Depot existed and recommending that the Russian Armed Forces should investigate the transfer as a possible theft. He put a copy in the depot's files and sent another, along with a copy of the transfer order to the Organizational and Inspector Department at the Defense Ministry in Moscow.

In the paranoid world of the Russian Army, copy machines were carefully controlled. Anyone who made a copy had to fill out a log kept by the machine noting the day, time, type of document copied, and the reason for the copy. He filled out the log saying that a copy of the shipment orders must be returned to Moscow.

Gregori figured there was a 50 percent chance his memo would start an investigation. The question was, by whom and who would be investigated? Would the first officer given the note recommend it be investigated internally within the Russian Army? Or would he turn the memo and shipping document over to the FSB, the agency responsible for monitoring arms shipments? Or would he send it to the GRU as an intelligence matter? Or would the person who received the memo the one who created the fake papers, assuming they are forgeries, and try to investigate him.

Tzuri believed it would take days before someone reacted, if at all. He was within a year of retiring, and when he did, he planned to emigrate. He did not know, but he was legally or illegally leaving Mother Russia.

Since he had no specific instructions on what to do with the fifth copy, he folded it in thirds and then in half before sliding the document into one of the pouch pockets of his fatigues.

THE SAME DAY, 4:56 P.M. LOCAL TIME, WASHINGTON, D.C.

The sun was already well down on the horizon, and from the office's door, the shafts of light coming through the windows turned anyone standing by the windows into a silhouette. As Adnan Maalouf closed the curtains, he felt the heat of the sun. He then locked the door and headed down the hall.

In his hand was a number 10 envelope. When he reached the floor-to-ceiling glass partition at the end of the corridor, Adnan stopped where his administrative assistant sat. Molly Lights was a career FBI staffer who'd applied for a job in the National Counterterrorism Center after being with the Bureau for over 20 years because the center was closer to where she lived. Despite several attempts to encourage her to become a special agent, Molly resisted. Her rationale was simple. "When I leave at the end of the day, I don't have any homework, and I don't get middle-of-the-night calls to respond to a crisis. That makes my time off my time, not the Bureau's or the Center's."

Molly looked up from the desk where she was filling in as what the admin's referred to as the "gate guard." This desk had a button allowing the admin to open the door to anyone whose badge didn't provide access.

"Adnan, have a good vacation."

"I plan to." He put the envelope on the desk. "In here are copies of my leave papers and my itinerary. I'll be back a week from Monday."

"I've always wanted to go to Greece. Enjoy."

"I'll bring you something back." Adnan was referring to the bookcase behind Molly's regular desk bookcase with figurines from around the world. If Molly worked for you and you went out of the country, the tradition was that you brought back something for her collection.

SATURDAY, OCTOBER 22ND, 2016, 11:39 A.M. LOCAL TIME, MOSCOW

Most of the long train ride from Pochep to Moscow was in the dark and the rocking and swaying of the train, made Tzuri sleepy. He found a compartment with just one another occupant sprawled on the bench seat on one side, so he flipped down the backrest that became an upper bunk and laid down. He'd slept in worse places. His folded coat made a perfect pillow. Within seconds, Tzuri was fast asleep.

Light streaming though the corners of the window around the shade woke him. After washing and shaving in the bathroom at the end of the car, Tzuri made his way to the dining car for a breakfast of eggs and toasted and buttered black bread. He loved the crunch of the crust and the meaty dough soaked with fresh butter.

The reason to take the train to Moscow was the walk he took Thursday night after work. There was a section in Pochep where during the war, the Germans put the 2,300 odd Jewish residents—about fifteen percent of the town's total population—into two small ghettos, one for men and one for women. At the time, the town was swollen with Russian and Polish refugees fleeing the advancing German Army. The Nazis reached the Pochep on August 22nd, 1941, just sixty days after their invasion of the Soviet Union began.

Gregori stood in front of the small stone that marked the March 1943 massacre of the Jews imprisoned in the ghetto by the Nazis. Tzuri closed his eyes for a few seconds as he tried to imagine the horror the ghetto's occupants felt as the Germans shot everyone they could find. Only a few escaped.

While he was a Moldavian by birth, Tzuri's father was drafted into the Soviet Army in 1939 and came home a changed man in 1945. His grandfather and mother joined a group of Moldavian Jews that lived in caves and in the forests, hiding from the Germans who would, if they were caught, shot them immediately. Forty years after the war, his parents were among the lucky 79,000 Soviet Jews allowed to emigrate to Israel in 2000.

As a member of the Rocket Artillery Forces, Gregori would never be allowed to leave. Since he hugged his parents just before they boarded the plane that would take them to Israel, he had not seen them since except through pictures. That date, he sadly remembered was sixteen years ago.

Before he left, his father gave him the name and address of a person in Moscow he could contact and be trusted to talk about anything. About once a year, his father would mention in a letter that he had heard from his friend in Moscow and that he was well which meant to Tzuri that the man had not been co-opted by the KGB or now, the FSB. Meeting this man was the only reason Tzuri made this trip.

The address was in the western part of Moscow, about halfway between the Third Ring Road and the Autobahn like highway known as E-105 that formed the 'fourth ring road.' Using a tourist map he bought at the railway station in Moscow, Tzuri guessed that the address was close to the Tushinskaya Metro Station on the purple or Number 7 Tagansko-Krasnopresnenskaya line.

At this point, Tzuri decided he would go no further without confirmation that the address was (a) real and (b) there was a person by the name of Zelek Naidich living there. After looking around, he found a small bank of pay phones and pushed the requisite number of kopeks into the slot. He knew the number by heart.

After a few rings, a deep masculine voice answered. Gregori had rehearsed in his mind what he would say when a human answered the phone. "Zelek Naidich?"

"Who's asking?" The voice was guarded, almost hostile.

"Gregori Tzuri. My father Sameuil gave me your address and phone number." He figured he had about thirty seconds to get the man's interest.

"Tell me something that I would know about your father?"

The man wanted him to prove himself. His father gave him a date and a few words. "July 26th, 1944. Our grandfather and our fathers killed all the SS guards from Sobibor they could find and vowed to shoot every SS officer they captured."

A few seconds of silence followed that felt like an hour. Finally, the voice on the phone asked. "Where are you?"

"Tushinskaya Metro Station."

"Which entrance?"

"I am by the entrance to street with the same name."

"Good. Walk to the northwest corner of Proyezd Stratonavtov and Tushinskaya and wait for me."

"How will you know who I am?"

"My secret." Then there was a dial tone.

At a brisk, military pace of 76 centimeters (29.9 inches) per stride, Gregori needed eleven minutes, according to his watch to reach the southeast corner of the intersection. Not wanting to look too much out of place, Gregori crossed to the side where he was supposed to wait and watched passengers going to and from the subway station.

He tried not to be too obvious and stare at the man approaching him who was, he guessed a decade younger than he was. "Gregori Tzuri?"

"Yes."

The younger man didn't identify himself but held up a black and white picture of three young men in Army uniforms sitting on top of a destroyed German Tiger tank. Gregori instantly recognized the photo as one his father kept in a frame in their living room. "Which one is your grandfather?"

Get this wrong and Gregori knew that there would be no further conversation. He'd risked carrying the shipping documents for nothing. "My grandfather is the officer on the right, holding the Pep Pe Sha. My father is the young man holding the German MP-40 submachine gun." He used the nickname for the Soviet Army's PPSh-41 submachine gun that was easily identified by its round 71 round magazine.

"Excellent. My name is Sol. Our fathers knew each other. Not knowing my last name is safer. Zelek sent me."

Tzuri was skeptical, but Sol's answer made sense. Zelek was his father's age and would be, by now, in his 60s. Gregori left the man's comment hanging in the air. He expected some sort of skullduggery so he decided to let the man make the next move.

The man pointed up at the sign that read Proyezd Stratonavtov. "Shall we take a walk?" Gregori knew a command when he heard one.

After about 100 meters of walking in silence, Sol turned to the Moldavian. "Why'd you come?"

Gregori long thought Zelek Naidich was somehow connected to the Israeli embassy or maybe even Israeli military intelligence. "Good question. I really don't know other than I don't trust my chain of command."

"How so?"

Gregori gave Sol a précis of the delivery of the missiles and chemical weapons. Then, he added his analysis of the route the convoy would probably take to Rostov, an 1,100 kilometer-trip from Pochep. Best case, Tzuri said, was that it would take them two days to get to Rostov, but most likely, three.

He concluded by saying. "Three things made me suspicious. One, was the size of the shipment. By Russian Army standards, the size was very small. Two, the destination—the 195th Weapons Storage facility—doesn't exist. Three, the officer in charge of the convoy spoke Russian like a Chechnyan. I spent two tours in that god-forsaken country and I know a Chechnyan when I see one. He smelled like one, looked like one and spoke like one. His name tag was Nabiyev which is Uzbeki but he wasn't an Uzbeki, trust me."

"So why do you think Zelek Naidich would be interested in this?"

"Because my gut tells me that either he or you or both have connections with the Israeli government." Gregori was looking right at Sol's face when he spoke. The flash in the man's eyes and movement of his cheeks told him that he was right.

"When do you have to be back in Pochep?"

"I have to catch a train Sunday morning."

"Do you have a place to stay?"

"I have reservation at a hotel near the station because the train back to Pochep leaves very early."

"When we get back to my flat, we have much to talk about. You can stay with us and cancel your hotel reservation. I'll make sure you get to the train on time."

TUESDAY, OCTOBER 25TH, 2016, 10:26 A.M. LOCAL TIME, BONHAM

The four-room office suite was the entire third floor of the brick building on the corner of North Main Street and Highway 56, also known as Sam Rayburn Drive. Built back in the late 1880s, the historic building was right across the street from the Fannin County courthouse, administration building, jail, and police headquarters. The floor Derek rented had been the home to several legal firms that stayed until they outgrew the 1,100 square foot space.

To modernize the building, the building's owners installed a new air conditioning system, an elevator, new electrical wiring, and fiber optic cabling to handle a modern load of phone systems, faxes, printers, computers, coffee pots, and even small space heaters, which were provided by the landlord. When Derek signed the lease on behalf of Camelot International, Inc., he thought one of the best features of the building was that the stairway to the roof was only accessible through their offices.

The landlord agreed to let them mount satellite TV and communication antennas on the roof. The building's brick facia rose five feet above the roof, so the antennas would be hard, if not impossible, to see from the street.

Derek also liked the heavy solid oak doors from the 1880s. When the building was renovated, the owners left the original pine shiplap in place. They had the contractors screw five-eighths-inch thick drywall onto the wood. The extra material provided additional insulation that kept the noise out and negated the ability for someone to hide mikes and cameras in the walls.

The offices were, Derek thought, ideal for Camelot International. The realtor, who was also the owner of the building, was happy to rent the vacant space for six months with an option for a year. Some rental income is far better than no rental income.

A quick trip to an office supply company that sold used furniture provided the desks, a conference table, and chairs. Later in the day, an unmarked truck unloaded four grey, drawer safes that looked like they'd seen better days. On each, the combination was written on a yellow Post 'it taped to the bottom of the front of the top drawer.

The shipment also contained three secure desktop phones; six ruggedized laptops with encrypted hard drives; four secure mobile satellite phones; two color printers, and a wireless router that encrypted any data it processed. As best as Derek could tell, all were brand new.

After checking the serial numbers against the manifest, Derek signed it, signifying he'd taken possession of the material. He was the president and one of the two employees and shareholders of Camelot, International.

Earlier in the week, Eileen, as the president of Camelot, signed the contract with Logistics Support Corporation (LSC) in which they agreed to provide administrative support for Camelot International through one of LSC's "indefinite order, indefinite quantity" contracts with the CIA. The services LSC would provide to Camelot were defined as performing the administrative functions needed to ensure their individual and corporate clearances were current, providing equipment as requested, and processing Camelot's invoices to the CIA. For their services, Logistics Support would add four percent to each Camelot invoice.

When the equipment arrived, the landlines were turned on and the desk phones worked. When Camelot's employees came, the safe combinations would be changed, and Camelot would be ready for business.

Derek's Rolex chronograph said it was 10:36 a.m. Bonham time or just before lunch in D.C. Don Sanderson should be at his desk. The phone rang once. "Sanderson."

"Good morning, Don… As you can see, the regular phones work."

"Same to you, Derek. Are you in business yet?"

"Not quite. All the stuff we asked for just arrived. There is a minor, well maybe not so minor, problem with Logistics Support

Corporation. When I was at their offices in Fort Worth on Monday, I gave them all the clearance forms that had everyone's name, prior clearance info, and Social Security Numbers and authorizing Top Secret/Specially Compartmented Information and access to code word programs. The contract says LSC is to administratively support whatever levels of clearance we are granted by the government. Period, end of statement. Bill Roffe, our LSC contract administrator, says he needs special authorization from the agency granting the clearance to authorize anything above Secret. You need to have a word with Roffe to get it sorted out. I don't want to get our collective asses hung out because we're handling code word material and are only cleared for Secret."

"I'll take care of it. If I need to, I'll explain the facts of life to Roffe." Don paused for a second. "Seriously, how soon do you think you'll be in business."

"Assuming everyone gets here this week, and there are no hiccups with the equipment or the intel, we'll start work immediately. Monday would be a safe bet."

"Let's plan on Monday."

"Super."

"Until Jacob Sobrano returns from Afghanistan, Ed will be your contact at Special Operations Command and will have direct access to the commander."

Before Derek could speak, Don continued. "I'll send a shipment of classified material to be delivered by courier on Monday. Oh, and I'd like to come out next Wednesday to see the set-up and bring more stuff. It's part of my job as the program manager. Any chance you can pick me up at DFW?"

"Sure. No problem. Just let me know when you will arrive and you can stay as long as you like."

CHAPTER 8

RISK VERSUS REWARD

The gray sky had emptied itself of the rain, and the thinning clouds suggested the sun would be out in a few hours. That was the good news. The bad was that the humidity would get more oppressive for a few hours before the air "dried" out. Then moisture content would drop from 80 percent to a more normal, but still very sticky 60.

In the humidity and 32° Celsius (90° Fahrenheit) temperature, clothes that didn't fit loosely clung to one's sweaty skin like wet tissue paper. Everywhere one went in Karachi, body odor mingled with exhaust fumes, cooking spices, uncollected garbage, and smells from a busy port. Some found the scents intoxicating, but Fatimah Serraf, who grew up in a privileged world of well-to-do Saudis, the pungent smells of Karachi assaulted her nose. They were an unpleasantness she would never get used to.

When she became the CEO of the bank, Fatimah told the prior owners that she expected everyone, from secretaries to executives, to bathe every day. Talwar's employees were paid enough to rent modern homes or apartments. Body odor or clothing that stank from tobacco or sweat would not be tolerated in the bank's offices. To help, she had showers installed in the bathrooms. The bank contracted a cleaning service for those worried about their clothing. Those who wished to do so could have their clean clothing delivered to the bank and keep it in their offices or closets.

Her second significant change was to forbid smoking, even by clients, in Talwar's offices. At first, there was some resistance, but quickly even those who opposed the policy change grew to like the clean air. Once the smoking stopped, she replaced all the furniture, carpets, curtains, and anything else that reeked from tobacco smoke.

On Monday of last week, she called the number in London and arranged to have a man flown to Karachi, business class, of course. Gerrard Butler arrived Thursday just after supper, and his sole purpose was to satisfy her sexually.

Looking at the gray sky, Fatimah leaned back in her chair, still glowing from the lovemaking. By now, the man was at the airport with 10 extra 100 Pound Sterling banknotes in his wallet after fulfilling his contract with another session early this morning.

Butler was, Fatimah found out, very, very good at keeping her either on the edge of having an orgasm or having one. Finally, after hours of her begging, Butler finally slid his penis into her soaking-wet vagina. Over the weekend, Fatimah was sure she nearly passed out several times from the intense pleasure. Her first act, when she got to the privacy of her office, was to call the firm for whom Butler worked and leave a glowing recommendation.

Satiated, Fatimah was ready for the challenges of running the bank and helping her jihadist friends. Her first appointment of the day on her calendar was the chief financial officer, who was prompt, as was his custom.

Like most of the executives in the bank, Saad Nazari wore a dress shirt with cufflinks and dark slacks. Coats and ties were optional in the office, and most executives preferred not to wear them. However, if needed for a meeting, all had a coat, a spare shirt, and a tie hanging behind their door so they could quickly transform into a 'banker's outfit.'

Saad was one of the three founders of the bank. He'd spent 10 years in the U.K. working for Barclays before moving to Faysal Bank in Pakistan. After five years in Faysal's wealth management group and with the encouragement of several clients in Karachi, he joined two other men with clients who would follow them and started Bahar, Nazari, and Touma.

His role in the bank had evolved from client partner to CFO since he was a chartered accountant registered in both the United Kingdom and Pakistan.

He never wanted to give up his client-facing role. At his urging, the bank found a controller who would manage the accounting department. Nazari also held the title of chief compliance officer and managed the regulatory reporting in the countries where Talwar had offices through the contacts he made while applying for banking licenses inside and outside of Pakistan. If there was a problem, Nazari was the person the agencies would call, and so far, none had.

When the bank was formed, Nazari wrote off the lack of regulatory agency interest because they were very small. Now, with the clients Serraf had brought in, Talwar would soon be among Pakistan's top five private banks. Increased regulatory scrutiny, Nazari believed, was just around the corner.

In his late fifties, Saad Nazari and his partners were wealthy men, even by U.K. or U.S. standards. They lived well, vacationed in five-star resorts, and flew first class anywhere they went. Selling the bank to Fatimah was another transaction that added to each founder's net worth. For him, retirement in comfort was assured, and it was just a question of when.

"Good morning, Fatimah. I trust you had a good weekend."

"I did, Saad. And I hope you spent it with your family." She wasn't about to tell him that she paid a London-based escort firm to fly a man from London to Karachi for the sole purpose of fucking her brains out all weekend. No romance, no love, just continual sex. The stud's mission was to get her orgasmic and keep her there for as long as she could stand it. Then, let her come down, and when she was ready, get her going again. Food and clothing were optional.

Before Butler arrived, the refrigerator and freezer were stocked to minimize cooking. How the Englishman got the toys he brought with him through customs was a mystery to her, but she was glad he did.

"We had our usual dinner on Friday with our children and grandchildren. Life is good when you can watch them grow up. The nest, as they say in America, was full."

Fatimah pointed to the small conference table opposite her desk. Her administrative assistant had put a pot of tea and another filled with strong coffee on the table. Next to it were cups made from Wedgewood China Fatimah knew were the real, not locally made knockoffs.

Once they had served themselves, Fatimah slid her small 15-by-25-centimeter notebook off to one side. She waited for the paunchy Nazari to arrange himself in his chair. His girth strained against the buttons of his dress shirt.

"So, what do we need to talk about?" The note in her calendar said, "Potential compliance issue."

Saad looked down at the paper he'd brought with him, more as a gesture to give him time to frame his words carefully. "First, I want to say that I am impressed at the number of new clients that have come into the bank under your leadership. Our client list has increased by twenty-five percent and we have almost doubled the assets we are managing."

Fatimah nodded slightly to acknowledge the compliment. *So, what's the problem?*

"As you know, when we were Bahar, Nazari, and Touma, we carefully vetted each new client before they deposited money in an account for two reasons. One to ensure that we could meet their needs and two, meet our commitments to the regulatory agencies in the countries where we do business."

For a Pakistani, Saad was straightforward in dealing with difficult problems. He preferred to get all facts out on the table without sugarcoating them so all involved could discuss them. This simplified things because he often told his partners, "We didn't have to remember what set of lies we told who and when...."

"Fatimah, what concerns me is that accounts were opened, funds were deposited, and we started investing the client's money without going through the bank's normal vetting or research process. In the past, at least one partner would review the client's portfolio and his needs before we took them on. This is a clear violation of one of our compliance processes."

She knew exactly what the real issue was. None of the bank's founders knew the four oil-rich sheikhs from Saudi Arabia and Qatar, who each gave her 100 million U.S. dollars to invest. The unspoken agreement was that 70 percent of the income generated went back into their account, and 30 went to al-Qaeda bank accounts she'd set up scattered around the world.

"I'm sorry, but I know these men and have worked with them before. They came to Talwar because of my ability to make them money. Unfortunately, these men are also very secretive." Fatimah thought the fewer words about them she said, the better.

"I understand." Saad paused and then chose his words very carefully. "This bank's reputation is built on three things which I think are worth noting. Number one is service we define as giving them choices to make money legally and keeping them informed to carefully chosen clients. Number two is transparency, which we define as being open to our clients and the regulatory agencies allowing us to conduct business in their respective countries. And number three is we maintain an audit trail. To reduce risk to the bank and our clients, we document everything from client backgrounds and discussions with prospective and current clients to investment decisions and the execution of transactions."

Saad stopped speaking, looked at his chief executive officer's coal-black eyes, and didn't like what he saw. They were a cold, emotionless mask. Like the other two founders, his holdings were now only eight percent of the stock, and the employees held six. Fifty-one percent was held by Fatimah, and 19 by her investors.

With the subject broached, there was no turning back. If he was fired, Nazari didn't care. He had enough money to live comfortably. As the bank's chief financial and chief risk and compliance officer, Nazari felt compelled to say that the bank may be headed down a slippery slope that may not have a good ending. While he prepared for this conversation, he wondered if the time to retire had come.

"Fatimah, clients have been taken on, and purchases of investment vehicles were made without any record of analysis performed by you or by a senior analyst within Talwar who has the authority to approve an investment. In fact, no one at the bank knew about the transactions until they appeared on our books. That is most irregular and is a serious violation of our policies."

Saad waited a few seconds and delivered what he thought was the first of his punch lines. "Fatimah, these actions greatly increase the bank's exposure, and if the investments do not perform, we have no defense against a lawsuit. And, if any of the regulatory agencies receive a complaint from one of these clients, we have nothing on which to justify our decisions."

Fatimah waited until Saad finished before speaking in a soft, soothing voice. "Saad, let me put your fears to rest. These clients are all legitimate businessmen, and all know me. They followed me to this bank because of my ability to make them more money than they could get through other banks. Some of them provided the funds that enabled me to buy this bank. The portfolios I manage for them have grown and will continue to grow. They will tell their friends, and we will get more clients. I did what I did because I know them and wanted to get them results quickly to increase their faith in Talwar. If you wish, I will sign a memo saying I will write a check to the bank to cover any losses."

"Fatimah, I understand. Qualified new clients are welcome, but you must follow our procedures and policies. Surely, they could have waited a few days. Remember, one complaint to a regulatory agency and the reception area will be full of investigators. Neither of us wants that."

Very true, and I have a different set of reasons to go along with yours. "I will try to do better." *No, I won't, but I need to placate Saad in the short term.*

"Then, there is the movement of money. Seventy percent of the profits stay in their accounts, and thirty is sometimes sent to banks where we, until the transaction happened, never had a relationship. Often, they are small banks in countries known for ..."

"Secrecy of their banking laws?" Fatimah made the question sound more like a statement. She knew he didn't want to utter "laundering money" because the words could get them both in trouble. If the funds went through a bank located in a country that enforces strong anti-money laundering statutes and the money was earned by illegal activities, Talwar could, at the very least, lose its banking license and be forced to pay fines. They could even wind up in jail.

Saad replied flatly. If one didn't know him, the soft tone in his voice could have been taken as an indication of acquiescence. "Yes."

"The arrangement I have with my clients is that seventy percent of the profits stay here, and thirty goes to accounts they select. It is not up to you or me to judge where the money goes, but just to send it. After all, we're sending their money."

"But we need some documentation... An e-mail or a fax or something from the client that we can put in our files that authorizes the transaction."

"I will see what I can do in the future."

"Thank you."

"Anything else on your mind?"

"No. Thank you for your time."

The CFO stood up to leave, and Fatimah's professional voice stopped him. "Saad, I appreciate your concern. I will try to do a better job of complying with the Talwar's long-standing policies." *You are uncomfortably close to what I am really doing. None of the other partners are as deeply involved in compliance as you are. Maybe you should move on. Heaven would be a good place.*

THE SAME DAY, 1:56 P.M. LOCAL TIME, DOHA, QATAR

Adnan Maalouf was sure no one followed him to The Curve Hotel in Doha. His early morning Athens to Doha non-stop flight was about half full, and he zipped through immigration using his Lebanese passport.

Looking out the cab's window as it drove along al Corniche Street and the waterfront, Adnan was surprised by the number of Americans and other Europeans he saw in the bustling city. He wrote their presence off to their staying after the World Cycling Championships that, according to the signs that were still up, had just finished.

For him, this was more than a quick conversation at a restaurant. Adnan thought what was about to happen was more of a debriefing. He dared not copy files or mails from his work computer, so Adnan kept what he referred to as a work diary. Ostensibly it was his meeting notes. Buried in those notes were tidbits of highly classified information in a personal code on what the U.S. knows about al-Qaeda and who is the next target of a drone strike or raid.

On the way to Doha, he compiled the notes from the past three months and what he understood about the current plans against al-Qaeda and the Taliban. In his hotel room, he photographed each page with a burner phone he bought at a kiosk at the airport.

Now equipped, he waited to board a cab to take him to the house in Madinat Khalifa North on al Farkiya Street. When he checked into the hotel, the clerk handed him a sealed envelope containing a sheet of paper with the address.

At the gate in the front, Adnan rang the bell, and when the door opened, he stepped inside. Once the door was closed, two men, both with AK-47s, patted him down and then used a device to see if he had a chip embedded in his skin or was wearing a wire. With that done, they compared Adnan's picture to the one they were provided. Satisfied, the men apologized for the search and ushered him into the house.

Inside, he was directed to a chair in front of a tape recorder and handed a mike. The debriefing lasted almost to midnight when Adnan was driven back to his hotel. Before going to his room, he stopped at the front desk to ask for an 0430 wake-up call. His Qatari Airlines flight back to Athens left at 0715. The roundtrip flight to Doha was not on the itinerary he left with his admin, nor did he mention that he used a forged passport delivered to him in Athens.

THURSDAY, OCTOBER 27TH, 2016, 12:33 A.M. LOCAL TIME, HINDU KUSH, AFGHANISTAN

For the past two hours, Jacob had been lying on the cold earth, wedged between two rocks studying the mouth of a cave 9,000 feet above sea level and 200 yards in front of him. Whatever heat his body generated by the five-hour hike in the dark to this position had long dissipated. His sweat felt like cold water, and he could feel the rock's cold through his long underwear. He'd lost count of the times he shivered.

Spread out in the trees and rocks near him, 16 soldiers from the Army's 10th Mountain Division and, including Jacob, Chief Tomkins, and 16 SEALS commanded by Lieutenant Junior Grade Randy Sullivan, patiently waited for the word to start the raid. For the past two nights, Aazar Rahim guided the 34 men around paths used by al-Qaeda. They hadn't seen a soul since they entered the mountains east of the Asar River.

Jacob halted the group every hour to download the latest imagery from an MQ-9 Reaper unmanned aerial combat vehicle orbiting overhead with four Hellfire missiles. From 5,000 feet above their heads, the Reaper's thermal imager gave him a near real-time picture of how his 34-man force was deployed and any other humans, animals, or objects that showed up as heat sources. As their commander, Jacob worried they were a misstep away from re-enacting Custer's last stand.

Jacob looked at the young man sitting with his back to the rocks, staring at the night sky. He pointed at the rock outcropping. "You sure that is the cave?"

Aazar Rahim nodded emphatically. "Yes. There are two entrances. This one is where I made the deliveries, and the other is about two hundred meters down the cliff on the ledge."

Both the young man and his father readily agreed that Aazar wouldn't be armed. This way, if things went into the crapper, he could tell their attackers he was a prisoner of the Americans.

When they headed out, Qaeder took Jacob's hand and said as he looked into Jacob's eyes, "Kill the interlopers to my country and bring my son back alive."

Jacob remembered nodding yes. Qaeder's words reminded him of something his father would say in the same situation.

"Mister Sobrano...." Jacob recognized the whispered voice of Chief Tomkins. "The scouts are back."

He scooted farther down the hill to a small clearing in the rocks. The most recent Reaper pictures showed nothing they hadn't seen, so they accomplished the insertion successfully or had walked into a trap. So far, Mr. Murphy hadn't reared his ugly face. On missions like this, something out of the ordinary always threw a monkey wrench into the plan.

"Sir, we're about one hundred feet from the first machine gun emplacement right by the entrance to the trail that leads to the main cave entrance. Then, about halfway up, there are two more, staggered so they are mutually supporting. Each position has four men."

The speaker, a young first lieutenant on his second deployment to Afghanistan with the 10th Mountain Division, pointed to the positions on the screen of a ruggedized tablet that showed both their location and the al-Qaeda fighters. The nametag on his BDUs said his last name was Westerly. He introduced himself back at Bagram as Gary before saying that he was class of 2013 at Norwich. After the brief, Westerly said he was the school's mountain rescue team captain in his senior year.

Westerly jabbed his forefinger at the hot spots on the screen. "Here are their machine guns. We could see another couple of men on the ledge, and we're not sure if they are sentries or are just outside getting some fresh air."

"How many other fighters are in the area?"

"Not sure. We saw about two dozen, and there could be more we can't see. We should assume there are many in the cave."

"Gary, how do we get to the cave mouth quickly?" Jacob didn't want to ask the obvious question of once the shooting started, did we have to rush up the path? It could get them pinned down, people hurt, and prevent them from achieving their objective - capturing the missiles.

"Sir, my snipers think that if we set up positions on these two rock outcroppings, we could take out the machine gunners with a couple of shots. We'd need twenty minutes to set up."

Aazar pushed his head into the circle and spoke to Jacob in Pashto. "May I speak?"

"Sure." Jacob nodded as if to say continue.

"Are your men good at climbing rocks?" Jacob translated for the other Americans.

Westerly said, "Depends on what you want us to climb. Can we see the cliff before we say yes?"

Aazar didn't wait for Jacob to finish translating. "Yes. Small goats can go up. Your men should be able to as well. Climbing will be slow, and your men will have to go one man at a time, but you come out on a flat area a few meters from the cave mouth."

"Aazar, show Lieutenant Westerly and come back here with an answer. How long?"

"We need ten minutes."

Jacob nodded, and the lieutenant and his platoon sergeant followed Aazar into the darkness. As he leaned back against a tree, Petty Officer Braddock said, "Sir, our sitrep is past due. What do you want me to send?"

"In position, updating assault plan based on latest intel. More later."

"That's all?"

"Yup. Anymore, and the guys sitting in cushy chairs with nothing better to do will start asking questions. Ask for an intel update. If they don't have one, tell them to stand by. When you finish sending, I want to look at what the Reaper is seeing."

Jacob stared at the thermal image. The four figures at each machine gun position were clearly visible, two were on watch, and two were sleeping. A dozen more walked along the ledge where the cave entrances were located. The thought, "What was he missing?" kept nagging at Jacob as a plan began to come together.

"Sir…"

"Yeah, Braddock, what do the geniuses back at Bagram want?"

"An update on the pick-up time and any other resources you may need, sir."

"Tell them they'll have one in less than twenty minutes." He hoped he would know by then.

"Lieutenant Commander Sobrano…"

Jacob turned to see the smiling face of Lieutenant Westerly. "What makes you so happy."

"Sir, the climb won't be a piece of cake, but it is very doable, even with packs. We should be in position in less than twenty minutes from when we leave here until we're up on the ledge."

"Lieutenant, is that a realistic, optimistic, or pessimistic estimate?"

"Sir, the estimate is both Sergeant Haskell's and mine. We came up with the same number independently."

Jacob looked around. His first thought was "show time." All the squad leaders were arranged in a semi-circle. Inside, despite having led raids like this many times before, his stomach churned. Each man was betting their life that his course of action wouldn't get them killed. As the leader, he had to shove his fear into the back of his mind and exude confidence they had a good plan based on solid intel.

"As much as I would like to lead from the front, I will move the command post up the trail as a follow-on unit to support that attack. Lieutenant Westerly, your objective is climbing the wall and securing the cave entrance on the right, which we will call Cave 2.

Don't go too far into the cave until we are all up on the ledge. The main attack force will take on the main entrance designated Cave 1. Randy Sullivan's SEAL snipers will deploy as suggested. On my command, they will start the attack on the two lower positions using suppressed pistols and, if needed, knives. No one enters a cave until you ensure it is not booby-trapped. Lieutenant Westerly, if you hear rifle fire, go, don't wait for my command, just get control of the ledge. Chief Tomkins and Petty Officer Braddock, you're with me as the command and communications element. Understood?"

Jacob heard a series of murmured yes sirs, then turned to Aazar and said in Pashto. "You're with me."

"Assuming we capture the caves, we grab what intel we can and set charges on any missiles or weapons we want to destroy. Then, we move as a group to the clearing on the top of the mountain that we agreed was a perfect pick-up point."

Once he received a nod, Jacob looked at his watch. "It is, on my mark 0123. We move out in seven minutes and conduct a radio check. Attack goes down at 0155. Braddock, tell our friends at Bagram that we want the AC-130 gunship that is supposedly nearby on scene at 0155 and will advise on pick-up time once we secure the caves. For planning purposes, tell Bagram 0300. Good luck and good shooting. Hopefully, along with the missiles, we'll find a treasure trove of intelligence. To minimize casualties, put the bad guys down first. Worry about prisoners later."

Jacob was happy he didn't say let's send the bastards to Allah. Grim faces nodded, and within seconds, only Chief Tomkins, Braddock, Aazar remained nearby.

The last thing Jacob did before slipping his arms through the straps of his pack was to make sure the magazines were seated correctly and a round chambered in his M4 and his Beretta 92F. Once that was done, he cycled the safety on both weapons to make sure they were in the off position.

Braddock looked around to make sure they didn't leave anything behind. As he stepped on the path, the earphone hissed for a few seconds before he heard the voice of Lieutenant Sullivan. He whispered. "Boss, we got a problem."

Jacob's first thought was "oh shit, Mr. Murphy has arrived." He pressed the mike button. "What's up?'

"We're looking at twelve sleeping bad guys a hundred feet from us. They'll wake up when the shooting starts. We can take them out, but it will delay our rush up to the cave."

"Where are they?"

"About fifty feet up the trail from the lowest guard post."

"Take out the guard post first, then the second nest if you can, then these guys."

"Roger."

No sooner did Jacob start moving again than he heard a loud crack made by wood breaking, followed by shouting in Pashto. Jacob heard more shouts, then silence. By the time he took a few more steps, the unmistakable rattle of M4s being fired in single-round mode interspersed with the distinctive staccato of AK-47 bursts.

Jacob heard in his earpiece, "Tenth is at Cave 2." The zing of a round passing just above his head caused Jacob to duck, and he saw the tracers before they zapped into the dirt a few yards away from where he and Braddock were crouching.

Sullivan's voice came through his headset. "Moving up the trail."

Jacob visualized what the two-man SEAL fireteams were doing as they worked their way up the main path. "Snipers, can you cover the area around the mouths of the caves?"

"We can see the mouth of Cave 1 but don't have a shot unless they come out into the open."

Shit! He should have thought of that. "How long can you get in position to shoot into the entrance?"

"Wait one. Will report when we are in position."

Jacob listened to the sporadic firing. He could hear the occasional bark of an M4 carbine and the rattle of an AK-47. As hard as he tried, Jacob couldn't hear the suppressed sniper rifles. He tapped Braddock on the shoulder and used the extended palm of his hand to point in the direction of the trail up to the caves. Both Aazar and Braddock nodded, and Jacob keyed his mike. "Double zero actual moving up the trail to the cliff."

"Boss…. Stay where you are. We're making sure the tangos are out of action. We don't want to let one shoot you before he meets Allah."

"Any possible prisoners?"

Short three-round bursts from the M4s interspersed with fewer and fewer bursts from AKs answered his question. Jacob realized his question was a dumb one to ask in the middle of a firefight.

"Clear. No prisoners. Boss, meet me by the lowest guard post, and I'll escort you up" By the strength of Lieutenant Sullivan's voice, he wasn't trying to be covert.

Rather than charge ahead, Jacob kept moving carefully, searching the trees around him. He hadn't climbed 50 yards when a shape emerged from the trees wearing familiar gear.

"Sir, if you follow me, we'll hustle up the hill." Even though the figure was dull green, black, and white, Jacob recognized Randy Sullivan.

Despite his workouts and efforts to stay in tip-top shape, he was huffing and puffing when he reached the ledge as he kept up with Lieutenant Sullivan, who was probably 10 years younger than he was. The fact he was lugging a 50-pound pack, and they were at about 9,000 feet above sea level, didn't give him any comfort or make the climb any easier.

Rather than bend over at the knees and catch his breath, Jacob slowed and looked around. Lieutenant Westerly emerged from the shadows. "Both entrances to the caves are secure, sir. We've gone into the first large room, and I've got guys already collecting computers and drives. We also found some of the missiles. The bad guys didn't have time to set booby traps."

"Show me."

Jacob looked around the mouth of the cave. It looked like an electrical engineering lab from his days at Norwich University. Workbenches made from plywood and 2 X 4s, probably stolen from American bases, lined both walls. Someplace a generator was still pumping out electricity and outlets, fed by a thick cable, were screwed to a 2 X 4 that hung from the rock.

Jacob ducked into a room with cots and another with a small refrigerator, microwave oven, and hotplate. Packaged foods, paper plates, and plastic utensils were stacked neatly in the corner at one end, and boxes of ammo for AK-46s and grenades were in another.

As he came out, Sobrano paused momentarily to watch Chief Tomkins finish checking the serial numbers of the 12 Stingers in the cave against his list. Before touching a case, Tomkins carefully looked for signs of a booby trap. Finding none, he lifted the lid just enough to use his flashlight to see a trigger. Slowly, he lifted the lid off the case and studied the missile.

He turned, "Sir, come look at this."

Jacob peered into the case not sure what he was looking at. "Looks like the bastards are recharging the batteries and coolant units. It also looks like they were monkeying around with the circuit boards. If you look here, they broke open the case and then glued the piece back down, and you can see where the glue leaked out. Back home, that would never pass inspection. If I were a betting man, they were updating the software because if I remember correctly, if the missile isn't fired in ten years, the clock in the software shuts the system down, and the missile won't fire. That's one of the things they update when they bring them into the depots for maintenance. We need to see if they have any manuals or a computer with the software around here."

"Do you know what you are looking for?"

"No, but if we take all the hard drives, CDs, and thumb drives, we should find it. I'll put the 10th Mountain guys to work."

"Mister Sobrano…."

Jacob turned to look at Petty Officer Braddock, who was standing in the cave mouth. "Sir, the pick-up helicopters will arrive in thirty minutes or less, and it's a ten-minute hike up to the extraction LZ."

The SEAL yelled. "Chief, you have ten minutes max. Lieutenant Sullivan, search the caves and see if you can find another exit. Let's take one of the missiles we think has been modified after we make sure it is not a booby trap. Then set the demo charges on the ammo and missiles with fifteen-minute fuses."

Sobrano turned to look for Aazar. He was nowhere in sight. Shit! A wave of panic swept over him. "Westerly, is Aazar with you?"

"Negative, sir."

Shit, piss, and corruption! Where the fuck is he? Last time I saw him was when I ducked into the cave.

Jacob heard a single pistol shot as he went farther into the cave. The sound reverberated through the cave. Jacob started running to the sound, afraid he would find Aazar lying in a pool of blood. Instead, he saw Aazar walk out of a small room with a pistol in his hand.

Jacob took the Makarov from the 16-year-old. "Where did you get this pistol?"

"My father gave it to me before we left."

"Why?" Jacob expected Azar to say that the weapon was for protection.

"To kill any of my father's relatives, I found and both Tomkins and you if you were about to be captured. My father feared that if you were tortured, you'd reveal he helped you."

Jacob was not shocked by the typically Afghan answer and peered into the room with a ladder leading up to a hole which he suspected led to the top of the cliff. Lying with his back to the far wall was a man with blood draining from a single hole in his head.

"Who is he?" Jacob assumed the Azar knew the man.

"My uncle. He had brought great embarrassment to my people in many ways. If you didn't do what he wanted, he whipped you." As he spoke, Aazar unbuttoned his perahan tunbun and down vest and turned away from Jacob. On the young man's back, Jacob could see the scars and welts from a beating.

THE SAME DAY, 12:48 P.M. LOCAL TIME, ISLAMABAD

The summons came late last week via a message on her mobile phone. Fatimah had no option but to comply and took Pakistani Airlines Flight 300 from Karachi which landed in Islamabad at 9:00 a.m. Fatimah's administrative assistant arranged for a car to take her to the hotel, where she planned to wait until the meeting started at 1130 and would go through lunch. To return to Karachi, she was booked on Pakistani Airlines Flight PK-304 leaving at 3:03 p.m.

Fatimah assumed the hotel was selected because her client, a man named Sameer, was not worried about surveillance in Pakistan's capital. She was sitting in a chair in the corner of the lobby sifting through the blizzard of emails that arrived in her inbox every day, when a male voice interrupted.

"I hope you saved enough room for lunch."

Fatimah looked up to see Sameer standing on the other side of the coffee table, which had an empty bowl of yogurt, a pot of tea, and a plate with the juices from fresh fruit puddled in the middle. She almost didn't recognize Sameer, who'd let his beard grow, but she knew his eyes were as cold as lumps of unburnt coal. "I was hungry."

"You could have used the conference room, ordered lunch up there, and had more privacy."

"This was fine. I've paid my bill, so we can meet." *I wanted to be out in the open as if I was not hiding.*

Sameer pointed in the direction of the door. Rather than leading like most Muslim men and expecting the woman to follow, he followed Fatimah. Two other men, she presumed were his bodyguards, opened the door, and searched the conference room, which had a table and eight chairs, before nodding to Sameer.

Again, Sameer followed the Western custom and let Fatimah enter first. She picked a chair next to the head of the table, so she sat on Sameer's right and opened her portfolio, which had a blank pad with graph paper. Inside were several folded sheets summarizing the investments she was managing for what Sameer called his "firm."

"Please, Fatimah, no notes."

"Of course." She closed the portfolio. *So, he will give me directions, or what he called 'guidance.'*

"An Omani friend of the firm wants to meet with you in Riyadh to arrange some investments. He is very, very observant...." Sameer let his words trail off.

He's telling me to wear a burka for that meeting at Talwar's Riyadh office.

"And he is uncomfortable dealing with a woman, even though I have assured him that you have been very valuable to the firm. He has heard good things about your work from his friends and wants to meet you."

Translation—Sameer's friend believes women should be home having babies. Not this one. I wonder how many wives this man has.

"Do you have any specific guidance for me?"

"Yes, the sheikh wants assurance that you can get money to bank accounts held by Russian citizens in non-Russian banks with branches in that country. The money will be used to purchase specific types of weapons."

"I've already done that for the firm. That you could have told him."

"I did, but he wants to hear how from you. He is giving us a substantial sum for a weapon that will devastate our enemies and bring the infidels to their knees. He wants assurances that the money goes directly to the sellers, not to intermediaries who will take a percentage."

"I understand." *That is very hard to do and increases my risk. Everyone wants a piece of the action to make the transaction disappear or be hard to trace. Maybe the total will be enough.* "I can limit the additional fees to a couple of percentage points. How much is he going to invest?"

"Initially, two hundred and fifty million."

Even Fatimah had to nod at the size. "Does he realize Talwar will want a fee for managing his money? We will only ask for one and a half percent for this size investment, and anything less is not worth the risk."

Sameer thought she was going to ask for two percent. This was good news. "I will let the sheikh know, and he will be pleased."

Fatimah nodded.

"I will contact you in the usual way to give you the meeting date."

"I'd like as much lead time as possible."

"I understand."

The rest of the meeting was spent going over the firm's accounts. Sameer was happy that despite all the spending, the principal had yet to be touched.

CHAPTER 9

WIRING DIAGRAM

Each day that passed, Eileen was enjoying her new role as the head of Camelot International, Inc. more and more. Government contracting was an entirely new world for her, and she began taking online courses recommended by Logistics Support Corporation. Some were offered by LSC, and others were provided by outside companies.

She submitted a Form SF-86 used as the basis of a clearance request, and the other documents that LSC wanted to grant her a Top-Secret clearance supported by a special background investigation. The plan, with Don Sanderson's and SOCOM's sponsorship, was to grant Eileen an interim Top-Secret clearance while the formal process was underway. Until the interim clearance was approved, she couldn't go into Camelot's offices if classified material was out of the safes.

Now, without the press of client calls, internal meetings, and the ad and brochure design work she did, Eileen could spend several hours every week on their ranch's pistol ranges. The box she signed for before she left The Evans Group was from Remington and contained a brand-new R51 pistol. It was the second one she had. The first, serial number 758, had engraved scrolls on the slide filled with silver. It was given to her when The Freedom Group was awarded the Best

Booth at the 2016 Shot Show. The pistol came with a note asking her to consider replacing her Smith & Wesson 9mm M&P Compact with the R51 as her concealed carry weapon.

The other good news was while she hadn't received the money, Stan had sent her an email saying she would be paid in full. Avery Lundquist said this is as good as a contractual commitment, particularly since Evans agreed with Eileen's calculation of what she was owed was based on her employment contract.

This commitment let Eileen enjoy the legal fencing between The Evans Group's attorney, whom she knew well, and Derek's and now her attorney, Avery Lundquist. For whatever reason, Stan insisted through his attorney that Eileen sign a new agreement with onerous, unenforceable non-compete clauses. Stan was, she concluded, just being a jerk, insisting she agree to the clauses unmodified before he paid her a dime.

Not once was Stan on the conference calls about the separation agreement, which did nothing but run up his and her legal bills. Eileen knew eventually Stan would have to give in because her abrupt departure started a series of events within The Evans Group he did not anticipate.

On the Monday after Eileen left, The Freedom Group called Stan to terminate the agreement immediately. By Tuesday, two more of Eileen's clients did the same, and the three losses created a $90 million hole in The Evans Group's 2017 revenue forecast. Worse, three of his best copywriters resigned, and employees demanded a meeting to hear him explain why Eileen left suddenly.

Evans stood before his staff, trying to spin Eileen's departure as one caused by philosophical differences. He was quickly shouted down by those who knew the truth. And many, mostly women, had concealed carry permits and pistols in their cars, if not their purses. The loss of the three clients and the prospect of more of Eileen's clients leaving affected the agency's profitability and, ultimately, their bonuses.

Stan said that Eileen was no longer a team player and had become difficult to manage. He said clients were complaining, and those who knew the truth yelled bullshit. Faced with a hostile audience, Stan walked out, leaving April McClellan to pick up the pieces.

As she stood trying to explain the unexplainable, April fought the panic filling her brain spurred by the fear that The Evans Group could go down the drain. Her retirement nest egg was now at risk because she knew that, while the agency was doing well, there were fissures in the firm that Eileen's abrupt resignation would turn into chasms. Stan's attempt to paper over the reasons behind Eileen's sudden departure did not help and, in fact, caused some to fester. Changes she and Eileen had been discussing on and off over the past six months needed to be made. April hoped that by starting to make them, she was not too late.

Within minutes of the end of the meeting, which several employees recorded on their mobile phones, Eileen's phone began to ring.

THE SAME DAY, 12:46 P.M. LOCAL TIME, BONHAM

Climbing out of Montgomery Field, just east of San Diego, Derek kept the power at 33 inches of manifold pressure and the propellers turning at 2,400 rpm as his Aerostar climbed steadily at 150 knots. Once he leveled off the pressurized twin at Flight Level 200 and engaged the autopilot, Ed DeCosta reached behind his seat and handed Derek a sheaf of papers from his briefcase.

"Here's what I could legally copy out of the service records of the five guys who should be in Bonham by Sunday. The paperwork allowing them to work for Camelot has been signed off."

Derek glanced at the top name, and DeCosta started talking. "Petty Officer First Class Jefferson has family in the Dallas area. He spent the weekend with them and drove out to Bonham yesterday. He's going to see the Holiday Inn Express and Suites manager and see if we could get a better rate by committing to 240 room nights over the next three months."

The SEAL continued. "Jefferson has made four deployments to Iraq and Afghanistan. He's back in the U.S. for a break before his next assignment. I thought working for you would be good for him. He doesn't say much, but when he does, listen. He takes time to work through stuff, but when he comes up with a plan, it generally is a good one."

DeCosta went to the next name on the list. "All these guys, except for Petty Office Pillar, have worked for me. Pillar is fresh out of intelligence training and came down with mono right after he reported to us. He is on light duty as he gets his strength back. I thought this would be educational for him."

"Tell me about Senior Chief Norquist."

"He's been in the Navy for about fifteen years. He's good at looking at stuff from all sorts of angles. You and he should get along great because neither of you think linearly. And he's good at getting stuff through the system, if you know what I mean."

"I do." Derek looked at the next sheet. "So, who's Zack Neimeyer."

"I yanked Intelligence Specialist Neimeyer out of the SEAL shop at the Naval Strike Warfare Center after he told me he was tired of giving briefings and wanted to get back into the field. He knows where to get the good intel from those who know what they're talking about. He recommended I add Petty Officer Buckholz to the list. Buckholz was working for me and will ask you questions that cause you to think. When you reach the point you don't need to answer any more why questions, just tell him to shut up. Oh, and he reads and speaks Arabic, Farsi, and Pashto like a native and is an expert on their culture. He's married to an Iranian woman whose family are not fans of the current regime."

Derek made a circling gesture with his hand. "How much do they know about me?"

"Honest answer is not sure." Ed paused. "They all know who I am and what I do. I'd bet Senior Chief Norquist has talked to several chiefs to find one who knows you. Beyond that, I don't know how much research they've done."

"They all know the arrangements?"

"Not sure if they know every detail. That's one of the things we'll cover tomorrow when they all arrive in Bonham. I'll go through the wiring diagram, and we'll go through all the interesting stuff I brought with me. Oh, that reminds me, did you ever get a vault for code word material?"

Derek twisted as much as he could to face Ed. "Our friends at Logistics Support Corporation told me that since we only had Secret level clearances, we didn't need anything more than the safes they sent us, so I went out and bought two new Lincoln 50s from

Liberty Safes. They are very large gun safes and are bolted to the floor. Their insulation will keep paper from burning for ninety minutes in a 1,200-degree Fahrenheit fire. They meet DOD standards for code word material and have ten-digit codes."

"How much did that set you back?"

"With delivery, a little under twenty-seven hundred dollars each… Don't worry, if Logistics Support doesn't want them back, I know people who will take them off our hands. Or maybe I can give them to you. Moving them will be a bitch since each one weighs just over eleven hundred pounds."

De Costa made a note about the Liberty Safes in a 5" x 7" spiral-bound notebook. On one side of the yellow sheets, there were light blue lines. On the back, graph paper with quarter-inch squares. "That reminds me. When we land, I must call the folks at LSC. By now, they should have the paperwork for the code word access, and, if they don't have their shit together, they'll get a lot more help than they want."

The controller's voice clearing Aerostar N111DA to descend and maintain 15,000 feet, told Derek it was time to go back to flying. They were 20 minutes from the small airport he jokingly called "Bonham International." The official name of the airport was Jones Field. Like everything in Fannin County, the home of the former Speaker of the House, Sam Rayburn, one could see the benefits from his tenure in the house. One was the VA hospital in Bonham. Another was the six instrument approaches to this little airport.

Derek loved hand flying his Aerostar. The plane's pushrod actuated controls and well-balanced feel made the twin a delight to fly.

Ten minutes after Derek closed the hangar door, he parked his truck on North Main Street in the center of Bonham. Ed's bags were left locked in Derek's truck while each carried a box of classified material to Camelot's office.

Neither Ed nor Derek was surprised to find all four men waiting in the hallway when they walked off the elevator. He suspected they were eager to find out more about this unusual assignment.

They were amid introductions when there was a discrete knock on the door. The unmistakable odor of Mexican food filled the room as soon as the door was opened.

Derek smiled. "Welcome to Texas, everyone. I thought we'd start with Mexican food from the restaurant across the street. If I remember, I ordered fajitas, chips, dip, and sopapillas for lunch. Then, we can get down to business."

Ed DeCosta waited until everyone was well into his meal. "OK, everyone listen up. Time's a' wasting, so let's get started. I will kick this off with a quick overview of how we got here, the wiring diagram, and some rules of engagement. Then I will walk everyone through the intel on what we know."

Heads nodded, and the eating continued. "For starters, once you sign all the paperwork, you've been, as the Brits say, seconded to Camelot International, Inc. In other words, legally and operationally, you are no longer in the Navy. However, all your medical benefits will continue through a company called Logistics Support International or LSI which has a contract with the Navy Special Warfare Development Group. LSI has a contract with Camelot. So, you will be paid your Navy pay plus ten percent and all allowances. However, instead of the deposits coming from DFAS, they will be made by Logistics Support. To do that, Camelot bills Logistics Support for your salaries and expenses. For the record, you will not lose any longevity or miss any evaluations. Commander Almer and Chief Norquist will write your evals, and I will take care of it from there. That's the administrative side of it. Any questions?"

No hands were raised, and Ed looked around the room. "Now, the reason we're all gathered here is that many of us believe al-Qaeda is going to attempt to shoot down some airliners here in the U.S. using Russian or U.S.-made MANPADS. They've already tried once, but the missiles didn't fire. More about what happened later. Our good friends in the Middle East have very credible intelligence that al-Qaeda has either acquired or is in the process of acquiring Russian SA-24s to go along with the Stingers they already have. The current president doesn't believe this is a real threat and doesn't want to cause panic that will disrupt air travel. As a result, he directed the CIA to focus on other things, such as finding leaders of al-Qaeda and the Taliban to kill using drone strikes. His rationale is the assassinations will disrupt their operational planning. There are some of us in the CIA and Special Operations Command who have a different opinion so you will find the missiles, quietly. Then, if ordered, destroy them."

He let the implications of what he said sink in for a few seconds. "Operationally, Camelot works for me. I work, depending on the topic, for the head of the Navy Special Warfare Development Group or the four-star head of the Special Operations Command. He has a fair amount of latitude in what he can do to identify and eliminate threats to the United States homeland."

Ed took a sip of his Coke. It was a chance to take questions.

"Sir, are you telling me the CIA is not working on this?" Petty Officer First Class Jefferson shook his head as he spoke.

"Officially, they are not. Unofficially, they have a team working on the problem, but if the White House finds out about it, heads will roll. That's why we're here!"

Senior Chief Norquist tried not to sound skeptical. "So, how do we get intel?"

"Through me. Tell me what you want, and I'll get it. Or use your own sources. Depending on who they are, those who won't share, will have an uncomfortable conversation with either the Director or the head of SOCOM. If anyone checks, Camelot will appear legit and have the necessary access."

"What about individual weapons?" Petty Officer Pillar showed he wasn't shy.

Ed looked at Derek. "Great question. This is Texas. Through Commander DeCosta, we'll all have Federal permits to carry firearms along with Texas concealed carry permits. They should arrive any day. As far as weapons, that's up to you. My recommendation is that we all carry the same firearm. If you don't already have one, we can get them here in Texas. You'll be reimbursed for the cost. I know which stores have the best selections and prices. I have a Class III license, so I can purchase automatic weapons legally. The second safe will be used to store firearms and ammo."

"Commander DeCosta, would you mind telling me why we're out here in bum fuck Egypt? Why not someplace nearer civilization?" Buckholz's New York accent that told you he was from "da Bronx" was noticeable.

Derek held up his hand. "Ed, let me answer that…. There are several reasons. One is security. This is a very, very small town of about ten thousand so any strangers will be noticed. If they show up, I'll find out about it. Two, Bonham is well away from prying eyes on both sides of the game. We want to be low-key and stay well under the radar. Yet, we can go and come as we please. We're close to DFW, which means we're one or two stops from anywhere in the world. Or, if we want to take my plane, we just load and go. And last, we're standing about twenty miles from my ranch, which has gun ranges on which we can practice."

Ed stuck his finger in the air. "Buckholz, what the commander didn't say about his ranch is that he has a tactical gun range that will make you wet your pants and a rifle range where you can practice shots from up to five hundred yards. He has a nice pool, and his house backs up on a lake stocked with freshwater striped bass. If you are nice to him, he'll let you ride his horses, and if he really likes you, I'm sure he'll let you hunt white-tail deer on his land."

Buckholz and the other men were grinning when DeCosta finished speaking. Ed pulled the switchblade from one of the thigh pockets in his 5.11 Tactical pants and flicked open the blade. He was about to slit open one of the boxes when one of the secure telephones began ringing.

Derek reached for the phone, and when the handset was next to his ear, he said, "Camelot International." He then looked down, and the display said that the caller was using a phone that could be used for Top Secret phone calls. Derek didn't recognize the identifier for the location.

"I'm not sure if I dialed the right number. Is there an Ed DeCosta there?"

"He is. May I tell him who is calling?"

"Jacob Sobrano."

"Just a second, I'll hand him the phone." Derek pushed mute on the phone.

"I'm going to put him on the speaker. My guess is that he has something to tell us that relates to Camelot International's tasking."

Derek pushed the speaker button. "Jacob, this is Commander Almer along with Commander DeCosta, Senior Chief Al Norquist, IS1 Zack Neimeyer, IS2 Harold Buckholz, and SO3 Grant Pillar. I think you know most of these guys. Anyway, Camelot International was formed by me and hired by Ed and Don's organization to do some research into lost Stingers and other missiles of a similar ilk."

"Now it all makes sense." Derek wasn't sure if he heard a bit of annoyance in Jacob's voice from being "left out."

"Jacob, Camelot International is not a name you want to bandy about. We're trying to stay under the radar. I'm going secure."

The familiar beeping and hissing of secure phones linking up followed. The letters in the LED said TS/Bagram TOC, and TOC was short for tactical operations center.

"As Ed knows, I came over here to follow a lead on some missing Stingers that turned out to be a good one. In a raid on a cave complex a few nights ago, we found a dozen missing Stingers in an electronics workshop. What we liberated has been passed on to our technology exploitation team in Bahrain and should be on the way back to the States by now."

Jacob paused for a few seconds to let the encryption algorithm catch up before continuing. "Here's what we've learned so far. One, we managed to kill one of al-Qaeda's top logistics guys who has been helping them maintain the flow of weapons into Afghanistan. Two, al-Qaeda is attempting to update the software in their Stingers. Three, we dusted everything we got for fingerprints and found some from Neil Mirage, a former Army soldier. He entered the U.S. as the son of a Syrian immigrant as Na'il Miraj. Here's the punch line. The guy spent his time in the anti-aircraft artillery branch of the Army and qualified as a depot-level Stinger repair technician before his enlistment expired. Mirage earned an honorable discharge."

Ed held up his hand as if to say let me speak. "Jacob, do you have any pictures?"

"Yeah, tons. Before I go get some shuteye, I'll send them to you via secure email along with Mirage's photo from his personnel jacket."

Ed pointed to his chest. "Good. When are you coming back?"

"I'm going to Bahrain tomorrow for a formal after-action debrief before I catch my flight back to Tampa. Should be in Florida by the weekend, why?"

"You've been assigned to Camelot. I'll have your orders sent to Bahrain so you can book a commercial trip back to Dallas. Derek will pick you up at DFW. I'll send you his contact details. Get some sleep."

Ed ended the call and was about to say something when the phone rang, again. He picked up the handset. "Camelot International."

"Is a Mr. Almer there?" Ed recognized the accent as being either German or Israeli.

"May I tell him who is calling?"

"Zvi Rosenthal. He knows who I am."

"Just one minute, I'll put him on."

Ed handed the phone to Derek before facing the others and putting a finger to his lips.

"Zvi, shalom. How are you doing?"

"I'm fine. I have another package for you. When and where can I deliver it?"

"Same way as last time?"

"I will be flying into Love Field tomorrow. I'll send you the flight information by email."

"I'll meet you as you come into baggage claim."

"Thank you."

Derek placed the handset back in the cradle, wondering what the Israelis wanted to tell him. "Where were we?"

Ed laughed. "I was about to tell everyone that we will be receiving info from several foreign sources. One of them will be the Israelis, and I think you will find their intel very helpful."

SATURDAY, OCTOBER 29ᵀᴴ, 2016, 4:52 P.M. LOCAL TIME, AFGHANISTAN

The sun was almost below the horizon when Ghanem directed the column make camp under a rock outcropping. Smoke from earlier fires by others who stopped here had already blackened the back wall and top.

The dried wood the men had gathered crackled as it burnt and was hot enough to brew tea. The "they" were the small group that clambered out of the cave's back entrance when the Americans attacked. In their hike just below the tree line, Na'il and the others drank water from mountain streams and boiled it with pine needles and nuts for food.

Right after they finished their watery soup on the third day of their trek into Pakistan, two al-Qaeda fighters grabbed Na'il behind and forced him to the ground. Ghanem used the tip of his AK-47's barrel to raise the American's chin. "Are you working for the CIA?"

"No!!! I came here on my own."

"Why?"

"To help with the jihad."

"How did the Americans find us?"

"I don't know. Maybe one of the locals who deliver supplies told them. They know the caves, and many don't like us."

"We are deep in al-Qaeda and Taliban-controlled territory. No one gets in or out without our knowledge."

"Well, they did. There may have been a leak within al-Qaeda."

"Maybe." Ghanem leaned over until his face was just a few inches from Na'il's. "When we get back, I will have you X-rayed to see if you have a GPS locator implanted in your body. If we find one, you will spend your remaining days in pain until we are sure we know everything you know. Meanwhile, we will check out your theory."

THE SAME DAY, 6:30 P.M. LOCAL TIME, LONDON

The four-story townhouse on Marloes Road was in the heart of Kensington. Fatimah had stopped at a realtor's office to inquire about buying one of the homes in Kensington. She was not surprised when she was told they started at around 23,000 Pounds Stirling per square foot. The cost made Kensington one of the most expensive and exclusive neighborhoods in the U.K. and the world. Still, when she came to London, she looked at what was for sale in Kensington because she liked the neighborhood.

During a week with a full schedule of meetings and calls that had to be supported by research and analysis to support her recommendations, Fatimah forgot to make a personal phone call. With her feet curled up under her rear and a glass of wine on the end table, Fatimah dialed a number she knew from heart.

Kathryn Hollingsworth, the voice at the end of the phone when she called for what Fatimah referred to as companionship, worked out of her house in Kensington. Fatimah would leave her six-digit Smart Chic customer code and dates needed on an answering machine. An hour or so later, a pleasant voice called back with a name and a confirmation would be texted to her phone.

This time, it was different. A human being answered Smart Chic's phone, and Fatimah recognized the voice as the one who called back to leave details. Before Fatimah hung up, she said, "I need help."

"What kind of help?" The voice replied.

"You know my needs. I need to talk to someone."

"I'm not a shrink."

"I know that, but I think you can help me."

Kathryn Hollingsworth was not just successful; she was also cautious. Before she took on any client, the individual was thoroughly vetted through her law enforcement and business contacts. These checks corroborated information from the background research services to which she subscribed and allowed her to quickly check out prospective clients.

Her escort and modeling business paid the bills and turned a tidy profit. Still, the call person, as she referred to the third leg of her business because she provided both men and women, is what made her real money. Sex was very profitable and always in demand.

Her "resources" were also carefully vetted. She was paid well, and so were they. Working for Kathryn came with perks such as access to the best medical care in the U.K. Those who were not discrete or violated her strict rules were not given a second chance.

Something in Fatimah's call struck the "mother chord" in Kathryn. She was interested in meeting this very, very successful woman. Kathryn toyed with giving Fatimah a portion of her portfolio to manage. In the end, she decided that a commercial business beyond her fees for services entailed way too much risk.

Now 52, Kathryn was 5' 11" in her stocking feet, and her blond hair, mixed with a little gray, gave her a distinguished as well as very attractive appearance. How much was gray, blond, or tint was her secret. Those who knew the blue-eyed woman thought her to be 'aristocratic' in bearing, but Kathryn had a way of making people feel comfortable and "open up" to her.

Her late husband liked to date models, and that's how they met. Kathryn became a trophy wife who soon realized her well-connected husband and partner in one of the U.K.'s largest and most prestigious law firms couldn't keep his pants zipped. After a string of affairs, she demanded he buy her a modeling business as the price of not filing for divorce.

When he died of a heart attack banging a woman a third his age, Kathryn inherited his investment portfolio in offshore banks in tax havens. She negotiated a full buyout by the law firm that netted her £12,000,000 after taxes.

Fatimah pressed the button at the door, and the speaker came alive with a soft feminine voice asking her to open the door. She walked into a foyer where a well-dressed woman wearing a skin-tight, black leather pantsuit with the hair on the left side of her head shaved waited. "Miss Serraf, Kathryn will be down in a minute. I am Diedra. Please have a seat in the sitting room. May I make you something to drink?" The woman used her hand to show Fatimah which room was to be used.

"A dark red wine would be nice."

"We have a 2000 Merlot from Pavie that is open. The vineyard is close to the village of St. Émilion, and the year was one of the best in memory."

Fatimah nodded. Diedra poured the wine into two lead crystal glasses and swirled each.

"Diedra, what do you do for Kathryn?"

"I serve Kathryn." The woman's robotic answer and blank look made the Saudi woman feel uncomfortable as if she wasn't in the room. She handed Fatimah one of the glasses, and the other remained on the Sterling silver tray. Diedra bowed slightly from the waist and left, her chrome black leather three-inch heels clicking noticeably on the polished granite floor.

Fatimah used the time alone to study the room. She was sure the antique furniture was made during Queen Victoria's reign and the Matisse, Mondrian, and Picasso paintings on the walls were originals.

The sound of another set of high heels on the stone floor alerted Fatimah to someone coming. Thinking Kathryn might be coming, Fatimah stood.

The Englishwoman wore a mid-thigh black leather skirt and a slate gray blouse buttoned almost to the top. A string of gray pearls Fatimah guessed were six millimeters in diameter were visible. Black pumps with two-inch heels completed the woman's outfit.

"Hi Fatimah, I'm Kathryn." After they shook hands, Kathryn turned to Diedra who followed Kathryn into the room. "Diedra, thank you. Please get the tray in the kitchen."

Diedra nodded as she bowed. "My pleasure to serve, Miss Katherine." The woman bowed, turned, and disappeared down the hall.

"My chef has prepared something for us to munch on, and then, if we want, we can go out to dinner. Please."

Fatimah took one end of the loveseat, and Kathryn sat in the chair at right angles. When Diedra returned, she placed a tray with an artfully plated assortment of cheeses, vegetables, dried fruit, and nuts on the table with wood inlaid in intricate squares made from different woods.

"Fatimah, I must tell you that if you wanted, you could be a model."

Fatimah lowered her eyes at the compliment. "Thank you."

"So, I'm dying of curiosity… What kind of help do you need?"

Both women knew there was no need to beat around the bush. Smart Chic provided men who had the necessary stamina and control and who would do whatever Fatimah wanted to satisfy her sexual needs.

"I need something more than a good fuck."

"Something as in romance?"

"No. A man in my life and line of work would be a complication I don't need at the moment." *He would also be a risk.*

"Would you like to experiment?"

"In what way?"

"Well, knowing what you have requested in the past, there are several options. I could arrange a threesome. You get to pick between two men or a man and a woman or one or two women. Trust me, making love to another woman, particularly one who knows what she is doing, can be quite satisfying." Kathryn stopped for a few seconds. "Those are the traditional answers or suggestions."

"I hear an 'or' in your answer."

"Yes, there is more. Fatimah, before I make those suggestions, tell me why you are bored. Are you under so much stress you can't relax?"

I've never thought about it that way. Yes, there is stress from hiding the fact that I am the banker for the most hated terrorist organization in the world. There is stress from running the bank. There is stress from trying to make sure that the banks, and most importantly, its clients get the return she promised. So yes, there's lots of stress.

"Yes, my work is stressful. My father has come around to accept me for what I am, which is a professional businesswoman who runs a private bank. But he still thinks I should be married, wearing a burqa, and making babies."

"Tell me about your father?" Kathryn thought she sounded like a psychiatrist.

"He is a chartered accountant who started working for the finance ministry. As a young man, he helped members of the royal family make millions more than they were earning from the advice given by their financial advisors. From that point on, the royal family bestowed favors on him. Over time, he too became wealthy." Fatimah realized that that was the first time she'd talked about her family to a stranger. She'd never have this conversation with anyone at Talwar, where she preferred to remain aloof.

"Brothers? Sisters?"

Fatimah drew in a deep breath. "My father has only one wife. My mother gave him four children, three boys and me. My oldest brother is a Saudi Air Force fighter pilot, and the two others work for the Saudi government."

"Do you talk to your father?"

"Occasionally. When I call my mother, he often gets on the phone, but the conversation is…. Is…." Fatimah struggled for the right word. "… stilted. He asks the same things each time and congratulates me on each promotion. He does not ask about my social life."

Kathryn refilled both glasses of wine. "Here, have another glass and some food."

Fatimah spread some warm brie on a soda cracker, then added a bit of honey and jam before popping the combination in her mouth. She sniffed the wine and enjoyed the rich aroma. Fatimah wasn't a wine snob, but she could smell the oak and hints of plums, blackberries, and chocolate. In her first sip, Fatimah thought she tasted fennel or licorice.

Kathryn pointed to the bottle. "Pavie, I learned, is in completely renovating the winery. Their wines are almost opaque, which I am told comes from the minerals from the limestone and chalk in the soil, but what do I know. I just like their wines."

Fatimah took another sip and felt the alcohol warm its way down to her stomach. Talking to Kathryn was easy. Being a terrorist's banker is lonely work, and she had no friends or anyone she could confide in. "Me too. This is lovely."

"Has your father taken on another wife?"

"My mother is always worried that he may, but he hasn't yet. You would think a man in his sixties would want to slow down."

Kathryn giggled. "Trust me, I've been there."

"What do you mean?"

"I married the man who is now my late husband when I was an up-and-coming model in my middle twenties. He'd been divorced, and I knew he married me for my body and looks, not my brains. By the time I was thirty, I'd confronted him with evidence of three affairs. He wanted a wife to parade at company events or meet with clients so he had the look of stability. I was his trophy, and after I caught him the third time, I forced him to give me the money to buy what is now Smart Chic."

Kathryn held up her glass of wine, tiled the top toward Fatimah, and took a sip before she continued talking. "He was in his late fifties and told me that he would be working late in Manchester and would be home the next day. He came home alright, this time in a bloody box. He had a coronary while fucking a client's wife."

"Ouch."

"It wasn't traumatic as one might think because Smart Chic was off and running by then. He left me a pile of money, but I really wanted his business contacts to support what I call the companion business. You're considered a companion client. To be blunt, the companion business gives me leverage, so if anyone ever complains, the names in my little black book will come in handy. Unless something odd or scandalous that happens, I am confident the police look the other way. Girls and the blokes from Smart Chic are discreet and expensive. Most work for a few years, make a pile of money and then go on their merry way."

Fatimah leaned back. Between the wine and the conversation, she was more relaxed than she'd been in months, maybe years. "So, what do you do for sex?"

"That is not an appropriate question to ask one of London's leading and most respectable madams." Kathryn giggled and finished her glass of wine. She topped off Fatimah's glass before emptying the remainder in hers. "Enough about me. Let's go back to you. My guess is that with you, everything is all about control."

Fatimah furrowed her brow. She'd never associated the word sex with the word Kathryn used. "Control?"

"Yes, control… You want to be in charge and in command to control everything. And that goes for sex. You buy dicks from me, and they do what you want them to do. In other words, you are in control."

"I never thought of it that way. But you have a point."

"What if you could increase the amount of control but simultaneously increase the intensity of each orgasm. Would you be interested?"

Fatimah took a sip of wine to keep herself from saying "yes" immediately. She savored the taste of the burgundy-colored liquid. "Yes, yes, I would."

Kathryn stood up and held out her hand. "Great. Can you stay in London until Sunday?"

"Yes, I am booked on a flight back to Karachi on Sunday night that I can change." She knew she could skip the Monday a.m. staff meeting.

"Great. Let's go have dinner, and I'll share my idea. Then, if you're still interested, we can go from there?"

"Perfect." Fatimah could feel the pressure in her loins. She was sexually excited and didn't know why.

SUNDAY, OCTOBER 30TH, 2016, 10:22 A.M. LOCAL TIME, KENNEBUNKPORT, ME

From where the stocky, broad-shouldered Abbas Salib stood on the dock, the fishing boat *Mary Beth* rode easily in the calm, cold gray water. Despite his ski jacket, Abbas shivered in the damp, chill air as he admired the sturdy construction of the boat's steel hull and large winches used to haul in fishing nets. He loved the salty smell of the ocean that, at this pier, was tainted with a faint smell of diesel fuel and rotting seaweed wrapped around the dock's pylons. Along with the faint smell of cleaned fish, the pier reminded him of his father's boat back in Umm Qasr, only bigger and much more modern.

According to the ship broker's website listing, *Mary Beth* was five years old. When he called, the broker claimed the fishing boat had been well but lovingly used by its prior owner, who had died suddenly of a heart attack. No one in the family wanted to keep fishing or make the payments, so *Mary Beth* was on the auction block.

The broker offered interested buyers a short cruise to see that all the systems worked. The engines purred, and the generator provided enough electrical power to run all the winches and hoists. *Mary Beth* had a separate diesel generator that could power anything on the ship if the captain didn't want to run the main engine. The bridge of *Mary Beth* had the scope for the mast-mounted radar and another for the GPS that portrayed the ship's position on a moving map display. The boat also had VHF radios and an HF one for long-distance communication. None of the boats his father owned back in Umm Qasr, Iraq's primary port, had this equipment.

Salib asked if the family would take $100,000 plus the balance of the banknote and offered to close before the next payment was due. The broker, William Bryce III, said he would present the offer to the owners. Salib was prepared to go to a quarter million to buy the perfect boat for his mission.

Looking down the harbor toward the Atlantic, Salib thought *Mary Beth* looked out of place amongst all the sailboats and cabin cruisers in the broker's yard. The *Mary Beth* brought back many pleasant memories of working in the northern end of the Arabian Gulf, often in sight of the oil platforms operated by his native country and those of its mortal enemy, Iran.

Abbas stood at the aft end of the bridge as the man hired to take the boat out shifted the screw into neutral so the fishing boat could coast toward the dock. He heard the rubber fenders groan as they were compressed.

Once the boat was tied up, Bryce III left and walked down the pier. Salib was headed to his car when he saw the broker approaching him. Salib was asked if he was flexible in his cash offer. He nodded saying "within reason."

"The owners want two hundred thousand over the banknote. If you can agree to that number, we have a deal."

Salib looked away and then at *Mary Beth* without responding. He wanted to make the broker squirm. "How about one-fifty?"

Bryce said, "Let me make a call." He turned and walked away, dialing his mobile phone. Salib could see him wave his arms and nod several times before returning to the Iraqi native.

"The owner will take one eighty plus take-over the payments."

After waiting about 15 seconds, Salib stuck out his hand. "Deal, and I want to take possession as quickly as possible."

"Mr. Salib, how much are you willing to put down?

"I can have an electronic transfer of twenty thousand initiated today as a deposit. I would like to close in a week."

The sale for *Mary Beth* was closed on October 21st. Today, Salib and Kamil Nassar cell would take the *Mary Beth* to the berth they had rented in Portland, and Tawfik Tomas, the third member of his al-Qaeda cell, would meet them in Maine's largest port.

A shout caught Salib's attention. It was William Bryce III, who was walking down the pier pulling a small cart.

The broker handed Salib the boat's new registration in the name of IQ Marine and laid out all the manuals he'd kept in his office on the chart table next to the wheel. He also gave Salib the lien release from the bank, a bill of sale, and a statement that all the necessary fees and taxes had been paid to the State of Maine.

Once both *Mary Beth's* Caterpillar diesel engines rumbled into life, Bryce helped Tomas untie the lines and toss them to Kamil Nassar on *Mary Beth*.

Salib let the *Mary Beth* drift in the outgoing tide that pulled the boat away from the pier before he spun the wheel and shifted the gearbox into reverse. The water churned behind the fishing boat, and *Mary Beth's* stern moved slowly away from the pier, pulling the boat into the harbor. Once he was well clear of the pier, Salib shifted into neutral, paused for a second, and then shifted the transmission into forward. As *Mary Beth* began to move forward, he turned the wheel to the right to point the fishing boat into the channel.

Bryce gave them a salute, and Tomas stood as instructed to wait until *Mary Beth* was out of sight. Then, he would drive to Portland, roughly 30 miles by car to the north. Salib figured that Tomas would be at their new berth in Portland 40 minutes after he and Nassar left Kennebunkport. *Mary Beth* would need about three hours. Salib was happy to be at sea again.

CHAPTER 18

TEST RUN

Given their tasking, Camelot International's working hypothesis was that al-Qaeda's next major attack would be an attempt to disrupt the world's transportation system. What better way than launch MANPADS at airliners taking off or landing from airports in the U.S.?

The team studied images on Google Maps of the top 50 U.S. airports and divided them into two categories. The airports were listed on the four-by-six-foot whiteboard in the largest room in the office suite.

Category I had those that had clearings within three miles from the ends of the runway from which a shoulder-mounted surface-to-air missile could be fired. The clearings had to be large enough to give the shooters an unobstructed view of arriving and departing aircraft. Category II were airports where a missile could be shot from a rooftop.

In Derek's mind, a rooftop launch was riskier for the shooter because hauling a missile to the rooftop increased the risk of being discovered. It also made the shooters more visible to neighbors and escape more difficult.

DeCosta and Neimeyer contended that the shooters were on one-way missions and may be wearing suicide vests to kill as many first responders as possible. However, Derek insisted that the shooters would make some attempt to get away, even if their goal is to create more mayhem.

For each airport, they collected a National Oceanographic and Atmospheric Administration (NOAA) airport diagram which they used to plot the arrival and departure routes on Tactical Pilotage Charts. Google Maps provided enough resolution to identify buildings and clearings. When they finished, they had the potential launch site locations plotted with range circles drawn for Stingers and SA-24s and the flight paths to and from each of the runways. The completed charts for the airports told strongly suggested where the most likely launch locations would be.

Ed downloaded electronic versions of the TPC charts on which they could plot the information collected. This enabled them to easily update the charts projected on a Sony 80-inch LCD TV hung on a wall.

They also collected information on MANPADS missile performance, primarily Stingers and the Russian-made SA-14s, 16s, 18s, and 24s. The paper documents, plus other information on the missiles, were scanned and kept in Camelot's encrypted server. Two encrypted backups were made at midnight. The next day, one was put in the gun safe, and the other was transmitted electronically to a server designated by Ed DeCosta.

A discrete knock on the suite door stopped all work. A black drape was dropped over the whiteboard, and more than one person reached for their sidearm.

As per their procedure, Derek looked through the peephole in the door. He wasn't worried about someone shooting him through the wooden door because the door had a sheet of case-hardened 3/8ths inch steel bolted on the inside.

When he saw Zvi's scarred face, he opened the door. "Zvi, how are you?" Each time Derek saw the man, he was reminded of his ordeal of escaping from a burning M113 armored personnel carrier set on fire when it rolled over a mine. The scars on his face and his hands from the burns that cost him two fingers on his left hand were the only ones visible. Derek assumed there were more but never asked.

"I'm fine. I hope this is not an inconvenient time, but I have relatives in the Dallas area so I rented a car."

"Not a problem. Driving out here saved me a trip to DFW."

With a clunk, the door closed behind Zvi, and Derek turned to the group. "Let me introduce you to everybody."

After the handshaking, Derek handed a Fairborn-Sykes fighting knife to the Israeli. Its razor-sharp blade made the knife an ideal tool for opening an envelope. Zvi hefted the knife and noticed the balance. "Derek, where did you get this?"

"A Royal Marine Commando gave the knife to me as a present after I pulled their team out of a shitty situation."

The Israeli smiled as he nodded and then dumped out a pile of photos. "Let me start with these. I understand you read and speak Russian."

"I do. It's a bit rusty…." Derek took the sheets of paper. "What am I looking at?"

"A shipment order for Iglas which we know as SA-24s, code name Grinch by NATO, and chemical bombs."

"This is the man who bought the weapons." Zvi laid out five surveillance photos of a man as if he was dealing a blackjack hand. "His real name is Dawuud Ghanem. He was born in Lebanon, went to your American University in Washington, D.C., and graduated with a degree in mathematics. He was a member of the PLO, but that organization wasn't radical enough for him, so Ghanem joined al-Qaeda. We think he is now their weapons buyer."

"And you know this how?" Zack Neimeyer said what was on everyone's mind.

"He showed up in Moscow where these photos were taken where he met with this man …" Zvi slide several other photos on the table taken by a camera with a long telephoto lens. "… Serik Saliemenov. He is the commander of a weapons storage depot in Pochep, and I can show you where the depot is on the map later."

"How do you know his position?"

"We have a source inside the facility who gave us this document and identified Ghanem and Serik. Earlier this month, Ghanem showed up with a group of men to pick up the missiles and chemical weapons. His travel authorizations and orders are part of the documents our source gave us."

Derek put the photo he was looking at on the table. "Where are the weapons now?"

"On a ship in Rostov-on-Don. Based on the type of cargo, we have narrowed the number of possible ships down to six, and I have the manifests for each as well as their supposed routes."

"So, what you are telling us is that twenty-four brand new SA-24s and an unknown quantity of chemical bombs that can be loaded with the components to make Sarin gas are on a ship that left Rostov-on-Don on the 28th of October, destination unknown."

"Yes."

"And you want us to help you find them?"

"Yes. Ari said that's part of your tasking."

Derek made a face. *That's a stretch!* Camelot is under contract to determine if there is a credible terrorist threat to the U.S. from shoulder-fired anti-aircraft missiles. It is not in their brief to help the Israelis find some missing MANPADS. This was a gray area, but the quid pro quo was that the Israelis were providing useful intelligence. Any MANPADS on the loose could be headed to the U.S., which puts them squarely in the heart of Camelot's tasking. "OK. Let's start with Ghanem Dawuud. What else can you tell me about the man?"

"One thing we know is that he speaks Russian, Arabic, and English. He has a valid Lebanese passport and American Green Card. We don't know how Dawuud got into Russia or where he acquired the documents to acquire the weapons, but we have our suspicions. We suspect he has a Pakistani passport as well."

"Is he on the freighter?"

"We don't know where he is. We just know he left Moscow recently."

TUESDAY, NOVEMBER 1ST, 2016, 1:56 P.M. LOCAL TIME, PESHAWAR

Now safely in Pakistan, the two dozen al-Qaeda fighters that escorted Ghanem and Na'il to the safe house were fed and housed on the first floor. After two days of rest, they would begin the trek back to al-Qaeda's base in Afghanistan.

Once inside the house, despite Na'il's protests that no tracking device was in his body, Ghanem used a hand-held metal detector to check Na'il's body for a locating device. None was found.

Still, Ghanem didn't believe him, so with the help of a sympathetic technician, Na'il was escorted to a medical center and x-rayed from head to toe. Again, nothing was found, forcing Ghanem to accept that Na'il was telling the truth.

This left the matter of what to do with the Afghanis who helped the Americans. That was a more delicate issue because they would lose support if the word got around that al-Qaeda was killing Afghans.

Ghanem was trimming his beard, which was streaked with gray, when his cell phone rang. He recognized the number and accepted the call.

"Allo…"

"I'm glad you are back. I hear you were almost killed."

"Yes. We were lucky to get away."

"What do you need?"

"Krugerrands to buy some loyalty."

"How many?"

"A hundred thousand U.S. worth plus some toys to replace what they use."

"Whatever you are planning must look like a tribal feud."

"Understood. I know who to call. Many don't like Qaeder Rahim because he supports the Americans."

"How soon do you need the coins?"

"Within a week. We need to teach both Rahim and the Americans a lesson."

"Agreed. I will have a courier deliver the gold to you in a few days."

"Excellent."

"When this is done, you will return to America with Na'il Mirage. He is not the source of our leak, and I have decided on the mission for both of you."

Before Ghanem could say, "Allah be praised," he was listening to a dial tone.

Since the caller's number was in the database, the conversation was recorded and downloaded to the Echelon station in New Delhi, India. Within two minutes, the recording was sent to NSA headquarters at Fort Meade, Maryland, for analysis.

Echelon is a signals intelligence program run by Australia, Canada, New Zealand, the U.K., and the U.S. that collects signals from ground-to-ground microwave stations and mobile and satellite phones. Software algorithms loaded into high-speed computers determine if the transmission should be recorded or, at the very least, the particulars—time, date, participants—should be kept.

Since the caller was in Lahore, the recipient in Peshawar, and one of the phone numbers was in the database as "a phone number of interest," the recording was searched for keywords. While none were found, the text was flagged for an analyst to review.

THURSDAY, NOVEMBER 3RD, 2016, 11:00 A.M. LOCAL TIME, FORT MEADE, MD

One message in the stack of transcripts kept nagging NSA linguist and analyst Kevin Rathburn. Several times, he listened to the call. Then he read the transcript in the original Pashto and the English translation. Rahim was a name in the database because a Provisional Reconstruction Team gave him a satellite phone. Three questions needed answers.

What did the recipient of the call barely escape from?

Who were they buying loyalty from?

Why did they want to teach Rahim a lesson?

Kevin Rathburn picked up the handset. The button he pushed for Central Command was well used.

"CENTCOM, J2 watch officer, Major Julio Hernandez. This is not a secure line."

"Major, this is Kevin Rathburn at NSA. Let's go secure."

"Roger that."

Both men waited until the secure telephone LED told both they were speaking to each other in facilities authorized for top secret, specially compartmented information discussions.

"Julio, I have two questions for you. One, who is Qaeder Rahim? I suspect he is an Afghani. Two, what did he do that would lead us to believe that several tangos who just escaped from what I am assuming was a raid of some sort would want revenge?"

"Can you give me a time frame?"

"I'm guessing within the past week or two?"

"Stand-by. Let me look up Qaeder Rahim in our database."

Kevin cradled the handset between shoulder and neck while he flipped through three other transcripts. None were as interesting as this one.

"Found him. Rahim is a friendly tribal leader in Kunar province working with one of our Province Reconstruction Teams. He's provided us with good intelligence in the past and, as a young man, fought to get the Russians out of Afghanistan...." Hernandez's voice tailed off. "Oh, here's something interesting. He provided some info on a stash of Stinger missiles. Raid went down last week. Do you want to speak with the action officer?"

"I do."

"Let me see if he is in the building. Call me right back if you get disconnected. If I don't pick up, ask to be switched to Lieutenant Commander Jacob Sobrano."

Kevin went back to reading another transcript. He heard a synthetic ringing in the background.

"Lieutenant Commander Sobrano." The LED on Rathburn's screen said they were still TOP SECRET/SCI.

"Hi, my name is Kevin Rathburn, and I'm an NSA analyst. I was passed on to you by CENTCOM's J2 watch officer as someone who might be able to shed some light on the conversation in a transcript that caught my eye."

"Shoot."

"Does the name Qaeder Rahim mean anything to you?"

"Yes. He is a tribal elder who dislikes the Taliban or al-Qaeda. Rahim gave us a tip that led to a raid that destroyed a cache of Stinger missiles. Why?"

"I think the Taliban or al-Qaeda want revenge. I'm looking at a phone call transcript suggesting that al-Qaeda is planning to take him out."

"Kevin, can you send the transcript to me?"

"Sure. Let me finish my analysis, and I'll pass the info up the chain of command to you. Look for my email in about thirty minutes. I'll also tweak the system to see what else we can find or if we get any more calls. What's your email address?

As Jacob rattled off his email address. The clock on the wall of the small room he shared with another SEAL officer said the time was 1922 at Bagram Air Base in Afghanistan. Until he talked to Rathburn, Sobrano thought he was about to get on a plane to come home, and that evolution will have to wait.

SUNDAY, NOVEMBER 6TH, 2016, 9:26 A.M. LOCAL TIME, LONDON

The crack in the curtains let the fall sun stream into the bedroom. Fatimah groaned as the light pierced her eyelids. When she rolled on her back, the beige satin sheets rustled seductively.

Now fully awake, Fatimah looked around the room at Victoria House and then fell back against the pillows, sexually satiated. The bedroom was painted and furnished in a tasteful Victorian style with eggshell white paint and furniture with soft reds and pinks.

On the nightstand was an envelope under a single, long-stem rose. The envelope had a gold paper liner, and the note on heavy linen paper looked like a calligrapher wrote the words.

Fatimah,

I hope you had a wonderful time during the past two days. It was my pleasure to be your host, and I hope to have you as my guest in the future. When you are awake, pick up the handset, and when someone answers, tell her what you want, from food to whatever.

Let's have a late lunch today before you go back to Pakistan.

Kathryn

Fatimah thought for a few seconds. After a quick trip to the bathroom, she picked up the phone. A proper British voice answered and asked what Fatimah needed. She asked for a continental breakfast, and then, if Mistress Danica was available, she wanted another bondage session with her and two male slaves.

MONDAY, NOVEMBER 7ᵀᴴ, 2016, 12:07 P.M. LOCAL TIME, KARACHI

Saad Nazari waited patiently at the curb. He'd just said goodbye to an old friend from school with whom he'd had lunch when a man on a motorbike stopped at the light two meters away. The driver, wearing a full-face helmet, pulled a Soviet-made Bizon PP-19 submachine gun out from under his light jacket. He fired a short burst into Nazari's chest before he sprayed what was left of the 64-round magazine of 9X18mm Makarov rounds into the crowd at the corner and drove off.

THE SAME DAY, 4:08 P.M. LOCAL TIME, KARACHI

During dinner on Thursday night, Kathryn opened Fatimah like a book. Their table at the five-star Mediterranean restaurant was secluded, and the staff attentive but discreet.

When as she got out of the cab at her hotel, Kathryn pecked Fatimah on the cheek and said, "Get your work done early, and I'll pick you up at your flat at three." Kathryn gave her a knowing wink and closed the door to the cab.

Kathryn was right. From that moment on, every detail of the weekend was etched in Fatimah's brain. As she exited her apartment building at three, she saw Kathryn standing by the back door of a black Daimler DS420 sedan. "Where are we going?"

"To a private club in Ascot."

"Near the racecourse?"

"Close…. Victoria House is an old mansion on a few acres. Membership is very exclusive and very private."

"What's there?"

"Anything you want or desire."

"How do you know about it?"

Kathryn smiled and caressed Fatimah's arm. "This is the perfect place where in complete privacy, someone like you can explore your wildest fantasies."

"What about you?"

"Me too."

The car crunched noticeably on the gravel driveway as it stopped under a portico. Fatimah could see that the building was an old stone manor house, probably built in the 1800s. A man dressed as a butler with a starched shirt, white tie, and tails met the two women at the door. "Welcome, Lady Kathryn. And this is?"

"Fatimah. She is my guest and may become a member."

The butler smiled. "Wonderful. Welcome Fatimah, and I hope you enjoy your time with us."

A familiar voice interrupted Fatimah's replaying the sessions at Victoria House as she looked out the window. Already, she'd made her mind that she would spend a weekend a month at the Victoria House. "Miss Serraf?"

Fatimah spun around in her chair and saw Hadiya, her administrative assistant standing in the doorway with a horrified look on her face. "The police just called to tell us Saad is dead."

"What happened?"

"Some madman fired into the crowd, and Saad was one of those killed. He never came back from lunch, and now I know why. At first, I wasn't worried because Saad often spent hours with his friend Kamran." Hadiya controlled a sob and wiped the tears from her eyes. "We have the news on in the conference room."

"Oh my god, Hadiya, this is terrible news." *For me, this is good news. That's what Saad gets for sticking his nose where it didn't belong.*

As they walked to the conference room, Hadiya spoke in hushed tones. "Al Jazeera says that Karachi has the highest murder rate of any major city in the world. The commentator said that we have twelve-point-three murders per hundred thousand residents, and no other city comes close."

Fatimah put her arms around Hadiya, one of the bank's first employees. "What happened?"

"Saad was unlucky. Someone in the crowd was the target of one of those motorbike assassins. He just got in the way."

Fatimah's voice oozed sympathy and compassion. "Poor Saad."

"How many people were killed?"

Hadiya sniffed. "At least seven, including Saad. Twelve more were wounded. But you know, first reports are always wrong."

"Please have the partner who knew Saad best call his family. The bank will do whatever we need to do to help them." *Meaning the buy/sell agreement stipulates that upon the departure of one of the founders, the bank will buy the shares based on the average of three formulas outlined in the agreement. Saad's family will be happy because the value of the bank's shares has increased by at least 15 percent. I will be happy because my investors and I will own more shares.*

The middle-aged woman pulled back and wiped the tears from her face. "I will call. I worked for Saad before he came to Talwar and know his family well."

THE SAME DAY, 6:04 P.M. LOCAL TIME, AFGHANISTAN

Because the command center at Bagram worked around the clock, Jacob wasn't surprised to see the hallways and offices filled with his fellow officers and enlisted men. He found an empty cubicle, connected his ruggedized laptop, and dialed in. Chief Tomkins put a bottle of cold water on the table and sat next to him, and both wanted to see what Rathburn had sent.

Lieutenant Commander Jacob Sobrano had been in the Navy for almost 10 years after being born and raised in Charleston, South Carolina. He graduated from the Virginia Military Institute with a degree in international business which was a logical major considering his family had been in the import/export business since his forefathers arrived in the colonies in 1733. His ancestors left Spain in 1588 and, when they arrived in England, joined the British East India Company. They stayed in England for almost 150 years before leaving for the New World.

Since the Sobranos could not own land in Spain or the United Kingdom, the family bought land as often as possible. The first Sobrano who came to America bought 5,000 acres near what is now known as Summerville, SC. By the time the Civil War broke out, the Sobranos owned 12,000 acres and managed to hold onto the land and their business after the war.

Over the years, the family kept expanding its land holdings throughout the state, particularly along the South Carolina coast. After World War II, the family began to develop the land, adding to the family's sizeable fortune.

Despite his noticeable Southern accent, Jacob spent a year, with the Navy's blessing, at the University of Madrid. Besides being fluent in Spanish, Jacob learned Pashto and Arabic at the Navy's language school in Monterrey, CA. During his tours in Iraq and Afghanistan, he perfected his ability to speak both.

After studying the material Rathburn sent him, Sobrano looked at Chief Tomkins. "Here's what I think. After talking to Rathburn, I called that ring knocker colonel who leads the PRT team for Kunar province. He said he'll do what he can but needs direction from higher authority, and that means someone at ISAF must tell the idiot what to do."

"I know how that goes, sir."

Sobrano rubbed his chin, which was clean-shaven for the first time in months. Whenever he was in Afghanistan, he let his dark beard grow, and along with his skin color, he could pass as a local, "I gave the J2 himself a heads up, and he said that they get lots of intelligence like what Rathburn sent us which never amounts to anything. I got pushy after trying to be polite because you and I know what is coming. No tango worth his salt will risk making a call like that unless the discussion is so important there is no other way."

"So, let me guess, sir. ISAF is not going to do anything until they get more intel." ISAF stood for International Security Assistance Force which in 2016 consisted of soldiers and airmen from 13 nations.

"Pretty much."

Chief Tomkins smiled "Sir, do you know when the attack will happen?"

"No, but my guess is within a week." Jacob let some time pass to let his mind work.

Before he could speak, Chief Tomkins was already thinking ahead, "Sir, I'll get a team together, and if the request comes through me, the guys at Special Ops Command know what we are doing and why and will approve. I'll call a friend so he has the scoop what and why. We will, of course, coordinate the op with ISAF to keep them in the loop and keep them from getting their feathers ruffled."

"Thanks, Chief."

"No problem, sir. Like you, I don't like hanging friends out to dry. Do you have a way to reach Qaeder Rahim?"

"I have his satellite phone number, and when we are on the way, I'll call him."

"Yes, sir."

"Chief Tomkins, one more thing. I hope we're not too late."

"Me neither. I don't want this to be a replay of the movie, The Magnificent Seven."

Jacob chuckled. "Let me know if you need my help. I'd like to get moving sometime tomorrow."

THE SAME DAY, 7:07 P.M. LOCAL TIME, BAGRAM

A smile came across Sobrano's face as he read the mission plan and justification Chief Tomkins created. The only change the chief made was rather than flying in by helo, they would drive in by large mine-resistant, ambush-protected (MRAP) trucks during daylight instead of in the wee hours of the morning. As a practical matter, Jacob didn't think the daylight insertion would change their plan, and neither did Tomkins.

Sobrano was studying several images of Rahim's village when his satellite phone rang. The caller was the aide to the Commander, Special Operations Command, who said the four-star wanted to speak to him.

"OK, Sobrano, what is so hot that you absolutely, positively had to talk to me."

"Sir, I am not sure where to turn, but this has been eating at me since I read the report on the shootdown earlier this month."

"Why?"

"Sir, I was told by the operations officers here that they were not listed as combat but as operational losses." Jacob stopped for a second. "Sir, we had two surface-to-air missiles shot at us. The other helo was hit by at least one. We pulled shrapnel out of the gunner that came from a Stinger, and there were no friendly forces in the area, so there is no way this is a blue-on-blue engagement."

"So why are you telling me this?"

"Sir, someone on the Central Command staff told ISAF to list their deaths as an operational/non-combat losses even though they were shot down! Sir, that's unmitigated bullshit which also means the men killed or wounded won't be awarded Purple Hearts."

"Who did you speak with at ISAF?"

Jacob took a deep breath. "I talked to the J3 out here, and he gave me the name of the officer on your staff. Both told me that having two helicopters listed as being shot down by a U.S. surface-to-air missile wouldn't align with the President's position that al-Qaeda and the Taliban don't have these weapons. Apparently, President has stated publicly that the Stingers left over from the Soviet-Afghan war are all out of date and incapable of being used."

There was what is known as a pregnant pause before the four-star spoke. "Both men are political bastards and will do anything to get another star. Sorry, Jacob, you didn't hear that." Another pause. "I'm in a difficult position."

"I'm sorry, sir. I didn't mean to do that to you."

"Yes, you did. This is an ethical as well as morale issue."

"As in intelligence analyses and mission reports, sir?"

"Yes. Now that you have told me this, what's bugging me is what else is being covered up or distorted. But that's my problem, not yours."

"Sir, I don't want to mention names, but I can tell you that the SEAL community out here doesn't like working for the ISAF J3 or his J2. Net-net, they don't trust either man's judgment. The J2 reports stuff that they find, which comes back as an analysis that makes you wonder where they got the intelligence. The J3 won't act unless someone lights a fire under his ass, such as what we're doing to help Rahim and his tribe."

"I was afraid of that. I've heard this before."

Jacob sat quietly, waiting for an answer.

"Don't talk to anyone about this. Jacob, if someone asks you about the helo shoot down, refer them to me. And, if someone forces you to change what you've reported or puts pressure on you or threatens you with your career, you come to me right away."

"Yes, sir."

"Thanks for ruining my lunch. Now get your Navy SEAL ass out of the command center and go help Qaeder Rahim and his people!"

TUESDAY, NOVEMBER 8ᵀᴴ, 2016, 9:07 A.M. LOCAL TIME, AFGHANISTAN

Afghanistan is one of those countries where one doesn't have to train most of its citizens on how to use a rifle or an AK-47. They're as common as soccer balls, and boys beginning as early as age 10, learn how to fire one. And, if they live in the hills, many are combat veterans by the time they are teenagers.

Being proficient with a gun is a matter of necessity. Even before the Soviet invasion, what the West would call tribal warfare was the norm in Afghanistan. The Russians invaded because the government, first under Mohammed Taraki and then under Hafzullah Amin, began implementing economic and cultural reforms against Soviet desires. The Soviets assassinated Amin and invaded.

Ten long bloody years later, the Soviet Army left Afghanistan. The civil war continued, and the shaky central government, weakened by defections, fell to the Taliban bolstered by an estimated 35,000 foreigners who came to fight a jihad against the Soviets and stayed.

The Taliban imposed strict sharia law, exterminated their enemies, and allowed Muslim terrorist organizations such as al-Qaeda to operate training camps in the country, which set off another conflict. Most Afghans didn't like the Taliban or al-Qaeda any more than they did the Soviets.

One of the groups fighting the Taliban was the Northern Alliance, which was struggling until after 9/11 when the U.S. began to provide air support. The Taliban faded into the hills to wage a guerilla war. Between bribery and assassinating tribal leaders who opposed the Taliban coupled with the average Afghani's traditional hatred of invaders developed over centuries, the Taliban regained control of parts of Afghanistan.

Some tribes resisted their efforts because they saw that the work of the International Security Assistance Force was making the country a better place to live. Others played both sides, and their loyalty was the subject of negotiation and how much gold or dollars one would give them.

Most Afghan males had to be proficient in using rifles, pistols, and machine guns to survive. On his first tour in Afghanistan, Jacob concluded that most houses had at least one AK-47. Ammunition was as much a priority as food, and the 30,000 rounds for their AK's he was about to deliver would be received by Qaeder Rahim as manna from heaven.

The village was at the end of a small valley aligned essentially north/south. On the western side, the green meadows were perfect for grazing cows and goats. They provided clear fields of fire against anyone coming from that direction. The valley's eastern side gradually increased in elevation until ending in a steep, almost impossible to climb, 100-meter rise that towered over the town. Access to the world from the village was a road built along a stream that led down to the valley floor.

Looking at a map and overhead imagery, Jacob thought that generations earlier, the village elders had chosen well. Holding the high ground that was 1,000 meters from the village was a key component to winning any battle for the town. So, Jacob believed unless the bad guys brought heavy weapons, this battle would be fought at close range.

The 16 SEALS in Randy Sullivan's platoon, Chief Tomkins and Jacob flew to the Kunar Provincial Reconstruction Team's helipad. He was not surprised that the lieutenant colonel commanding the base didn't come out to greet them. Still, as promised, four mine-resistant vehicles were waiting to carry them, their additional equipment, and the AK-47 ammunition most of the way to the village.

At the drop-off point, the SEALS clambered out of the vehicles, and the Army drivers helped unload the munitions, which were stacked in a collection of rocks by the side of the road Jacob picked because it was a strong defensive position if they were attacked while waiting for Qaeder Rahim to show up with his promised transportation.

Chief Tomkins spotted the four white trucks coming down the road from the town. The ubiquitous white Toyota Tundra's pulled off to the side and parked in a ragged row.

Jacob watched as Qaeder and Aazar got out of one of the trucks. "Chief, cover me." He stood up and slung his M4 carbine over his shoulder so the barrel was pointed at the ground.

"Qaeder and Aazar, I am glad to see you again." The SEAL put his hand over his heart before he stuck out his hand.

The tribal leader took Jacob's hand in both his. "Did you bring the weapons?"

Jacob showed Qaeder the weapons and ammunition that were quickly loaded onto the trucks. So far, so good. Now, they would find out the answers to the questions that Jacob and Chief Tomkins discussed most. Were they being lured into a trap? Or would the bad guys show up? And, if so, when?

THE SAME DAY, 10:36 A.M. LOCAL TIME, PORTLAND, ME

The first time Abbas Salib visited the small warehouse, the real estate broker apologized to Salib, saying that he had better, more convenient facilities. Salib listened patiently, thinking this place was perfect.

The garage door would allow them to bring a 20-foot-long box truck into the building and pull out the ramp to load and unload.

There were two rooms, one was at the front with a door to the street just inside the small 10-by-15-foot waiting room. The other was a large storeroom lined with steel shelves bolted to the floor that ran the length of the building.

Right after he signed the one-year lease, he called the telephone company, who turned on the phone. The heater for the office and the storeroom worked perfectly, and overhead, there were heaters for the loading and unloading area. Salib wondered if the heaters in the warehouse would keep it warm in a Maine winter.

Abbas "Abe" Salib was 18 when his family arrived in the U.S. as Iraqi war refugees in 2005. The U.S. government "settled" them in the Houston area, where his father was trained to check documentation and manifests of cargo coming into the Port of Houston.

College, despite his father's urging, was not for Salib, who went to sea with Royal Caribbean as a 'Junior Engineman.' He moved to Miami, and, after three years, he qualified as a second engineer. He loved the work because he spent six months on a ship, followed by six months off.

Over the years, culturally, Abbas became at odds with his family. They were more concerned about assimilating into American society than what was happening in Iraq and Afghanistan.

During one of his leave periods, Salib flew to Jordan and then to Bagdad. From there, he took a bus to Umm Qasr and was astonished by the changes in Iraqi society. Nothing was as he remembered, and he blamed it all on the American invasion that deposed Saddam Hussein. He was no fan of the dictator but didn't think Iraqi society should remain secular.

When he got off the plane in Miami, he was taken by immigration to a separate room. There, the officers wanted to know why he had gone to Iraq, where he went, and with whom he met.

Although he was allowed back into the U.S., Salib felt violated. In his mind, he had done nothing wrong. He just visited the land of his birth. After his next tour of duty with Royal Caribbean ended in the spring of 2013, he signed out, saying he would call when he wanted to work again. In his mind, he wasn't resigning; he just didn't want to work for the cruise line for a while.

He moved his few belongings into a small five foot by ten-foot storage area and took his car to CarMax. Some of the cash was used to buy a ticket to London. After spending two days in the English capital at a small bed and breakfast in the Bayswater area, Abbas called a number he was given by a colleague at Royal Caribbean who, as he left, said to call if he ever wanted to serve Allah. The voice on the phone instructed him to walk to a particular travel agent near the hotel.

The agent, a man in his forties, looked at Salib carefully. He issued the ticket and gave him an address on paper. "Go here. When you knock on the door, give them your name. Bring your passport as identification; they will expect you around eight p.m. The rest is up to you."

That day was in the fall of 2008. For the next six months, he was in one firefight after another. Toward the end of 2009, a man asked what he knew about ships while he was sitting in a cave in Afghanistan. Salib said he had an engineering officer's license, was a qualified Royal Caribbean bridge watch stander, and worked on his father's fishing boat as a teenager.

He remembered the man's gaunt face, sallow complexion, and height but never got his name. He said, "We have a mission for you in the United States."

Two weeks later, after flying from Pakistan to Toronto via London, Salib drove across the U.S. border just north of Niagara Falls using his valid American passport that showed only stamps saying when he arrived and left the U.K. His job was to rent a warehouse, find a suitable ship based on the specifications he was given, and, when tasked, take it to sea. He didn't ask what the cargo was but assumed it would be people and weapons.

THURSDAY, NOVEMBER 10TH, 2016, 5:26 A.M. LOCAL TIME, EASTERN MEDITERRANEAN

The 555-ton coastal freighter *M.V. Abdul-Muqaddim* wallowed as it plowed through the two-foot, quartering sea heading east toward the Syrian port of Tartus. The churned-up wake behind the ship gave no indication of that the boat was making its best and most economical speed of nine knots through the water.

Built in 1946 for the Dutch government by the Higgins Corporation, *Abdul-Muqaddim* was based on the U.S. Army's 381 design specification for small coastal freighters. Known as FS or freighter supply ships, 318 were built by 25 different shipyards. Their 180-foot length made them ideal for getting into smaller ports. After the war, most 381s were either abandoned or bought by companies who took advantage of their low cost of operation to make money moving small loads.

Captain Qasim Boutros took off his sunglasses and cleaned them, knowing that for the next five hours, they would be steaming east into the rising sun. Putting them back on, he turned to what he was sure was the sound of a helicopter hovering alongside the ship. A man in the open cabin door pointed a machine gun at the bridge that appeared to be pointed directly at him.

The Star of David in a darker shade of gray than the light grey paint that covered the rest of the helicopter was clearly visible. This far from land meant there was an Israeli warship close by.

The radio crackled inside the bridge on an international VHF communications frequency. "*Motor Vessel Abdul-Muqaddim* heave to at once and prepare to be boarded. I repeat *Motor Vessel Abdul-Muqaddim* heave to at once, or you will be fired upon."

Boutros muttered, "What do the fucking Jews want now?" He turned to the helmsman and ordered, "All stop." The bells clanged, and the wheel man acknowledged, "All stop."

As the *M.V. Abdul-Muqaddim* slowed, a second helicopter positioned itself over the deck, dumped out a thick rope, and six heavily armed men slid down.

Abdul-Muqaddim's captain jammed his dirty white bridge cover down on his head and watched an Israeli warship close on his ship. It had what destroyer captains loved to describe as a "bone in its teeth." The expression came from the white water rising along either side of the bow made the ship appear to be carrying a white bone.

The senior Israeli commando spoke in Arabic, "Captain Boutros, please order every member of your crew to immediately muster on the forward part of the deck."

Boutros nodded and picked up the microphone connecting him to the ship's main communication system. By now, the *Abdul-*

Muqaddim was almost stopped, and as the sailors came up on deck, they were quickly directed to the bow. From his position on the bridge, Boutros did not see the large rubber inflatable boat pull alongside the 67-year-old freighter. But what he did see were another half dozen armed men climbing onto the main deck. From the bridge, the overweight, some would say fat, Boutros watched as his 15-man crew assembled, guarded by four Israeli commandos.

A man, Boutros thought to be in his early forties, came onto the bridge and saluted. Boutros returned the gesture, but his salute was not nearly as crisp as the Israeli's. "Captain Boutros, I am Commander Yitzhak Malkah of the Israeli Defense Forces. I would like to see your manifest, ship's log, registration, insurance documents, passports and identity documents for every crew member and any passengers. The *Abdul-Muqaddim* has been stopped because my government believes that your ship is carrying chemical weapons and surface-to-air missiles."

Boutros looked at the slim man standing in front of him. Instead of wearing battle dress, he wore an immaculately clean white uniform. He probably had a waist size of 60 centimeters, maximum. The Israeli held a radio in his right hand and was unarmed. "Impossible. We are carrying fertilizer, farm machinery, and several pallets of barrels of 100-weight oil. I can assure you that there are no weapons on board."

"Captain Boutros, if that is the case, then when we finish inspecting your ship, you can proceed to Tartus with our apologies. If we find what we believe is on board, the ship will be seized, and you and your crew arrested. If our investigation determines that you were not involved in smuggling weapons, you will be set free. If not, you will be tried in an Israeli court."

Malkah pointed at the door as if to say, "After you, Captain, let's start the process." Boutros headed down the passageway, followed by Malkah and two Israeli commandos. Others were already in the ship's hold using equipment that would detect traces of the precursors needed to make Sarin and VX nerve gases and tools to open crates.

With the passports, ship's log, manifest, and insurance documents in hand, Malkah spoke into the radio. Within a minute, a man appeared and took the bundle of passports with him. In addition to matching crewmembers to the documents, each would be photographed. Malkah was reading the ship's log that showed that *Abdul-Muqaddim* stopped in Thessaloniki and Istanbul on the way to Rostov-on-Don when his radio crackled.

Rather than continue the conversation in Boutros's presence, Malkah stopped in the passageway. A minute later, a grim-faced Malkah walked back into Boutros's cabin. "Before I arrest you, would you like to see what we found?"

THE SAME DAY, 12:46 P.M. LOCAL TIME, WASHINGTON, D.C.

The president was clearly not happy. Just a few moments ago, his chief of staff whispered in his ear at a fund-raising luncheon at the Hyatt Regency. "Mr. President, you are needed in the White House situation room immediately."

"Can't this wait?"

"No, sir. The chairman of the Joint Chiefs of Staff, the National Security Advisor, the Director of the CIA, and the DNI are already there. The Secretary of State is on his way, and he'll be there by the time we arrive."

The president turned to his host. "I'm sorry, I must go." The commander-in-chief got up and left, leaving 250 people who paid $50,000 apiece to hear the president speak and informally meet him were left holding the bag.

In the presidential limo, the president turned to his chief of staff. "What the fuck is going on that is so important that you need to pull me out of an important fundraiser? Hell, the people in that room are the moneymen behind the PACs who will ensure that the Democrats retain the White House in 2016, despite Comey's announcement to re-open the investigation into Clinton's emails."

"Mr. President, all I know is that the Israelis have seized a freighter in the Eastern Mediterranean headed to Syria that has chemical weapons on board. They are towing it to Haifa, and Netanyahu is about to hold a press conference and show pictures. Our ambassador to Israel has been told that the Israeli government will fly any journalist out to see what they found. Fox News and Sky News have already accepted, and CNN, CBS, and ABC may accept. They're waiting for some guidance from your press secretary."

"Did the Israelis provide us with an inventory yet?"

"I was told there were several pallets of 250-kilo bombs designed to spread Sarin or VX nerve gas in the hold along with the precursors to make the gases along with Russian-made shoulder-fired surface-to-air missiles. They have more info in the situation room."

CHAPTER 11

FIREFIGHT

Their command post was set up in the corner of a compound surrounded by a six-foot-tall stucco and cinder block wall. While not in the center of the village, the house and compound were ideally situated so the SEALs could quickly move from one end of the village to the other without being seen. The walled-in area was also large enough to give their antennas a clear line of sight to the satellites so they could download images from the Predator that orbited overhead.

Earlier in the evening, Jacob spoke with Rahim and the other village elders. In addition to agreeing on how they would deploy the village men, he asked whether al-Qaeda or their Taliban friends would attack during the Muslim sabbath. Qaeder didn't reply at first, but one of the other men said al-Qaeda and the Taliban only respect the sabbath when convenient.

Jacob did not tell Qaeder about the Krugerrands. He forced himself to keep from smiling when another elder said, "If they were paid enough, they'd kill a Safi saint.

While he was not surprised by the answer, Jacob was surprised by their bluntness and the reference to a Safi saint who spread the word of Allah through Persia and what is now Afghanistan and southern Russia. With the meeting over, the men split up to get some rest, maybe even sleep.

Jacob lay back against the house wall Qaeder suggested that they use it as a command post. He knew he would not get much sleep, but some would be better than none.

The coolness of the mud, stone, and brick walls seeped through his clothing. At one end of the house was a ladder to the roof surrounded by a waist-high wall. From there, anyone could see the ledge and the entire village. Like the walled-in compound, they had an unobstructed view of the sky for their Satcom radio and link to the Reaper that was supposed to be overhead.

"Bingo. Boss, we have contact."

Petty Officer Eric Draeger's words roused Jacob, who had been asleep seconds before. Rahim thought that if the attack came, the Taliban would strike either early Friday or Saturday morning.

"What do you have?"

Sobrano stood behind Draeger, looking at the screen as he pointed out the white dots. "The Reaper is showing a column of a one hundred plus coming up this path. One of our outposts should be able to see them in about ten minutes. The RPV showed a column of trucks that dropped off another group near where we unloaded. I'm guessing that they will coordinate by cell phone before moving towards us."

Inside, Jacob's stomach was churning. *Al-Qaeda is coming to kill Rahim and anyone who resists.* Along with the other SEALs, his job was to prevent a massacre.

"Got it." Jacob paused briefly before keying the throat mike for his radio. "Everyone listen up. The game is on as planned, so far."

Rahim's house was next door. Jacob rapped softly on the door, and when he thought he heard a voice, he cracked it open. Qaeder Rahim was on his prayer rug praying. When he was finished, the older man turned to Jacob. "This is the time to show my enemies that we are right. Allah will be pleased, and he will provide victory. We have a good plan."

Jacob didn't want to say what was on his mind, that the plan was good only if it worked! *Allah won't help when the shooting begins.*

Half of the SEALs under Randy Sullivan and roughly half the men in the village were deployed up in the rocks defending the caves where the women and children were taken. After scouting the caves, Randy, Qaeder, and he felt they were easier to defend and would give Rahim's men more backbone when the battle was joined.

A whoosh of a rocket-propelled grenade fired broke the stillness and exploded near the entrance of the village. Three more were fired where the attackers thought there might be defensive positions. Jacob suspected the rockets were intended to intimidate the villagers. The explosions momentarily lit up the growing dawn.

The rattle of AK-47s from almost a quarter of a mile away was muted by the distance but was just as distinct as if the gun was closer. So far, Jacob heard the sharp bark of an M4 carbine firing the high-velocity M855A1 Enhanced Performance 5.56mm round only a few times. The differences and how they were being shot usually gave him some indication of how the battle was being fought.

As he climbed the ladder to the roof, Jacob heard four large explosions, one right after another. Even with binoculars, the fires from four burning pickup trucks dominated his view of the road. He pressed his throat mike. "Bill, what's going on?"

Bill was Petty Officer Second Class William Sweetman, the fire team leader deployed along the road. "Boss, we got four trucks, and they abandoned two more. Right now, about fifty bad guys have fallen back about five hundred yards from our position and are milling around trying to figure out what to do."

"Stay put. Conserve ammo."

"Roger that. We're out of LAWS but have a few 40mm grenades left. Each time they start coming forward, we pick the leader off."

Jacob turned to look up the hillside toward the caves where the women and children were. From his position in the valley, he could see the tracers going back and forth but not what was happening. Since the villagers and the Taliban fighters had AK-47s, it was hard to tell the two sides apart. In the noise, he'd hear an occasional sharp crack of an M4 carbine, then the faster, deeper rattle of their M249 Squad Automatic Weapon. "Randy, what's up?"

"Boss, we've got a problem. Two groups heading for the cave mouth are hitting us, and we're pretty spread out. I've sent 'The Kid' with Greenhorn and about half my men to stop them. We'll engage as soon as they make their move. My best guess is that we're facing about eighty to a hundred tangos."

Jacob knew 'The Kid" was Aazar and 'Greenhorn' was Petty Officer Third Class Grant Green, who was on his first tour in Afghanistan and fresh out of SEAL training. *Do I change my strategy? My total force, including the SEALs, is only fifty men.* Constant war since the 1979 Soviet invasion, forced conscription by the Taliban, and disease had robbed Rahim's village of at least two generations. Knowing Afghanistan as he did, their attackers were motivated by money, revenge, and probably hatred.

Jacob had five men and two SEALs by the road, and Sullivan had twenty plus two more SEALs up by the caves. Qaeder, five other villagers, Jacob, Chief Tomkins, and four SEALS were all left in the village.

Jacob turned to Petty Office Jack Arnold, who had their ruggedized laptop open. "What does the Predator tell us?"

"Nothing. The UAV was reassigned."

"Call them on the bat phone, tell them we're in contact with 150+ al-Qaeda and Taliban, and get us a replacement." Jack knew that the bat phone was their name for the satellite phones the team carried with them.

"I did, and all I got was a bullshit answer and think some shithead in Bagram gave them a new mission with a higher priority."

"Figures." Jacob took a deep breath. His options were limited. *In a firefight like this one, close air support will be dicey until daylight because both sides will look alike.* Jacob was afraid of what is euphemistically called a "blue on blue" engagement in which the good guys get bombed and strafed by other good guys. "Call the PRT's duty officer and tell them we're in contact with a force of about two hundred Taliban. Ask them to send out a couple squads at first light, along with a medical team. Then call our ops center and tell them what is going on. If that doesn't help, I'll call Tampa."

"Yes, sir."

Several volleys from M4s mixed with AK-47s caused Jacob to look toward the area where the caves were. The green and red tracers increased in volume, telling him the battle was on. He noticed Qaeder standing on the roof, looking in the same direction. "Qaeder, take the remaining men from the village and reinforce your son. He's on the left side, closest to the caves. I'll protect the village."

"Allah will bless you." The older man went down the ladder.

When Qaeder was out of sight, Jacob keyed the mike. "Greenhorn, Randy, I am sending the old man and five up to the kid. They'll be there in less than ten mikes."

"Got it." Randy replied. In the background, Jacob could hear gunfire.

"Thanks, boss." No matter how he tried, Green couldn't hide his Alabama drawl that turned one-syllable words into two.

"I hate this!" Jacob spoke to no one in particular.

"Hate what, sir."

"Hate sitting here and wondering if we're going to win. I'd much rather be up there on the hill engaged."

"Me too."

"Braddock, pack up. We're going for a walk around the village. If nothing else, moving around will give us something to do."

The sun was just starting to peek over the mountaintops, creating shadows along the village's main street. Something made Jacob stop and raise a closed fist, and both he and his radioman froze.

"Greenhorn, this is the boss. Any bad guys get past you, or did you send some folks back here?"

"Not sure, and no. Why?"

"I think we have visitors in the town."

Jacob resisted the urge to attack. He wanted to see what he was up against before he became the aggressor.

Two men peered around the last house on the street before they emerged carrying heavy-looking bags in one hand and AK-47s in the other. They were followed by two more men with AK-47s at the ready.

One man reached into a bag and pulled out a grenade that flew out of his hand when three bullets from Jacob's M4 stitched his face before he could pull the pin. While the grenade rolled on the ground, Jacob shifted fire to the second man and squeezed the trigger. The second man fell backward to the ground bleeding. He pulled the trigger on his AK-47 down, and 30 rounds were fired into the sky as he fell. Jacob was so focused; he didn't see or hear Braddock do the same thing.

Both SEALs waited about 30 seconds to see if there were more men. They started to move down the street when bullets kicked up a row of dirt plumes two feet away. Jacob pressed his back against a door and closed his eyes as the shooter fired a long burst into the compacted soil. He dropped to his knee as he peered around the corner and saw a man in the street with an RPD machine gun. Two more were moving down each side, close to the houses. Hand gestures communicated the situation to Braddock.

Jacob stuck his M4 around the corner, put the red dot on the man's chest, and fired a three-round burst. The machine gunner buckled at the waist and fell on a knee, struggling to hold the machine gun level. Jacob shifted to the man at his side and dropped him with a burst to the chest. The machine gunner fired another burst, and the bullets walked their way toward the doorway and suddenly stopped. He peeked around the corner, and the machine gunner struggled to change the box magazine with its 100-round belt with bloody hands. A three-round burst from his M4 into the man's chest caused him to fall on his face.

They checked each man. One was sprawled on his back, blood oozing from his chest and still alive.

Jacob spoke in Pashto. "Who are you?"

The man moved his head slowly, and then his eyes rolled back into his head. Jacob tossed the AK off to the side, pulled the unused magazines out of the pouches, and pitched them so they were near the rifle. Then, he patted the body down and found a small pouch. In it was a single gold Krugerrand.

While Braddock took pictures of the faces of the men they killed, Jacob studied the gold coins they took from each man. All were minted in the same year and looked brand new.

"Jack, take a close-up of one of the Krugerrands and send the photo back to our intel folks. I'm willing to bet that they will tell us something."

"Roger, that."

Jacob was enjoying the warmth of the early morning sun on his face when there was a brief burst of static and a voice. "Boss, this is Greenhorn. The tangos are running and leaving their dead. We're chasing them to make sure they are leaving."

"Randy, are you up?"

No response. Jacob tried again. No answer. "Greenhorn, when you can, check on Randy. He's not responding."

"Will do."

"Boss, this is Sweetman."

"Go."

"Tangos are leaving. A couple of them tried to get in their trucks, but we convinced them that it was a bad idea."

"Stay there until you are sure they are all gone."

"Will do."

"Boss, this is Greenhorn. Bad news. Eric took a round in the head and is dead. We have three walking wounded and two that we'll have to carry, and both should be OK if we can get them to a doctor."

"Bring them all down here. Break, break. Everyone, listen up. Search the dead and wounded tangos to see if they have gold coins. If they do, bring them to me. We'll take pictures of their faces before we leave them with the villagers to bury. The gold coins go to Qaeder."

Hearing the news about Eric Wendell hurt. They made three deployments to Iraq and Afghanistan together, and this wasn't supposed to happen. Jacob's eyes moistened, but he couldn't dwell on the loss. They had a mission to complete. When he returns to Bagram, he can grieve for his friend and comrade in arms. And visit Eric's wife when he gets back to the U.S.

An hour later, with fire teams posted along each attack route, Jacob stood in the same place he was when the fight began. In the compound, villagers were inspecting and dividing up the captured weapons that would go into their arsenal.

"Boss, look at this." The last word was pronounced "they-is" and told that it was Petty Officer Green. The young man was holding a small digital camera showing the image of a dead Afghan. "I've seen him before, and I'm sure this guy is a high mucky muck in the Taliban."

"Hold on." He took the camera and showed the picture to Qaeder. "Do you know this man?"

"Yes. He is Abdullah Quarishi, the local Taliban commander and, I believe al-Qaeda."

"You sure?"

"Yes. I have known this man all my life. I fought with him against the Russians, and he hates anyone who is not Afghani."

"Qaeder, do you think they will come back?"

"This group, no. They came only for the money. I believe they were given one gold coin before they left and told they would get another when they returned. Others, maybe. Al-Qaeda and their

Taliban friends will never leave us alone until they have been defeated. They now know that we are willing to fight them, so they will go to some other village. With the help of Allah, we will have some peace for a while."

"Good." Jacob turned to the young enlisted man. "Give your photos to Braddock to send with the rest."

"Boss, the cavalry has arrived." Bill Sweetman's voice came over on the radio. "We'll come in with them."

Jacob looked down the road and saw a convoy of eight mine-resistant vehicles making their way up the road. One was pushing the burnt-out trucks off the road.

Fatigue was setting in as the adrenalin flow slowed in Jacob's body. He leaned against the rough stucco and downed a water bottle in two gulps.

Qaeder put his AK-47 against the wall. "Thank you for coming. Allah will always bless you."

Jacob looked at Qaeder and could see both sadness and relief on his face. "You're welcome, and we cannot leave a friend to face al-Qaeda and the Taliban alone."

"War is nothing new to Afghanistan. You Americans helped rid us of the Russians. Will Allah's help, you will help us get rid of the Taliban and their al-Qaeda friends. And maybe then, my countrymen will stop fighting amongst themselves and see there is a better way."

Jacob felt sorry for Qaeder. In a few days, he would return to the safety and security of the U.S. The man and his village would be left in a war-torn country. "Qaeder, Afghan tribes have been fighting each other for centuries."

Qaeder made a wry face and smiled. "I know. That is the curse of my country. We can try to change our ancient ways. I want my youngest son to learn to be good at something other than war. With Allah's help and guidance, one day, my country will have peace in either my or my son's lifetime. We are all tired of the killing."

CHAPTER 12

NON BELEIVERS

Derek was in the middle of his breakfast when he picked up his cell phone. He was surprised he'd received a text during the night and didn't remember hearing the phone beep. If his wife Eileen was in the house, she'd have heard the phone and awakened him.

Instead, Eileen was at a one-week course at Logistics Support Corporation to learn their accounting systems and procedures, followed by a one-week Defense Procurement Agency course on government contracting and the Federal Acquisition Regulations. She would be back on Saturday.

Derek searched for the number in Tel Aviv, where the time was two-thirty in the afternoon. The phone rang twice before a voice answered.

"Allo."

"Good afternoon, Ari. It's Derek. What is so urgent?"

"You heard about the ship, no?"

"Yes. Details were passed on to us by our client. Anything new on the remaining missiles?"

"We don't know where they are, but we do know they were loaded on a ship in Rostov-on-Don and are eighty percent sure they are headed for the United States."

"Can you send me what you have and we'll see what we can find out."

"The material should be in your inbox."

"Thanks."

"Oh, your DNI was officially notified about both types of weapons we captured on *Abdul-Muqaddim*. Your secretary of state chewed out our ambassador because we told the world about the weapons and missiles. You'd think your president would be happy, but no, he sees us as the villain. Our ambassador politely told your secretary of state that Israel will continue to prevent the spread and use of chemical weapons."

"Are you telling me that the information was not well-received?"

"Yes and no. Analysts in the CIA loved what we provided, and the White House hated it."

"Figures. I'll call you later."

When Derek walked into the offices of Camelot International, Zvi Rosenthal was bent over a desk studying a picture with a loupe. "Zvi, you look like you've been here all night."

"Ari waited to call you after he figured you had gotten up. With me, he was not so polite. He called at midnight, and I've been here ever since." He was about to say something when the rest of the team members walked in with a box of donuts.

"Gather round, guys. Zvi is about to share some intel that will either make you throw up or be so motivated that you'll inhale all this sugary goodness."

With that, Derek waved at Zvi, who waited until everyone had a cup of coffee and those who wanted one had chosen a donut or cinnamon swirl.

Zvi finished chewing a crème-filled donut that he'd wolfed down. He added that the seized freighter had two tons of munitions, mostly ammo for AK-47s and 74s and RPG-7 rockets besides the missiles and bombs.

The Israeli looked at the others. None spoke so he continued. "The *M. V. Abdul-Muqaddim* has an interesting history. The ship was one of twenty built based on the U.S. Army's 381 Design by the Albina Engine and Machine Works of Portland, Oregon under a U.S. contract that would transfer the ships to the Dutch Government for service in Indonesia."

Zvi went through the ship's history from its launch in 1946. It was bought in 2002 by the current owner, Ottoman Shipping, Ltd. of Istanbul, and renamed the *M.V. Abdul-Muqaddim*. He took a deep breath and held up his hand. "As you Americans like to say, there is more to this story. Ottoman Shipping, Ltd. owns six of these ships. Some, we've suspected of carrying arms to the Palestinians, but we never had, until now, hard evidence."

"Do you have any info on the whereabouts of the other five?"

"Yes and no. We've found two others in ports around the Mediterranean, and one is in a dry dock in Sevastopol. So that's four. We're trying to find the other two—the *M.V. Abdul Zahir* and the *M.V. Abdul Basit*."

"What else?" Derek was about to ask the question, but someone asked it for him.

Zvi was about to answer when one of the secure phones rang. Derek was the closest so he picked up the handset. "Camelot International."

"Derek, you alone?"

Derek recognized Don's voice. "No, we're getting briefed by Zvi on the takedown of *Abdul-Muqaddim*, why?

"Ever hear of a couple of NSA programs called Echelon or Prism?"

"Yes, but I don't know much about them. Why?"

"Let's just say they suck up a lot of stuff off the internet and from telephone calls. There is a lot of chatter about *Abdul-Muqaddim's* seizure. What got everyone's attention was a call where one person told another not to worry. The missiles and other equipment will be delivered. And their mission is still on."

"On where and what weapons?"

"We don't know. The spooks at NSA think the U.S. is the target. The head of the CIA is in a difficult spot. He's got a boss in D.C. who told him that MANPADS are not a threat and not to spend any time looking for them. Now he knows better, but his hands are tied. SOCOM knows better, and he suspects he will be tasked to seize them before they get into the country. He's waiting for the where so he can pick the when." Don pronounced the acronym of the special operations command as "so-comm." "Would you fly to Tampa to give him some ammo?"

"Sure."

"I'll get the meeting scheduled."

SUNDAY, NOVEMBER 13ᵀᴴ, 2016, 10:17 A.M. LOCAL TIME, TEL AVIV, ISRAEL

Publicly, the Russian news organs did not report that chemical bombs, the precursors for sarin nerve gas, and Igla-S missiles were captured by the Israelis. Journalists from Western news organizations in Moscow were told curtly the country has no comment because "Russia has seen no concrete proof that the weapons were made in Russia."

Privately, the story was quite different. The Russian ambassador to Israel was summoned to the Israeli foreign ministry. There, he was shown video recordings and close-up photographs of the weapons that showed the data plates on the missiles and the markings on the bombs. At first, he tried to suggest that the photographs could have been taken anywhere.

The Israeli Foreign Minister replied that if the Russians wish to examine the weapons and take their serial numbers, a visit to the ship today could be arranged before the weapons were unloaded. The Russian ambassador called his embassy and ordered one of the military attachés to meet an Israeli officer at the pier where *M.V. Abdul-Muqaddim* was tied-up at one p.m. today.

MONDAY, NOVEMBER 14ᵀᴴ, 2016, 11:39 A.M. LOCAL TIME, AFGHANISTAN

Even after eight hours of sleep, Jacob was still tired as he sat in the building SEALs used for operational planning at Bagram AB. He drummed his fingers impatiently on the desk while waiting for two people to call him back.

One call would come from Kevin Rathburn so he could learn what NSA had on all the phones they captured. The other would come from the FBI. The special agent assigned to work with Special Operations Command gave him a number in the bureau to call. When the phone rang, his heart raced when the LED said, FBI. "Lieutenant Commander Sobrano."

"Good morning, sir. This is Special Agent Roger Harrison. We don't have much, but what we have is interesting."

"Shoot, Roger."

"OK. The South African government keeps track of when gold Krugerrands are sold and to whom. They have different individual and bulk sales processes; because you found more than one, I assumed someone bought a bunch. Sellers are required to report the person's name, the date and time of the sale, and information on the buyer. If the buyer is an individual, they record passport or national ID card numbers. Buyers are limited to the number of coins they can buy. Bulk buyers need licenses and follow a similar process that records the details of the sale. You with me so far?"

"Yup."

"Our office in Johannesburg talked to the appropriate people in the South African government. You captured bullion coins because they only have one hundred and sixty serrations on the edges. These Krugerrands most likely came from the two hundred and fifty sold by Bidvest Bank Limited in Durban ten days ago for two thousand dollars each. Gold is worth about nineteen hundred dollars an ounce right now. Our experts estimate the melt value is at least thirteen hundred dollars each."

"Wow. So, what you are saying is that these were not bought by a collector."

"Correct. Coin dealers are all licensed and must follow the rules from the South African Reserve Bank or risk significant jail time and fines. A sale of that many coins by a single dealer would be unusual and they would have to get them from the government because most dealers would not have that many in stock."

Jacob didn't say anything because he hoped Roger had more.

"In a few minutes, I'll be sending you the passport info used by the buyer and his photo, along with the data on the electronic fund transfers used to pay for the coins."

"Transfers, as in plural."

"Yes. Bidvest received the money from a bank in Lichtenstein which received the money from a bank in the Seychelles, which in turn received transfer instructions from a bank in Bahrain. We traced the original transfer order from a bank called Talwar, headquartered in Karachi. Talwar used to have three names, but a few months ago, the new owners changed the name."

"What do you know about Talwar?"

"Not much. Talwar is a small wealth management bank catering to wealthy Pakistanis and has offices in Karachi, Abu Dhabi, Cairo, and London."

"Did you say the name of the bank is Talwar?"

"I did. Why?"

"Roger, do you know what a Talwar is?"

"No. Again, why?"

"A Talwar is a curved sword used in Afghanistan and Northwest Pakistan. So, why would a wealth management bank take the name of a sword?"

"I don't know. Maybe someone in the bank collects swords."

"Can you get a list of the owners and executives?"

"Yes. The easiest place would be the Brits because they would be on their filings for a license to do business in the U.K. The Pakistanis are tightlipped when asked to provide information on their banks unless we have evidence of a crime being committed. Buying or paying mercenaries with Krugerrands is not a crime."

"I know. How long do you need to get what we can on the bank?"

"A couple of days. I'll call the guys we work with in the Treasury Department."

"Good. Call my satellite phone. I'm heading back to the States in a few days."

THE SAME DAY, 12:47 P.M. LOCAL TIME, JFK INTERNATIONAL AIRPORT

Na'il paused for a second as he stepped into the hall where the booths were for the immigration officers. Ostensibly, he was adjusting his backpack, but he stopped to check for surveillance in the large room that was more like a convention center with windows on the second story that provided natural light. He followed the crowd into the corral for U.S. citizens that S-turned back and forth to feed 20 booths where blue-shirted men and women checked the documents of the people entering the U.S.

Nervously, Na'il fingered his U.S. passport as he ran through his answers and entered the line. Two days ago, he shaved his beard in a small hotel room in London and went for a haircut. Instead of wearing traditional Afghan dress, he wore a turtleneck sweater and jeans he bought in London.

After being gone for over six years, Na'il had mixed emotions about setting foot on U.S. soil. His last letter to his parents was mailed in Switzerland for him by a member of al-Qaeda. He did not intend to call or see his parents. What would he talk about?

On the one hand, he was glad to be back. There was an allure of the U.S.'s open society and freedom that conflicted with his resentment of the country's wealth and its citizens' ignorance about the teachings of Allah.

Lost in thought, Na'il followed the line to a single opening where a person in a red coat directed an individual to a cubicle.

"Sir, number six."

Na'il slid his passport and customs declaration form through the slot under the thick glass. On the back, he listed the sweater he was wearing and a brass teapot he bought in Egypt on the back of the form. The total was less than $400.

The agent looked at his passport and noted stamps for Morocco, Jordan, Saudi Arabia, the U.K., Germany, Turkey, and Egypt. "You've been out of the country a long time. Why so long?"

"I always wanted to bum around, so after I was discharged from the Army, I went where I wanted to go until my money ran out."

"How'd you get to Egypt?"

"I took a Limosol Cruise from Athens to Cyprus and then to Port Said because they were the cheapest." That was his only true statement. When he arrived in Cairo, Na'il was following the route to Afghanistan given to him and paid for by al-Qaeda.

"You go anywhere else?"

"The countries I visited are listed on the form." What wasn't on the form was Syria, Afghanistan, and Pakistan.

The agent waited for his computer to respond. A code flashed on the customs officer's screen saying Neil Mirage was on a watch list and to report his entry immediately but not detain him. The agent, who had been screening entrants to the U.S. for 10 years, knew that he was to slowly process Na'il so a tail could be set up. He flipped through his passport again, compared the photo to the man and what was on the screen, and then typed his notes. While he did so, Na'il shifted his feet as he stared into space and then back at the immigration officer.

Once the immigration officer pushed send on his notes, he flipped through Neil's passport, searching for a blank page. Finding one he liked, he stamped Na'il's passport and customs declaration. Sliding the documents back through the slot, he said, "Welcome home."

THE SAME DAY, 1:46 P.M. LOCAL TIME, DULLES AIRPORT, VIRGINIA

The airport had changed considerably since Ghanem left the U.S. A train now connected the main terminal with the outlying ones. When he and his parents first arrived, the FAA used futuristic-looking buses with four horn-like devices sticking up from the roof to take passengers and flight crews from the main, modern-looking terminal to the outlying ones where passengers boarded or deplaned from most of the flights.

Ghanem followed the signage that followed the same style used by international airports in the rest of the world to immigration where there were at least 100 people ahead of him in the line for "non-U.S. citizens." He handed the immigration agent his Pakistani passport, valid U.S. visa, and green card. The officer thumbed through his passport before sliding it into a scanner and swiped the green card. Both matched, and there were no notes.

"How long are you planning to stay in the U.S.?"

"About a month?" *The 'about' could be a few weeks or several months, depending on how long I need to carry out my mission.*

"Where are you staying?"

"Initially with friends here in D.C., and then I have some business in Boston."

The agent seemed satisfied and stamped Ghanem's passport and customs declaration before returning the documents to him. "Welcome to the U.S."

TUESDAY, NOVEMBER 15ᵀᴴ, 2016, 8:30 A.M. LOCAL TIME, TAMPA

Jacob felt excited because there would be a new sheriff in town. He dreaded the possibility of a Hillary Clinton presidency. He was seriously considering resigning from the Navy if she were elected.

When he stopped at the officer of the day's desk to have his orders stamped, Jacob was handed a message telling him to report to the SOCOM's commanding officer immediately. As he entered the office carrying his laptop and notebook, the general's admin smiled and pointed to the door. "The general will see you know."

The general was on the phone and grim-faced. He ordered, "Close the door."

After doing what he was ordered, the general sat back in his chair. "What the fuck did you do?"

"Do what where, sir?"

"Afghanistan. I spent thirty minutes on the phone with my cohort at Central Command, who wants your ass run out of the Navy. He's already made a similar call to the head of NATO because that's where ISAF reports. The head of ISAF is pissed at you. So, tell me your side of the story before I do anything I'll regret."

"Sir, here's what happened…." Jacob gave him the sequence of events starting with the NSA transcript and his call to ISAF's head of operations, who told him that they get similar intelligence all the time and what he knew was no big deal. He reiterated how he notified the ISAF operations officer so he knew what they planned to do and recounted his conversation with the local PRT team leader, who wouldn't do anything without direction from ISAF. "Sir, I thought we don't hang our friends out to dry, so I acted. The good news is that we chewed up a Taliban unit, killed the local commander, and collected some fascinating and valuable intelligence."

"Tell me what kind of intelligence."

"One, we know someone very high in al-Qaeda wanted Qaeder Rahim, the tribal leader, dead. Two, we know they paid the Taliban in Krugerrands to do it, and each fighter got at least one. Three, we've added several phone numbers to track on the list. And four, we have the money trail."

"We lost a good man."

"Yes, sir, we did."

"So, here's ISAF's story. One, the operation was unauthorized. Two, they were trying to turn the Taliban commander that the ISAF's J2 was sure was about to flip. Three, the head of the local, provincial reconstruction team thought you unnecessarily put his men and the villagers at risk. And four, the Taliban will be back to exact their revenge."

"I disagree with that assessment, sir. They sent between one hundred and fifty to two hundred to Rahim's village. The villagers buried fifty-six, and blood trails suggested many more were wounded. Given the state of their medical care, most of those will die. So, let's be conservative and say we killed a third of the attackers. First, the Taliban must find replacements which, despite the influx of foreign fighters, is getting harder and harder. Second, they know the villagers have been reinforced with additional weapons, which makes them a tougher nut to crack. Net net, the Taliban acted because they were bought and expected an easy op. We made them pay, big time."

The general looked at the young SEAL. He was full of what was known as "piss and vinegar," and it reminded him of when he was that age. "Jacob, O-4s don't make these kinds of assessments and judgments. Decisions on whether or not to go on those types of operations are made by the theater commander and his staff, not you, not O-4s who are there TAD."

"Sir, I had the flexibility in my mission tasking to take appropriate action before I left."

"Maybe... The operational authority to execute a mission like this would come from the ISAF commander or his designee. If he doesn't give his OK, those of you below in the change of command have to live with their decisions."

"Even when they get our friends killed?"

"Yes... I know, the idea sucks... But that is the way the system works. If not, we would have chaos."

Jacob bit his lip. He was about to say something and then realized he might piss the general off."

"Out with what you are thinking. I can see your mind working, and you disagree."

"Sir, with all due respect, we're in Afghanistan to defeat al-Qaeda and the Taliban and help the Afghans rebuild a nation torn apart by a war that has been going on since 1979. That's forty-seven years. Yet, when we have evidence that the Taliban will attack a village that provided us with valuable, accurate, and actionable intelligence and enabled us to destroy a bunch of Stingers that were being updated, we hesitate to lift our finger to help them. That, sir, is not right. That's not how we should treat a friend, much less a man who risked his family and the lives of his village and tribe for us."

"Welcome to my world. I deal with this every day."

"Yes sir… That's because the shoe clerks are in charge." The words popped out, and Jacob regretted saying them and expected a harsh comment from the four-star.

Instead, the general laughed. "I didn't hear that." He let a few seconds of silence act as a natural break before he continued. "Jacob, I just got off the phone with our JAG office. I'm not going to cashier you, nor will I discipline you mainly because you are too good an officer, and I agree with your assessment. I'd probably have done the same thing if I were in your shoes. All I'm interested in is did we win on the battlefield. The armchair assholes, or shoe clerks as you called them, always wait until the shooting stops. Then, they give us their assessment from ten thousand miles away in the calm, cool air of an air-conditioned office. When those at the pointy edge of the sword read or hear their analysis, we do our best to keep from puking. If you ever attribute what I just said to me, I'll deny it."

Jacob grinned and looked around the room. "Did you say something, sir?"

"Good…. here's the plan. You get your ass out of town ASAP and work for Derek Almer at Camelot International like we originally planned so Ed DeCosta can come back here. Just get out of Dodge quickly and quietly."

"Yes, sir."

THE SAME DAY, 7:07 P.M. LOCAL TIME, CAMELOT

Darren rocked back on the couch and clasped his hands behind his head. By pushing back, he could arch and stretch his back now that his laptop was closed, his time entered for the day, and his email inbox empty.

Seeing he was finished, Eileen sat crossways in his lap, waving an envelope. "Guess what came today?"

"I'll bite. A notice from the IRS saying we owe them a lot of money...."

She kissed him on the lips. "Bite your tongue, but what's in here will increase our 2016 tax bill."

"By how much?"

"At our tax rate of thirty-three percent, about thirty-seven thousand. Don't worry. The Evans Group took out twenty-eight percent. Apparently, when The Evans Group attorney saw the court filing, Stan gave in. I insisted he pay for my legal costs, or we were going to court and ask for triple damages plus legal costs."

"How big is the check?"

"Gross is one hundred and forty-eight thousand, six hundred and twenty dollars. After taxes, Medicare, and social security, I netted ninety-six thousand, six hundred and three buckaroos."

"Fantastic. Send the check to your broker."

"I will, but I can contribute to the family pot."

"No, the money goes to your nest egg. Camelot will generate a healthy profit for us."

"Are you sure?"

"Yup, because we'll get a healthy twelve percent over our salaries, rent, and other allowable costs. You, my love, just need to send the bills in on time that are documented properly so Camelot International can mint money while providing a valuable service to our country. What could be better?"

CHAPTER 13

DUEL IN THE DESERT

Talwar's London office took up the entire fifth floor in an office building near Canary Wharf that was rebuilt after World War II. Physically, their offices on the south side of the building were as large as the bank's headquarters in Karachi since most of their clients had business relationships, investments, and property in the U.K.

Floor-to-ceiling windows let employees see the Thames River and South London, and the sky. The day was typical for London in November, gray, overcast, and rainy, with a temperature hovering about five degrees Celsius (41° Fahrenheit). By four in the afternoon, the dark clouds accelerated the sense that night was coming.

The man sitting on the couch wore a traditional white agal with two black bands on his head. The cloth came down to the shoulders and contrasted with the charcoal gray fabric of his custom-tailored western suit from, Fatimah guessed, a shop on Savile Row. She could relate because her clothes came from a tailor and dressmaker who catered to wealthy women.

Out of respect for the Saudi businessman who was close to the Royal family, she wore a simple black chador that covered her shoulders and a black pantsuit with a light gray blouse. Before she put the chador on, Fatimah buttoned the jacket and the top two buttons on her blouse to appear modestly dressed for the Saudi.

Right after Saleh El-Amin sat on the couch in Fatimah's office, the receptionist brought in fresh coffee, dates, and sweet rolls. Meetings with Fatimah were by introduction only, and El-Amin was neither a client nor a prospect. He was a middleman who approached her on the recommendation of her father. El-Amin's job was investing money for members of the Royal family, but, like her father, he was not a member of the House of Saud. Out of courtesy, she addressed him as "your highness," knowing the title incorrect. Still, inside her office, no one would hear or take notice of her flattery.

The traditional family discussions that open Saudi business meetings took just a few minutes because there wasn't much to discuss. Fatimah had no children and was, for all practical purposes, estranged from her father.

Fatimah waited for El-Amin to explain why he wanted to meet with her. She forced herself to hide her impatience because each minute with El-Amin delayed her departure for Victoria House. El-Amin had been living in London for at least 10 years, and his children went to an English school. She suspected he was never moving back to Saudi Arabia.

"I have a very observant client who has a very traditional view of the role of women in the kingdom. He has also heard of your work from members of the Royal family. He would like to open an account in Talwar and ask you to make investments in causes important to him."

Translation... My client is a member of the royal family who wants to support those who oppose the West. He probably stopped giving money to the Palestinians when they supported Saddam Hussein and his attempts to overthrow the House of Saud.

Fatimah nodded as a signal that she understood and for him to continue. "My client would like to see more Muslim influence worldwide."

Translation... Neither Hamas nor Hezbollah will get his client's money because they are focused on the destruction of Israel. He wants someone who will attack the West.

"Does your client have a desired return on his investment?"

"Yes. He is very generous but does not want to lose the principal. Any excess money less, of course, your fees, would be donated."

Translation... Make him money, and the profits go to terrorists.
"I can arrange that." *Not the bank, but me—Fatimah. The bank will make money, I will make money, and al-Qaeda will get money.*

"Excellent." El-Amin's one-word answer meant negotiations on the fees had just begun.

"Can your client invest a minimum of fifty million pounds sterling?"

El-Amin didn't react. He was in a difficult position. His fee was one percent of the investment, and the larger the investment, the more money he made. His client hadn't given him a maximum number, saying only to transfer a "reasonable" amount. In the past, his client never invested more than U.S. $25,000,000. "Can you work with twenty-five million U.S.?

"Yes, certainly. Unless the markets crash, I can guarantee a five percent short-term and twelve to fifteen over three years."

El-Amin nodded. Perfect. His contract gave him one percent of the retained return, which must be noted in the contract. "I'll have my client transfer $25,000,000 for three years. Donate seven percent of the return, and he will be happy with five to eight percent in his pocket." *And I will receive a nice check every year.*

Fatimah picked up the man's card. Her administrative assistant had placed the card on the table before her when he was escorted into her office.

"Your highness, I will call you when I have the accounts set up and have the wiring instructions. Is three p.m. on Monday afternoon a good time?"

El-Amin smiled and nodded. "Perfect." He stood up; business completed. The meeting made his week.

Fatimah waited until El-Amin had left their offices, then she handed the card to her administrative assistant and asked her to do two things. One, set up an account at Talwar for El-Amin's client whose name was on the back of the card and prepare the wiring instructions. Two, to change her Monday flight to Karachi to the first one out on Tuesday.

That task done, Fatimah answered the emails in her inbox and left Talwar's office. Her loins throbbed as she rode the elevator down. Fatimah took a cab to her flat, and the concierge waved at her when she arrived. "Madame Serraf, I have two packages and a letter for you. Would you like me to give them to you now or bring them to your flat?"

"Please bring them up in ten minutes."

"Yes, ma'am."

The first thing to come off was the chador. Fatimah shook out her long hair and pulled off her shoes. She was pouring herself a glass of wine when there was a discrete knock on the door.

"Madame Serraf, Harold here from the concierge desk. I have the packages."

Fatimah undid the deadbolt and slid back another security latch. The man held a silver dress box with a pink ribbon and bow. The smaller box was wrapped in silver paper with another pink bow and a large envelope that typically contained a greeting card.

She said thank you and handed Harold two five-pound notes. The boxes sat next to each other on her coffee table, and Fatimah debated about whether to open the letter or the boxes first. The big box won, and slowly she unfolded the tissue and lifted out a light gray dress. It was simple yet elegant, and the label was from one of London's better bespoke woman's tailors.

How did the buyer know my size?

Fatimah used a kitchen knife to slit open the note.

Fatimah,

Wear this dress and only this tonight. Nothing else. When you are ready, call my number, and I will have a driver pick you up. When you enter the grounds, put on the items in the smaller box before you exit the car.

I look forward to having you serve me.

Lady Danica

Weak-kneed with anticipation, Fatimah sat on her couch and pulled the silver-wrapped box toward her. Neatly pulling off the wrapping paper, she took a deep breath before she opened the lid.

There was a leather drawstring bag under a pair of four-inch patent leather heels with thick leather straps to keep them on. Fatimah found a leather collar with four chrome steel loops, leather ankle and wrist cuffs, and two chrome steel chains inside the soft leather pouch. A leash with a leather handle was also in the box.

Fatimah put the collar on and buckled it. Then, she put the cuffs on above her ankles and buckled them before clipping the chain between them. The shoes followed them, and the half-meter-long chain only allowed her to take half her normal stride. Smiling, she could feel the wetness in her crotch as she made her way to her bedroom.

The gray dress had a square-cut neck and three-quarter sleeves and fit perfectly. Fatimah took everything off and headed for the bathroom.

After picking Fatimah up in a Daimler DS420 limo, the driver lowered the partition slightly to let her know they were 15 minutes or less from the mansion. This was Fatimah's signal to put on what she called the accouterments. When the Daimler pulled up to the door, she saw Lady Danica waiting on the steps.

The driver held open the door while Fatimah swung her legs out. The silver chains glistened in the soft light, and the rain had stopped. Fatimah ignored the cold because inside, she was on fire. She bent her knees as she handed Lady Danica the handle on the leash.

"Fatimah, are you ready?"

"I am ready to serve, Mistress Danica."

FRIDAY, NOVEMBER 18TH, 2016, 10:26 A.M. LOCAL TIME, BROOKLYN, NY

The Thanksgiving Day holiday is uniquely American. Besides the traditional family gathering, it is the day before Black Friday, which is the busiest shopping day of the year. And it is the signal to all shoppers that Christmas and Hannukah are just a few weeks away. With all the holidays coming, the sidewalks of Manhattan were crowded with people. The other boroughs were less so, but still, there were more out than usual.

Na'il suspected he was being tailed, and each time he looked down at 38th Street from his hotel room, he always saw a man either standing on the street or sitting in a car. He wanted to find out, so he hailed a cab on 9th Avenue and wedged himself in the corner of the cab's back seat, diagonally behind the driver. When he got in, he plopped his backpack down on the back seat and said, "La Guardia, American Airlines."

The cabbie gave him a dirty look because, despite the 30-plus dollar fare and tip, he had two choices after he dropped Na'il off. One, get in line and wait about an hour for a fare at the cab stand, or head back to the more lucrative streets of Manhattan where 10-dollar fares and two-dollar tips were the norm.

The FBI agent watching the hotel noted the cab's medallion number and called it in. The FBI command center called the cab company, who gave him the destination reported by the cabbie.

When Na'il got out of the cab, he gave the driver a five-dollar tip, entered the terminal, took the escalator down to the lower level, and joined a crowd waiting for the rental car buses. When the black and yellow Hertz bus arrived, he got on. He didn't know that the man sitting in the back of the bus, wearing a suit, and holding a briefcase, was an FBI agent.

By the time Na'il pulled out of the Hertz facility just west of the airport, two cars, each with two FBI agents, were waiting.

Na'il drove south on the Van Wyck Expressway, wondering if he should just drive around or do something that would confirm the tail. The abruptly slowing traffic gave him a chance. He cut in front of a cab and two other cars to get onto the exit for the Long Island Expressway generating blasts from the horns of the vehicles he'd cut off. Thankfully, the cars were moving quickly, and he looped around and headed east on I-495/Long Island Expressway or what he'd heard a local refer to as the world's longest parking lot.

Frustrated, the FBI agents called in to say they lost Na'il and described the car and the direction where Miraj was headed. The command center called Hertz, who said they would notify the FBI when and where the car was turned in. Apparently, the tracking device in Mirage's car was not working. Neither the FBI nor Hertz knew that Mirage had disconnected the power cable and the one to the NeverLost's® antenna.

He drove down the Cross-Island Parkway toward Kennedy Airport and the Belt Parkway. Then, he exited at Cross Bay Boulevard and turned south. At 159th Avenue, Miraj turned right and pulled into the first open spot he could find. He waited for 15 minutes and, satisfied no one was following him, drove down 159th Avenue to where it entered Spring Creek Park.

Miraj drove slowly along the narrow park road and stopped where he could see the hangars at the Floyd Bennett Coast Guard Station on the other side of Jamaica Bay. To the northwest, he watched thousands of seagulls and other birds cawing at each other as they orbited the landfill.

Na'il took a deep breath to inhale and enjoy the smell of the salty air from the Atlantic Ocean just a few miles to the south. Back in the car, he drove until he found a wide spot in the road and stopped to watch a Boeing 747 thunder overhead. At this point in the plane's climb from the 11,411-foot-long Runway 13 Right, Na'il estimated the four-engine airliner was less than 1,000 feet above the bay. Smaller airliners taking off from the shorter Runway 13 Left climbed much faster.

He walked toward the water bordering the park, searching for a small area hidden from the boat landing and the houses to the east, where two men could fire two missiles quickly. Where Miraj was standing was too far out in the open. East of where he parked, Na'il found a grove of trees that would shield the shooters from the homes bordering the park.

As an American Airlines Boeing 777 whined overhead, Na'il held up his arms as if he was holding a Stinger missile and tracked the large twin-engine jet and then a smaller MD-80 taking off from the shorter, 9,999-foot-long 13 Left.

Perfect! They could fire at one climbing out from Runway 13R and shoot the one that took from Runway 13L in the ass. Done right, both missiles could be launched simultaneously. The only bad news about this site was that there was only one way in or out. However, he was confident that by the time the police arrived, his men would be in a car headed for a safe house in Brighton, where they would hole up for at least a week before driving to Canada.

Satisfied that he was not followed, Na'il called the main Hertz number and asked if he could drop the car at Newark Airport. He was told yes, and there would not be a drop-off fee. Thinking it was an invasion of a person's privacy, the individual who took the FBI's first call didn't put a note in the file to contact the FBI if they heard from Miraj.

Na'il's next call was to the hotel to tell them he would not be returning and to charge the day to his credit card. By the time he finished, Na'il was driving over the Verrazano Narrows Bridge to Staten Island.

At Newark Airport, Miraj hailed a cab to take him to Union Station in downtown Newark where he boarded the Acela high-speed train to Washington, D.C. On the train, he tilted back his chair and closed his eyes, thinking this was a good day. One site was found and the tail, which he presumed was the FBI, was gone.

MONDAY, NOVEMBER 21ST, 2016, 11:31 A.M. LOCAL TIME, MOSCOW

Federal Security Service Colonel Mikhail Zabara wasn't surprised that it was snowing. While his office didn't have a window in the hallway, he could see the large snowflakes through his door and out the window. When he walked across Lubyanka Square from the metro station to the front door of the building that housed the headquarters of Russia's secret police earlier in the morning, there were two centimeters on the ground. More was expected, and it was only November!

The pale-yellow building known as the Lubyanka was built by the All-Russia Insurance Company in 1898 as its headquarters. After the Russian Revolution in 1917, the building was seized, and the Cheka, the communist country's new secret police organization, appropriated the structure as its headquarters.

In 1922, the Cheka was renamed the "Peoples Commissariat for Internal Affairs" better known as the NKVD. A year later, the name was changed to the "Joint State Political Directorate" or the OGPU. That lasted until 1934, when the agency was given the name NKVD and the OGPU was absorbed into an organization that could investigate, arrest, and interrogate anyone in the country.

During World War II, the NKVD was reorganized and emerged as the Ministry of Internal Affairs or the MVD. In 1953 when the head of the MVD, Lavrentiy Beria, was purged after Stalin's death, the agency became the Committee for Internal Affairs, a.k.a. the KGB. After the attempted coup led by the head of the KGB that failed to overthrow Gorbachev in August 1991, the KGB was split into three organizations—the Federal Security Service (FSB) to handle internal security; the Foreign Intelligence Service (SVR) to gather intelligence overseas; and the Federal Protective Service (FSO) assigned to protect high ranking Russian politicians.

Through all those iterations, the country's secret police headquarters remained in the Lubyanka. The building had been expanded several times, and the section where Colonel Zabara's office was renovated in 1983. He thought the new paint was an effort to cover up the fact that the building desperately needed another upgrade.

The first major winter snowstorm made Zabara remember the FSB's standing joke about the Lubyanka. Some wag said the Lubyanka is the tallest building in Moscow because from its basement, one can see all the way to Siberia.

After watching the early winter snow for a few minutes, Zabara turned his attention to the documents at the center of his desk, most of which came from the Russian embassy in Tel Aviv. All had been handed to him at the meeting that started at 0830 in the office of the chief of the FSB's Investigation Directorate. He was given a stack of documents and told to investigate how these missiles were stolen. More documents, but not what they were, Zabara was told were coming, and both the head of the FSB and Vladimir Putin, a former KGB officer, wanted answers and wanted them soon.

This investigation, along with the other half a dozen he was pursuing, was, in the words of the head of the Investigation Directorate, his "number one priority!" He was not dumb enough to ask, "What about the others that were also supposed to be his number one priority?"

Instead, Zabara did what he had in the past, juggle, make a little progress, report what he now knew that was new, and go on to the next project on his list. He would handle this one no differently but was intrigued by the sheer brazenness of the crime.

His first call was to the headquarters of the Russian Armed Forces to ask for the paperwork that documented the chain of custody for the missiles and bombs. This would lead him to where they were stored, and that would give him names and a place to start.

When he rattled off his authorizations, the colonel at the other end of the phone said he would dig out the information but might need two weeks. Zabara pushed by mentioning Putin's interest, and the colonel agreed to a week which, if his experience was any indicator, the colonel would fail to meet.

THE SAME DAY, 3:32 A.M. LOCAL TIME, SONORAN DESERT, AZ

The bright full moon and a cloudless sky lit up the desert, and there was almost enough light to read a book. All around him, Saguaro cactus stood like sentries and cast shadows on the light brown dirt.

From his perch on a rock outcropping, Border Supervisory Border Patrol Agent Gary Lonewolf looked up as he remembered his days as a Recon Marine. Helicopter pilots who inserted his unit deep in Taliban-controlled territory referred to the light coming from the full moon as a "colonel's" moon because the additional light made it easy for the older Marine Aviators to see at night. In the Sonoran Desert, just like in Afghanistan, the bright moonlight made Lonewolf's job easier.

The full-blooded Mescalero Apache was on his favorite kind of patrol, tracking smugglers coming across the U.S.-Mexican border. Already, he'd found a set of fresh tracks of at least five men, and, based on their footprints, they were heavily loaded.

Once he established the group's general heading, Lonewolf moved quickly through the cactus and scrub brush to a rock outcropping he guessed was about a quarter mile ahead of the smugglers. He eased up to the edge behind a small bush. He slowly scanned the valley with his night vision goggles, focusing on a dry creek bed.

Bingo! Five men with large packs and slung AK-47s followed a leader carrying a smaller pack and an assault rifle. Lonewolf studied the men who had stopped to take a break and were leaning against their backs for support. He touched his earpiece to ensure it was in place, and the volume turned down before turning on his radio.

Overhead, about two miles to the south, the crew of a Border Patrol Sikorsky flying an ex-U.S. Army Blackhawk heard his call. Lonewolf waited until the group began to move out. He confirmed to the agents in the helicopter that he thought these heavily armed men were drug smugglers, not illegal immigrants.

He took one last look before stuffing the night vision goggles into his pack. The radio was left on as he trotted northwest to intercept and arrest the smugglers.

At his next observation point, again on raised ground, Lonewolf noticed that the group now numbered seven, and the new man was, like the leader, carrying a small pack and an AK-47. Lonewolf moved farther away before making another call while paralleling the smuggler's route. Two miles to the north, there was a culvert under a dirt road where he suspected the group would spend the day or wait for pick-up. The dry riverbed widened 200 yards south of the culvert before it turned east, making the spot perfect for an ambush.

Lonewolf was moving faster than the column and confident he was not making any noise. When he reached the road, four agents were waiting with their Ford Broncos parked in a stand of trees. Each had six spare 30-round magazines for their M16s and two spare 15-round ones for their Beretta 92F nine-millimeter pistols.

As they checked the weapons, Lonewolf estimated that he was about 30 to 45 minutes ahead of the smugglers. He was told that four more agents were on the way via car, and the Blackhawk had gone to Ajo to pick up six more. The first group would arrive in about 10 minutes, and the Blackhawk would be back in 15.

Two agents set up so they could fire down the ravine while Lonewolf and another agent, another former Marine, set up where they could shoot into the ravine where the dry river widened. They planned to wait for the smugglers to be in the open area before they announced themselves.

Laying on his stomach, Lonewolf pushed the switch on the portable speakerphone an agent who arrived in one of the Broncos had given him to the on position. The smugglers were now less than 100 feet away. Lonewolf could see their familiar-looking, standard-issue U.S. Army packs in the bright moonlight. "Halt. U.S. Border Patrol."

The leader turned to the noise and raised his AK-47. The five men with the big packs bent forward and ran toward the culvert, unslinging their AK-47s. Tail End Charlie knelt and fired a series of aimed bursts at where he presumed Lonewolf was.

The two border patrol agents at the bottom of the L-shaped ambush opened fire, dropping two men. The smugglers started leapfrogging, with one man moving and the other firing aimed bursts at the Border Patrol agents.

Lonewolf heard two sickening thuds in rapid succession. The agent next to him rolled over, and he could see a hole in the man's forehead and blood gushed out of his neck. He tried not to stare but couldn't help but notice that the back of the man's head was blown off.

Tail End Charlie lobbed a grenade in Lonewolf's direction before he turned and sprinted for the culvert. The grenade landed 25 yards from Lonewolf, and he shot the man as sand and bits of cactus rained down on him.

In front of him, there were four bodies—the leader, two of the smugglers, and Tail End Charlie. The other three reached the culvert and were using their packs for cover. What impressed Lonewolf was their fire discipline. They weren't blazing away like the typical drug smuggler. These men were well-trained soldiers.

The two agents had moved to cover the north end of the culvert. Lonewolf had the south end.

Once again, he keyed the loud hailer. "This is the Border Patrol. You are surrounded. Throw out your weapons and come out with your hands up." He waited a few seconds and repeated his order. His answer was two bursts that tattooed the dirt uncomfortably close. Then, the desert was silent.

They were at an impasse because Lonewolf had nothing— grenades or tear gas—heavier than a 5.56mm bullet other than time which was on his side. Lonewolf assigned two men to guard the north end of the culvert. A tap on his boot told him that the reinforcements had arrived. One motioned for him to pull back from the ledge and showed him six flash-bang grenades. Perfect.

Lonewolf asked for a volunteer from the four on the north side. John Green, a 20-year veteran of the Border Patrol who refused promotions because they might take him out of the field, met Lonewolf 30 yards to the east of the culvert.

The sun was now rising, and dawn in the desert is very transitory. One minute there is half-light, and then there is bright sun.

Lonewolf was tired, hungry, thirsty, and angry. He hadn't eaten or slept since the early evening and was angry at the smugglers for killing one of his fellow officers.

Over the center of the culvert on the south side, Lonewolf pulled the pin from one of the three flash-bangs. He raised his hand with three fingers held up, then two, then one. He flung the grenade, which bounced once off a smuggler's pack and into the cave. The delay gave him time to put his hands over his ears.

Screams came from the cave, but no weapons, no people. The men looking into the culvert could see movement and men. Lonewolf took out both remaining flash bangs and held them up.

He pulled the pin on one, released the spoon, and threw the grenade as hard as he could. Then he threw the second, as did the other agent. Lonewolf's first bounced off one side of the culvert and exploded, sending a cloud of dust out both ends.

The four explosions reverberated in rapid sequence. Lonewolf hoped that the flash and concussion would disorient, blind, and deafen the men inside the culvert. They didn't. The smugglers sprayed a magazine of bullets from each end of the culver. They were not giving up.

Lonewolf saw the Blackhawk lifting off in a cloud of dust after six more agents jumped off and jogged toward him. As the Blackhawk circled overhead, Lonewolf relayed a quick overview of the firefight to the crew, who passed it on to the local headquarters. The Blackhawk headed back to Ajo to get more equipment, and the only advice the watch officer could give Lonewolf was, "Don't do anything stupid that gets more agents killed."

Great, Lonewolf thought. That's why you're at a desk, and I'm out here in the desert.

As the officer in tactical command, Lonewolf met with the newcomers and went to each position to brief them on his latest plan. With Green in position on the north side of the culvert, Lonewolf counted down over the radio. Both Green and Lonewolf, had their M16s slung over their shoulders shoulder and their Beretta pistols drawn.

When he reached zero, the teams on both sides of the culvert began firing three-round bursts into the opening. The return fire was sporadic, and Lonewolf thought he heard a scream as he slid down the dirt to get to the bottom of the ravine and the edge of the entrance to the culvert.

Lonewolf jumped around the edge and came face to face with a man bleeding from a shoulder wound trying to load an AK-47. He pumped two rounds from his Beretta into the man's chest.

Officer Green fired only once and his bullet hit his target in the face. Both men kicked the weapons off to the side, away from the dead men. Lonewolf stared at the corpses shaking his head. He'd seen men like this in Iraq and Afghanistan, who were either Taliban, Fedayeen, or al-Qaeda.

Forty miles northwest of Nogales, Mexico, and 120 miles from where Lonewolf stood, six more men made their way through the Coronado National Forest. When they reached Route 82, they lay in a ditch until a Suburban stopped 100 feet from where they waited. They quickly loaded their packs into the sport utility vehicle. They drove off, leaving the two Mexican guides with a wad of cash and several extra bottles of water. An hour later, they were in a safe house in Tucson.

TUESDAY, NOVEMBER 22ND, 2016, 7:39 A.M. LOCAL TIME, LANGLEY, VA

Don Sanderson started paging through the National Counterterrorism Center's online daily brief with a one-sentence reference noting that today was the 53rd anniversary of the assassination of John F. Kennedy. Lonewolf's report caught Don's eye, and he clicked on the link that provided the complete report. When he finished, three facts stood out.

One—the men were carrying forged green cards and genuine Saudi passports with American long-stay visas showing they entered the U.S. at Kennedy Airport.

Two—they were equipped with fully automatic AK-47s and explosive vests, and each man carried 20 one-pound bricks of U.S. manufactured C-4 and detonators. The batch numbers on the packaging matched C-4 shipments sent to Saudi Arabia.

Three—Lonewolf's description of the firefight convinced Don that Lonewolf knew what he was doing and the men killed were well-trained soldiers.

The report had the Border Patrol base's name and phone number in Ajo, Arizona. Don's finger tapped out the digits on his secure phone. When an agent answered, he asked for Officer Lonewolf.

His shift over, Lonewolf was about to leave when he was told he had a phone call. On a secure phone. Don asked for details about the firefight that weren't in the report and to think as a Recon Marine as he answered his question, "How would he use the C-4 to cause as much damage as possible to the U.S.?"

Lonewolf didn't hesitate. "Sir, if it were me and I'm just a lowly E-6, but if I wanted to really hurt the U.S., I'd drop as many towers that carry high voltage lines out here in the desert as I could. Just go a few miles from any power plant, and they're unguarded. Bring down enough of the lines crossing the desert, and you'll cause the lights to go out in Phoenix and LA for weeks. This is easier than trying to smuggle a bomb onto an airplane. Or they could use the C-4 in car bombs and set them off in crowded places."

Don took a deep breath. "Lonewolf, have you shared these theories with anyone else?"

"My boss. He agrees, but the higher-ups took my ideas out of our report."

"Can you send me what you wrote originally?"

"Yes, sir. If you give me your secure email address, you'll have them in a few minutes."

Don did as he was asked. "Is there anything else I missed?"

"Maybe, sir. That night, our sensors picked up two groups. The one we caught and another one. All this is in what I will send you, but about forty miles east of where I was, other agents found tracks of what we think was a Suburban along a desert road. The vehicle tripped a camera going in and coming out. We got the license plate, and despite the bad quality pictures, there was one guy going in and eight coming out in the vehicle. This had to be another team. The guys in D.C. pooh-poohed our analysis."

"Have you tracked down the plates?"

"Yes, sir, they're fake."

"And the geniuses in D.C. don't think that is unusual?"

"No, sir. They say smugglers do this all the time. Someone way high in the food chain is looking the other way or doesn't believe we know a trained soldier from a drug smuggler or a coyote with illegals when we find them. Get my drift?"

"I do."

"Sir, if you need anyone to help track these bastards down, we've got a lot of ex-Marines and Rangers down here, and they'd love to go huntin'. They'd take personal time off if needed. We all left buddies behind in Iraq and Afghanistan who died thinking they'd rather die there than on our streets if we could keep the bastards out of our country. Unfortunately, I don't think anyone in D.C. sees this situation that way anymore."

"I do, and I have friends who do, and we're all trying to stop these guys. I will certainly keep your offer in mind. Let me know if you see or hear anything more."

"Yes, sir."

Don waited until the promised email arrived, devoured the contents. After forwarding to Derek, he dialed a number in Bonham, Texas.

"Camelot International."

"Derek, is that you?"

"Yup. What's up?"

"Let's go secure." Don recounted what he learned, his suspicions and Na'il Miraj was now in the wind. The FBI said no other action would be taken unless Neil Mirage, a.k.a. Na'il Miraj committed a crime.

"Good grief. The man's fingerprints were on the thumb drives captured in Afghanistan."

"Yeah. Welcome to my world. In Washington, I deal with the three monkeys—hear no evil, see no evil, and speak no evil—daily. We're forbidden to use the words Islamic terrorism or terrorist in reports."

Zvi opened the door to Derek's office, holding a picture and a folder, and pointed to his chest. Derek took the hint and pushed the button on the speakerphone. "Don, this is Zvi from our friends in

Tel Aviv. We just got word that Dawuud Ghanem entered the U.S. a few days ago using a valid U.S. green card and a Lebanese passport."

He slid the photo of Ghanem waiting for his luggage at Dulles Airport in front of Derek. "Ghanem wears many hats in al-Qaeda. Before Bin Laden was killed, he was his chief procurement officer, so to speak. Hezbollah and Fatah were not radical enough for him, and the next place he turned up was in Afghanistan to fight you Americans."

Zvi dumped several more photos on Derek's desk. "We're pretty sure he's the guy who bought the missiles. Mossad doesn't believe he is in the U.S. for a vacation."

Don waited a few seconds to make sure the Israeli was finished speaking. "Zvi, I know this is a dumb question. Have you guys shared this with the FBI and the Counterterrorism Center?"

"Yes. From what I was told, they said thank you, and we'll look into the matter."

"Shit, shit, shit...."

"Don, give me until the end of the week to come up with a couple of hypotheses we can run up the flagpole."

"Done. Call me when you have something."

THE SAME DAY, 9:20 A.M. LOCAL TIME, WASHINGTON, D.C

The daily intelligence brief was postponed until after the President's early morning phone calls with two European leaders. When the President finished, the briefing team, along with the National Security Advisor, the Director of National Intelligence, and the Director of the CIA, were ushered into the Oval Office accompanied by the President's press secretary.

At the end of the briefing, the press secretary spoke up. "Mr. President, I've had several calls about the gun battle in southern Arizona. Based on the questions, they've gotten some details from the Border Patrol agent's report. We need to get ahead of this story."

"First, keep pushing the message that Bin Laden is dead and al-Qaeda is not an existential threat to the United States. Second, make sure your contacts know the President and the heads of the nation's intelligence agencies think this is an isolated incident. Third, I will inform the head of the Department of Homeland Security to tell the Border Patrol that any agent who leaks information on this will be dealt with harshly."

The press secretary nodded. "Sir, I've also taken calls from reporters with excellent contacts with the Israeli intelligence community. Their questions suggest that al-Qaeda and their affiliates are preparing a major attack on the U.S."

The President shifted in his chair as he flushed, trying to control his anger. "Goddamn them. They need to be taught a lesson and mind their P's and Q's. Tell them the Israelis see a terrorist on every corner and tend to overestimate the threat. Also, say that our intelligence community doesn't give much credibility to their perspective."

"Yes, sir. You know this is a hard message to sell because the goddamn Jews and their Israeli friends have sympathetic ears in the media who push their talking points. Also, the President-elect may see this differently and open his big mouth."

"Well, do what you can to change their perspective. That is part of your job! I'll have my chief of staff ensure this is left out of any intelligence briefing given by the president-elect."

The head of the CIA lingered after the briefing team left. "Mr. President don't discount what the Israelis are telling us. They have better sources than we do in some areas and are right more often than wrong. We need to listen."

The President was in no mood to listen. He had an agenda to pursue. "They are trying to push us into a position we may not want to take."

"Yes, sir, they do play the PR game well. But this is not about PR. This is about American lives and the security of the nation. We need to listen and maintain our bridges with Shin Bet and the Mossad."

"Noted. We should cultivate similar relationships with the Arab countries to give us a different perspective. I don't trust the Israelis."

The head of the CIA realized the meeting was over and left thinking that after eight years in office, the President of the U.S. didn't understand the importance of the country's relationship with Israel. There was about to be a new sheriff in town, and he was sure that his replacement would be encouraged to expand information sharing with the Israeli intelligence agencies.

CHAPTER 14

BOAT TRANSFER

The *Mary Beth* had been loitering around the point in the ocean almost 100 nautical miles east southeast of Portland for almost an hour. The 70-foot-long fishing boat rode easily with the bow pointed into the long swells as the ship barely made steerage way through the charcoal-blue Atlantic.

Abbas Salib, with both Tawfik Tomas and Kamil Nassar aboard, left Portland on the afternoon of November 15th. The ship's autopilot, coupled to the GPS navigation system, brought the boat to the planned latitude and longitude for the rendezvous.

The surface search radar showed only one ship anywhere near *Mary Beth*. The rendezvous was supposed to be at 8:00 a.m., so Salib advanced the throttles and turned toward the radar target 11 miles away.

At three miles, through his binoculars, Salib recognized the *M.V. Gwadar III* from the picture he was sent. Neither crew was supposed to use a radio and Salib, in the more maneuverable *Mary Beth,* took up station 100 yards from the 10,000-ton freighter.

The 300-foot-long freighter was a general cargo ship that went back and forth between European and U.S. ports. Registered in Liberia by a Pakistani shipping company, *Gwardar III*'s last port of call was Rostov-on-Don, where the ship filled its holds with pallets with rolls of thin sheet steel covered with a preservative to prevent rust. *Gwadar III* stopped for a day in Benghazi, Libya, ostensibly to take on fuel, with the real purpose of the stop being to allow 16 passengers to board. They'd been flown from training camps in Afghanistan to Syria and then on to Benghazi.

While *Mary Beth* was getting into position alongside the *Gwadar III*, Tawfik and Tomas untied the lashings that held the Zodiac Pro 6.5 across the fishing boat's transom. The inflatable rubber boat had a wide-open area forward of the small 'bridge' and only two seats. The five-bladder boat was powered by a 115-horsepower Mercury Marine Optimax engine which could push the Zodiac to 30 knots.

With the Zodiac tied alongside, Tomas climbed aboard, turned on the ignition, and pushed the starter. The fuel-injected, three-cylinder engine roared to life.

Tawfik, tossed the untied lines onto the floor of the Zodiac Pro 6.5, and Tomas sped toward the Jacob's ladder on *Gwadar III*'s starboard side. Once the Zodiac was positioned at the bottom of the ladder, the first six men wearing orange life vests climbed down carrying backpacks.

Born and raised in the Syrian port of Tyre and the son of a fisherman, Tomas was an expert in handling small boats. He looped a line through a stanchion on the platform at the bottom of the Jacob's ladder, and the first man tossed his pack into the boat and jumped in. The other five quickly followed.

Tawfik kept the Zodiac at about 15 knots as he sped back to *Mary Beth*. He made a second trip to bring six men to the *Mary Beth* before returning to *M.V. Gwadar III* for the last four.

Once they were on board the Zodiac, the Syrian held the Zodiac 6.5 Pro in position about 20 feet from the side of the freighter. Much closer, and the RIB was in danger of being sucked alongside the bigger ship and dragged back to where the screw would chew the boat to pieces.

On *Gwadar*'s main deck, the crew of *M.V. Gwadar III* lowered eight olive-drab-colored boxes lashed together to the Zodiac. Unlike the men, the boxes had no flotation gear. If they were dropped into the water, they would sink like stones to the bottom, 300 meters below.

With the first boxes lashed down, Tawik returned to *Mary Beth* where the boxes were lifted on board before being taken to the hold and lashed down. By the end of his twelfh-round trip, 16 men and their backpacks, AK-47s, and GSh-18 pistols. The 9mm pistols, designed by Gryazev and Shipunov were unique in that they only contained only 17 parts compared to a Glock 17, which had 34.

Also transferred to *Mary Beth* were crates containing 16 RPG-7 launchers with eight missiles each, 4,000 rounds of 7.62 X 39mm ammunition for the AKs, and 1,000 rounds of 9mm ammo for the pistols along with 24 containers with MANPADS—12 with English and 12 with Cyrillic markings.

Abbas gave a long blast from this ship's horn and turned the wheel as he broke away from *M.V. Gwadar III*. *Mary Beth* had been alongside the freighter for four hours. As he turned the fishing boat west, Salib eased up the throttles on the twin Caterpillar diesels so *Mary Beth*, according to the readout on the screen, was moving across the bottom at 12 knots. According to the GPS, *Mary Beth* would arrive at its destination at 2333.

Each of the 12 boxes with English markings had an FIM-92E Stinger missile. The olive-green crates with Cyrillic markings had Russian made 9K388 Igla-S missiles. One of which was 9K-338-S-004546-VAD-16. The crates with the RPGs and their rockets had Chinese characters and the ammunition came from North Korean factories.

In the hold, the 16 newcomers had arranged the cargo into five stacks. Four had 1,000 rounds of ammunition for the AKs, 200 for the pistols, two RPGs and eight rockets. Two of the four had Stingers, and the other two had Igla-S'. The remaining eight MANPADS and RPGs and their rockets were set aside in the fifth group and would be stored in the warehouse Salib had rented.

At 2315, Salib eased back on the throttles so that it was creeping along at three knots. Already, the Zodiac was tied to a cleat on the starboard side, and the first team to go ashore was loading the boat.

Mary Beth was less than a half mile from an isolated cove with a rocky beach less than 50 miles from the Canadian border. The GPS and Salib's National Oceanic and Atmospheric Agency marine chart said the fishing boat was off Buck Cove near Winter Harbor, Maine.

The muffled Zodiac cast off when Abbas saw the three short flashes of white light followed by a longer one. The signal meant four vans were parked in the woods off Schoodic Road that paralleled the coast a few hundred feet from the water's edge.

Each time the Zodiac headed toward the beach, it was crowded with four men, their gear, and four missiles, firearms, RPGs, and ammunition. On the way to the Maine coast, Tawfik gave each team the color of their van and $2,000 in cash. They were all given credit cards, driver's licenses, and Green Cards when they boarded MV *Gwadar III*.

In the glove box of each van were the keys to the vehicle, a map, and directions to their safe house. In a pouch under the seat, Tomas put a Garmin GPS system they could plug into the cigarette lighter.

With the teams ashore, Abbas sailed south down the Maine coast and anchored in 50 feet of water off one of the Cranberry Isles. With the generator on to provide heat and electricity, Tawfik, Tomas, and Salib climbed into the bunks and slept.

THURSDAY, NOVEMBER 24TH, 2016, 11:39 A.M. LOCAL TIME, CRYSTAL CITY, VA

Dawuud leaned back in his chair and looked out at the Potomac River. From his hotel room, he could see airplanes taking off to the south from Reagan International Airport every 30 seconds. He couldn't help but smile, thinking he was sitting about seven miles as the crow flies from the White House, the center and heart of the American empire. The country's military nerve center—the Pentagon was less than three miles from where he sat in his room on the top floor of the Hyatt Regency. And, because this was a national holiday, the watch teams were reduced to a minimum.

The phone rang. Dawuud listened carefully and hung up the phone. Five teams, along with their MANPADS were on their way to the safe houses. So far, the first phase—insertion—was complete. Dawuud wanted to get six, four-man teams into the country in his original plan. One was lost in the desert, so only five made it. Once they were in their safe houses, he would send them instructions on what he wanted done when the time was right.

Lesson learned—insertion by sea was safer than through the American desert Southwest.

CHAPTER 15

VULNERABILITIES

A passing motorist called the Tennessee High Patrol District Three office to report a white van that looked abandoned by the side of the road. The report said the vehicle had a flat tire.

When Trooper Bill Murphy received the call from the dispatcher, the mile marker given in the call indicated that the van was in a rural section of I-40, about halfway between Nashville and Jackson. To the agent in the 911 center, the call seemed routine. To Billy Murphy, now a 10-year police veteran who was an infantryman with the 70th Armored Regiment during the 2003 invasion of Iraq and now in a Military Police unit in the Tennessee National Guard, one never knew.

As he approached the van, Murphy flipped on the flashing lights and kept his bright lights on. He stopped 100 yards away to survey the scene through the steady rain. Between the sweeps of the wipers, he could see the back two doors of the van were cracked open enough so he couldn't read the license plate. From what he could see, the van wasn't on a jack on either rear side.

Murphy always wore his Kevlar vest. As a precaution, he unbuttoned his blouse and felt the Velcro attach as he pressed the chest plate against his body that would stop rifle caliber rounds. After calling the dispatcher, Murphy turned on the dash camera. When the green light indicated an image was being recorded, he put the patrol car into drive and let it roll forward.

Thirty feet away, Murphy stopped, reported what he saw, and was about to get out of the car. Suspicious, Murphy drew his pistol and kept it by his side as he peeked around the door and saw a stack of long olive drab boxes with yellow markings.

Instinctively, Murphy brought his issued full-size Glock 31, which contained 15 rounds of .357 SIG ammunition in the magazine and one in the chamber, up to a ready-to-aim and fire position. The .357 round developed by the German-Swiss firearms manufacturer SIG-Sauer was a way to provide the power and accuracy of the .357 Magnum cartridge in a semi-automatic pistol. Before coming into wide use in semi-automatic pistols like the Glock 31, the .357 Magnum could only be fired from a revolver.

Murphy took one step out from behind the door of his cruiser when he saw what he knew was a muzzle flash, followed by two more. The first bullet slammed into his body armor, and the shock knocked the air out of his lungs. As he fell backward, another round came through the door and hit him in the thigh. A third bullet hit him in the side, as Murphy fell to the ground.

Before Murphy could fire, the shooter emptied the rest of the magazine into the front grill of his patrol car. The engine stopped in a cloud of steam.

Murphy dragged himself to his knees, and as the back door to the van slammed closed, Trooper Murphy emptied his pistol, firing the first eight shots into the left side of the door and the rest into the passenger side. He had the satisfaction of seeing the back window on the driver's side craze and small gray circles appear where the .357 rounds went through the thin metal of the van.

Weakened from a loss of blood, Murphy made a crude bandage out of two rags on the front seat. As he talked to his dispatcher, Billy Murphy passed out from blood loss.

Three hours later, the white van was found in a Walmart parking lot just off I-40. The bullet holes in the back door caught a shopper's eye. When the Jackson Tennessee police officer arrived, he found two dead men on the van's floor, both of whom died from gunshot wounds, and the front two seats were soaked in blood. No identification was found on either man, the license plates were removed, and there was no registration or proof of insurance. A quick search for the VIN showed the van had been stolen in Arizona two weeks prior.

The forensic team found scrapes of olive-green paint on the van floor that was later determined to be Russian. Footage from the lot's black and white security cameras showed another van back-up to the one Murphy saw. With the doors on both vans open, there was a gap of over a foot between the sets of doors, and the security camera recorded the men transferring eight long crates from the shot-up van to the new one. They could not be identified because the men never looked toward the camera. What was noted was the second van didn't have license plates. To the police officers watching the footage, the crates' size meant they could contain rifles, RPG launchers, or even small rockets or missiles.

The imagery was forwarded to the Bureau of Alcohol, Tobacco, and Firearms, who used a computer software tool to determine the crates probably contained MANPADS. The officer who conducted the analysis sent a copy of his report to the National Counterterrorism Center, the CIA, and the FBI.

SUNDAY, NOVEMBER 27TH, 2016, 2:00 P.M. LOCAL TIME, KARACHI

Running a bank with branches in the Muslim world and one in London meant Fatimah worked six days a week. Fridays and Saturdays were days off for the Karachi, Dubai, and Riyadh offices, while the London office was closed on Saturdays and Sundays.

The only blessing about working on Sundays in the Karachi office was the slower pace. During the average Western workweek, Fatimah was often speaking with correspondent banks in North America, Asia, and Africa. Only a few clients had either her direct or her office number. Potential new clients had to be vetted before Talwar's CEO would consider accepting a meeting. Therefore, an unannounced visitor asking for time with Fatimah was most unusual.

When told that Fatimah was busy and didn't accept walk-in appointments, the man handed the receptionist his card. Underneath his name were his rank and organization, Inter-Service Intelligence, a.k.a. ISI—Pakistan's intelligence and internal security agency.

Before Colonel Ali Zain entered her office, Fatimah had slipped on a niqab. Fatimah nodded to her secretary, who closed the door after the ISI colonel entered. Fatimah pointed to one of the two chairs in front of her desk and waited for the colonel to sit down before she sat in the other chair next to him rather than sitting behind her desk. "What can I do for you, Colonel Zain?"

Fatimah wanted to send Ali two messages by skipping the traditional small talk. One, she was a busy executive with a bank to run, not that he cared, and two, she wanted to find out why he was in her office.

The Pakistani officer's head moved forward several times before he spoke. "Ms. Serraf, you seem to travel a good deal. In the past two months, you have been to Dubai and London several times and Peshawar at least twice."

I wonder if he knows I have also been to Paris and Tehran. "True. That kind of travel is not usual for the president of a private bank, who prefers to frequently meet in person with large clients. We have offices in London, Riyadh, and Dubai as well as here in Karachi. I am sure that you know that...." Fatimah let her voice trail off.

Zain didn't take the bait, which would either demonstrate his lack of knowledge of what an investment bank does or those trips were of no interest. "Your visits to Peshawar are the ones that interest me the most."

The colonel let the statement hang in the air for about 15 seconds so that Fatimah could process the implication of his statement.

"May I ask why?" *I didn't break the law. I met with a client.*

"ISI is interested since one of the men you met with is affiliated with al-Qaeda. We believe, as do the Americans and British that he is what a business would call their chief financial officer."

Fatimah let out a soft "oh." *I knew that.* "I'm just a banker. The man wanted to take advantage of our investment services."

Zain pursed his lips. "I see." He waited a few seconds. "You may be interested to know that Talwar's name has popped up several times in ISI's conversations with the CIA. We can only assume that the Americans are becoming interested in your bank's activities. So, if I were you, I would be cautious of who Talwar takes on as a client."

Fatimah forced herself not to react. She smiled as innocently as she could. "Why?"

"I think you can imagine why?"

"Actually, I can't. Talwar invests money on behalf of our clients to earn them a return. We move profits, as do all private banks, to avoid taxes when possible. And we transfer money at the behest of our clients. To my knowledge, we haven't broken any laws, so humor me."

"The Americans think Talwar and you may be one of al-Qaeda's bankers. I also believe you are on their watch list, and they are probably monitoring your travel. As far as ISI is concerned, if you do not violate Pakistani laws, we're not interested. As you know, sometimes we don't agree with the Americans or the British."

Fatimah laughed. "The Americans have vivid imaginations. Talwar invests and moves money legally. Let me repeat that word, legally, around the world. Yes, my clients take advantage of bank secrecy laws and tax havens, which is their right. Talwar's job, which is, therefore, mine, is to generate healthy profits, minimize the share government taxmen can take, and protect the funds from being stolen. You may want to pass that on to the Americans. They have large firms who are experts at this."

I wonder if ISI or the Americans know about Victoria House and Lady Danica. They could try to use that as blackmail.

Zain put the palms of his hands on the armrests. "Well, I thought you would like to know." He stood up. "Thank you for your time, Ms. Serraf. I hope Talwar continues to be successful. Good day."

After Colonel Zain left, Fatimah's mind raced. *Was Zain sent to deliver message? If so, why and from whom? How much did he or ISI know? How much do the Americans know? My only conclusion is that now I am a target.*

MONDAY, NOVEMBER 28ᵀᴴ, 2016, 4:47 P.M. LOCAL TIME, MOSCOW

Colonel Zabara thoughtfully stirred his tea and watched the second lump of sugar dissolve. The ritual gave the investigator time to let his mind shift gears. Of the six investigations he was pursuing, four were "all stop," i.e., he was at a dead end. He was wondering if the Russian army colonel would keep his word and send the promised documents about the missile and chemical bomb transfers. The sky was already getting dark because sunset was around 4:20 p.m. today. Winter was fast approaching.

The jangling of the phone surprised Zabara. He answered using his rank and last name.

"Sir, we have a courier here at the entrance with a large box of documents. What do you want us to do with them?"

"Bring them to my office immediately." Zabara wanted to add the word idiot but didn't. He used the time to make a space on the table, which was pushed against the wall.

The courier who brought the box to his office handed Zabara a clipboard with forms. Each one needed his signature signifying that he had taken possession of the documents noted on the forms that they were the "originals."

Zabara carefully went through the accompanying inventory to ensure that what was in the folders was in the box. He was impressed that someone took the time to catalog the information he requested.

One folder had the original weapon transfer order. Another had the shipping documents showing the chain of custody from the missile factory in Kovrov to Pochep. He put aside the one with the paperwork allowing a transportation unit to take possession of the bombs and missiles to which someone attached a handwritten note. The last two folders were copies of the personnel files of Colonel Serik Saliemenov and Lieutenant Colonel Gregori Tzuri, the commander and his deputy of the weapons depot.

TUESDAY, NOVEMBER 29TH, 2016, 3:30 P.M. LOCAL TIME, LIBERTY CROSSING

Once the head of SOCOM had been briefed on Camelot's conclusions, he decided that he would call the head of the CIA and set up a meeting for Derek. This was to keep Don Sanderson out of the firing line in case there was some blowback by the Director of National Intelligence or someone in the lame duck administration.

Before Derek left to fly to D.C., the commander of the U.S. Special Operations Command told them, "I'll have the appointment set up by the time you land along with a staff car to take you to the National Counterterrorism Center. Trust your instincts. I agree with you and so does the guy who works for me at the center. So, let's run what you know up the flagpole and see who salutes. By the end of January, we'll have a new boss and hopefully, things will be better. They can't get any worse!"

That conversation was seven hours ago at Special Operations Command headquarters at MacDill AFB. Within half an hour of walking out of the general's office, Senior Chief Norquist and IS2 Harold (don't call me Harry) Buckholz were airborne in Derek's Aerostar 701P for the four-hour flight to Reagan International. Sobrano was also on board because he saw the MANPADS al-Qaeda had in Afghanistan and used his contacts to help refine their analysis. The two enlisted men were with him because they had the detailed knowledge of the intelligence and the sources on which they based their analysis that led to the hypothesis just shared with the commander of Special Operations Command.

As a former member of Seal Team Six, Norquist had unquestioned counter terrorism credentials. He was on the team because he was technically on "light duty" because he was still recovering from a chest-wound he'd received in Afghanistan.

When the men from Camelot walked into the Signature Flight terminal at Dulles, a driver with a van was waiting. Badges were also waiting in the lobby of the headquarters of the National Counterterrorism Center.

Because their briefing and supporting material was on a laptop not issued by the National Counterterrorism Center, a technician used another laptop to run a virus scan which took ten minutes to complete. Two of the meeting's invitees—Paul Bricker and Adnan Maalouf—came in right after an administrative assistant notified them that the visitors were here and their laptop was clean. Bricker was assigned as the senior FBI special agent to the National Counterterrorism Center.

Maalouf said when he introduced himself that all the analysts studying intelligence on al-Qaeda, the Taliban, Shia, and Sunni terrorist groups reported to him and he reported to the center's Director of Intelligence. The third individual who came in a few minutes later was Allen Hunter-Bayer, the most senior State Department counterterrorism expert assigned to the counterterrorism center.

Hunter-Bayer, they learned from their sources at SOCOM, came from a wealthy family, went to the right school, i.e., Princeton, and they should not allow themselves to be bothered by his effeminate mannerisms. His father was a senior executive for Shell U.S. and he lived in Saudi Arabia and Iran. He was fluent in Arabic and Farsi and a hard man to read.

Eight minutes after the meeting was supposed to start, Lawton Evergreen, a political appointee, walked into the room. His title said he was a deputy director and Derek learned at SOCOM that the administration plucked him out of a think tank that supported all the current president's positions on foreign policy. They were warned that Evergreen felt the average IQ in the room jumped up by at least thirty points when he entered.

Evergreen sat down at the head of the table, looked at his watch and then glared at Derek. "I've got a hard stop at 1600 so let's get going. Let's start with the punch line of why you are here."

In other words, who the fuck are you and why are you here wasting my time?

Derek summarized what they knew and ended with the statement that the likely timing of an attack would be heavy travel days before Christmas until after New Year's.

"So, you believe al-Qaeda could do three things. One, shut down the electric grid that supplies New York and LA. Two, set off car bombs in crowded malls. And three, shoot MANPADS at airplanes leaving Atlanta, DFW, LAX, JFK, O'Hare and maybe Boston or Dulles. This option is, based on the weapons smuggled into the country, the most likely scenario followed by the bombs in shopping malls. Did I understand you correctly?"

Derek nodded his head emphatically, "Yes sir, you do."

"And how did you, a private citizen, gather the highly classified intelligence to support these fantasies?"

"Mr. Evergreen, they are not a wild dream Camelot International pulled out of thin air. My firm has a contract to evaluate intelligence and come up with a hypothesis. Camelot used information provided by the U.S. intelligence community, open sources as well as other contacts that provided information we verified. We think the threat is real and believe that the U.S. can stop al-Qaeda before the attacks are carried out. May I remind you, sir, the fingerprints of Na'il Miraj, a U.S. Army trained Stinger repair technician were on a computer keyboard on which there was the software needed to update a Stinger missile that was beyond its end of use date."

The State Department officially tilted his head back so he could look down his nose at Derek. "Mr. Almer... You're, what, an O-5. What the hell do you know? You're not trained to look at this data; you're not even a trigger puller. You're just a goddamn helicopter pilot. So, let me give you a clue... Bin Laden is dead. Neither the DNI nor the head of the National Counterterrorism Center believe that al-Qaeda can carry out such a complex operation in the United States. They see far more intelligence than you could as a contractor. More importantly, the president doesn't think they can."

Derek bristled as he controlled his growing anger. Jacob put a hand on his friend's shoulder, afraid that Derek's mouth would speak before his brain fully vetted his words. He was too late. "Mr. Evergreen, I wish I shared your optimism. We missed all the clues that led to 9/11 and then we missed all the signs with Major Hassan, San Bernardino, Orlando, and a host of others. As tragic as these may be, they were pinpricks and might have been prevented if we were more open to new ideas and theories. Maybe the new administration will have a different view, or maybe, if there is an attack such as we think is possible, you can visit the families of the victims."

Evergreen stood up fuming. "Commander, let me give you some advice. You're in way over your head. Go home. You're playing in a sandbox where you don't even know the players, the rules, or where the landmines are. Do what you were doing before you started this think tank called Camelot. If not, you may, no, you will regret ever starting the business."

After Maalouf followed Evergreen out, Paul Bricker motioned to Derek to stay. Hunter-Bayer remained seated and busied himself reading a document in a folder with red and white stripes that Derek could see was stamped Top Secret.

"Evergreen doesn't speak for us. However, he is the number two man at the center and, unfortunately, we work for him until he is replaced. We, that's Hunter-Bayer and me, agree with you. Something's brewing and we've not been able to figure out what. Your analysis and scenarios connect a lot of dots for us."

"Thank you."

"Technically and officially, we can't work with you which is bureaucratic bullshit. So, through Ed DeCosta we can continue to share information. I'll send you a group of intercepts and other material that you can evaluate to validate or change your theory."

Derek nodded. "Thanks. I'm sure they will help." There wasn't anything else to say. So, he let Bricker continue.

The FBI agent pulled a photo from the leather portfolio he had on the table. "I understand that you flew here in your own airplane, is that correct?"

"Yes."

"Good. If you want, I'll set up an interview the Tennessee State Trooper whose dash cam took this picture. He swears he saw Cyrillic markings on these cases and says he's seen these kinds of crates in Iraq and Afghanistan where they contained RPGs and SA-7s."

Bricker slid the picture across the table that was a blow up of what the security cameras photographed. There was not enough detail to see, much less read the stencils on the side of the cases, but the shapes and sizes were discernible.

Derek passed the photo to Chief Norquist. "We'll spend the night out near Reagan and fly down early in the morning."

"How about I set up the visit for 1030?"

"Perfect."

"Good, I'll send the address and room number to Ed's e-mail. Officer Murphy is out of the ICU and is being guarded by his fellow troopers."

THE SAME DAY, 7:26 P.M. LOCAL TIME, CRYSTAL CITY

Since it was cold and rainy outside, they - the employees and owner of Camelot International - decided not to go out to dinner. The dining room at the Crystal City Marriott was relatively empty, and the maître d' put them at a table in the back of the restaurant to give them privacy and room to spread out. Halfway through their main courses, Jacob turned to Derek. "You've been awfully quiet since we left National Counterterrorism Center. What's up?"

Senior Chief Norquist and Petty Officer Buckholz looked at each of the two officers. As enlisted men, the normal order of the day was that when an O-4 talks to an O-5, enlisted people keep quiet.

Norquist had heard many stories about how the two men operated and bounced ideas off each other. His look at Buckholz was meant to convey, listen, and speak only when spoken to. The following wink suggested this could be fun.

Derek put his knife and fork down on the top of his plate. The filet—medium rare—was almost gone. "I've been thinking...."

Jacob cut him off. "That's both worries me and gives me hope. About what?"

"Two things. If I were Mr. al-Qaeda prime and wanted to create the maximum amount of havoc, what would I do with a limited number of men? Bombs and SUVs in the mall are the easiest to execute but won't kill hundreds, much less thousands. Our theory about bringing down the power grid is interesting, but, again, based on what the guys who work for Texas Utilities, Con Edison, and Pacific Gas & Electric told us, dropping a dozen powerlines in the right sequence and destroying the right sub-stations requires expertise and knowledge that al-Qaeda probably does not have. Plus, many of the power stations in the grid have been hardened against such an attack."

Derek took a sip of his wine. "Soooo, this brings me to the MANPADS option as the most likely one. Our challenge is to whittle down the number of potential locations, and two, how do we get the manpower to protect them." Derek cut a piece of the filet and then held the chunk of medium-rare meat in the air while he finished his thought. "If we could narrow the number of possible airports to less than a dozen, then we have a fighting chance. I'd like to get the list down to six. If al-Qaeda wanted to make the biggest splash, my guess is that they are looking at ten possible airports. Starting with Logan in Boston, JFK in New York. La Guardia is out because the planes only carry 180 or so people. Then there's Atlanta, Charlotte, Philadelphia, Chicago O'Hare, Dallas, Denver, LA, Seattle, and San Francisco. All of these have Transatlantic or Transpacific flights or both. If I was a shooter with a Stinger, I would want to be at the takeoff end of the runway because the airplanes would be full of fuel. When they shoot them in the ass, there will be a spectacular, fiery crash. So, if we use Google Maps, we can narrow down those launch locations along the departure routes in the heart of a Stinger's and SA-24's envelopes."

Derek popped the chunk of meat into his mouth and chewed it without saying anything. After he swallowed, he spoke. "Am I crazy?"

Sobrano smeared white horseradish on a piece of rare roast beef. "No, Derek you're not, but let's not underestimate al-Qaeda. They've surprised us before, and I don't want to be looking under one rock and not another. If we task a few reservists who work for utilities, we can run the power grid idea to ground. We owe it to ourselves to find out. As far as the malls go, we'd be spinning our wheels trying to figure out the top mall targets. Like you, I believe they're the easiest to hit, but have the least long-term bang for the buck."

Jacob put the roast beef in his mouth, chewed it before speaking. "The question in my military mind is where do we get such reservists?"

Derek made a half laugh and then grinned. "The Seventh Fleet reserve unit at the Joint Reserve Base in Fort Worth has many officers and enlisted men who are employees of Texas Utilities. Several have designed power lines and stations, and there may be more in other reserve units. We need to activate them so they can help us. I'll task Ed with that job...."

Sobrano swallowed. "OK. That's assuming they're willing to take time off for active duty."

"Well, they can always drill with us. The next issue is manpower. At the moment, just can't go to the local police departments with our theory because we'll get blown out of the water. This is where it gets dicey, so don't freak out. We need to run the legal traps to find out what states allow when and where concealed carry holders can use deadly force to prevent a crime. We all have Texas Concealed Carry Licenses, so we need to research the details of the reciprocity agreements between the states that recognize the Texas CCL. In a perfect world, we want SEALS, Army Green Berets and/or Rangers or Marine Recon and infantrymen who have carry permits and are combat veterans."

Jacob reacted visibly at the suggestion. As a SEAL, he was very aware of the Posse Comitatus Act of June 18th, 1878, which restricts the use of the military to enforce domestic policies. "You're creating a posse or a militia."

"Call it what you want, Jacob. My gut tells me that a state which gives a concealed carry permit holder the right to act to prevent a crime gives us a legal basis to act even if we don't have a law enforcement officer with us. Whether or not he is a veteran or in the Guard or Reserve is irrelevant. In other words, if I saw someone shoot a MANPADS at an airliner, I could, in the words of my concealed carry permit instructor, stop him from shooting a second."

Jacob shook his head in wonder. "Only you would think of something like this. The rub is we want to prevent someone from shooting the first missile at an airliner."

"Yeah, I know, defense attorneys and prosecutors will have a field day with questions about how we knew the poor victim was about to shoot a missile. We'll cross that bridge if we come to it. So, the job is to figure out which airports and power stations. That will tell us how many additional men we need."

THE SAME DAY, 7:43 P.M. LOCAL TIME, GEORGETOWN IN D.C.

Adnan Maalouf slid into a booth at a crowded restaurant on M Street N.W. in Georgetown. Even though he worked at Liberty Crossing, Maalouf preferred to live in "The District" and drive 45 minutes to Liberty Crossing. In D.C., there was no such thing as going against traffic during rush hour.

Maalouf was nursing a glass of lemonade at the back of the small restaurant specializing in falafel, shawarma, and other Middle Eastern foods. When he saw Ghanem, he stood up, and the two men embraced before sitting on opposites of the table.

Ghanem leaned across the table and whispered. "What's so important that you had to text me?"

"There are some Americans who suspect you are about to strike."

The other man at the table ran his tongue along his lips and looked away for a few seconds. "What do they know?"

"They suggest the attack will likely use MANPADS to shoot down several airliners. Another choice would be explosives to cause a massive blackout on both coasts that will take months to repair."

Ghanem clasped his hands in front of his face and rested his elbows on the table's edge while the waiter put plates of food in front of him. He waited until the waiter was out of earshot. "Do they know where and when we intend to strike?"

"No. The Americans who came today had a preliminary list, but they are not sure of where."

"Are they CIA?"

"No, they are independent contractors, and no senior executive at the National Counterterrorism Center gives their ideas much credibility. But there are some at CIA and Special Operations Command who do." Adnan slid Derek's business card across the table. "They are from Texas."

They ate in silence for a few minutes before Ghanem spoke. For safety reasons, neither man used names. "This gives us another opportunity to kill infidels. We will take care of these people because they are too smart for their own good." The man paused while he noisily chewed on his food. "Adnan, what did your boss think?"

"He is like the American president who thinks al-Qaeda is too weak to mount any kind of attack."

"Did you delete the texts?"

"Yes, yes, of course."

"Destroy your personal phone and get a new one with a different number."

Adnan nodded. "I will."

"Inshallah. God willing, the attacks will go forward, and we will show the Americans and the rest of the world that al-Qaeda is alive and well."

Adnan finished his dinner and left. What neither man knew was that one of the two men who followed Adnan's guest into the restaurant recorded their conversation. Back at the Israeli embassy, a technician cleaned up the recording in a basement lab before sending the file to Mossad's headquarters and Unit 8200 for further analysis.

CHAPTER 16

STUFFED CABBAGE ARREST

For Derek, the morning started off well. After a few minutes of conversation, a reservist who worked for Oncor Electric Delivery called and said he and another reservist would drive to Bonham tomorrow. Both had the necessary clearances and expertise.

Derek no sooner put down the phone and set up a meeting note in his calendar when his personal cell phone buzzed. "Derek, it's Billy James."

The hushed tone in James' voice set off alarm bells in Derek's brain. He knew the ex-Marine gunnery sergeant had a voice like a drill instructor. James was now the head of the small Fannin County SWAT team that used his ranch's gun range to practice long-range shooting.

Before Derek signed the lease, he called James to ask for the Sherriff Department's recommendations on how to make the offices physically secure. At the time, Derek was worried about an attack by al-Qaeda or a gang looking for weapons to steal. The visit served another purpose which was to let James know that if their alarm system went off, they needed to come running fast. Once a gunny, always a gunny, James was sure classified material would be kept in the office.

"What's up Billy?"

"The FBI called to ask us to provide security because they're coming to raid Camelot in a few minutes. Gotta go."

From the front window, Derek could see the Fannin County offices across Fifth Street. The sheriff's offices were less than 10 minutes away. He went to the center of the room and yelled. "Everybody listen-up. Shut down your laptops and put every sheet of paper that's classified in the big safe. Once that's done, lock both safes. We're about to be raided by the FBI."

Once everyone started moving, he told Jacob and Zvi to leave via the back stairs and call Don and Ed to let them know about the FBI raid once they were on their way to his ranch. When Jacob started to protest, Derek shook his head. "Zvi is liable to get stuck in some kind of trumped-up immigration fuck up while his status is determined, and an arrest will ruin your career."

If they had poker chips in the office, they could have used them. Instead, the cards were dealt, and there was a foursome three tricks into a game of hearts when the buzzer at the front door went off, followed by a shout, "This is the FBI. Open the door."

Feigning annoyance, Senior Chief Norquist put down the paperback book he was ostensibly reading and shouted back. "We're coming. Don't get your panties in a wad."

When he opened the door, an FBI agent in full battle dress shoved a pistol in his face and shoved Chief Norquist who had raised his hands back and away from the door. The agent was followed by four more men carrying M16s, wearing helmets and FBI in big yellow letters on their Kevlar vests. They swept their M16s back and forth across the room, looking for threats, while the lead FBI agent went from office to office, looking for other people.

Derek slowly put his cards face down and looked at the lead agent. "Would you mind telling me what is going on? If the FBI wanted to pay us a visit, all you had to do is call."

"Are you Derek Almer?"

"I am. Who are you?"

"Special Agent Daniel Randolph. Mr. Almer, I have a warrant for your arrest."

"For what?"

"Illegal possession of classified documents."

Derek had to keep himself from laughing. Out of the corner of his eye, he could see the others at the table turn their heads so the FBI agents couldn't see their smirks and stifled laughter.

"So, you need FBI agents armed to the teeth want to make an arrest on a bogus charge."

"We were told you were heavily armed and would possibly resist."

Derek turned around and picked up the opened box of donuts. "Here's our armament. Do you want one? They're really good and were hot when we picked them up a couple of hours ago."

Randolph made a face as he holstered his pistol, and Derek wondered if he was debating if he should take one of the glazed donuts. "I need to handcuff you and take you to our office in downtown Dallas and seize all your classified material."

"Assuming I have classified material that I am not supposed to have, there's no way I can turn the documents over to you until Camelot International has one, verified your clearance. Two, we have verified that you are authorized to have access to the material, and three, whether you have the proper facility to store what I turn over to you. Whether I go with you is a matter open to discussion."

"No, it is not. I have a warrant for your arrest."

"The charges are bullshit. What if I refuse?"

"Then, we will add resisting arrest to the charges. And I will handcuff you and drag you down the stairs at gunpoint if I have to."

"I've not said I am not going with you, but the charges are bogus."

"That's not for me or you to decide. The Attorney General of the United States filed them."

"You mean to tell me that the attorney general of the United States personally signed off on sending an FBI SWAT team out to Bonham, Texas to seize classified material."

"I am." Randolph looked unsure. He looked around, hoping he didn't look stupid to the other agents.

"I hope you have better evidence than the last time the AG pulled this stunt. That day, he got embarrassed in Federal Court. I suspect this going to happen again." Derek turned to Senior

Chief Norquist, who was noisily shuffling the cards. "Senior Chief, would you be so kind as to get the contract that authorizes Camelot International to use and store classified information from our unclassified files."

Senior Chief Al Norquist, a very un-Scandinavian, dark-haired, 5' 6" and 150 pounds, whispered something in the second FBI agent's ear as he went to one of the gray four-drawer safes. The agent's eyes widened as they followed the SEAL. Norquist shielded the dial as he spun the numbered knob left and right. The safe unlocked with an audible click, and Norquist pulled out a file folder about a quarter inch thick.

With the contract in front of him, Derek pointed to the pages covering the handling of classified information. "Here…. Read this." He wanted to say that the FBI was misinformed but didn't.

"I need a copy of this contract."

"You can't. The contract is classified as Secret NOFORN. I took a risk that you are cleared for Secret matcrial and not an agent of a foreign government by showing you this. I am happy to give you the contract number, and you can have someone at the FBI who is properly cleared download the entire document. Now, you wouldn't want me to break the law, would you?" Derek gave the FBI special agent a toothy smile and waited a few seconds. "Special Agent Randolph, what level of a clearance do you and your men hold?"

"Secret."

"Good. I'll take your word on that. Please read this document." Derek watched as Randolph read the document that clearly stated that the Camelot was authorized to receive, store and, as appropriate, classify material that was Top Secret, Specially Compartmented Intelligence with specifically authorized code words. He guessed that the agent suspected where this discussion was headed.

"This doesn't prove anything and could be a fake document." Randolph glared at Derek. "Where is all the material covered by the contract?"

Derek waved his hand toward the two large black Liberty safes. "In those safes."

"You need to pack the classified material so we can take what you have back to our offices."

"Not a chance, Special Agent Randolph. Everything we have is TS or higher, and you're not authorized to see, much less handle, store, or carry it."

"Yes, I can. I can have my men open the safes with a cutting torch if needed."

"That would create a shit storm I don't think the FBI wants to start...."

The ringing phone on the desk stopped the discussion. Randolph nodded, and Derek spoke in a pleasant voice. "Camelot International.

He listened for a few seconds and then offered the phone to Randolph. "This call is for you."

Randolph was clearly hostile. "Who is this?"

Derek barely heard the female voice say, "Special Agent Randolph, please hold for Mr. Grady Gibson, the assistant director at the FBI in charge of counterintelligence. He would like to say a few words to you."

"Bullshit. This is a ruse."

Derek forced himself to sound firm, conciliatory, and helpful. "Not true. I suggest you talk to this man. And I'm sure he'll give you a callback number. Or you can call your office and have them call. Your choice."

Randolph glared at Derek and then looked at the other FBI agents who appeared unsure of what to do in this stand-off. Their strategy to use overwhelming force to intimidate the employees of Camelot International had failed. Their raid was about to be hijacked, and the FBI would not get its man.

Derek held out the phone. "Special Agent Randolph, are you going to talk to Assistant Director Gibson?"

Randolph hesitated and then grabbed the phone. He glared at Derek as he listened for a few seconds and then said, "Yes, sir. At once." With his free hand, Randolph unbuckled his helmet and handed the phone back to Derek. "Deputy Director Gibson would like to speak with you."

"Derek Almer."

"Commander, on behalf of the FBI, I apologize for this intrusion. This was not initiated by the FBI. Any records will be properly noted that there was no basis for the warrant. I will find out who requested the warrant and deal directly with that person. I can assure you this won't happen again. If you need help from the FBI in what you are doing, please do not hesitate to call me. We'll be happy to listen and, if warranted, take action."

"Yes, sir. Thank you." Derek hung up the phone and slid the box of donuts toward Randolph. When he did, he wasn't sure if he was spitting in the man's eye or making a peace offering. The special agent glared at each Camelot employee in the room before turning around to tell his men to stand down and return to Dallas.

Senior Chief Norquist watched the FBI agents walk past before they trudged down the stairs unstrapping their body armor and taking off their helmets. As he came back into the room, the phone rang. Again, Derek answered it.

"It is Don. Are the FBI agents gone yet?"

"Yup, they just left. Who'd you call?"

"Paul Bricker, the FBI agent we met at the National Counterterrorism Center, and he called Gibson. Ed called the head of SOCOM, and I have no idea who he called."

"Thanks. This could have gotten ugly."

"Amen. Did the FBI see anything?"

"Nope. We were playing cards when they banged on the door. A friend in the sheriff's office gave me a heads up."

"Keep going. SOCOM's intel folks think you're onto something. The chatter on the Internet and several recent intercepts supporting your hypothesis are on the way to you. That political hack Evergreen thinks otherwise, and he has the ear of both the president and the head of the center. Bricker thinks Evergreen is behind this. However, he will be gone by the end of January, I hope."

"That would be good news."

"Different subject. When do the reservists get there?"

"Tomorrow."

"Good. Keep plugging." Dial tone.

As they opened the safes to get back to work, Derek turned to Senior Chief Norquist. "What did you say to that FBI agent?"

"Just that if he ever pointed a gun at me again, I would rip his balls off and shove them down his throat while he was still alive."

THE SAME DAY, 12:26 P.M. LOCAL TIME, STATEN ISLAND, NY

The Boston Whaler pitched down noticeably when Daniel Morcos reduced the rpm on the twin Mercury Verado outboard motors from 4,500 to 2,000. Earlier in the day, he'd taken a bus to Toms River, N.J., and then a taxicab to the marina, where he signed the documents that gave him possession of the boat called Outrage by the maker.

After a brief checkout and a promise to return for the trailer, Morcos headed south on Barnegat Bay at a sedate five knots to Barnegat Light. Once through the narrow passage and into the Atlantic, he turned north and opened the throttles. During the demo on the bay, the salesman let him run the Mercury Verado engines up to 4,000 rpm for a short period but quickly had him pull the twin 250-horsepower outboards back to a more sedate 3,000 rpm because the boat was making too much of a wake and they could get a ticket.

In the Atlantic, Daniel opened the throttles first to 3,500, letting the boat cruise for about 10 minutes before pushing the two powerplants up to 4,500, their most economical cruising speed. The salesman warned him that at full power of 6,200 rpm, the engines would go through the 150 gallons of gasoline the boat carried in about two hours. At that power setting, the Outrage 280 would make around 50 knots. And, he said, unless the water was relatively calm, he would feel as if the boat was trying to beat him to death. Daniel took the warning as a metaphor but was anxious to find out for himself.

The boat was a quarter mile off the sandy beaches of the Jersey shore as Daniel increased his speed in 500 rpm increments. The salesman was right, lightly loaded as the Outrage 280 was, the v-hulled Boston Whaler banged through the waves in a hurry. Spray went everywhere, and he slid forward on his seat to get closer to the small windscreen to keep from getting soaked. With the boat bouncing around, he had trouble maintaining a constant heading and was afraid he'd be tossed off the seat, so he throttled back to 3,500 rpm. The ride became much more comfortable, and the boat's instruments said the Outrage 280 was making 22 knots.

Out in the Atlantic, the boat's thermometer said it was 45 degrees Fahrenheit, five degrees cooler than it was in Barnegat Bay. Supposedly, the temperature would reach the mid-fifties before the sun started to go down.

Daniel had been at sea for under two hours when he turned west just north of Sandy Hook. The course he'd plotted on the National Oceanic and Atmospheric Administration chart #12331 for Raritan Bay and the Southern Part of the Arthur Kill indicated he had another six miles to the mouth of the Arthur Kill River that separated Staten Island, NY, from Perth Amboy, New Jersey. From there, the Tottenville Marina on Staten Island, where he reserved a slip, was a mile further upstream. Officially, his slip rental started on December 1st.

In Raritan Bay, the water calmed as the Atlantic swells disappeared. Daniel eased the throttles back to 3,000 rpm, and the Boston Whaler's bow pitched down as the Boston Whaler Outrage sliced easily through the calmer water. When he turned north into the Arthur Kill River, he pulled the engines back to 2,000 rpm to ensure the boat was moving at under 10 knots.

A dock boy helped him tie up the boat and fill the tanks before pulling the Outrage into his slip. In the two and a half hours, he'd burned one-third of the fuel on board or about 50 gallons.

The receptionist called him a cab, and Morcos walked into his furnished apartment in Jersey City, NJ, 12 hours after he left at 6:00 a.m. Daniel smiled when he thought that today, he traveled by train, bus, and cab to the marina in Tom's River and then by boat, cab, subway, and train to return to his apartment.

THE SAME DAY, 6:47 P.M. LOCAL TIME, CAMELOT

During dinner, Derek could sense Eileen was upset. The conversation was monosyllabic, and she responded with terse answers to his attempts to start a conversation.

Knowing his wife liked bluntness, Derek took the bull by the horns. "OK. Eileen, what's eating at you?"

"Nothing."

"Bullshit. Something I did or something someone else did, has you really upset."

Eileen deliberately put her knife and fork down on either side of her plate. The slices of grilled flank steak were barely touched, as was the rice pilaf on the side. "Derek, when will you realize that you cannot take on the world? Today was the second time in our relationship in which you were paid a visit by FBI agents with a warrant for your arrest. After the first time and several frantic phone calls, I watched you walk into a courtroom in an orange jumpsuit with manacles and chains. Today, the FBI sent a SWAT team. Thankfully, I didn't have to ask Avery to drop what he was doing so he could defend you at a bail hearing."

Derek knew better than to answer. Better to let the love of his life continue to rant.

"At times, I think you are oblivious that you put everyone's career at risk to say nothing of me. I'm just collateral damage. Sorry, that was cruel."

Eileen paused, took a breath, and continued. "I can deal with you risking your scrawny ass in a helicopter or getting into a firefight with a terrorist, but I'll be damned if I will visit you in jail."

Nothing was said for what seemed an eternity but was probably less than 20 seconds. Derek, now sure that Eileen was finished, spoke softly. "First, the FBI didn't do their homework. Again! If they had, they would have learned that we had been granted access by the CIA and the appropriate clearances. Just like the last time, this was a political stunt by an asshole bureaucrat who saw Camelot International as a threat because his or her pet hypotheses were challenged with facts. This ended, just like the one last year, with egg on the face of the bureaucrat."

Eileen wasn't about to give up. "And that's the problem., Derek. They don't care about the truth. They only care about justifying their existence or keeping their contract if they're from one of the high-priced think tanks. You've got to be more careful. Everyone who is working at Camelot believes in you. They're risking their careers, to say nothing of their lives. Neither you nor any of them have the money to take on the Federal Government to defend yourselves in court. And, if LSI thinks you will affect their relationship with the

DOD, they will find some contractual technicality to dump Camelot International in a heartbeat."

She looked Derek in the eyes and saw that he was listening. "These people who tried to shut Camelot International down don't give a damn about whether if their or your analysis is right. What they care about is their position and power. If something bad happens again, like 9/11, they'll still be in their nice offices, doing their PowerPoints and wringing their hands while they blame someone else. You know how the game is played. You saw it firsthand in Afghanistan."

Derek nodded and clasped his hands behind his head for a few seconds while he arced his back, more to relieve stress than to stretch his muscles and spine. Then he leaned forward, "OK, I get it. We'll try to be more careful, but the facts are the facts, and what they tell us won't change. That's what Camelot International was created to do and what we will do."

Derek took a sip of his wine and said wistfully, "Hopefully, the current crop of assholes has learned a lesson and will, in the future, listen with open minds."

Eileen smiled. "We can only hope."

SATURDAY, DECEMBER 3ᴿᴰ, 2016, 11:46 A.M. LOCAL TIME, POCHEP

Right after Mikhail Zabara received the first batch of documents, he asked for a map showing where Pochep was located relative to Moscow. He remembered growing up hearing stories that maps were considered classified documents and that Stalin went so far as to order landmarks—bends in rivers, mountains, and cities be "misplaced" on the printed maps and allowed to be released. Stalin's rationale was that by making them inherently inaccurate, invaders couldn't use them to navigate accurately or find targets to bomb. The advent of satellite mapping changed all that.

Rather than wait for the Defense Ministry to respond, Zabara sent one of his staff members to the Intourist office on Shabolovka Street to buy a road map of Russia with Pochep on the map. He had to chuckle thinking that Stalin must have rolled over in his tomb when the agency he ordered formed in 1929 was privatized in 1992. He probably had apoplexy when the British Thomas Cook Group bought 50.1 percent of the shares in 2011.

Pochep, he learned, was 468 kilometers southeast of the Russian capital. Way too far to drive. He didn't want to bring Saliemenov to Moscow by train because the trip would be public and take too long, which left traveling by plane.

The nearest airport to Pochep was in Bryansk, roughly 82 kilometers away. At first, he wanted to fly to Bryansk, helicopter to Pochep, and land on the helipad in the center of the depot. That option was not feasible because there were no military or civilian helicopters to commandeer in Bryansk.

Logistically the solution was simple if one lived outside Russia. In Russia, it was a bureaucratic mess requiring approvals from the FSB, the Russian Air Force for the airplane, and the Ministry of Transport for the flight clearances. Getting the authorization to fly him to Bryansk and back took a week, then he had to negotiate a date with the unit assigned to fly him.

With that information on hand, he notified the Bryansk office of the FSB that he needed two vehicles and four men to accompany him to Pochep and back on the same day. That tasking was easier than getting the authorization for the plane.

Chkalovsky Aerodrome, where the 8th Special Purpose Aviation Division was based, was 34 kilometers to the northeast of the Lubyanka. When he left Moscow at 0600, the ride normally took about 45 minutes. Along the way, he wondered if the pilots would be drunk as had happened before. Not so, this time.

They were waiting when he arrived at 6:50 a.m. and ushered him out to an Antonov AN-72, which had its jet engines mounted on top of the wing. Zabara learned on an earlier trip in the plane with the NATO code name of Coaler was selected to take advantage of the tendency of a stream of air to follow a curved surface.

First discovered and presented in 1800 by Thomas Young to the Royal Society of London for Improving Natural Knowledge, the principle has become known as the Coanda effect after the Romanian mathematician and aerodynamicist Henri Coanda who patented the aviation application in France in 1934. The concept is used in many airplanes today, particularly those with multi-section flaps, to increase lift at slow airspeeds and high angles of attack. The Antonov Design Bureau applied Coanda's principles in the AN-72 to improve the plane's short takeoff and landing characteristics. Another benefit was that placing the engines high off the ground reduced the chances that the engines would ingest rocks and other debris when the plane was operating off dirt, ice, or gravel runways.

Zabara was pleased to see two VAZ-2110 cars with no markings waiting when he walked off the AN-72 45 minutes after the plane took off from Chkalovsky.

FSB captain Pyotr Yozhin wasn't wearing a coat as he held the door open to the VAZ-2110. Zabara learned as they drove that Yozhin grew up in Magadan, a port on the Sea of Okhotsk. This explained why Yozhin didn't consider the minus 2° Celsius (28° Fahrenheit) air cold.

Yozhin sped down Highway A-240 at 110 kilometers an hour, traffic permitting. When the Siberian had to slow down, he switched on the blue light on the dash. If that didn't clear the way, a short blast of the siren did.

While they made small talk for most of the trip, Yozhin had two questions of importance. One, did Zabara think that Saliemenov would resist arrest. Zabara didn't know but said they must be prepared.

He suspected Yozhin knew the answer to question two which was implied but not asked, i.e., how did the FSB know Saliemenov was still in his flat? The implication could be that Zabara didn't trust the local FSB office, so he didn't use them to make the arrest. The reality was both.

Once Zabara believed that either Saliemenov or Tzuri or both were involved, he sent a surveillance team from Moscow to Pochep. Yozhin's office wasn't notified.

Zabara rapped on the door to Saliemenov's apartment, holding his Makarov pistol behind his back. Yozhin was on the other side of the door behind what they hoped was a concrete wall. Down the hall, the other four FSB officers were in full battle gear with their assault rifles ready. However, Zabara wanted Saliemenov alive and, preferably, unhurt because he felt they had much to discuss.

Saliemenov opened the door, and Zabara held up his bright red folder with his identity card and gold FSB badge. "Colonel Saliemenov, I am Colonel Mikhail Zabara. May I come in?"

Serik Saliemenov tried to hide the fear coursing through his body as he stepped back. He held a chunk of coarse black bread in his right hand. "Of course."

Resisting arrest by the KGB or its progeny, the FSB, was usually fatal.

Zabara nodded to Yozhin as if to say, wait here and stepped into the apartment that smelled of cabbage, sausage, and rice being steamed. "Sir, I am here to place you under arrest for allowing and profiting from the illegal sale of Igla-S missiles and chemical bombs. Please turn around so I can handcuff you."

Saliemenov waved his hand toward the stove. "Colonel, the steamed cabbage is almost ready. I have enough for your whole team. Can we at least eat and allow me to clean up my flat before you take me away?"

MONDAY, DECEMBER 5TH, 2016, 1:58 P.M. LOCAL TIME, LONDON

When Fatimah returned from lunch, Denise Hildegaard, the receptionist who doubled as her administrative assistant when she was in London, was beaming. "Miss Serraf, there is a surprise for you on your desk delivered by a courier right after you left for lunch."

A large glass vase with 12 long-stem roses sat on her conference table next to a box of chocolate from Galler, one of Belgium's best. Fatimah leaned forward to sniff the flowers and picked up her saif letter opener. This one was plain looking compared to the scimitar shaped Talwar with diamonds and rubies on the hilt of the one she used in Karachi.

The penmanship on the card was exquisite.

Fatimah,

Our mutual friend Katherine believes we have many common interests and should meet. I would like to suggest a lunch or dinner if not tonight or Thursday, or the next time you are in London? Please call me at 44 20 1130 4722 to let me know if you are interested.

Lord Haversham

Since they had dinner several weeks ago, she and Katherine had become friends, and the Englishwoman probably knew more about her than her parents. The last time Fatimah was in London, Katherine asked if she could give her business address to an individual she might like. Fatimah took the question as more than a suggestion.

Lord Haversham, according to Katherine, was a widower, well-connected, extraordinarily wealthy, and helped her set up Smart Chic. What piqued Fatimah's interest was that Katherine believed they shared many common interests.

Since the Industrial Revolution, the firms owned or controlled by the Haversham family were focused on mineral exploration and mining. They owned copper, nickel, platinum, chromium, and aluminum mines that went along with their extensive holdings in coal. The only significant natural resource that the family missed out on was oil.

Research led Fatimah to conclude that the Haversham fortune was around four billion pounds. As much as she tried, the closest she could come with her estimate was plus or minus half a billion. The lack of information was a testament to how well the family protected its wealth.

Her Internet search and the tools Talwar used to vet clients, she learned Lord Haversham was in his early forties, and his wife died from leukemia 11 years earlier. They had two boys in their twenties, and both were working in one of the family companies.

Fatimah looked at her watch, hesitated, then dialed the number.

THE SAME DAY, 11:58 A.M. LOCAL TIME, LOS ANGELES

Bahir Shaloub, an Omani who led the team that survived the trek across the southwestern desert, stopped for a second as he looked at the safe house. The house, with its light gray paint and white trim, looked small from the street, even though the garage would easily hold a large passenger van.

Once inside, the house was larger than anything he'd ever seen growing up in Muscat, Oman. His father managed Oman Air's catering services for the airline's aircraft and others whose flights departed from Muscat International Airport. Bahir started learning English in his first year of school. His father told him that if he wanted to succeed in life, he needed to speak English because few outside the Arab world spoke Arabic.

As an executive with the airline, Shaloub's could take advantage of discounted airfares and hotel rates, and the family went on extended vacations in Greece, Spain, and Switzerland. He was 10 on the family's first trip to Switzerland, and the holiday was exciting and frightening. He felt as if he was transported to another planet.

Instead of the flat, dry land along the Omani coast, Zurich was surrounded by tree-covered mountains. Instead of the sand of the desert, the fields were dark green with shades of brown where they had been recently plowed.

Something was missing in Bahir's life, and he started studying Islam to find answers. The more he delved into the religion's history, the more he became convinced that now was the time to stop the exploitation of the Arab world by the major Western powers.

After 10 weeks of training at a camp inside Pakistan, Bahir was sent to Kandahar, where he distinguished himself in several skirmishes. Because he spoke English well, Bahir was trained by Na'il Miraj on how to fire a shoulder-fired anti-aircraft missile.

As the team leader, Bahir had the master bedroom, and seniority left the junior man sleeping on the couch in the second bedroom. Also, in the master bedroom were the crates for four Igla-S missiles—serial numbers 9K-228-S-004550-VAD-10 through 9K-228-S-004553-VAD-10.

Bahir was standing in the kitchen when his new cell phone rang. "Allo."

The familiar voice on the other name sounded cautious when it asked. "Is everything in order?"

"Yes, you have been very generous." The caller at the other end of the phone took that proper code to mean yes and no threats.

"Excellent. Always keep this phone with you. Do not go anywhere without it." Then there was a dial tone. Bahir recognized the voice of Na'il Miraj.

TUESDAY, DECEMBER 6ᵀᴴ, 2016, 8:38 P.M. LOCAL TIME, LONDON

Several of her clients from Fatimah's days at Citibank in London wanted to meet with her, so she decided to spend the week in London rather than fly back to Karachi. Wanting to meet Lord Haversham again was a major factor in her decision to stay. Fatimah was clicking through e-mails on her iPhone as she walked through the door held open by the doorman. She said good evening and looked up just in time to see the concierge waving at her. He came from out behind his desk and bowed slightly.

"Madam Serraf, a chauffeur came by this afternoon at about four and dropped off three boxes and long stem roses already trimmed and in a vase. I put the roses on your kitchen counter and the boxes on your dining room table. I hope you didn't mind."

She gave a 10-pound note she took from her wallet to the man. "No, that is fine. Thank you." She didn't want to tell him she hadn't ordered anything, but the roses probably meant the packages were from Lord Haversham.

Fatimah sniffed the roses as she walked past them, noticing the three gift-wrapped packages, and plopped her briefcase on her desk. Fatimah put the vase with the flowers on the coffee table before retrieving the card and the boxes she laid out by size in a neat row.

Fatimah sat down and used her toes to pry off her shoes before opening the card in the same find hand as the note asking her to call. Like the first note, this one was written with a fountain pen with a thick point. As she began reading, the words 'very old fashioned and very traditional' ran through her mind.

> *Fatimah,*
>
> *One box has things to enjoy while you are dressing for dinner. The items in the two other boxes are for you to wear to dinner. I will pick you up at 7:30 p.m. Reservations are at Cheneston's at the Milestone Hotel, one of London's oldest hotels. The décor is very Victorian, and the food is five-star.*
>
> *Lord Haversham*

A very Western notion went through her head—Fatimah's mind was that she had nothing to wear. In Saudi Arabia, the choice would have been which colored niqab, chador, or jilbab. In London, her choices were much broader. Fatimah opened the middle-size box first and found herself looking at box of Waller chocolates. She popped one piece into her mouth and savored the orange liqueur inside the creamy Belgian chocolate.

Gently, she pulled off the bow from the largest box and undid the gold-colored wrapping paper. When she lifted the lid, she found a set of black lingerie. The first piece she pulled out was a body stocking that ended with garters, then carefully wrapped in tissue paper that muted the color was a matching bra, panties, and stockings.

Fatimah nodded in approval as she laid them on the coffee table, wondering how he knew my size. Katherine must have told him! Now, at least, I know what goes under my dress.

She looked at the third and smallest box was a long rectangle. Before she unwrapped it, she took a bite of a chocolate truffle filled with a strawberry liqueur. Fatimah held the uneaten half for a few seconds as she enjoyed the taste and then put the remainder in her mouth.

The wrapper on the smallest box came off quickly, and she rested it on her lap before slowly lifting the lid. Inside was a jewelry box in which one carries expensive necklaces home from the jewelry store.

Fatimah pulled out the gold pins at the end, and the lid popped open. Inside were four sterling silver bracelets adorned with diamond chips. Each had a small loop at the opposite end of the clasp. The writing was familiar.

The bracelets are for your wrists and ankles.

She sat back and closed her eyes, enjoying the feeling in her loins. She knew a command when she read one. This will be, if nothing else, a wonderful evening.

At precisely 7:30 p.m. the concierge called and asked if Lord Haversham should come up or wait in the lobby. She asked him to send him up.

Moments later, the door chime went through its five tones. Fatimah spoke softly. "Please come in. The door is unlocked."

She stood at the end of the hallway, silhouetted against the bright light of her living room. *Two can play the seduction game.*

Lord Haversham had longish hair that was starting to gray. He wore an Edwardian double-breasted suit with subdued pinstripes showing through the gray fabric. She recognized the Eaton school tie.

He came forward with his hand out, then stopped abruptly. "Oh my, you are gorgeous. Stunning!!!"

Fatimah nodded slightly. "Thank you." Her shoulder-length hair flew out as he spun around so her date could see the black designer dress with the square cut neck and half sleeves that came down to just above her knees. She was wearing three-inch black heels to match. Her shoes had straps wrapped around her ankles and clasped at the bottom of her calf. The diamond and silver chains around her ankles glistened in the light.

Around her neck, Fatimah wore a diamond and silver choker necklace from which hung a 10-carat oval diamond. Her dark skin provided a subdued but contrasting background to the glitter. The necklace was a present to herself when she became the president and CEO of Talwar.

Fatimah gave Lord Haversham a modest curtsey and held out her arm. "Your lordship, shall we…"

Heads turned when they walked to the table, arm in arm. Already, Fatimah was relaxed and comfortable. Dinner was a blur. At first, there was a fair amount of verbal fencing as she probed on how the Havershams made their initial pile of money mining iron ore. Then, as the industrial revolution went on, the family business—British Minerals—began to find and mine other metals. They were the first firm to find the enormous iron, zinc, and bauxite deposits in Australia, along with precious metals such as gold, platinum, nickel, and silver in South Africa.

Lord Haversham now sat on the board of directors, and his family had positions throughout the companies in which they were the largest shareholders but no longer controlled. As a family, they were amongst the richest in the world.

They'd talked for over an hour when Fatimah realized she hadn't used his first name. "So, what do I call you?"

"In public and in the business world, British society dictates that if one has a title as I do, then I am Lord Haversham. In private moments like this one, my first name is Edward. Before we became the Haversham's, the family name was Marston. Why King George changed the family name, I do not know."

Fatimah giggled. "I like Lord Master Marston …"

Lord Haversham smiled. "Me too…"

The waiter brought two sniffers of Courvoisier 21. He placed one in front of Fatimah and the other in front of Lord Haversham. The cognac stopped their conversation, and he held up his glass. "To many more enjoyable evenings."

Fatimah nodded and sipped the Courvoisier, letting the liquid sit on her tongue. The aroma of pears, raisins, and orange filled her nose. Neither said anything for a few seconds.

Edward tipped the top of his brandy sniffer toward her. "I guess this is where I ask you what you want to do with the rest of the evening."

Fatimah decided to be a bit coy. "I think you already know."

"Wonderful." Lord Haversham reached into his suit pocket. "In that case, I have another present for you." He slid the small box across the table and waited for her to open the box.

"What is this?"

"That is a butterfly. The panties I bought you were designed to keep such toys in place. I suggest you go to the ladies' room, put the butterfly on, and when you come back, you can sample the pleasure the device creates."

Lord Haversham took a small remote control out of his pocket and flipped a switch. Fatimah could feel the box vibrate.

"Then, we'll go to either your flat or my house in Kensington."

Fatimah nodded, and he stood up as she did. On her way back to their table, she felt the soft nub of the butterfly rubbing against her clitoris. When he saw her returning to the table, Lord Haversham turned the butterfly on. Fatimah had to force herself not to react to the surge of pleasure coming from her groin.

Lord Haversham held the chair for her to sit down and gently kissed her on the cheek before whispering. "Slave Fatimah, do not cum. That is an order."

Fatimah nodded sharply. The pleasure from the vibrating device in her vagina was making it hard to speak, but she managed to say, "Yes, Lord Master Marston."

THE SAME DAY, 3:48 P.M. LOCAL TIME, BONHAM

Before they could start, Senior Chief Norquist was required to go through the paperwork drill to verify the two naval reservist's Top Secret/SCI clearances and "read" them "in" to the project. By the time this was completed, it was almost lunchtime. Both officers understood that nothing said while they were at Camelot International could be shared with anyone at any time without specific authorization from the Navy. This restriction would last for 20 years.

Spread out on the table was a high-level diagram of the power grid that delivered electrical power to the New York and Boston metropolitan areas. The two reservists marked main power and sub-stations on an FAA VFR Sectional Chart and TPC charts that showed the powerlines so they would have the geography to go with the diagram.

Zvi came up to Derek, holding a strange-looking phone. He pointed to Derek's office. "A word in private with you, sir."

"Sure, what's up?"

"Tel Aviv would like to talk to you." Derek had learned a long time ago when a member of Mossad referred to the organization's headquarters, they always used Tel Aviv.

Zvi handed Derek a satellite phone and noted the encryption was incompatible with his U.S. government phones. The Israeli closed the door. "My boss wants to talk to you along with someone from the prime minister's office.

Zvi put the phone flat on the desk and pushed a button labeled with the letters 'SPKR.' "Derek Almer is with me. We are the only ones in the room."

A gruff voice with an accent that was either German or Israeli. Derek, if asked, would guess, German. "Commander, thank you for including an Israeli on your team. My government has all a great deal of faith in you and your judgment."

"Thank you…" Saying anything else would cheapen his response. What was just said was also scary.

"Commander, my government is prepared to provide men to help you. Just tell us how many and when and where you need them."

"Sir, I am not sure how that would work. I would be worried if something happened to them."

"They would be Camelot International employees."

"This is a very generous officer. Thank you. I don't know how many men we would need. Right now, planning any direct action is premature and not in the scope of our work." The legal issue of having Israelis in the U.S. shooting at U.S. citizens, or even terrorists, was so far off the chart he could not conceive of a possible scenario where it might be possible.

"There is one more thing."

Ahhhhh, I knew it. The Israelis want to task me with something to do.

"We know one of the men involved in the plot is Dawuud Ghanem, who was spotted in Washington, D.C., a few days ago. We are following him. The other is Ra'b Kassab. We believe he just landed in the United States using a valid Kenyan passport. Kassab is a former member of the U.S. Army who has been fighting in Syria. We think Ghanem is one of Ayman al Zawahiri's top lieutenants."

"Have you passed this on to the CIA?"

"Yes, and your Immigration and Naturalization Service. All we received was a polite thank you after we were told that neither man was on a terror watch list. We even sent the CIA our files on the men."

"Can you send them to me?"

"Yes. They were just sent to Zvi, who will give them to you."

"Thank you."

"A beneficial outcome to all concerned would be if you could take care of these men."

As in kill. "If Kassab and Ghanem are involved and if we are involved in any direct action, then we will do our best."

"Thank you, that is all we can ask. Shalom."

Zvi looked at Derek and opened his laptop. "My guess is that by the time I go through the security protocols and get logged in, the file and photos will be in my inbox."

Derek looked at the young Israeli. "Look, right now, we only have a hypothesis of what al-Qaeda is planning. We think they will use missiles and not drop the power grid or set off bombs in crowded shopping malls. However, I don't want to rule those options out. Our job is to gather and analyze intelligence and attempt to predict what may happen. We don't have permission to act!"

"Neither those in my government who worked with you nor I believe you will sit on the sideline and let an attack happen. So, yes, I believe you and every man in the office, along with others, will do their best to stop an attack."

"Am I that predictable?"

"When you need to protect your friends and your country, yes."

Derek made a face and walked out of the office. At the table, the senior reserve officer, Captain Elliot Grantham, tossed his pencil on the top chart and said to the other officer, "Nine's the magic number."

"Why nine?"

Grantham turned around. "Sorry, Derek...."

"Don't apologize, sir. You think the number nine is important. Why?"

"The U.S. power grid is designed to accommodate downed power lines, damaged power stations that are forced to shut down, and transformer failures. The control stations are on a secure network and are not connected to the internet. There's no physical connectivity, so those working in the control station can see an outage and re-route power as needed to maintain the supply. If an event or a series of events make the grid unstable, the goal is to resolve the outage in less than thirty minutes. A stable grid is known as N-1. Are you with me so far?"

Derek nodded and noted that all the Camelot employees standing around the table did likewise.

"If the control center can't maintain an N-1 condition, then the operators have a series of protocols they follow to maintain the integrity of the grid. As an aviator, you would call them emergency procedures. These procedures include options such as getting power from another source; shutting down power generating stations; switching transmission lines routes; even cutting off power to customers. Once they start this process, they are in an N-2 situation."

Derek looked at the captain, knowing there was more, so he kept quiet.

"So, I asked myself, what would it take to shut down Texas, and by that, I mean, turn out the lights of Dallas, Houston, Austin, San Antonio, and as far west as Amarillo. I picked this area because I know the grid best. The number I came up with was any combination of cutting nine key power lines, shutting down nine power generating stations, and taking nine major substations offline would create an event from which the grid couldn't recover. The problem is you must have inside knowledge to know which nine to take out. Even then, unless it happened simultaneously or within minutes, the watch standers in the ERCOT command center could react and prevent a total failure."

Grantham took a deep breath. "I then called a friend of mine at New England Light and Power and ran my theory by him, and he said the number they use is six to seven, depending on which power-generating plant goes offline. He put me in touch with the guy who manages Southern California Power's grid, and he said their magic number varies from four power stations to nine depending on whether the outages include sub-stations and power lines and which ones they are. I also talked to the guys at Exelon in Chicago and received the same answer."

Grantham looked at all the men around the table. All were paying rapt attention. "Here's the bottom line. Depending on the combination of what goes offline and when in an area, by the time you get to nine, the grid is hard down, and it will take a long time to get the electrical power supply back to normal."

"OK, Captain Grantham, here's the sixty-four-thousand-dollar question... Do the bad guys know this?"

The reserve captain took a deep breath. "Short answer is I don't know. To make the calculation, they'd have to have someone on the inside who has detailed knowledge of the grid, and that person would have to have the training to conduct the analysis or gather the data to give to someone who did."

Derek wasn't about to give up. "If you were a betting man, what are the odds that al-Qaeda has such a person?"

"Sir, I'm not a spook." Grantham looked at Jefferson, who was black and flushed. "Sorry. Old terms die hard."

"No offense taken, Captain. I always use it when I refer to our intelligence folks."

"Derek, my bet is they don't have the data, and they are guessing because you need an engineer who is well-versed in power transmission networks and has detailed knowledge of the network you trying to destroy along with a very sophisticated computer program to run the analysis that is only viable with accurate data. I guess they think they can drop a few power lines, blow up a power station or two and drop the grid. If so, there may be short-term outages, but nothing catastrophic. However, I wouldn't underestimate al-Qaeda."

"Give me a percentage?"

"I'll be safe and go with the eighty/twenty rule. By that, I mean that there's less than a twenty percent chance they've done the analysis."

"Captain, if you looked at the New York/New England and LA power grids, could you pick likely targets?"

"I couldn't, but I know who could. Do you want me to make the calls?"

"Well, Captain Grantham. Both you and Commander Barstow have a new task. I need a list of likely targets. I'm sure your counterparts in other utilities have played with similar scenarios. Use the 2013 attack on the Metcalf Power Plant in California as a model if you want. I want the list by Friday, if possible, Sunday night at the latest. We assume the attack will occur over the holidays, just in time to ruin everyone's Christmas and Hanukkah."

Derek walked away from the desk, and Zvi stood off with his back against the wall, smiling. His laptop was cradled in his arm. "Derek, this is a picture of Ra'b Kassab taken a few weeks ago when he visited Hezbollah's offices in Damascus. We have more photos of Kassab now that he is in the U.S., and they're coming."

What struck Derek about the man was not his face but his eyes. Even in the photo, he could tell they had a hardness behind them.

"Why doesn't Mossad just take him out?"

Zvi just gave Derek the "that was a dumb question look."

"OK, Mossad doesn't want to risk killing an American citizen in the U.S. even though he is a suspected terrorist. What else do you have?"

"And this photo was taken a few days ago in a restaurant in Georgetown. "Ghanem is having dinner with a friend. We don't know who he is."

Derek looked at the photo. "Holy shit." The words came out of his mouth. "That's Adnan Maalouf from the National Counterterrorism Center. We may have a fucking traitor in our midst."

CHAPTER 17

ALARM BELLS

WEDNESDAY, DECEMBER 7ᵀᴴ, 2016, 6:16 P.M. LOCAL TIME, POCHEP

Streetlights four floors below cast a dull, yellow glow on the ceiling of Gregori Tzuri's flat, which was pitch black at this time a day. The streetlights usual glow was dimmed by the heavy snow. Before Tzuri turned the lights on, he picked up the two bags of groceries he'd placed outside the door and put them on the small table. Next, he hung his uniform cap on a hook, shrugged it off, and shook his heavy woolen overcoat to remove snow that hadn't melted.

Now that he was home, he unbuttoned his collar and loosened his tie. He was about to turn on the lights when something made him hesitate. Burglaries were uncommon in Pochep, and if anyone was in his flat, he would assume they were from the FSB.

At first, the message left at his office was that Saliemenov had been called to Moscow on an urgent matter. There was no other info, a phone number, or where Saliemenov was staying. Tzuri knew the way the Red Army worked and assumed Saliemenov was arrested. This suggested he was next in the queue, so to speak, and it was only a matter of time before the FSB came looking for him. He wondered where the note he wrote wound up. Thankfully, he kept two copies. One in his office and the other in his flat.

In Russia or, before, in the Soviet Union, in situations such as this, it wasn't a matter of if one was guilty. What mattered was how many people the government wanted to punish. The notation in his FSB files that his parents emigrated to Israel would automatically make him a suspect. He was surprised that the FSB didn't arrest him at the same time they took Saliemenov.

Sensing the presence of someone else in his flat, Gregori hesitated before he reached for the switch as a friendly voice came from the darkness. "I was wondering when you would get home from work."

The light went on, revealing the man he knew as Sol. Since Gregori spent the night at Sol's apartment in Moscow, neither risked talking on the telephone, much less sending a letter.

"What are you doing here?"

"I've come to get you out of Russia."

"How?"

"My secret."

"What about my wife Elana? She is still in Kiev." When he took this assignment, he had the option of bringing his wife and living in Pochep for two years or accepting a one-year assignment, and she could stay in Kiev with his two boys. To both parents, the one-year deal was a no-brainer.

"She is already in Israel. We got her out a month ago."

"Elana has been sending me letters postmarked from Kiev.

"The letters were written by her, and we had them mailed in Kiev."

"How do I know this is not some kind of FSB ruse."

"You have to trust me. Or, if you want, you can wait for the FSB. They just picked up Maxim Novokov. Saliemenov may throw you under the bus to save his own skin. Remember, you signed the shipping documents when the missiles were picked up."

"When do we leave?"

Sol looked at his watch. "You have fifteen minutes to change clothes and pack a small bag so we can make the next express train to Moscow. We'll get there early in the morning, take the metro to a station a short walk from the Israeli embassy where you are expected. There, you'll clean up and be given an Israeli passport. Later in the day, you'll board the El Al flight to Tel Aviv where your parents and wife will meet you at Ben Gurion Airport. On the way to Israel, you'll be one of many former Russians who came to visit relatives in Mother Russia..... Do you have an iron?"

"I do. Why?"

"Heat it up. I will take a picture of you. Within seconds, you will have the necessary travel documents to go to Moscow."

Tzuri's flat only had two rooms, three if one counted the bathroom. They were sitting in a 10-meter square space with an alcove with a sink, stove, and refrigerator. Gregori lit a match and then turned on the gas. The burner lit with a soft whump. Gregori took an old-fashioned iron and a base plate from a shelf on the other side of the alcove that provided storage for pots, pans, food, and dishes. Both items went on the burner. Satisfied they were in the proper position; Tzuri rotated the knob so the burner was at its maximum.

Gregori turned to Sol, who was still sitting. "The iron will take a few minutes to heat up. I'll go pack."

"Good."

"How often do you do this?"

"All the time." Sol didn't want to say that this was the first time he'd helped a Russian lieutenant colonel escape from the clutches of the FSB.

"Am I under surveillance?"

"Not that I could tell. I wouldn't have waited in your flat for you if you were. Go, you're wasting time!"

THE SAME DAY, 6:30 P.M. LOCAL TIME, WASHINGTON, D.C.

Sunday was not a normal workday, but the call from Grady Gibson came as Andrei Kovalenko and his wife were headed out for dinner and a movie. To Special Agent Andrei Kovalenko, if the man on the phone was not God speaking, Gibson was damned close.

Gibson thought what he was asking might only take an hour or two of Kovalenko's time and to call him from the bureau's headquarters when he finished. Specific instructions sent via the bureau's secure internal email system would await him at his desk.

Kovalenko, the son of Russian immigrants from Rostov-on-Don, loved serving his adopted homeland. He still vividly remembers arriving wide-eyed in 1993, seeing the Statue of Liberty and the New York skyline silhouetted against a bright blue sky.

His father—Asher Kovalenko—a captain in the Soviet and now Russian Merchant Marine known as Morflot began applying to Western shipping companies but none would offer him a job. He believed the rejections were because they feared he would spy on their operation. By chance, in Norfolk in early 1992, right after the Soviet Union collapsed and became the Russian Federation, Asher met a captain of a container ship operated by Zim. Over dinner, he told the captain that he'd been trying to find a job with a Western shipping company that wasn't owned by the Chinese. And he and his family wanted to emigrate to the West, preferably the United States. When he learned that Zim was an Israeli-owned company, Asher Kovalenko casually mentioned his KGB file contained the notation he was "of Jewish origin."

The Israeli captain, whose family left Germany in 1933, just after Hitler came to power, knew what that meant and smiled, saying those words will make things easier if Asher Kovalenko could prove his claim because he would be entitled to emigrate to Israel under the law of return. Kovalenko had both his out-of-date Soviet and his newer Russian internal identity books as well as his passport with him. Both had the notation "of Jewish Origin."

That led to a series of interviews the next day at Zim's Norfolk office that Kovalenko thought were promising. His ship was headed back to Rostov with oil field equipment and when it arrived, it would be sent out when to who knows where. Asher Kovalenko was told that Zim's agent in Rostov would contact him when he arrived.

In June 1993, eight months after his first conversation, Asher, his wife Rita, along with eight-year-old Andrei arrived at JFK, their Israeli passports and immigration documents allowing the Kovalenkos to live in Norfolk. Asher had just finished training as an engineering officer for Zim.

Every day in America brought new and exciting things to Andrei. He played soccer (a.k.a. football) in Rostov and became a starter on a local club team. His halting English quickly became fluent. At home, his mother Rita struggled with English, and Andrei would go shopping with her so he could, if needed, translate.

At home, Asher kept telling Andrei, "In America, anything and everything is possible." His soccer skills and finishing number three in his high school class of 550 helped him win a full scholarship at the University of Virginia. He was thinking about joining the American Navy when he met the recruiter for the FBI visiting the school.

In 2008, he graduated number one in his class at the FBI Academy and asked to be assigned to counterterrorism. In his second year, he took a lead everyone thought was a waste of time and turned it into an arrest of two Chechen terrorists about to attack Russian embassy officials living near Coney Island in New York. While he had sympathy for the Chechen cause, he did not approve of their methods nor the heavy-handed tactics used by the FSB and the Russian government against to suppress their rebellion.

At his desk, Andrei opened the email from Gibson marked Top Secret/SCI. Besides the instructions, four pictures of three men at the table were attached. The note instructed him to dive deeply into the background checks and travel history of Adnan Maalouf, an intelligence analyst at the National Counterterrorism Center. The email had Maalouf's Social Security and passport numbers, address, home, government-issued, and personal mobile phone numbers.

The first thing Kovalenko checked were Maalouf's travel plans reported to his employer. Immigration records showed he left the country about a year ago for two weeks. The entry was associated with a flight from London and his U.S. passport. This was his third London visit in five years.

Curious, he opened Maalouf's personnel file looking for a trip report. Anyone with Maalouf's clearance level and position in the intelligence community, he needed permission to go abroad. Depending on where they went, they were required to check in with a designated official at the closest embassy or consulate.

Since Maalouf's was born in Lebanon, he checked the manifests for flights from London to Beirut. Six airlines—British Airways and Middle Eastern Airlines—had non-stop flights. Lufthansa, Alitalia, Turkish, and Air France had ones that connected through their main hubs.

Maalouf had flown to London on American Airlines so Andrei checked to see if he had a codeshare ticket on British Airways. Nothing. He then searched for a British Airways ticket, and again nothing.

Andrei called the FBI liaison at the U.K. Immigration Service. After a short explanation, the woman on the other end asked him to hold on. A minute later, she came back on and said an Adnan Maalouf has, over the past eight years, boarded flights to Beirut. The first two had different passport numbers and expiration dates. Maalouf used a valid Lebanese passport for the last two tickets that expired in 2019. She also had the information on the return flights and volunteered to send him the files. Seconds later, they appeared in his inbox.

Kovalenko made several notes in the Word document he started to document Maalouf's unreported travels. He looked at the three pictures, and in two, Adnan Maalouf was sitting at a table with Ghanem Dawuud on two occasions. In the third had Maalouf, Dawuud were with a man identified as Ra'b Kassab.

Encouraged that he was on a roll, Kovalenko entered the name Ra'b Kassab into the FBI database. The machine asked for his access number and posted a warning that he was about to enter a Top Secret Specially Compartmented data base.

After entering his access number, he clicked submit, and a progress bar slowly marched across the screen. The dropdown box said the search would take about 10 minutes.

He went to get a soda, and when he came back, the screen saver with the logo of the FBI was on, so he pressed the return key. The computer asked him to enter his username and password, and he was rewarded with several photos of Ra'b Kassab and a summary of his life.

Date of Birth—(U) January 28th, 1976
Birthplace—(U) Port Sudan, Sudan
Status—(U) refugee, naturalized citizen
　　June 15th, 1988
Last known U.S. address—(U) 2106 Vassar Drive,
　　Irving, TX 75062
Father—(U) Okot Kassab
　　(U) Occupation—Pharmacist
　　(U) Status—refugee, naturalized citizen
　　June 15th, 1988

Mother—(U) Talia Kassab
(U) Occupation—administrative assistant
(U) Status—refugee, naturalized citizen
June 15th, 1988
Parent's address—(U) 2106 Vassar Drive,
Irving, TX 75062
Passport—Current U.S. passport, expiration date
12/08/22. Number 1519862. Revoked on 7/1/96.
Military—(S) enlisted May 30th, 1984, Honorable
Discharge, June 30th, 1988. Served in 10th
Mountain Division, MOS 89D (Explosive Ordnance
Disposal Specialist). For complete service record,
contact the National Military Personnel Center
Notes: (TS/SCI) Suspected of having joined al-Qaeda.
No known location. Name has been linked to the
following terrorist attacks:
(TS/SCI Code Word Vixen Orange) 4/8/94—Arfur Bus
attack in Israel. Suspected of helping Palestinians build
the bomb. Immigration records show he used his U.S.
passport to enter Israel 3/26/94 and left on 4/9/94.
Entry allowed because he was not on a watch list.
Source—Mossad.
(TS/SCI Code Word Vixen Orange) 8/18/94—
AMIA bombing in Argentina. Suspected of helping
build the bomb. Immigration records show he used
his U.S. passport to enter Argentina on 8/1/94
and left on 8/19/94. Entry allowed because he was
not on a known watch list. Source—Gendarmerie
Nacional Argentina.
(TS/SCI Code Word Vixen Orange) 6/25/96—Khobar
Towers. Now suspected of helping build the bomb
that destroyed the building. Immigration records
showed he used his U.S. passport to enter Saudi
Arabia as a potential employee of Aramco on 6/1/96
and departed on 6/27/96. Aramco has no records

of a job application, interview or offer. Warrant issued as person of interest and wanted by Saudis. Warrant canceled in November 1999. Source—Saudi Ri'āsat Al-Istikhbārāt Al-'Āmah, Mabahith/General Investigation Directorate.

(SECRET NOFORN) 6/30/96—At request of the Saudi and Israeli governments, Kassab's U.S. passport revoked as of 7/1/96. Added to terrorist watch list. Interpol note issued requesting countries to detain for questioning by either Israeli or U.S. law enforcement agencies. Source—U.S. State Department.

(TS/SCI Code Word Vixen Orange) 6/1/05—Kassab is believed to be living in Afghanistan and helping al-Qaeda fight U.S. forces. Intercepts suggest he helped create/perfect detonation methods of what are now known as IEDs. Source—DIA, NSA.

(TS/SCI Code Word Vixen Orange) 3/28/04—seen in Madrid on several surveillance tapes at the time of the bombings. Wanted by Spanish police. No records of legal entry or exit from Spain. Source—Cuerpo Nacional de Policía.

(TS/SCI Code Word Vixen Orange) 5/6/06—Surreptitiously taped by a student while conducting a bomb building class in Kandahar, Afghanistan. Student was later beheaded after al-Qaeda discovered the video was passed to U.S. forces and is now in CIA and Army EOD archives. Source—DIA.

(TS/SCI Code Word Vixen Orange) 8/8/08—Kassab was photographed in two locations. One in the Bekaa Valley at a Hezbollah training camp teaching bomb-making. Second sighting was at a meeting of al-Qaeda and Hezbollah leaders in Damascus. Source—Mossad.

Action—Detain upon entry for questioning for possible extradition.

When he finished reading, Andrei sat back in his chair thinking the last data entry was almost nine years ago. *So Kassab, where have you been between June 2008 and December 2016?*

There was still one unknown person in the photos. Andrei copied the photo and then cropped the unknown person's face he dubbed Stranger #1 and entered the image into his computer and went through the screens answering whatever questions he could before he pushed search. The machine whirred, and then the progress bar showed an estimated wait time of 15 minutes.

While he waited for the computer to answer, Andrei entered Dawuud Ghanem's name into the terrorist database and paged down through two screens to read the long list of operations like Kassab's, but with noticeable differences. He was stunned to learn that Ghanem still had a valid Green Card that had not been revoked, had been educated in the U.S., and was already on the terrorist watch list. *How the hell did he get into the U.S.?*

Ghanem's file was longer than Kassab's. He joined al-Qaeda and was linked to Hezbollah. Andrei cross-checked the information in the file with that of Maalouf. He found they attended the American University in Lebanon at the same time. *I'd bet money that the two men knew each other.*

Andrei's laptop beeped, and when he changed screens, the computer said the facial recognition software had found a match and asked did he want the file? *Of course, he did!* He entered his secure FBI address and pressed send.

His laptop beeped, and when he opened the email file, Andrei found himself staring at the face of Na'il Miraj. A link took him to Miraj's file in the terrorist database, where he found another link to the National Military Personnel Archives. There, he learned that Miraj made two one-year deployments to Afghanistan as an infantryman (MOS 11B) before qualifying as a MOS 14S and 94T. MOS 14S was given to qualified Stinger missile crew members, and 94T meant he was a qualified missile maintenance technician for Hellfire and Stinger.

Miraj/Mirage's file showed that he left the Army with an Honorable Discharge in 2004. A note at the end said Mirage was suspected to be in the mountains of Pakistan, just east of the Afghan/Pakistani border, helping al-Qaeda refurbish Stinger and other surface-to-air missiles left over from the Soviet-Afghan War. As a result, his passport was revoked, and he was put on a watch list.

Kovalenko clicked on a link to known associates and found himself looking at Ayman al-Zawahiri. The words "Holy Fuck" came out of his mouth. He was tempted to call Assistant Director Gibson but decided to check one more thing—Maalouf's job description—and his background investigation. *Maalouf, associating with Dawuud, Ghanem, and Miraj makes your actions suspicious, if not traitorous. You too, came to America where the streets are paved with gold. And now, you stupid idiot, you've fucked up.*

Kovalenko dialed the cell phone number of the assistant director of the FBI. Gibson, seeing the letters on the caller ID said, "Andrei, what did you find?"

"Sir, since this is not a secure line, let's just say the person of interest keeps very interesting company. You need to see what I found. The sooner, the better."

Gibson said, "I'll be there in fifteen minutes" followed by a dial tone.

The son of a Russian immigrant thought, at least, he'll have time to get his research organized.

THURSDAY, DECEMBER 8TH, 2016, 9:46 A.M. LOCAL TIME, FARMERS BRANCH, TX

Janey Humphries stared at her phone, thinking what a strange call that was. The man at the other end of the call was the one who signed the lease to rent one of her houses for four months. Since the three-bedroom, two-bath, 1,800 square-foot house was empty at the time and Janey didn't have any prospects for it, some rent was better than no rent. The lessor agreed to a 25% premium, and she continued advertising the home north of Valley View Lane and east of I-35E.

After looking at the house, the man gave her the needed information, including a Social Security Number. His credit score was close to 700, and experience told Janey that home renters with scores over 680 were less likely to trash a house. He sent her a personal check for the first month and a security deposit of another month's rent, so she left the keys under the front door mat the night before he said he would move in.

What puzzled her was that he said she could keep his security deposit. Usually, when a tenant notified her that he or she was moving out, Janey would walk through the empty house to determine if she needed to use some or all of it to make repairs.

Curious, she drove to the house and opened the front door. She was entitled to inspect the home at any time as per the lease. As she walked through each room, she was convinced no one had been inside. The lines in the carpet from the professional cleaning service were still there, and the toilets hadn't been flushed for weeks.

The last place she checked was the garage, where most renters leave their trash. Janey saw a tarpaulin-covered, chest high stack on one side. Curious, she pulled the tarp back, and what she saw took her breath away.

Not knowing who to call, Janey dialed 911. Once the operator determined that Janey was not in danger and had police cars on the way, she connected Janey to the Dallas office of the Bureau of Alcohol, Tobacco, and Firearms. The agent listened to her patiently describe in detail the four AK-47s and four Glock pistols on top of another tarp.

When the agent on duty asked the 53-year-old Humphries if she was sure they were AKs, she tersely answered, "I've been in enough gun stores in my life to know an AK-47 from an M16. Plus, I go duck hunting every year with my husband, who was before he retired after twenty-seven years, the Command Master Sergeant of the 75th Ranger Regiment. Just so you know, I use a Remington Auto 5 that was my grandfather's that he gave the shotgun to me as a birthday present. The shotgun was made in 1908 and should be in a museum, but I love shooting the old gun. I also have a concealed carry permit. Before buying my Smith and Wesson MP-9 Compact, I tested a bunch of pistols. One of them was the Glock 19. So, yes, Officer Barden, I know what an AK-47 is."

Chastised, Agent Barden apologized. He forgot he was in Texas, not downtown Chicago where strict gun laws kept honest citizens from owning firearms. Gangs used stolen handguns and rifles to give the city one of the highest murder rates in the country.

Barden had been with the Bureau of Alcohol, Tobacco, and Firearms for 10 years and had just transferred to Texas from Chicago because his wife was a native Texan who grew up in Richardson and didn't like Chicago winters.

Agent Jeffrey Barden and his partner Sam Schiller, III pulled their black Ford Crown Victoria into the driveway of Humphries' rental property. Already, there were four squad cars and eight police officers guarding the house.

The agents looked for signs that there might be a bomb. Finding nothing suspicious, the agents took pictures of the pile from all four sides and corners. Before they took the next step, Barden turned to Janie. "Mrs. Humphries, have you touched these weapons?"

"No. As soon as I saw them, I called 911."

"Good. Would you come down to our offices to provide a statement?"

"Sure. Just let me know when."

"Can you describe the man who rented this house?"

"I can, and when I come to your office, I'll bring copies of his check, credit report, and his signed lease. I even have a photo."

"That is fantastic." Experience told Barden that the bank account was probably closed by now, and the addresses on the credit application were probably fakes. The credit report might be an interesting avenue to follow along with the photo. If they are lucky, they may get a fingerprint or two.

Then, Barden and Schiller checked the AK-47s and the Glocks to make sure they were not loaded before they were set in a neat row at the back of the garage. With a nod, Barden pointed to one of the two top boxes. Schiller slowly unlatched the top and lifted it off.

"This is going to ruin the day for many people…." The words just popped out of Barden's mouth. He pointed to the Cyrillic on the four long cases underneath four smaller ones.

After, Barden called his boss in Dallas, who told him to babysit the weapons until he got back to him. Barden suspected his boss called D.C., where he was referred to the Bureau of Alcohol, Tobacco and Firearms agent assigned to the National Counterterrorism Center. Eventually, someone would call him. Until then, he had to wait.

Meanwhile, an armored panel van arrived to transport the weapons to the BATF gun vault in Dallas. Before they were taken away, Agent Barden took pictures of the crates, specifically the serial numbers, and popped them all open. His hand-written inventory on his notepad said they found four AK-47s and 4,000 rounds of ammunition already loaded into magazines; two RPG-7 launchers and eight rockets; and two brand new, right from the factory, SA-24s serial numbers 9K-338-S-004548-VAD-10 and 9K-228-S-004549-VAD-10.

THE SAME DAY, 8:09 P.M. LOCAL TIME, KARACHI

When Fatimah arrived back at her apartment just after eight p.m., the concierge came out from behind his desk to greet her. "Miss Serraf, I have three packages for you. They were delivered by an Englishman. Do you wish for me to bring them to your flat, or do you want to carry them up?"

"How big are they?"

"Let me show you?"

The concierge walked briskly back to his desk, and Fatimah followed at her own pace. Her heels clicked loudly on the marble floor.

He put the gift-wrapped boxes on the counter and handed her a card with a familiar script. "Please bring them to my flat."

The trip up the elevator gave Fatimah time to fish out a 500 Pakistani rupee note. She started to take off the light gray hijab that complimented her dark gray pantsuit with subtle pinstripes. She then stopped, deciding to wait until the concierge delivered the packages.

A discrete knock at the door suggested that the concierge had arrived, and Fatimah could see him through the peephole. Opening the door, she pointed to the coffee table in the living room. On his way out, she pressed the banknote in his hand.

Boxes from Lord Haversham required a glass of wine in celebration. Fatimah went to her refrigerator and uncorked a half-finished bottle of Pouilly Fuissé she started the night before.

Fatimah,

As promised, I have sent you some things to wear. From this time on, you are required to wear the body harness at all times. In the evening and in the privacy of your flat, I expect you to wear the cuffs on your ankles and wrists and connect them with the provided chains along with the collar. In my next package, you will receive several jeweled leather collars that I expect you to wear during the day either under an abaya, chador, or niqab or out in the open, your choice.

And, last, there is a chastity belt. It, too, is to be worn except when you bathe.

Enjoy. And I expect to see you on your next trip to London to continue your training.

Lord Master Marston

THE SAME DAY, 11:42 A.M. LOCAL TIME, BONHAM

The bombshell Richard Barstow dropped on the table on Sunday afternoon kept rattling through Derek's mind. Barstow said that if you really wanted to create a big bang and screw up the U.S. energy business, blow up one of the U.S.' liquefied natural gas (LNG) processing plants. Putting an RPG into one of the tanks would set off a series of explosions that would devastate the area around the plant for miles.

Barstow suggested that if he were a terrorist, he'd run a boat up the Arthur Kill River between Staten Island, N.Y., and Perth Amboy, N.J. firing RPGs as they went. Both sides of the river were lined with natural gas, crude oil, and gasoline tank farms. Barstow opined that even if the terrorists didn't hit an LNG tank and the refiners turned off the natural gas, the tank farms would burn for days and put a crimp in the Northeast's gas and oil supplies.

Derek was looking at a Google Maps image of the Arthur Kill River when Buckholz stuck his head in the door to his office. "Sir, There's an FBI agent on the phone for you for you."

He gave the 23-year-old enlisted man a quizzical look and picked up the secure telephone. "Derek Almer."

"Commander, my name is Andrei Kovalenko. I am a special agent with the FBI and Mr. Grady Gibson, the FBI's Assistant Director for Counterterrorism and Espionage, told me to call you. Do you have a few minutes to talk?"

"Good morning, I do. Do we need to go secure?"

"Yes, sir. I'll initiate."

Derek waited for the phones to get their secure algorithms in sync. On his phone, the letters TS/SCI showed on the LED display. He assumed that Kovalenko saw the same letters.

"My boss wants me to meet with you as fast as we can set it up. Based on the photographs you gave him and what we uncovered, we've begun an investigation into Adnan Maalouf, who may be a traitor. I understand you have a theory about what al-Qaeda is planning."

"I do. I think it will occur sometime around December twenty-third."

"That is what my director said. I spoke with Mr. Sanderson earlier, and he provided your clearance information. Can you be at FBI headquarters around 0800 tomorrow?"

"I can. I will bring four people with me. One of whom is Mossad. Is that OK?"

"Does he have a clearance?"

"I'll send the authorization that gives him access."

"Excellent."

Derek hung-up and walked into the main area. "Everybody listen-up. Sobrano, Jefferson, Buckholz, and Rosenthal, we have a meeting with Grady Gibson, the FBI's Assistant Director for Counterterrorism and Espionage, tomorrow at 0800. He wants to hear in detail what we know. We need to get our shit together and bring a suit and tie. If you don't have one, I can loan you one. Senior Chief, you, Pillar, and Neimayer need to stay here and mind the fort. Wheels up in my Aerostar at 1700 tonight. Sobrano, you and Jefferson start pulling together the briefing. I want to go over the outline in thirty minutes."

Because his laptop had gone to sleep, Derek keyed in his password. The top e-mail was from Don.

> Derek,
>
> They just found two SA-24s in Dallas so incorporate them as an option to Stingers. I will provide more details as I get them. Gibson is a professional FBI agent, not a political appointee. Breakfast in the concierge lounge at the JW Marriott in DC tomorrow at 0630? The hotel is short walk from the FBI HQ. How many rooms do you need?
>
> Don

FRIDAY, DECEMBER 9TH, 2016, 8:07 A.M. LOCAL TIME, WASHINGTON D.C.

The five men from Camelot International were led by Special Agent Kovalenko to a secure conference room two floors below the street. It was just like the ones in the Pentagon—concrete walls, no pictures, a government-issued table with gray government-issued chairs. Overhead, fluorescent lights provided plenty of light. At a small table in the back, there was a coffee pot and Styrofoam cups, creamer, and sugar.

Assistant Director Gibson arrived with another man, William Wiggins, a prosecutor with the attorney general's office. Derek looked at Gibson, who anticipated his question. "Bill Wiggins specializes on counterespionage and terrorist cases and has all the necessary clearances. He's worked for the Justice Department for ten years."

Derek nodded. "Thank you."

Gibson stood at the end of the table. "Before we begin, I will remind you of the obvious. Right now, only the employees of Camelot International, Don Sanderson, Bill Wiggins, Andrei Kovalenko, a judge on the FISA court, and I know there is an active investigation of Adnan Maalouf. Until further notice, this must stay that way. Mr.

Almer, before you add to this circle, please check with me. For the record, everything we cover is TS/SCI Code Word Excalibur Sword for the investigation into Maalouf's potential treason."

Derek and the others from Camelot all nodded and acknowledged Gibson by saying. "Yes, sir."

"Good. The purpose of this meeting is two-fold. One, better understand what you think al-Qaeda is planning and for us to share what we know."

The director looked down at his legal pad. "The second is for us to start figuring out how to stop al-Qaeda. Failure is not an option. I realize that some American citizens may die, but I want to keep the body count of the good guys as close to zero as possible. So, part of my desire to meet with you today is to identify potential targets and determine what resources we need. Several people I trust believe that Camelot International's missile scenario is the most likely."

Gibson nodded in the direction of Andrei Kovalenko. "Andrei, why don't you share what you know about Maalouf, Kassab, and Miraj. Derek, then you're on. I have nothing on my calendar until noon. If this goes on longer, those calls and meetings will get canceled. This is, until we run these bastards down, my number one priority."

The Q&A on Maalouf, Kassab, and Miraj had died out when an agent knocked on the door and provided a detailed summary of the weapons captured in Mrs. Humphries' rental house. The FBI ran the photo she took through its facial recognition program and came up empty-handed. Gibson suggested a break so Zvi could be escorted to where he could connect to the Internet and send the photo to Mossad so it could be run through the Israeli databases.

When they restarted, Derek explained how Camelot International came into existence. Neither Gibson nor Wiggins had any questions, so he shifted gears, and he stated that if he were al Zawahiri, he would want to accomplish two goals. One, attack symbols of American strength to send a message to the world that the U.S. is weak and can be attacked successfully.

Two, disrupt the American economy and kill as many Americans as possible.

Given those two goals, Derek explained why he eliminated chemical and biological weapons, i.e., they are hard to build, deploy, and may or may not work. Both men were familiar with al-Qaeda's failed attempt to attack the Texas-Oklahoma football game using a Piper Pawnee ag airplane to spray the crowd with Sarin gas.

Dirty bombs are hard to create, fuse and deploy and are often lethal to their creators. Unless heavily shielded by lead, they are easy to detect because they leak radiation. Derek concluded by saying they are sexy to talk about and create fear in the minds of the uninformed but may not accomplish either of al-Qaeda's objectives.

Derek stopped for a few seconds so Gibson, Kovalenko, or Wiggins could ask questions. They had none.

"Everything we analyzed was viewed through the lens which is what will al-Qaeda do to achieve their two goals. We kept returning to three—the power grid, air transportation, and oil and gas storage facilities. Liquefied natural gas—with one exception—was ruled out because the large facilities in the U.S. are in remote locations, so even if they explode, the number of people killed may be in the hundreds, not the thousands or tens of thousands. The al-Qaeda benchmark, we believe, is 2,996, i.e., the number who died on 9/11."

Derek tapped the forward key on his laptop. Up popped a map of the United States on the 80-inch monitor mounted on the wall at the end of the table.

"The blue stars are the eight airports we think are the most likely targets because they have the most international flights using the largest airplanes, i.e., 747s, 777s, Airbus 340s, and 380s. The 777 is the smallest of these airplanes, carrying about two hundred and fifteen passengers and ten to twelve crewmembers. The rest can carry over three hundred passengers, plus the cabin and flight deck crew. The range domes, by that I mean the height and distance the Stinger or Igla-S can fly, limit the launch locations which require line of sight to the airplane taking off or landing. The starred airports are Los Angeles, JFK, Logan, DFW, Dulles, Atlanta, Chicago O'Hare, and San Francisco. Denver and Seattle were ruled out because they had less than a quarter of the international flights compared to the others. Just for the record, if al-Qaeda shoots down ten airplanes with an average of two hundred and seventy-five people on board, that's twenty-seven and fifty hundred victims. Add in another couple of hundred on the ground, and you're close to the number of those who died on 9/11."

Derek paused and took a breath. "If the terrorists are smart, they will shoot at airplanes taking off because they are full of fuel and climbing slowly. Shooting the missiles within seconds of each other minimizes their exposure. Based on what we heard today, Dallas may be off the list because replacing the missiles we captured may be hard, if not impossible, for al-Qaeda. We also believe they'll view the loss as a cost of doing business."

Before Derek pushed the forward button again, he looked around the room. "I don't mean to be optimistic, but we think they'll only get one, maybe two missile shots off at each location which puts only one or two airplanes at risk. Pilots on the runway may see the missile trails and abort if the tower doesn't suspend takeoffs."

The next map showed the United States, and there were five stars, two in Arizona and three in the Northeast, one in Vermont, one in New York and one in Connecticut. "if al-Qaeda goes after the power grid, we think New York City and Los Angeles would be the primary targets. D.C. is a distant third. New York because it is the center of the world's financial industry, and if you shut down the banks and exchanges, you create a typhoon that affects other financial markets. L.A. because it is a cultural icon and home to the movie industry that the fundamentalists hate. We think D.C. could be a target but could be collateral damage if they shut down the New York power grid. Again, if the U.S. government shuts down, the world isn't affected as much as if Wall Street was down for several months. Sorry, I know Federal employees think they are the center of the universe. Still, in this scenario, they take second fiddle."

There were soft chuckles as heads nodded. Derek then described what he called the "rule of nine" as he pointed out how combinations of shutting down power stations and sub-stations and dropping power lines could end electrical delivery to New York and Los Angeles.

He said that IS2 Buckholz would cover why they thought that the electricity generating plants were probably too hard for al-Qaeda to attack and that they would concentrate on the lightly protected power stations and power lines. When Buckholz finished, there was silence in the room.

Gibson ended the quiet. "We'll need several thousand men to protect all those substations and the power lines. That means we'd have to call out the National Guard. The president would never go for that."

Derek put his hand up. "No sir, I don't think that is necessary. We don't have to cover every line. We need to protect only those critical to stopping the "rule of nine" from happening. We need only to protect a few power stations in the Northeast and Arizona. The power lines can go down and, as long as the utilities maintain the integrity of the grid, they'll be able to deliver electricity."

"Says who, Derek?"

"The two guys who design power grids for a living who we called in. Both are naval reservists and had the necessary clearances, so we read them in. They don't know about Maalouf, Kassab, and Miraj."

"Are they available to help?"

"All we have to do is issue the recall orders. They know they might be coming."

Gibson turned to Don. "Recall them." Then, he turned to Derek, "So what's the plan to keep the "rule of nine" from happening and minimize the number of airplanes shot down?"

"Sir, I thought you would never ask. It is a mix of deterrence and surveillance. Then, if needed, direct action. Jacob, you're on."

THE SAME DAY, 2:56 P.M. LOCAL TIME, LIBERTY CROSSING

Adnan swore in frustration. All day long, his computer was slow. Processing that usually took fractions of seconds now took 10 - 15 seconds. Downloading files and sending emails with attachments took even longer. He took a deep breath and called the IT help desk.

The person on the other end listened carefully and offered some suggestions. None satisfied the IT-savvy Maalouf.

At the end of the conversation, he asked for a new computer. His rationale was that his Dell tower was three years old and was due for a replacement. The help desk technician told him that the request was submitted and, if approved, he would have a new computer by the end of the week.

Adnan rung off and fired off an email telling his boss that he needed a new computer ASAP. In the note, he restated his reasons.

Adnan didn't know that every keystroke was being recorded, slowing its processing speed. The tapping of his computer was based on an FBI warrant that authorized the FBI to record all Maalouf's emails, texts, and telephone conversations. The downloading of his computer usage history was completed during the night.

SATURDAY, DECEMBER 10ᵀᴴ, 2016, 9:36 A.M. LOCAL TIME, NEW YORK CITY

The two things that were the most important to Na'il Miraj were sitting on the desk in his room at the one-star hotel in lower Manhattan. One was the "burner" phone he bought with 100 minutes of "talk time." When he ran out of minutes, he'd buy another.

The other was a sheet of paper with the phone numbers for each team leader and the addresses of the safe houses. He also had written the current burner phone number for Dawuud Ghanem on the sheet and when either man changed phones, one would call the other using the new phone to exchange numbers.

Changing phones and phone numbers gave Na'il a sense of security. Every day at a specific time, he called each safe house except for the one in Dallas since that was for the team killed in Arizona. So far, none reported anything out of order other than each asking for their go date and instructions.

There were five four-man teams left. If they followed their orders and didn't do anything stupid, they would be ready to go when Na'il sent them their targets.

Carefully prepared packets were locked away in a safe deposit box in a New York City bank Na'il rented for a year. Each had specific instructions for each team and maps to help them reconnoiter their targets. He planned to drop them off at a Federal Express office on Saturday, December 17ᵗʰ, for delivery on Monday so they could rehearse their entry into their assigned launch area and escape. During their practice runs, they were not supposed to leave their vehicle or do anything that would draw attention to themselves. Once they reported they were ready, he would give them the date.

THE SAME DAY, 9:48 A.M. LOCAL TIME, BONHAM

Deterrence started with a copy of the cashier's check given to Janey Humphries before Derek and the others flew to Washington. The FBI had a warrant within minutes of their application to contact Bank of America which provided them the branch address where the check was issued. An FBI agent was sent to interview the teller who processed the transaction.

Bank of America provided information on all the checks drawn on the account. All were within a month of the one given to Janey Humphries.

Based on the interview of Janey Humphries, the FBI now had a profile of the type of home, the story Morcos told, and a list of real estate agencies who cashed the checks. FBI agents were dispatched, with warrants, if needed, for a copy of the leases and restraining orders that prevented the realtor from speaking with anyone about the FBI's investigation.

All the realtors cooperated and spoke at length with the FBI special agents. All identified Morcos as the lessor and gave the FBI addresses of the houses which were placed under surveillance.

On his daily call with Gibson and Wiggins, Derek suggested that if they raided the houses immediately, they would get the weapons and the teams and not get the real prizes - Maalouf, Ghanem, Miraj, and Morcos.

Gibson's voiced his strong opinion. "Let's capture the teams and get the weapons first while continuing the manhunt for the three men. Maalouf, we can arrest at any time."

Derek countered. "I believe Mossad is keeping tabs on Ghanem, so Zvi will know where he is. We know Miraj is in the country, but not where. We don't have a clue where this guy Morcos is or if he is in the country. Once the raids happen, they will be hard to keep out of the media, and Miraj may change his plans. That means he must move or run."

"Agreed. To conduct all the raids at once so, we'll have to bring in the locals and use BATF."

"Yup... I figured that. I'd also suggest that someone from Camelot International be assigned to each raid."

"Good idea. When I know when they'll go down, I'll let you know."

CHAPTER 18

PREVENTATIVE MEDICINE

Fatimah walked into Haandi's Indian restaurant in Knightsbridge 10 minutes early rather than be fashionably late. The Haandi's chain of five-star restaurants specializing in North Indian cuisine started in, of all places, Nairobi, Kenya. Number two was opened in Kampala, Uganda, before the chef opened his London restaurant.

As she walked in, the maître d' came around from his podium. "Miss Serraf, Lord Haversham is waiting for you. Please, come with me."

Fatimah nodded, thinking that his being here shot her plan to hell. She followed the middle-aged Indian through the tables to one in the back corner. Like the others, the table was separated to give diners privacy.

When she approached, Lord Haversham, stood. At a 190-centimeters tall, he was almost a head taller than Fatimah. She held out her hand, which he took with a nod. "I am so happy to see you again."

Fatimah nodded as she sat down. Show time. "Me too!"

She was wearing a custom-made pantsuit that was one of what she referred to as her banker suits—medium gray, double-breasted with subdued white pinstripes. Her white blouse had ruffles down the front and opened enough to reveal one of the collars Haversham sent.

The gift bracelets were on her wrists and ankles, and if she pulled down her pants, he would see the chastity belt. The device took several attempts to fit before she locked the chrome steel belt with gel liners in place. At first, the belt was uncomfortable, but within a day or two, she began to enjoy the feel of the steel belt around her waist. The belt, along with the harness to which it was attached, was a constant reminder of the pleasure Lord Haversham gave her.

Fatimah wore two-inch spool heels, like the rest in her closet, with wide bases because she was afraid she'd sprain an ankle on London's uneven sidewalks wearing spike heels. Her shoulder-length hair was stylishly streaked with gray and hung loosely.

After pleasantries and an offered but declined glass of wine, Lord Haversham waited until she finished stirring sugar into her glass of tea. "I would like to talk business first if that is acceptable to you."

From what I learned, your family is both secretive about their financial dealings and business ownership, and from what Katherine told me, you are also discrete. We both have sexual tastes that are not the norm.

"Of course. Always." *I wonder if this about his family business or he wants me to do a favor for him.*

"First, just so you know, Katherine and I are involved in several very successful business ventures."

Like what? I'll ask Katherine if you don't tell me.

"As an investment banker, you have had a most interesting career and many satisfied clients."

So, you've checked out my CV. I'm not surprised. Where is this going?

"I think we can serve each other outside the bedroom."

That's an interesting choice of words. The implication is that this is more than sexual, and my master doesn't want a favor. The sex we've had has been intense, and I want more. Speak to me, Lord Master Marston. Fatimah found her tongue. "In what way?"

"My family has a fair amount of money, and I manage the family portfolio. Other family members work in or run the businesses we control and give me the profits to invest. We would, as you can imagine, like to increase the size of our holdings. To that end, a couple of years ago, after going through the usual bureaucratic drill, we were awarded an investment banking license but have done nothing with it."

You have more than a bit of money. You're personally worth billions, and your family has billions more. Fatimah nodded, wanting Lord Haversham to continue.

"I would like to move half of our portfolio into our bank, which would, at least initially, just manage our holdings. This way, the fees we pay would go to the bank we own. My brothers and sisters agreed to this plan when we applied for the banking license. We would like you to run our own private investment bank."

"Interesting. Does the bank have a name?"

"On the license, it says Haversham and Partners, but that can be changed."

Before Fatimah could ask her next question, her host continued. "We would make you president. Are you interested?"

Fatimah stirred her tea and felt the stirring in her loins. Lord Haversham had not specified what she should wear. "I am, but of course, the devil is in the details, and I have a very nice compensation package at Talwar."

"We would be much, much more generous."

"Would you put your thinking in writing?"

"We already have." Lord Haversham pulled out a sealed envelope from his suit coat and put the envelope with the family crest on the table. Fatimah let the envelope with her name hand-written on the front sit, untouched for a few seconds before she reached out. Lord Haversham put his hand on top of hers. There was a glint in his eyes as he said what could be construed as a double entendre. "I think you'll find what we are offering to be very, very enticing."

Fatimah held the envelope as she looked at her master and sexual partner in a different light. Now, he would be her boss in every respect. "And what about our personal relationship? How would that change?"

"Ahhhhh, I suspected you would ask that. We have many options. You could move either into my house here in London or to my estate where Victoria House is located. You would, of course, continue to serve me, and we would be monogamous. I would dictate what you are wearing. If it interferes with your work, we will, of course, change it. You would have several maids in my service to take care of you."

Lord Haversham squeezed her hand. "We would go out as a couple to the many social events I have to attend."

She squeezed back. "Let me read this letter. I am sure that the changes I would request could be made if they are reasonable. And I think a separate contract governing my personal service to you would also be appropriate."

"Both are perfectly acceptable. I didn't expect a 'yes' today. When do you think you will get back to me?"

"I will need some time to read and think about this offer. If I accept, I must sort out how I leave Talwar and its clients, some of whom have been with me for many years. So, I will read the letter, and when we see each other again tomorrow, I am sure I will have some questions for you that may take time to answer before I accept. We can work on the second one once we have the business contract done."

"Excellent." Lord Haversham nodded to the waiter, and lunch was served.

THE SAME DAY, 3:31 P.M. LOCAL TIME, MOSCOW

An assistant brought Colonel Zabara another pot of boiling water, a tea bag, and four large lumps of sugar. He thought that the tea would help fortify him for the cold walk from the station on the Sokolnicheskaya or Red Line station to his apartment building. Open on his desk in front of him was Saliemenov's FSB dossier. So far, all they could get out of Saliemenov was that a man named Novokov had contacted him about the weapons and that he'd spent the money paid him.

Zabara didn't think Saliemenov was telling the truth about the money, but so far, he had decided not to get aggressive because there were still several missing pieces. One was who was this Dadiani fellow. Another was where did Dadiani get the necessary authorizations and paperwork. A third was, who helped him? The fourth was the disappearance of Lieutenant Colonel Gregori Tzuri. Where did he go and why?

The phone rang, and the colonel picked up the handset without looking. "Zabara."

The voice at the other end told him that Maxim Novokov was in an interrogation room in the basement. After telling the man at the other end of the call to let Novokov sit alone, untouched, until he arrived, Zabara hung up.

Zabara pulled out Novokov's FSB file from a box on the case and began reading. Although familiar with its contents, he wanted Novokov to sweat for an hour and a half before entering the holding cell.

The senior investigator stood back while the guard unlatched the steel door with spots of rust and peeling paint to a windowless room. Novokov was sitting in a chair bolted to the floor in the center of the cell. His hands were handcuffed to a bar that ran the length of the table. The rattle of chains told him that Novokov's feet were in manacles attached to the cold concrete floor.

Zabara nodded to the FSB captain, who followed him into the room. Zabara sat down opposite the prisoner and put his briefcase with Novokov's FSB file, the transcript from Saliemenov's interrogation, and his notes on the floor next to him.

In the beginning, Zabara was not going to touch him. Novokov's FSB file noted that he was to be detained but not harmed because he was an excellent and reliable source of information.

"So, Maxim, let's start with do you know a Colonel Serik Saliemenov?"

Before Novokov could answer, Zabara added, "We have already interviewed Colonel Saliemenov, who is in custody."

Novokov winced noticeably. "We served together in Chechnya."

"Did he approach you about the missiles or vice versa?

"I knew someone looking for missiles, so when we talked, he confirmed he had them in the depot. All I did was put him in contact with the buyer."

"Do you know who created the papers to take possession of the weapons?"

"No. The buyer took care of that."

"Who is the buyer? I want his name and where I can find him." The "or I'll beat it out of you" was unsaid.

"I don't know where he lives."

"What is his name, and how do you contact him?"

"I know him only by the Russian name he gave me, which is probably not his real name."

"Let's start with that."

"Andrei Dadiani."

"Have you met him?"

"Yes. Several times."

"Would you recognize him?"

"Of course."

Zabara opened the folder and slid the artist's sketch based on Saliemenov's description. The scar on the man's forehead was noticeable. "Is this Dadiani?"

Novokov studied the sheet. "Yes, that's him."

Zabara's mind raced. This confirmed the second alias for Dadiani. "How do you reach him?"

"I call a phone number and leave a message. Then, Dadiani, or someone he trusts, calls me."

"What number do you call?"

"I don't memorize phone numbers. They're in my phone book."

"Where is your phone book?"

"In a very safe place."

"Will you take me there?"

Novokov shook his head. "If I did, then my phone book wouldn't be in a safe place, now, would it?"

Zabara went to the next question on his list. "What else did this Dadiani want to buy?"

"Chemical bombs. Dadiani was most interested in them."

"What about the chemicals to use in them?"

"I am sure you know this, but Saliemenov made sure that the ones we sold him would not work."

Zabara nodded. "He did say that."

A heavy silence fell over the room. Novokov had been through this drill before, and each time, either the KGB, now the FSB, or the militsiya questioned him, they let him go without a beating since the information he provided was accurate.

Zabara stood up and slid one of his business cards across the table before he put his palms on the table as he leaned over to position his face 30 centimeters from Novokov's. "We are going to release you. After you leave this building, you have twenty-four hours to call me with all the numbers you use to call Dadiani. If you fail to call me at the number on this card, then I will have you arrested, and I promise you, you won't leave this building as a free man. Understood?"

Novokov looked down at the card with Zabara's number and nodded. "I do."

TUESDAY, DECEMBER 13ᵀᴴ, 2016, 11:26 A.M. LOCAL TIME, RIYADH

Talwar Bank's office in Riyadh was a small office suite with a conference room, reception area, and seven small offices. The largest one was for the branch manager. Three were used by what Fatimah referred to as the "relationship managers," the men who met with existing and prospective clients. Three of the other four were occupied by support staff, and one was kept vacant for prospective clients or visitors such as Fatimah.

Fatimah opened her laptop in the vacant office with a few hours to kill before she left for the airport to catch the evening flight to Karachi. The break gave her time to reflect on the meeting with Sheikh Gamal al Hamdi that occurred earlier in the day.

The man had asked her to meet him at his compound 68 kilometers east of Riyadh on Saudi Route 80 and offered a car to take her back and forth. Fatimah suggested that his driver pick her up at Four Seasons Hotel at seven so she would arrive on time for the 8:30 a.m. meeting. Being late and knowing that the man was a very traditional Saudi and observant Muslim and reluctant to work with a woman, Fatimah did not want to give him any excuse to cancel.

Fatimah watched the gate open and suspected it was made from heavy steel that only a tank or armored vehicle could knock down. Her belief was reinforced when she saw armed men patrolling the thick, four-meter (13.1 feet) high concrete and brick wall surrounding the compound. In the courtyard, there were patrols of well-armed two-man teams. As Fatimah was escorted into the building, she spotted other armed men in the halls.

Rather than wear Western-style clothes, Fatimah wore a traditional dark gray, ankle-length burqa over her pantsuit. Although she preferred one or two-inch heels, she wore a black pair of flats. Fatimah was guided by whom she assumed was one of al Hamdi's administrative assistants and trailed by two armed guards from the car to a door just inside the gate. Once inside the building, the man pointed to a small room off the hallway.

"Please, we must search you."

As Fatimah entered, the door was closed behind her, and another door opened, letting two women wearing black burqas enter. Fatimah wasn't sure if they were members of his harem or women employees.

"Miss Serraf, please take your burqa off." The woman's voice was soft but conveyed a command through her diction and tone.

Fatimah did as she was told, and the women were surprised that she was wearing pants and a blouse under the burqa. They expertly patted her down before they looked through her briefcase, which contained her laptop, a portfolio with a pad, and business cards. Her wallet and phone were in a small, leather Mouawad purse. The Emirati-owned brand was known throughout the world for its expensive products.

Her phone and computer were placed in a small X-ray machine. Still, the woman commanded. "Please turn your computer on and open a file." Fatimah complied. "Now, your phone."

Satisfied she was not wearing a wire or an explosive vest or that her phone and computer were bombs, one of the women handed her the charcoal gray burqa and left the room.

Seconds later, the door she entered opened and revealed the same unsmiling, unfriendly aide. Fatimah suspected he was uncomfortable with a woman here to do business with his boss. His voice was flat, lacking warmth, "Come with me. The sheikh is waiting."

Fatimah was not surprised when she was ushered into a large room with a raised platform at one end and cushions arranged in a U in front of the platform. A heavy-set man with a gray beard sat on what looked to be a small bench. Next to him was a table with a plate of fruits and a pot Fatimah suspected contained tea.

Sheikh Gamal al Hamdi pointed to several cushions to his left. Fatimah took that as where he wanted her to sit. She was not offended that he didn't ask her to sit on his right side where custom dictated his most trusted advisors sat. After putting her briefcase on the marble floor, Fatimah sat and pulled her legs under her.

The man was wearing a traditional ghutrah with an agal made from two black bands holding the triangular headpiece on his head. His white thwab—a loose-fitting robe—was trimmed in gold. He turned to the assistant and said, "Leave us."

Fatimah noted there was no please in the command. She sat with her hands in her lap.

"I am Gamal al Hamdi. I understand that you are a mutual friend's banker. He thinks very highly of you."

Fatimah nodded. *He'd better. I've made his family hundreds of millions so they don't have to dig into their principal. And I've hidden the profits legally in tax-free locations so any regulatory agency will find it very difficult or impossible to figure out how much the man made.*

"I am not accustomed to working with a…. woman."

You mean a mere woman.

"However, because I am about to give my friend a substantial gift and, since you and my friend have already negotiated the reduced, fee, I am willing to work with you."

So, because I offered a discount, you are willing to work with a woman? You keep the principal, and al-Qaeda gets the return on the investment from which Talwar deducts a fee of one-half percent.

"Miss Serraf, do you know the terms under which I am making this gift?"

"No, I do not." *I don't want to know. All I do is handle the money Sameer tells me where he wants funds to be sent, and I send them. I have a feeling you will tell me whether I want to know or not. That makes me complicit.*

"Our friends need money to buy weapons, not just AK-47s, but weapons that will make the infidels stand up and take notice. The Americans call them weapons of mass destruction. I am funding the purchase of weapons that will destroy New York and London. Our friends believe they will have them next year."

Fatimah tried her best not to react but she was sure she did.

"Do you not approve?"

How do I answer that? A suicide bomber in a crowded marketplace is one thing. Destroying an entire city is quite another. These people are nuts. Setting off an atomic bomb in either city will set off a firestorm and a chain of events that will be hard to predict. If nothing else, the bomb will destroy the value of many of my clients and my investments. "Sheikh, I do not discuss or judge how my clients spend their money."

"Then, you do not approve." His words were a statement, not a question.

"I didn't say that. The confidential nature of my dealings with a client is not something I discuss with anyone. Whether I approve or not doesn't matter."

In this case, it does! This is the desire of a madman or madmen! Should I tell him what a nuclear bomb going off in London or New York will do to his investment portfolio?

Al Hamdi looked down at Fatimah, who looked right back. She could tell Al Hamdi wasn't used to being challenged, nor did she want to discuss the effect of such a device on his wealth.

"Very well." Al Hamdi handed picked up a cylinder with a red button. Seconds later, the man who led her to the room entered.

Al Hamdi pointed at Fatimah. "She will tell you how to transfer fifty million U.S. dollars to her bank."

"Yes, your excellency."

Al Hamdi picked up a document from the small pile beside him and a date from the tray. His gesture meant the meeting was over.

In another office, Fatimah went through the drafting instructions with the assistant. She would call him when he could transfer the money into the new account. Fatimah said Talwar would have the account open within 24 hours when asked how long that would take.

On the way back to the office, Fatimah's brain kept returning to the more than generous offer from Lord Haversham. The salary was one million pounds per year, net of taxes. She would be gifted five percent of the stock in Haversham Private Bank, Ltd. In addition, based on the bank's performance, she would be eligible for a bonus equal to one-half of her salary over and above the profit sharing.

One question she asked was where would the bank have its offices? Lord Haversham smiled when he answered by saying, "That depends on you and if we have a second contract."

The more she thought about the lord's offer, the more she wanted to accept it as a way out of Talwar. Being al-Qaeda's banker was making her nervous. Technically, she has done nothing illegal, but today's meeting about weapons of mass destruction changed that.

Hamdi was not being hypothetical; under oath, she would have to tell the court what the man said. Accepting the deposit, assuming a prosecutor could prove where the money went, made her a criminal.

Fatimah was also afraid that at some point, al-Qaeda may decide she knew too much and have her killed. She believed the counterterrorism agencies worked 24 hours a day to stop the money flow to al-Qaeda. Soon, they would conclude Talwar was one of their banks.

The time was now, Fatimah concluded, to get out. The only question was how fast. Lord Haversham provided the answer to the first question. She had to determine the answer to the second.

THE SAME DAY, 4:42 P.M. LOCAL TIME, MOSCOW

Zabara was frustrated because the discussion in the meeting he just left was more about politics and perceptions than finding traitors to Russia. Frustrated, Mikhail dropped the handouts on his desk, stared at them for a few seconds before dumping them in the trash.

He plopped down in his chair and looked at the stacks of folders on investigations he had to review. In the center of his desk, he saw a note asking him to call an officer in the Federal Customs Service at Sheremetyevo International Airport outside Moscow. The note said that their agents remember a man fitting Dadiani's description entered the country a few days ago, right after they received the sketch. There was number and name.

The FSB Colonel dialed the number that rang and rang and rang. No one picked it up. Frustrated, he called the FSB switchboard who connected him to the customs service office at the airport. The operator offered to connect him to the man. She came back on the line when no one picked up. Trying to be helpful, the woman suggested that she would put a message on his desk or maybe he should call back in the morning.

THE SAME DAY, 3:16 P.M. LOCAL TIME, NEW YORK CITY

The three FedEx packages were laid out neatly in a row. In each package, there were flight paths, the best time of day to launch, and what airliners to look for as targets. He had the launch times set so the missiles would be fired within minutes of each other at planes leaving JFK, Dulles, and Atlanta would fire. He presumed that the FAA would shut down the airline system for a few weeks before pressure from the airlines would force the FAA to allow them to begin again. That's when his last two teams would drive to Charlotte and Dallas to make their attacks.

The preferred targets were large aircraft such as the Boeing 777 and 747 or the Airbus 340 or 380. Once the missiles were in the air, the teams would return to their safe houses to await further instructions. His note emphasized that if they were not being chased, they would drive as if nothing had happened. If they were engaged by the police, they were to kill as many policemen and civilians as possible. No one was to surrender.

Na'il clicked on the first number on his mobile phone. Each conversation was the same, and the day the first three teams were waiting for had come. The other two would have to wait until it was their turn.

THURSDAY, DECEMBER 15TH, 2016, 4:43 P.M. LOCAL TIME, LIBERTY CROSSING

Andrei Kovalenko waited until Grady Gibson and Paul Bricker, the head of security for the National Counterterrorism Center, entered and closed the door. Paul Bricker asked what the purpose of the meeting was, and after listening to Kovalenko for five minutes, Bricker interrupted by saying, "Let's go get the bastard."

When Bricker walked into Adnan Maalouf's office, the analyst was tossing papers into his briefcase. Kovalenko, at first, saw hostility in Maalouf's eyes that softened to annoyance at the intrusion at the end of the man's day.

Bricker, who spent 20 years in the New York Police Department, stood in the doorway, just outside the door, with two more security guards. They were there as reinforcements if Maalouf reacted violently and to secure his office. After the arrest, no one was to be allowed in without Kovalenko's express permission.

"Paul, what do you want?" Maalouf didn't acknowledge Kovalenko, who stood behind and slightly to the side, his hands crossed just below his belt, holding a Manila file folder.

"To have a short chat. Oh, by the way, this is FBI Special Agent Andrei Kovalenko from FBI headquarters. He'd like to ask you a few questions."

Annoyed, Maalouf looked at the desk clock. "I'm late for a dinner appointment. Again, what do you want?"

On cue, Andrei stepped forward and pulled a close-up of Dawuud Ghanem's face out of the folder. "Do you know this man?"

Adnan glanced at the photo forcing himself not to react. "No."

Andrei's had a smile on his face. "Are you sure?"

"Yes, why?"

"You do realize lying to an FBI agent is a felony."

Annoyed, Maalouf responded. "Of course I do."

"Good, then how do you explain this?" Andrei laid two photos on the table showing Maalouf and Ghanem at a table in a restaurant with plates of food. One was taken in Syria, and the other in the United States.

"The man just sat down at the table. The restaurants were crowded."

Kovalenko let himself sound incredulous. "Really? The same man in two different countries? Doesn't that seem odd to you?"

"It is possible."

"How many times have you been to Syria?"

"I went several times as a child before my family emigrated to the U.S. Why?"

Kovalenko ignored Maalouf's attempt to gain control of the discussion. "How many passports do you have?"

"One."

"Are you sure? Again, may I remind you that lying to an FBI Special Agent is a felony."

"Yes."

Kovalenko took three sheets out of the folder that were copies of the identification pages of a Syrian, a Lebanese, and an American passport on the desk next to the photos. "That is odd. All three of these have your picture, and immigration records show that you have been a frequent visitor to both Syria and Lebanon."

Maalouf remained standing and glared at Kovalenko. His forefinger tapped the desk impatiently. "If that is all you want to show me, then this meeting is over. I have an appointment."

"Oh, Mr. Maalouf, we have much more to talk about." He placed a copy of the arrest warrant for espionage on Maalouf's desk. "This is a warrant for your arrest so you are not going to make your dinner because this discussion will continue at FBI headquarters. Espionage is just the first charge."

Kovalenko reached behind his back and pulled out his handcuffs. He came around the desk and grabbed Maalouf's arm. Adnan tried to pull away, but Kovalenko's grip was too strong, and he forced Maalouf's arm up toward his shoulder blades.

"I want to speak to my lawyer."

"Absolutely. We'll let you make that call when we get to FBI headquarters." Kovalenko read Maalouf his rights using a card to ensure they were read perfectly.

With Maalouf handcuffed, Bricker tossed Maalouf's overcoat between his hands to hide the handcuffs. However, anyone who has seen the "perp walk" on a TV crime show knows the position. Kovalenko and Gibson had a hand on each bicep as they led Maalouf through the National Counterterrorism's office. Heads turned, and mouths dropped in surprise.

Paul Bricker waited until the lock on Maalouf's door was rekeyed by the in-house locksmith waiting outside the door. Then he followed the two FBI agents, and when they got to the door, he handed the key to Kovalenko. "Thank you, Paul. A team is on the way to inventory everything and provide you with a list of everything taken for further analysis."

"Perfect. And the IT guys will have the CDs with all his emails ready when they arrive. Thanks for finding this bastard."

Kovalenko stuck out his hand. "Thanks for your help. Please pass my thanks and appreciation on to the IT staff as well. Thanks for the background info on Maalouf."

"My pleasure."

Maalouf was loaded into the car, and Kovalenko slid onto the front passenger seat. Another FBI agent sat in the back with Maalouf.

At headquarters, while Maalouf was being processed and allowed to call a lawyer, Andrei went into the FBI command center which was designed with small mini centers in separate rooms so that several independent operations could be managed simultaneously. Kovalenko found the one assigned to his next operation, keyed in the six-digit access code, and walked in.

Two technicians were already inside. He sat in the center seat where he could watch video feeds for up to six different locations. The man and a woman were hooking up additional monitors so the command center could switch between cameras at any location. Whether shown or not, the video and audio feeds would be recorded.

Kovalenko felt tired and drained. Arresting a traitor like Maalouf was more fatiguing than he thought. He took a long sip from the bottle of water he found next to the chair and then dialed a number from memory.

Caller ID told Derek who it was. "Hi Andrei."

"We need to go secure. I'll initiate."

Kovalenko waited until the two phones finished synchronizing their security algorithms, and the letters TS/SCI appeared on the small LED screen.

"Maalouf is in the bag. I'll start alerting the local SWAT teams. Are all your people on-site or enroute?"

"Yup. Jacob should be in Phoenix by now, and I just talked to Chief Norquist, who is at his hotel outside Boston. Jefferson is already in Atlanta, and Buckholz should be landing in Chicago soon. I just landed at Republic Airport in New York. Pillar, Neimeyer, and Rosenthal should be in the lobby of FBI headquarters any minute."

"Good. The briefing is still on for ten p.m. Eastern time. If anyone is delayed, let me know. We can slide the start time back an hour or two."

"No problem. I should be in downtown Manhattan in about an hour."

"Great. Call this number if you are delayed." Kovalenko rattled off a ten-digit number which Derek read back.

"Talk to you in a couple of hours."

"Yup. It is going to be a great day for the United States."

"Amen."

CHAPTER 19

TAKE DOWN

When the limo driver closed the door and headed toward Karachi's Jinnah International Airport, Fatimah looked forward to dinner with Lord Haversham. Unfortunately, bad weather in most of Europe delayed many flights. By the time Pakistani Airlines canceled her flight to London three hours after the scheduled departure time, Fatimah was already booked by her assistant on an Emirates flight to London via Dubai.

With the late departure, the stop-over, the flight time, and the time change, she arrived at her flat around three in the morning, London time. While in the first-class lounge in Dubai, she called Lord Haversham and promised to let him know when she arrived.

On the trip, she had permission from Lord Haversham to take off the chastity belt so she could go through security without any problems. She had to promise to put the device back on in the first-class lounge before she boarded her flight which now turned into flights. Since she agreed to wear the device, Fatimah felt naked when she couldn't feel the pressure from the polished stainless steel against her body.

Groggily, Fatimah rolled out of bed when her alarm went off at 7:00 a.m. She logged into her personal e-mail account and started to write a note to Lord Haversham. Fatimah decided that an e-mail was too impersonal. From the center drawer of her desk, she pulled out a sheet of 100-pound paper with a high linen content and her name and address embossed on the thick paper.

She unscrewed the top of her Sailor fountain pen thinking the wide, 21-carat gold point was perfect for penning a personal note.

Lord Haversham,

Getting to London yesterday was a nightmare. Between weather delays and flight cancellations, I arrived in the middle of the night. Due to the private nature of the conversation, I didn't want to call from an airline club lounge or my office.

All this is a preamble to saying that I am accepting your generous officer to lead Haversham Private Bank as soon as I can extract myself from Talwar. I will not know how long until I formally resign and work out the transition which may take two or three weeks.

Over dinner tonight, we can work out the details of my dual service to you.

Fatimah

She scribbled a flourish under her name. After folding the note and addressing the envelope, Fatimah called the concierge to arrange for a courier to deliver the note to Lord Haversham no later than 9:00 a.m. today.

With that task done, she took a shower and dressed, confident that her days in Pakistan were over. Now all she had to do was figure out how and what to tell Lord Haversham about her Talwar clients.

SATURDAY, DECEMBER 17ᵀᴴ, 2016, 3:30 A.M. LOCAL TIME, FRANKLIN SQUARE, NY

From where Derek knelt at the Y-shaped junction of Catalpa Drive, Hewlett Street, and Shelburne Drive, the 1,200-square-foot house looked just like the photos in the realtor's listing. The house was built in 1951 and sold to a World War II Army Air Force veteran and had three bedrooms and only one bath. Records showed that the original owner listed his occupation as an air traffic controller. Since then, 909 Catalpa Drive has been bought and sold over the years, and today, a buyer would have to fork over about $450,000, considerably more than the $11,000 the first owner paid the developer.

Through Derek's night vision binoculars, the driveway that led up to the house was a lighter shade of green than the lawn. Standing behind him was the FBI SWAT team leader, Scott Blasingame. Between the FBI, ATF, and the Nassau County police departments, they had 24 men arrayed around the one-story house. Six were hiding in the woods on the south side of the house to keep anyone from escaping in that direction. Traffic on the westbound side of the Southern State Parkway was down to one lane courtesy of the Nassau County police, who also set up roadblocks on all three streets—Catalpa, Hewlett, Shelburne—about a quarter a mile from the house.

Behind Derek and away from the sightline of anyone in the house, an armored car coasted quietly to a stop. A member of the FBI SWAT team opened a hatch in the top and pointed an M60 machine gun at the house.

A box truck fitted out as a command center parked farther away from the target house provided radio communications to the teams about to move in and to Andrei Kovalenko in the FBI's headquarters in Washington, D.C., who was coordinating all the assaults.

Derek's earpiece crackled with Andrei's voice, "All teams, repeat, all teams, execute, execute, execute!!! Good luck, everybody."

Teams in five other cities began to move in on homes where they suspected Igla or Stinger missiles were being stored and where the men who would fire them were staying. Police officers knocked on the doors of the adjoining houses to alert the residents, who were quickly taken to nearby fire stations for, as one office said, "the duration of the fight."

As a "civilian," Derek was an observer and not allowed to go in with the raiding force. Blasingame, the senior FBI Special Agent, tapped Derek on the shoulder and pointed to the front door to watch the attack. Then he jogged over to join the assault team.

First up, an agent let his dog sniff the door. The all-clear sent an eight-man team assault team toward the door and another armored car onto the driveway. Because Derek was convinced the terrorists probably had RPGs, he warned the driver to get out once the vehicle was in position.

Through the green-black image of his binoculars, Derek watched each of the two, four-man teams take cover on either side of the house. Blasingame had each team report they were in position before he signaled the front man on the team to break open the front door. Based on his position in the stack, Blasingame a stocky, muscular five-foot-eight, would be the fourth man to enter.

The ram buckled the door in the middle, and it swung open letting the first man shoulder his way in. In the quiet of the night, the traffic on the Southern State didn't drown out the sound of gunfire. Derek heard the rattle of AK-47s mixed with the sharp retort of the M4 Carbines carried by the FBI agents.

Blasingame's voice was loud as he shouted over the gunfire. "One tango down. One officer injured. Taking heavy fire from the back of the house. We've got them pinned down."

During the briefing, Blasingame said the one thing he wanted to avoid was a protracted gun battle. Derek saw a familiar arrowhead shape shoved out of a window and yelled, "RPG, get down…."

The rocket missed the armored car in the driveway and bounced off the driveway before hitting a Ford 350 Dualie parked on the other side of the street. The explosion and fire lit up the night sky, and lights came on all over the neighborhood from the houses still occupied.

Derek ran back to the armored car just behind him. "Do you have any anti-personnel grenades?"

The Nassau County New York police officer nodded. "Sir, we do, but we can't use them without the governor's permission. Too big a risk of civilian casualties."

Derek held out his hand. "How many do you have?"

"Twenty-four."

"Give me six."

"Sir, I am not sure I can."

"Just give me the goddamn grenades, and if anything goes wrong, it is my ass, not yours."

The round grenades looked familiar. Each weighed just under a pound and was the modern version of the pineapple grenade used during World War II. The spherical shape made the grenade easier to throw accurately. Theoretically, when the pin was pulled and the handle released, the grenade exploded four seconds later.

As Derek shoved the grenades into his jacket pocket, the policeman pulled a 9mm SIG Sauer P226 from a rack, shoved in a magazine, and jacked the slide back to load a round in the firing chamber before he handed him the pistol along with an in the waistband holster. Once the gun and holster were secured on Derek's wide leather belt, he handed him three spare magazines. "There's fifteen in each magazine."

Derek ran to the large tree in the front yard and heard Blasingame report over his headset that the bad guys were barricaded in the back bedrooms.

"Scott, it's Derek, I'm at the tree by the side of the house. I can put an end to this nonsense."

"What are you going to do?"

"Drop two grenades in each bedroom window, starting with the one on the west side."

"Let me know when you are in position."

"Roger that."

Derek zig zagged as he ran hunched over. Underneath the window, he felt safe.

"In position."

"Stand-by. Break, break. Friendly on the west side of the house!!!"

The window shattered when it was hit by a short burst of 5.56mm bullets. An AK-47 was stuck outside the window and turned parallel to shoot down the wall. Empty brass rained down on Derek's head as bullets chewed up the grass along the side of the house. Derek grabbed the weapon by the stock and shoved it skyward. The owner tried to wrest control of the gun without exposing himself to return fire.

The struggle gave Derek a chance to pull the pin of one grenade with his teeth, let the handle fly, and toss the olive-drab globe into the window. The man let go of the AK-47 just as the grenade went off, causing a section of the brick veneer to fall to the ground.

He took a second grenade, pulled the pin, counted to three, and tossed it into the room. More bricks fell to the grass, but insulation, wooden studs, and sheetrock blocked his entrance to the room. He ran around to the back of the house. At a back window, he radioed that he was in position by a window shattered by gunfire.

Blasingame responded with the same set of commands. This time, Derek had a grenade in each hand and let the spoons fly, counted to three before tossing them into the room. He heard yelling and then two booms followed by screams.

From where he was crouching below the window, he could hear the staccato bark of the M4s followed by a short burst from an AK-47. Then nothing.

About 10 seconds later, Blasingame came on the radio. "House is clear. Send in the meat wagon and an ambulance. We have two dead tangos and two barely alive. One of the good guys got hit."

Once the wounded FBI agent was carried out of the house, followed by the two severely wounded terrorists, Scott Blasingame allowed the forensic team to come in and examine the bullet-riddled house. Inside, the terrorists used dressers and tables to block the hallway. In the bedroom where Derek had tossed grenades, the occupant had pushed the mattresses against the wall and propped them up with the box springs. Each room was well stocked with loaded magazines for the AKs, and empty shell casings littered the floor.

Blasingame led Derek to the garage. Stacked on the floor next to a white panel truck were two Iglas and one RPG launcher. One of the terrorists had run into the garage and gotten a rocket launcher and four rockets. Two had been fired, and the other four were left in the crate.

Outside the house, Derek watched Nassau County police officers keep the nearby residents away from the battle scene. A fire engine was pumping water on the burning truck, now a mass of blackened, twisted steel.

Blasingame's face showed the tension and strain of the firefight. He wearily sat at the small table reserved for the on-scene commander in the command vehicle. He picked up the handset that connected him to the FBI's headquarters. "Andrei, we got the missiles and a shitload of AK-47 ammo, killed two, and captured two terrorists. It's a crapshoot if they survive. One FBI agent took a round in the leg, and he should be OK."

The FBI agent listened for a few minutes before he hung up and turned to Derek. "Andrei said it was a good night. We raided six homes. One was unoccupied. In each of the others, we captured RPGs and two SA-24s. None of the good guys were killed, although four were seriously hurt in Phoenix because the front door was booby-trapped. Out of the twenty tangos, only four are alive. The two here and one in Chicago and the other in Atlanta."

Derek nodded. "So, I wasn't crazy."

"Thanks for thinking of using grenades. We were out of flash bangs, and when I saw the guy we killed in the living room, I knew tear gas wouldn't work. He had a gas mask with him."

"No problem. I'm glad I could help. What's next?"

"Writing the after-action report. I'm glad I'm not the director who will have to face the press."

"Me too."

"Oh, I almost forgot. Andrei said that Maalouf was in custody, and the FBI put out an APB on Miraj, Kassab, and Morcos. The names mean nothing to me, but he said they would to you."

SUNDAY, DECEMBER 18TH, 2016, 9:29 A.M. LOCAL TIME, BASINGSTOKE, U.K.

Fatimah smiled as she sat up in bed. She could see the manicured lawn and flowerbeds three stories below through the maize curtains. After going to the bathroom, Fatimah she heard a soft feminine voice.

"Lady Fatimah?"

The native Saudi cracked the bathroom door. Standing in the middle of the room was a young woman holding a silver tray, and a teapot, along with freshly baked croissants, butter, and jam. "Yes?"

Fatimah opened the door a little farther to get a better look at Maid Daphne. She was average height with short, brown hair, and her traditional maid skirt with its white front apron came down no more than 10 centimeters below her crotch. Maid Daphne stood easily on three-inch spike heels, and a chrome chain connected the leather cuffs around her ankles. Fatimah saw a similar chain hanging below the tray that connected her wrists. The chains between her feet and hands were attached to a third chrome chain clipped to a ring on the eight-centimeter-wide collar around her neck.

The young woman Fatimah guessed was in her twenties, bowed slightly at the waist. "I am Maid Daphne. Lord Haversham ordered me to be your personal maid and to serve you. With Lord Haversham's and your permission, I can take care of you in many ways. This morning, I have been instructed to help, if you wish, bathe, shave your legs, armpits, and groin. Lord Haversham directed that when you are dressed, I will lead you to his sitting room on the second floor."

"Thank you."

"There are new clothes for you in the closet that are your size."

Maid Daphne draped a towel over a stool next to the large bathtub. "Please sit here so I can shave you."

While applying the cream to her legs and groin, Maid Daphne's touch was more of a caress than one applying the cream. She expertly used the razor, rinsing after every few strokes.

Fatimah reveled in the clean feeling of having her legs and armpits shaven. When she stepped out of the shower, Maid Daphne helped dry her off with a soft towel. When she was finished, she held out her chastity belt along with the leather harness given to her by Lord Haversham.

"Maid Daphne, do you wear a similar belt?"

"Lady Fatimah, I do. All Lord Haversham's maids wear harnesses and cuffs that restrict our movement. Yours is much more stylish and less restrictive than the tight leather corset and chastity belt I must wear with lubed dildos in my anus and vagina."

Fatimah didn't know what to say, so she said nothing. Having a woman attend to her who was also a "slave" was all new to her.

Maid Daphne bowed her head, "Lady Fatimah, Lord Haversham has already started to build your wardrobe."

"What are my choices in dresses?"

Maid Daphne's stride was noticeably shorter than normal because the chain between her ankles was only 40 centimeters long. She held out a black slip and two dresses, one light gray and the other bright blue with square cut necks and sleeves that Fatimah guessed would end halfway down her biceps. "Lord Haversham only provides designer clothes. These are from Chanel."

"The gray one."

"Yes, Lady Fatimah."

When she exited the bathroom, Maid Daphne smiled as she admired Fatimah's toned body. The collar Lord Haversham gave Fatimah to wear in the house was the same as the one she wore, except instead of chrome metal studs, Lady Fatimah's had large Swarovski crystals to go along with the same four chrome rings.

The dress went over her shoulders. It was mid-thigh in length.

Maid Daphne disappeared back into the closet and hung up the black dress before re-emerging, holding two pairs of shoes. "Lady Fatimah, Lord Haversham was not sure of your shoe size, so there are several pairs here. What size do you wear?"

"U.K. six point five."

She heard a shuffling of boxes. "I think Lord Haversham would like these." Maid Daphne opened a box with open-toed shoes with three-inch heels and long leather straps that would wind around her calves until buckled just below her knees.

When Fatimah hesitated, Maid Daphne spoke. "Please sit, Lady Fatimah, allow me."

Fatimah backed up and sat on the edge of the bed. When her butt touched the bed, she shivered from the sensations coming from her groin. Living and serving Lord Haversham is going to be wonderful.

Maid Daphne knelt in front of Fatimah, careful to keep her knees together. As she slipped the first shoe on, Maid Daphne's touch was soft and gentle as she wound the straps around Fatimah's calves. By the time Maid Daphne finished buckling the two-centimeter-wide straps, Fatimah was even more sexually aroused.

Maid Daphne stood, picked up her tray, and motioned to the door. "Shall we? Later today, I am sure Lord Haversham will have me give you a tour of the house. You can easily get quite lost here."

At the door of the sitting room, Maid Daphne tapped the frame. Lord Haversham, seeing Fatimah, stood up smiling. "I see you have met Maid Daphne. If you like her, she will be your personal maid."

Fatimah turned to Maid Daphne. "I do. She has a wonderful touch."

Lord Haversham nodded. "Done. She can take care of your needs when I am away. Have you had breakfast yet?"

What does he mean by needs? He knows I have a healthy sexual appetite and what my preferences are. I am not going to ask now. "No. I'm famished. Maid Daphne served me tea and a croissant, but I want something more substantial."

"What would you like?"

"Fruit, yogurt, and some orange juice. Maybe another croissant with butter and jam. Then I'll have some coffee." *I really would like to be tied up and fucked in different positions after I suck your cock.*

Lord Haversham laughed. "Hungry, are we?" He turned to the third woman in the room, dressed precisely like Maid Daphne but had not been introduced. "Maid Stephanie, go to the kitchen and fetch what Lady Fatimah wishes."

Maid Stephanie bowed stiffly and left, followed by Maid Daphne. When she did, Fatimah could see the stiff leather corset the woman was wearing. Maid Stephanie too had chains connecting her ankles and wrists.

"Did you have a good time last night?"

"I did."

"Excellent."

"Where are we?"

"At Haversham Estates. My family owns about forty square kilometers around this house between the city of Basingstoke and the town of Hook. Most of the land is a working farm and one of our many enterprises. In the southeast corner of the estate, separated from the grounds by a four-meter-tall stone wall, are the four-square kilometers Victoria House occupies. We're about seventy kilometers from London which is, as you know, the center of the English universe."

"I don't remember much after we got in the helicopter."

Lord Haversham smiled. He knew the reason. She dressed as was told, and then they rode in his chauffeur-driven Rolls-Royce to the Battersea Heliport on the south bank of the River Thames between the Wandsworth and the Battersea Railway bridges. The Sikorsky S-76 took 15 minutes to reach the estate's helipad.

When Fatimah entered the house, she was trussed, gagged, and stimulated by several women whom she guessed were Lord Haversham's maids. Then she was left alone, tied, spread-eagled on his bed before he caressed her body before entering her. Fatimah did not remember much more.

Maid Stephanie knocked, and when told to come in, she bent her knees as a courtesy bow before placing the silver tray on the coffee table in front of Fatimah. "Thank you, Maid Stephanie."

Another bow.

Lord Haversham nodded toward the door. "You may go. We will call when we need you." Haversham waited until Maid Stephanie left the room. "The accommodations are agreeable?"

"Oh, yes."

"Excellent. So, all we have to do is discuss our other arrangement."

"Yes. In my mind, one cannot be dependent on the other."

"Agreed. If you left my service, you would have to find a place to live and commute to the estate."

"Not London?"

"No. The headquarters and nerve center of the Haversham empire is on the estate about a kilometer from here on the edge of our property. It is where we have our corporate offices and a staff of about one hundred and fifty. Next door to it, we have set aside a separate building that is currently being renovated for the bank."

"May I ask what the status of Maids Stephanie and Daphne are?"

Lord Haversham smiled. "Of course. They are in training and are being watched over by a woman you know as Lady Danica. They are here only to serve my needs as well as those of my special guests, which, I hope for long into the foreseeable future, is you."

"Have you had sex with them?"

"No, I don't have sex with my maids."

"So, I am going to be your only lover?"

"That is the plan."

"So, how do we keep our unusual taste in sex out of the office?"

"Simple. You live here with me. In the office, you will be the President and CEO of Haversham Private Bank. The fact that we are sleeping together shouldn't raise any eyebrows. I am, after all, a bachelor, and when I attend social functions of which there are far more than I like, I expect you to be on my arm. Except for the help, I am the only resident of the house. Maids Stephanie and Daphne, along with one you have not met, Maid Christine, are here to do the housework. Maid Christine is a chef by training and runs the kitchen. Lady Danica provides me with instructions on their training and sexual needs. Each maid is here by their choice and survived a thorough vetting and selection process. they are paid handsomely for their services. By the time they are in their forties, they will be quite well off. Once that was completed, they spent about a year at Victoria House learning how to take care of a woman's and a man's sexual needs and perform other household chores. Their residence here is a graduation exercise before they are placed with a wealthy caring gentleman or woman who appreciates their needs and whom they will serve. Or, if you wish, they can remain here."

By placed, Fatimah assumed Lord Haversham meant a fee was paid to Victoria House.

"Since you are now the Lady in residence at Haversham House, you can help in their training and benefit from their skills which, I am told, are quite exquisite. However, if you wish, I can arrange with Lady Danica for you to train one of your own."

"Maid Daphne seems to be fine." Fatimah spread soft butter followed by apricot jam on a crusty roll and took a bite. She let Lord Haversham continue.

"Here in the house, I will prescribe to Maid Stephanie what you will wear. She will bathe, shave you, help you dress, and care for your personal needs. If you need clothing, ask Maid Daphne. You will always wear the harness and chastity belt you are wearing, even to work. Rest assured that I will not embarrass you publicly or in front of your employees."

Fatimah smiled at his reference. *She suspected she'd seen only a part of what was coming.*

Haversham continued to lay out his thoughts. "Later, I may decide to fit you with a more restrictive harness to wear in the house. I will, from time to time, ask you to wear certain devices you will wear without question. If you want to be pleasured by any one of the maids, that is your choice. However, if you want to touch them in any way, you must ask permission. I, then, must get permission from Lady Danica, who will decide, based on their daily performance reports, if you can please them. However, under no circumstances will you allow them to reach orgasm, which Lady Danica strictly controls. If they have one, Lady Danica must be notified straight away."

"Have you put this in writing?"

"Funny you should ask." Lord Haversham opened a leather folder with the family crest embossed in color on the cover. "This document has all the details and specific rules. I suggest you commit them to memory."

Fatimah smiled as she read, thinking this will be wonderful. During the day, I will make millions, and in the evening, I will enjoy sex like I never have had before. What's not to like?

"Do you have a pen?"

"I do." Lord Haversham pulled out a Waterman fountain pen, put the cap on the back, and handed the writing instrument with a wide, gold point to Fatimah. She scribbled her name on the two copies.

"When do we start?"

"Right now. Slave Fatimah, on your knees in front of me. I need to be taken care of, but only when you are properly trussed."

"Yes, Lord Master."

Lord Haversham pressed a remote, and Maid Stephanie came into the room with a tray of ropes made from silk.

THE SAME DAY, 5:56 P.M. LOCAL TIME, WASHINGTON, D.C.

The falafel restaurant was a small dive off Pennsylvania Avenue on 28th Street NW in Washington D.C. Dawuud walked with his head bowed against the cold, stiff wind that was accelerated in a flue effect created by the buildings and penetrated his jeans to make his thighs cold. He hoped to appear as just another one of the students living in Georgetown. The firefights around the country made the news. Still, in press conferences, the FBI was very tightlipped about who and what was captured and where. The thought that al-Qaeda failed again was depressing.

He wasn't paying much attention to the world around him as he walked toward his favorite place to eat. Head down, Dawuud didn't see the black Ford Crown Victoria pull up next to the curb 50 feet ahead of him nor did he pay attention to three men in overcoats get out. Nor did he notice the two men get out of another Crown Victoria behind him.

Andrei Kovalenko turned to Zvi Rosenthal, who nodded as he spoke. "That is Dawuud Ghanem."

Kovalenko positioned himself in Dawuud's path and held up his badge. "Dawuud Ghanem, FBI! You are under arrest."

Dawuud looked around, saw the two men behind him with their guns drawn, and decided that discretion was the better part of valor. Kovalenko read Ghanem his rights, and as he did so, Ghanem announced loudly that he wanted to speak to his lawyer.

MONDAY, DECEMBER 19ᵀᴴ, 2016, 9:26 A.M. LOCAL TIME, KARACHI

The nonstop, 6,300-kilometer (~3,840 statute miles) trip to Karachi from Farnborough Airport, near Lord Haversham's estate on his Gulfstream V, took just nine hours at Mach .83. Fatimah was the only passenger. The flight attendant had set up one of the couches in the cabin as a bed. While the first-class section on airlines was a pleasant way to travel, Haversham's tastefully appointed Gulfstream, one of several jets in the Haversham fleet, was several steps above anything offered by commercial air carriers.

Talwar Bank's executive staff meeting started promptly at 8:30 a.m. on Mondays, and the founders and all the department heads were expected to attend. The meeting was for coordination and project status rather than solving a problem. If a resolution couldn't be found in a few minutes, the parties involved were encouraged to devise a solution in a separate meeting and brief the bank's primary shareholders when a decision needed to be made or actions taken.

The meeting was scheduled for an hour and rarely ran that long. Forty-five minutes was the norm.

As the meeting came to an end, Fatimah nodded in the direction of the other two shareholders—Zahid Touma and Hamza Bahar. Bank's operations reported to Zahid, and Bahar was responsible for customer acquisition and retention. Functions such as human resources, finance, and legal reported directly to Fatimah.

As the last person left, Fatimah asked Touma to close the door. In her typically direct style, Fatimah jumped right into the topic she wanted to discuss. "I have decided to leave Talwar and turn the bank over to both of you."

Fatimah pulled two folded sheets of paper from her folder and handed one to each man. "This is my plan. Each of you will have your shares increased to forty-five percent, and the vested employees will receive another one percent. Financially, I don't expect either of you to write me a check, nor do I want to reduce Talwar's liquidity by paying me full value for my shares. Therefore, I propose that the bank pay me a separation bonus of five million pounds Stirling so the value of the shares is not diluted. The wire transfer can be made on my last day."

Hamza Bahar, the youngest of the founders and probably the one she would pick as the CEO, placed the letter on the table and smoothed the folds as he formulated his words. "Fatimah, why are you leaving us? You have done great things with Talwar."

Fatimah nodded slightly. "I have a much better offer; let's leave it at that."

Bahar viewed Fatimah as a much sought-after prize as a potential wife. Both men wondered when she would marry. She was wealthy, well-connected, and would be an asset to any family.

Hamza absorbed her response with a noticeable nod. "I have two questions. One, are you going to compete with us? Two, who is going to tell your clients?"

Fatimah smiled. "The answer to your first one is no. The answer to the second one is we, as in you and me, are. If you remember, I insisted that two of the bank's primary shareholders get to know each of our major clients. Since I have been here, we've done that. So, Hamza, you and I are going to do just that apart from two whom I will meet alone."

"What reason shall we give?"

"Just what I said, I received a much better offer and will not be working for a competitor, and I will make it clear that they cannot move from Talwar to where I will be working. Both of you are quite capable of running Talwar profitably."

"Is the bank London based?"

Fatimah thought for a few seconds before answering, knowing what she was about to say was true. "No, the bank is not headquartered in London." She wasn't lying, Basingstoke was 70 kilometers from London.

She had told them months before that she had written instructions on how to handle these special clients if she died suddenly. She could see that both men wanted to ask the one question on their minds and had nothing to do with the bank, i.e., is there a man involved. But neither asked.

"What are you going to do with these two clients?"

"Terminate their relationship with the bank because I believe they will be too risky for Talwar to continue as their private banker."

"Why? Are these the clients the colonel from ISI was inquiring about when you and he had a meeting?"

"Neither client was mentioned by name, but I think so."

"Why is ISI interested in them, and why do you want to terminate the relationship. If we're not doing anything illegal, then there is no risk to the bank."

"I suspect one is a member of a major terrorist organization, and the other is one of their major sources of funds. For Talwar to survive, I don't want the bank splattered with mud if either man is arrested. All we've done is invest their money to get better returns and move money around the world to banks in countries where their secrecy laws protect the transactions. However, my departure is an excellent time to end the bank's relationship with them. However, if you want to continue, then you are free to do so, but then you must come with me to the meeting, and they will want to vet you. There will be no guarantee that the relationship continues."

Both Hamza and Zahid didn't say anything for a few seconds. Fatimah suspected they were weighing the risks and rewards of being al-Qaeda's investment banker. One after the other, they both shook their heads and said, "Agreed. End the relationships." Zahid, the more risk-averse of the two, added, "Make sure you tell them that after we return their money, they do not contact us ever again."

Fatimah responded, "Of course. I will schedule the meetings as soon as I can." Fatimah knew contacting Sameer may take days.

What Fatimah didn't want to tell her two partners was that she created a complicated web of corporations that owned the accounts, and one needed a chart to understand. That chart sat on a thumb drive along with the written instructions she gave to the law firms to use in case of her death. A third set was kept in a bank vault in her safe deposit box at Coutts Bank in London. She had a second on a thumb drive she kept hidden in her apartment in Karachi.

Zahid asked the next logical question. "How soon do you want to leave?"

"I would like my last day to be December thirty-first. I will personally pay to hire a private jet to fly us around. Most of our clients are based in Karachi, Riyadh, Dubai, and London, so the travel should be easy. I will have my administrative assistant start making the appointments and those will have priority to whatever is on your calendar. We will make the announcement to our employees this afternoon."

Fatimah made tea on her way back from the conference room. As she sipped the cup in her office, she ran through her mind what she wanted to say. With the "script" outlined in her mind, Fatimah took a long drink before picking up her purse and headed out the door. She stopped at her administrative assistant's desk and told her that she would be out for about an hour. No reason was given, nor was one asked.

She'd used the PCTL payphone on a side street two blocks from Talwar's office before. Fatimah put a small drawstring purse on the shelf and dialed the number in Peshawar. The operator came on the line and asked her to deposit 250 Pakistani rupees.

Fatimah listened as the tones registered each 10-rupee coin. When she finished, the operator reminded her that she had three minutes. Fatimah asked for six and was told she needed to add another 200 rupees. The extra money took the rest of her coins.

As the phone rang, Fatimah looked around. No one seemed to be paying attention to the woman wearing a hijab standing at a payphone in the heart of Karachi's financial district.

The phone rang four times. "Allo."

"We need to talk." She assumed the male voice on the other end of the phone knew that there was only one woman who would be calling him. If she wasn't to Sameer, one of his assistants was on the phone, and he would pass the word.

"In person?"

"Yes, I have a package and must explain its contents."

Silence. Fatimah was sure Sameer was at the other end of the call.

"How soon?"

"By this Sunday at the latest."

"Do we need to see what is in the package before we talk?"

"No. That is why a face-to-face meeting is preferable."

"I will let you know where and when by the usual means."

Dial tone.

What Fatimah did not know was the phone number she called was on one of the many phones collected when bin Laden was killed. Once the operator dialed the number, Echelon flagged the call and began recording. The metadata noted that the call was made from a pay phone in the financial district of Karachi to a mobile phone in Peshawar.

Jim Birdwell, the NSA analyst to whom the call was forwarded, spoke both Urdu and Punjabi, along with Arabic, and didn't need a translation. He was surprised that a woman telling a man what to do. Clearly, there was some type of unique relationship.

After a few minutes of thought, Birdwell started typing a note to one of his fellow analysts. In it, he wanted to know the answers to four questions that he wrote out on a piece of paper.

His first question was what was the history of the conversations using these phones? Birdwell's second asked if any of the participants in earlier calls a woman?

Birdwell paused for a few second before he added question three, i.e., what were the topics discussed on the proper calls? Last, he wanted to know what did NSA and CIA know who the participants were and what information did they have on them?

THE SAME DAY, 7:30 A.M. LOCAL TIME, WASHINGTON, D.C.

The Israeli embassy's senior Ministry of Justice liaison officer arrived at the Department of Justice's offices at 950 Pennsylvania Avenue seeking an immediate meeting with its head of international affairs. When granted an audience at 8:00 a.m., he handed the attorney a formal extradition request for Dawuud Ghanem.

The papers stated that the man was wanted for planning and committing terrorist attacks in Israel, Lebanon, Afghanistan, and the U.K. The Israelis wanted him extradited so they could try him for murder.

THE SAME DAY, 9:32 A.M. LOCAL TIME, WASHINGTON, D.C.

Of the eight men in the conference room at FBI headquarters, Derek only knew three - Assistant Director Gibson, Andrew Kovalenko and Scott Blasingame. As the introductions were made, he realized he was the only non-FBI agent there.

Gibson said the raid pulled off by the men in this room was one of the bureau's finest moments. They are all to be congratulated. He also thanked Derek for helping develop the intelligence that led to the raid.

Somberly, Gibson noted that the FBI was given intelligence that 24 Iglas were in the hands of al-Qaeda. Twelve were seized by the Israelis earlier in the year, and the U.S. raids only accounted for 10 more. He looked down and read off the serial numbers from a list:

9K-338-S-004548-VAD-10—Captured in the raid in Farmer's Branch, TX
9K-228-S-004549-VAD-10—Captured in the raid in Farmer's Branch, TX
9K-228-S-004550-VAD-10—Captured in Los Angeles, CA

9K-228-S-004551-VAD-10—Captured in Los Angeles, CA

9K-228-S-004552-VAD-10—Captured in Worcester, MA

9K-228-S-004553-VAD-10—Captured in Worcester MA

9K-228-S-004554-VAD-10—Captured in Des Plaines, IL

9K-228-S-004555-VAD-10—Captured in Des Plaines, IL

9K-228-S-004556-VAD-10—Captured in East Point, GA

9K-228-S-004557-VAD-10—Captured in East Point, GA

"Gentlemen, this means that we don't know where two of the missiles are. That assumes that there are twelve. We cannot discount the possibility that the intelligence is wrong, but our going-in assumption is that there are at least two more that have not been found or accounted for."

Andrei was about to speak when Derek held up his hand. "The source is impeccable. We know twenty-four were stolen, and we can account for only twenty-two. If I were a betting man, I think there is a phase two to this attack. So far, no bombs have been found on power line towers or stations even though we found several hundred pounds of SEMTEX in Worcester. We certainly disrupted phase one, what we must do is figure out what phase two is."

The FBI agent from the Counterterrorism task force spoke up. "With all due respect, no source is perfect. Even the Israelis. They make mistakes, as does the CIA. Second, al-Qaeda never has, in its history, thrown, if I may, a one-two punch. 9/11 was four airplanes at the same time."

Derek was not put off. "You are making an assumption that may kill many Americans. Al-Qaeda has surprised us on many occasions. Six months ago, if I asked you if they could get twenty-plus MANPADS into the U.S., you would have said I am crazy."

The FBI Agent made a face, so Derek continued. "With all due respect to our intelligence community, I think they will hit us again before Christmas."

Assistant Director Gibson frowned. "You do know that the President is going on national television tonight to talk about the raids and assure the American people that we got all the bad guys and they are safe."

Derek shook his head. "Sir, I urge you to ask the director to counsel the president against making that kind of statement until we find the last two Igla-S's. If not, his words may come back and bite him in the butt."

Gibson put his hand on Derek's forearm. "I hear you and agree with you. However, as you know, the president has a narrative, and he's going to stick with it even if the facts tell him otherwise."

CHAPTER 20

WHOSE SIDE IS HE ON?

The attorney general of the United States was finishing the last of her agenda items. After she was satisfied that her staff knew how to handle each topic, she walked out of the conference room leaving her chief of staff in charge.

One of the staffer's spoke up. "I've got one more thing that will take just a minute."

"Shoot."

"The Israelis filed extradition papers on that suspected terrorist who was arrested on Saturday by the FBI. He's not committed any crimes in the U.S. He's Lebanese and went to American University on a student visa."

"Who else wants him?"

"Interpol says no one other than the Israelis."

The chief of staff started sorting through his emails on his iPhone and was facing the screen when he spoke. "So, the bottom line is that the Israelis are the only ones who want him, and they have a list of acts for which they suspect he was involved. Are their allegations and the evidence listed in the filing?"

"Yes."

"And the Israelis will seek the death penalty?"

"Yes, under their laws, if convicted—Dawuud Ghanem—could face the death penalty."

"Has the FBI learned anything from their questioning?"

"No, he asked for a lawyer and hasn't said anything. His lawyer is demanding that he be released or charged."

"This president and the attorney general are philosophically opposed to the death penalty. So, unless the FBI or another U.S. law enforcement agency has a warrant for his arrest, release him."

"What about the Israeli request?

"Deny it."

"Netanyahu will be pissed."

"Too bad, so sad. I'll let the AG know." The chief of staff walked out of the room.

THURSDAY, DECEMBER 22ND, 2016, 9:00 A.M. LOCAL TIME, WASHINGTON, D.C.

The head of the international affairs division of the Justice Department was instructed to send a terse response to the Israelis that stated that the extradition request was denied. The attorney was instructed not to call the Israeli embassy or discuss the denial. If asked, he was to say the request was reviewed by the highest levels of the Justice Department and turned down. The officer signing the letter was also instructed not to tell the Israelis that Dawuud Ghanem was released at 1600 on Wednesday, December 21st.

None of the Israelis staff members knew that Andrei Kovalenko called Zvi the moment he learned Ghanem Dawuud was about to be released. When Ghanem walked out of the FBI building, the first member of the Mossad team assigned to tail him followed about 50 feet behind him. Their instructions were not to lose him.

THE SAME DAY, 11:07 A.M. LOCAL TIME, FORT MEADE, MD

Jim Birdwell was translating a message for one of his colleagues when the upper right part of his screen flashed red telling him that a phone number he had flagged had made a call. He waited a few seconds before downloading a copy of the file to his computer.

Then, he listened to the call between two men setting up a meeting with another unnamed person. He copied down the address of a hotel in Rawalpindi, Pakistan.

He logged his analysis of the call and then forwarded his reports to the station chief to see if he could have an asset observe the meeting and, if possible, take pictures. He gave a short history of the use of the phone and why the CIA should be there. His role finished; Birdwell went back to the translation he'd been working on.

FRIDAY, DECEMBER 23RD, 2016, 3:39 P.M. LOCAL TIME, NEW YORK CITY

In the second bedroom of his apartment, Kassab set up two tables. One was a mini electronics workshop. At one end, 12 pale orange, clay-look-alike bricks wrapped in clear plastic were neatly stacked. Each brick weighed one kilo.

On the other end of the table, three boxes of Hornady 00 Buckshot used for reloading shotgun shells sat, waiting to be opened. Each box contained five pounds of .35-inch diameter lead balls hardened with antimony.

Kassab's first step was to unwrap and flatten a SEMTEX brick on a parchment paper sheet into a one-centimeter-thick sheet. The 00 buckshot was sprinkled on the explosive and then pressed into the clay-like material. The sheets were used to line the inside of a cardboard box.

The box, now with two sheets of SEMTEX and buckshot, was placed in the center of a hard-sided, expandable suitcase around which Kassab wedged rolled-up t-shirts to keep the box in place. Satisfied, he closed the lid and swung the suitcase around to see if the load would shift. It did not.

Five more boxes were made, and Kassab laid the open suitcases in a row on the floor and sat at the electronics bench. He dialed the five cell phones to ensure they worked before he finished building the bombs.

All that was left to do was insert the detonators into the plastic explosive and connect the triggering devices. That Kassab would do just before he went to place them.

THE SAME DAY, 4:58 P.M. LOCAL TIME, WASHINGTON D.C.

Ghanem walked out of the apartment he had been renting on P Street NW for six months carrying a backpack and towing a roller bag. He stopped at the curb to wait for the cab he called whose dispatcher said it would arrive at 1700.

He looked down at his watch and then up the street. The last sound he heard was a faint zzzzzzip just before the 5.56mm M855A1 round entered his forehead. Ghanem collapsed, blood leaking from the hole made by the hollow point bullet that shattered as it went through his skull and destroyed his brain. A passerby started screaming when she saw the growing pool of blood.

CHAPTER 21

PLAN B

After he watched the news reports and read what was in the papers, Na'il felt he failed. He could easily blame American intelligence or a traitor within al-Qaeda. If he returned to Afghanistan, he would be blamed for its failure, rightly or wrongly. He could turn himself in as an al-Qaeda defector, but that would be giving up. What kind of deal would the FBI give him? Plus, defecting put a target on his back. Or he could modify the plan. To Na'il, there was no choice.

Early in the day, he called Abbas Salib to instruct his team to lay low and they will be contacted. He was sure that none of the men captured knew how the missiles and equipment got into the country. Salib and his crew would be funded, and the *Mary Beth* used again.

Then, Na'il called Qusay Jabbor, the man he thought was most at risk because he had set up the bank accounts. Na'il suggested he return to Saudi Arabia and go to Pakistan or Afghanistan, where he could manage the funds. For Jabbor, the priority was escape.

Na'il used the subway ride out to Long Island City, and the 13-block walk to the small warehouse rented to act as a temporary storage facility gave to think through a new plan. He suspected he was now a wanted man and leaving the U.S. on his valid U.S. passport or the Syrian or Pakistani ones given to him by al-Qaeda was much too risky. Anyway, where would he go? What would he do for money?

He was a soldier in a war with a mission to accomplish. Even though many, if not all, the troops under his command were either dead or captured, Na'il owed them to carry out their mission.

The conclusion gave him a sense of purpose as he connected the battery to the panel van and turned the key. The van fired right up, and after a quick inspection, Igla-S serial numbers 9K-338-S-004546-VAD-10 and 9K-338-S-004547-VAD-10 appeared untouched. The missiles went in first, then two crates, each with 30 loaded magazines for an AK-47. An AK-47 and a Glock went on the floor next to the crates wrapped in a blanket. Another AK was laid in the passenger's footwell, and a second Glock 19 was shoved into a holster on his right side. Six extra 15-round magazines for the pistol were stuffed into the pouch pockets in his 5.11 Tactical parachute pants.

The work had, according to his watch, taken him 22 minutes. After driving out of the storage area, he pulled into a supermarket parking lot, loaded each AK, and slipped nine magazines into the tactical vest. Ten spare loaded magazines for the assault rifle went into a small duffel bag and 10 more in another.

Na'il knew where he wanted to go, and getting there would take about an hour. Once in the vicinity, he would find a place to park and wait before moving into position.

THE SAME DAY, 11:46 A.M. LOCAL TIME, STATEN ISLAND

The two RPG launchers fit easily in one of the bags used to carry the Outrage's cushions, and the 12 rockets fit into another. Morcos had a third duffle filled with two AK-47s and 30 full magazines. He had a Glock 19 pistol in a holster under his coat and three spare magazines in a pocket.

Daniel Morcos nodded to the young man who wanted to become a shahid or suicide bomber. When they were introduced, Daniel said that he had something much more important that would cause more damage than blowing himself up inside a crowded store. The young man he knew only by his first name, Mohammed, readily agreed.

The 20-year-old was excited even though it was probably his last day on earth. If Daniel's reconnaissance was accurate, within an hour, they would both be martyrs after hurting the American economy.

The duffle bags went along the sides of the Outrage's raised platform that was its 'bridge.' Mohammed cast off and did as he was told - sit down and wait. They would unpack the weapons and get them ready once they were out in the river and away from the Tottenkill Marina.

THE SAME DAY, 12:36 P.M. LOCAL TIME, HOWARD BEACH, NY

On the way toward Spring Creek Park, Na'il noticed that the airplanes taking off from JFK were using the longer 11,411-foot-long Runway 31 Left rather than the shorter, 9,999-foot-long 31 Right. Based on studying a map, Na'il estimated the heavily loaded airplanes taking off from the longer runway would be climbing slowly, roughly 3,500 to 4,000 meters from where he planned to fire the missiles. Perfect.

Na'il entered the park at the end of 159th Avenue and followed the gravel road along the bay until the road turned east. Just before an intersection with another park road that paralleled the houses that bordered the park, he left the gravel road and drove toward a clump of trees.

A 747 whined overhead, and Na'il stopped to watch the slowly climbing airliner before driving to the place he had found earlier. His watch said it was 12:45 p.m. and figured that by 1:30 p.m., he'd have launched both missiles.

He laid the two crates on the ground and opened them before leaning the missile launchers against a nearby tree next to one of his two AK-47s. Na'il donned the bullet-proof vest and the load-bearing harness with six magazines for the AK. Satisfied, he again looked at his watch, which said it was 12:55 p.m.

Now, he had to hide while he waited for the next Airbus 380, Boeing 747, or 777 to pass by. The first Igla-S, serial number 9K-338-S-004547-VAD-10, went onto his shoulder after he turned the missile on so that the nitrogen could cool the seeker. Once the missile was ready to fire, Na'il pointed the launcher toward the end of JFK's runway. Through the sights, he could identify the airplane as another 747. He couldn't tell the airline markings, but the shape and silhouette were enough to identify the airliner.

Na'il watched the airliner rotate. Right after the 747 left the ground, the landing gear retracted. Its nose was pointed to the sky when Na'il squeezed the trigger. The launcher bucked as the missile was ejected out of the tube. The rocket motor ignited a few feet in front of him with a whoosh, and the plume of spiraling smoke told Na'il the missile was on its way. Now was the time to get the second Igla-S ready.

THE SAME DAY, 1:03 P.M. LOCAL TIME, ARTHUR KILL RIVER

The Outrage plowed through the calm, gray-brown water at what Morcos estimated was about 15 knots. He was not worried about getting a ticket for exceeding the posted five-knot limit as he steered the boat toward the line of fuel storage tanks. When the Outrage was about 50 yards from the unloading pier, Morcos pointed at the cluster of smaller tanks as he eased back on the throttles to slow the boat. "Mohammed, shoot one rocket at those tanks and then another at the bigger tanks."

The RPG-7 rocket whooshed away, and the recoil almost knocked Mohammed over the side. The rocket's 730-gram high explosive, anti-tank warhead went through the side of the gasoline storage tank like a hot knife through butter. The explosion set off the gas fumes rupturing the tank, and the gasoline whooshed into a pillar of flame.

Morcos yelled. "Good shooting!!!"

Mohammed reloaded and fired another rocket at a larger tank, probably 300 yards away. The PG-7VL warhead penetrated the tank, and for a few seconds, nothing happened. Then the tank erupted, tossing large chunks of metal 100 feet in the air, and the concussion from the blast shoved both men backward. Shrapnel from this exploding tank sliced through the sides of the three nearby tanks, spilling more gasoline, and quickly becoming one giant fire.

Daniel shoved the throttles forward, and the boat's nose came up as the propellers dug into the water. The Boston Whaler Outrage accelerated, and he spun the wheel to head toward the next target, a quarter mile up the river, also on the New Jersey side of the Arthur Kill River.

THE SAME DAY, 1:05 P.M. LOCAL TIME, SPRING CREEK PARK

Na'il was so confident that the SA-24 would do its job and was so intent on getting the next missile into a firing position he didn't watch his first one. If he had, he would have noticed the 747 was still climbing away untouched by the missile. By now, the airliner had banked toward the east and was out of range.

Now with the new missile on his shoulder, Na'il searched the sky. Departures had stopped, and no airplanes were taking off from JFK.

Na'il didn't know that he fired the missile at an El Al 747 equipped with a directed infrared countermeasures system that detected the oncoming Igla-S. The system aimed a laser and flashing mirrors at the Igla-S' seeker head, confusing the missile's guidance software. Igla-S, serial number 9K-338-S-004547-VAD-10, passed harmlessly below and behind the 747 and headed southeast out over the water. When the motor ran out of fuel, the Igla-S self-destructed. Pieces rained down on the marshlands around Three Cornered Hassock.

Na'il knew what the lack of targets meant. He debated whether to toss the second missile into the van or leave it. He believed missiles were more expendable than people, so he dropped the SA-24, picked up the AK-47 and his satchel of extra magazines, and drove away in the van.

THE SAME DAY, 1:11 P.M. LOCAL TIME, ARTHUR KILL RIVER

Daniel had the Boston Whaler Outrage banging through the calm water at nearly 40 knots. Mohammed was sitting on the front bench, holding onto the railing to keep from being tossed around or, worse, over the side. When the boat approached the next refinery, getting close enough for a good shot with an RPG was impossible, so Morcos headed for the next one up the river with an empty pier.

Approaching the refinery, Daniel pulled the throttles back, and the Outrage pitched forward as the boat slowed. By now, Mohammed had both RPG launchers loaded. The first one missed its intended target, but the second one struck home. The tank exploded, and flames shot out from the ruptured sides. Mohammed quickly slammed another rocket into the launcher and squeezed the trigger. The missile flew true and impacted the original target halfway up the tank, which blew up and set two more tanks on fire.

Daniel gave a grinning Mohammed a thumbs up as he pushed the throttles forward and spun the wheel to turn the boat toward the east to the first target on the Staten Island side of the Arthur Kill. Looking over his shoulder, he could see the black pillars of smoke billowing into the sky. The very satisfying sight told him what he planned was working. Only two more tank farms, and they will beach the boat and get away.

The boat was almost at full speed when an orange and white helicopter flashed past. The U.S. Coast Guard had arrived!

After the first low pass, the twin-engine MH-65 Dolphin pulled up and circled well out of small arms range. Resolute, Daniel kept the Outrage pointed at the next tank farm, and Mohammed fired RPG rocket number six. He was right on the mark. A second followed, and quickly, the fire spread to two more tanks, bringing the total to four at this refinery.

Only two more rockets lay on the deck of the Outrage. When he left the marina, he thought they would be lucky to shoot six. Now, Morcos wondered if they could escape.

Daniel motioned to Mohammed to sit on the front seat and pushed the throttles up as far as they could. The tachometers showed that the engines were just below redline at 6,400 rpm, and the speedometer the salesman said was not very accurate, said they were plowing through the calm water at 48 knots.

I don't believe that martyrs got 700 virgins in heaven. I am prepared to die but want to escape. Mohammed preferred to die as a shahid, so I will do my best to give him that chance.

THE SAME DAY, 1:18 P.M. LOCAL TIME, HOWARD BEACH

Forcing himself to remain calm and drive as if he was not in a hurry, Na'il eased onto Cross Bay Boulevard, heading north, figuring that the sooner he was out of the local area, the safer he would be. He drove one exit to the west on the Belt Parkway. He exited at Pennsylvania Avenue when he saw a roadblock being set up.

Na'il turned onto the next street and headed north, hoping that a white panel van would be much harder to find on the streets than on the Belt Parkway. He did not know that a policeman at the roadblock spotted the van and called his command center.

THE SAME DAY, 1:28 P.M. LOCAL TIME, ARTHUR KILL RIVER

Looking over his shoulder, Daniel spotted a Coast Guard boat behind him that was losing ground to his Boston Whaler Outrage. Overhead, the helicopter was flying slowly but well out of range. He figured the helicopter's crew was directing a net of assets designed to capture them.

"Mohammed, I will beach the boat in a small inlet. You stay to defend the boat while I look for a way out. I'll leave you with one of the AK's, half the magazines, and the two remaining RPGs. Understand?"

The kid grinned back. Right after he spoke, there was a ripping sound, and plumes of water rose alongside the boat. Pieces of foam and fiberglass flew everywhere. Daniel looked up and saw another bigger helicopter he recognized as a Sikorsky Blackhawk flying parallel to his Boston Whaler. Sticking out of the cabin door, he could see a very large machine gun pointed at him. Daniel spun the wheel and another row of spouts 20 feet to starboard.

He was about to learn if the Boston Whaler's advertisements about their boats being unsinkable were true. One of the reasons he picked this brand was that the company put foam between the inner and outer layers of the hull so that if there was a puncture, the boat would still float.

As he steered the Boston Whaler Outrage in an erratic pattern, Daniel glanced at the Blackhawk and saw the gunner tracking his boat with the big machine gun. Anticipating the gunner was about to fire, Daniel yanked the throttles back to idle. The Outrage stopped as if it hit a wall, and the spouts of water made by bullets intended for them rose about 50 feet in front.

First, the wheel went to starboard at full throttle and then to the left. Frantically, Daniel mixed turns and changes of speed to avoid being hit. The Outrage took two more hits before the instrument panel dissolved in a mass of fiberglass, glass, metal, and other parts. So far, nothing vital like a fuel tank or an engine had been hit. By now, they were close to the inlet where he wanted to beach the Outrage where Daniel hoped to get out into the trees and underbrush and escape.

"Get ready. We're going to hit hard."

The Outrage skidded to a stop on the mud and sand just as machine bullets set the fuel tanks on fire. Both Daniel and Mohammed scrambled out with their weapons, and Mohammed found a defensible position amongst some fallen trees. Daniel patted him on the shoulder and pointed in a direction away from the water. Mohammed settled down to wait for the attack both knew would come shortly.

THE SAME DAY, 1:33 P.M. LOCAL TIME, EAST NEW YORK, NY

Na'il's heart was still racing as he sat at the light of Foster Avenue and Pennsylvania. He glanced at the street map, which told him that Route 27, the Jericho Turnpike was the next street. He debated whether to turn left or right when his senses said something wasn't right.

Looking out the side window, Na'il spotted a police helicopter. He couldn't tell if the helo was heading in another direction or flying over him. He reached down to make sure the AK-47 was within easy reach.

The light changed, and Na'il let the van creep forward. Seeing a gap in the traffic, he turned right on Stanley Avenue, figuring he could zig-zag on back streets to make his way back to Elmhurst. The plan worked until he turned onto Vermont Street and was stuck on the east side of Linden Park. In front of him, two NYPD squad cars blocked his path. He watched two more take up position behind him in his rearview mirror.

In the movies, Na'il had seen cars go up on the sidewalk to escape, so why not now? He could see a gap slightly ahead, so he slammed his foot down on the accelerator and aimed the van at the hole. The Ford bounced awkwardly onto the sidewalk just wide enough to let him slip through. He was surprised that the suspension didn't collapse.

Bullets started slamming into the car's sheet metal, and the windscreen had several holes before falling back into the driver's compartment. Na'il was past the police cars when he saw steam hissing from the radiator. The van was done, and now was the time to get out and fight.

THE SAME DAY, 1:46 P.M. LOCAL TIME, ARTHUR KILL RIVER

Daniel paused at the edge of the trees and studied the rail yard looking for signs of the police. Seeing nothing overt, he laid the magazines and the AK-47 down next to a track to make it harder to see. While the assault rifle gave him firepower, the distinctive silhouette of the weapon was also a dead giveaway that he was a terrorist.

In the background, he heard firing. First, the AK-47, then what he presumed was an American rifle firing the smaller, high-speed 5.56mm X 45 cartridge. Between the bursts of a firefight, he heard the whooshing sound of an RPG-7 followed by an explosion. Then, a rattle from the AK and a fusillade of barking bursts from the American M16s. Then silence. Now was time for him to move.

THE SAME DAY, 1:48 P.M. LOCAL TIME, EAST NEW YORK

Na'il didn't have too many choices. He could see Van Siclen Avenue and Linden High School on the other side of the park. The school would be an excellent opportunity to kill infidels, but he did not like the idea of killing kids. From where he stood, he gave himself a 30 percent chance to reach the trees.

The first targets were two policemen he cut down with two short bursts from the AK. His firing announced his hiding place, but if he didn't shoot, the cops would have stumbled on his position in a few minutes, and the results would have been the same.

Na'il jogged to the next place where he had a modicum of cover and spotted two policemen. When he was in the U.S. Army, every year, he qualified as an expert with the M16A3, the CAR-4, and the M94 Beretta pistol. His training took over, and two quick bursts cut them down.

From behind cars in the street, policemen were firing at him with pistols. Their bullets sang by but weren't close.

He eased out from behind the tree and fired the remaining rounds from the magazine at one of the police cars. One of the officers staggered back, hit by one of the 7.62mm bullets from the AK. From his position about six feet above the street, he could see policemen pouring into the area. Looking around as he dumped out the empty magazine and inserted a new one, Na'il spotted a concrete and brick building whose sign indicated it contained public bathrooms.

Running with slight changes of direction as fast as he could carrying the two duffle bags packed with loaded magazines, Na'il dodged a hail of bullets. Entering, he gunned down two men coming out of the men's bathroom. By his count, Na'il was down to 28 magazines for the AK and six for his pistol.

Na'il believed the odds were against him being able to fire them all. He pulled out the drawstring bag with a gas mask. If the police tried to flush him out with tear gas, they would get a nasty surprise. He checked to ensure all the stalls were empty and then stood on a bench along one wall that let him look out the window. Back on the floor, he thought the L-shaped entrance would keep grenades out of the main room.

He expected flash bangs and tear gas, possibly followed by a fragmentation grenade. Na'il already had foam earplugs in his ears and pulled on a pair of sound suppressors. He put on his gas mask and was ready for whatever came.

THE SAME DAY, 1:52 P.M. LOCAL TIME, PERTH AMBOY, NJ

At the intersection of ProLogis Way and Port Reading Avenue, Daniel had a choice to make. He could continue past what he recognized as the New Jersey Turnpike and keep walking until he found a place to call a cab. Or Daniel could turn either right or left on Port Reading Avenue. While waiting for the light to change, he spotted a convenience store on his right.

He had covered less than 150 feet when two New Jersey State Police cars came to a screeching halt in front of him. Both officers came out of the cars with their pistols drawn. Meekly, Daniel held up his hands, thinking he was way too young to become a martyr.

THE SAME DAY, 2:08 P.M. LOCAL TIME, EAST NEW YORK

The firefight between Na'il and the NYPD was going on in fits and spurts. Na'il used the same fire discipline he was taught in the army—short, aimed bursts only if you could see a target, most of which were well beyond 300 yards. The AK-47 was not an accurate weapon, and his had only one setting, full auto. The inaccuracy forced him to use up ammo to force police officers back.

Na'il was changing a magazine while a steady stream of fire aimed hammered the outside of the building. Those that came through the window sent chips of concrete and brick flying. Na'il knew that the 5.56mm rifle and the pistol rounds were chipping away at the bricks but didn't have the power to penetrate. If they had an M-60 machine gun, the 7.62mm rounds would quickly knock a hole in the wall.

Na'il shifted to the women's side and waited. He knew a direct assault was coming because he assumed the NYPD wanted to end the siege quickly.

The first man took a quick peek around the corner at the entrance to the men's room. He heard the clank as a flash bang was rolled into the men's bathroom, followed quickly by a second. The echoes from the grenades were still rattling around the structure as four men rushed into the men's bathroom leaving two behind to cover their backs. Na'il stepped out from where he was hiding in the woman's bathroom, and using his Glock, he shot them in the back of the head. Then, he jumped into the men's room and felled the other two.

After disarming the two who were wounded and tying their hands with zip-tie handcuffs he found on their belts, he took the weapons and ammo from the wounded and dead men. He dragged the dead men, so they were out of the way against the wall.

One of the wounded officers pointed to his side. Blood was oozing out from under his bulletproof vest. Na'il applied a compression bandage the police officer had in his first aid kid.

Na'il pulled the headsets off the wounded police officers and put one from the dead men on so he could listen. Whoever was at the other end kept asking for status. Na'il keyed the mike. "You want status, here's status. Four officers are dead, two are wounded, and I'm waiting for you."

"Who is this?"

Na'il ignored the call and covered the earpiece with his sound suppressors. He fully expected the NYPD to change frequencies and wondered if the NYPD would risk killing more of their officers just to get at him. He was betting that the answer would be no.

One of the dead men had a bottle of water in his vest that Na'il drained while he tried to figure out what was coming next. He didn't have to wait long. A canister clunked through the window and started to hiss, followed by a second. Na'il closed his eyes and held his breath as he ripped off his sound suppressors and pulled on his gas mask. He suspected it was knockout gas because he didn't believe the NYPD would use tear gas on its own officers.

More clumping. Na'il moved back to the ladies' room. The gas mask-clad men stopped when the first man in the stack saw the four bodies and retreated. He was sitting on the commode in the first stall in the women's bathroom when he was thrown across the room and slammed into the wall. Somehow, he held onto his AK-47, and even though he was dazed, he fired a short burst at a shape standing in the hole made by the breaching charge. The man staggered back, and two guns appeared on either side of the hole and raked the inside.

Na'il struggled to get away from the line of fire, but the bullets hammered at his vest. None that hit the vest penetrated, but one hit him just above the vest under his collar bone and the other in the groin, below his vest. They reloaded, and so did Na'il.

He struggled to move to get a better angle, knowing that his life was draining away quickly. Na'il fired half a clip at a shape and saw the man fall. One more killed. He wondered how many that made. He didn't see the man coming through the front door who shot Na'il in the side of the head.

THE SAME DAY, 4:26 P.M. LOCAL TIME, GRAND CENTRAL STATION, NY

As he walked into the Rotunda of Grand Central Station, his backpack sat comfortably on the top of one of the two roller bags Ra'b Kassab was pulling. He started on the upper level on the Vanderbilt Avenue side to look over the area to see if there were any bomb-sniffing dogs or policemen. Seeing none, he started to make his way down to the Rotunda's main floor.

His plan was simple. Place one bomb on each side of the open area, step into an alcove on the balcony, and set them off.

After Ra'b put the detonators in the bombs, he carefully washed his hands with vinegar and bleach. Then, he donned a pair of gloves and wrapped each bomb in the heavy-duty clear wrap that packers use to wrap skids. After each layer, he dabbed the mix of vinegar and bleach on the plastic. He hoped the chemicals would disguise the smell of SEMTEX and dogs trained to smell explosives would go elsewhere.

He was halfway across the Rotunda when an officer yelled out to him to stop. Ra'b tried to act as if he was focused on getting to his train.

"Hey, you in the black ski jacket. I said stop!"

Ra'b turned to the side where he thought the voice was coming from. He saw a transit police officer pointing his pistol at him. About 10 feet away, a dog was straining to get to the bag. The handler, knowing that the dog had picked up the scent, let the dog go and watched the animal run to the bag and sit down. This was all the officer needed to know.

"Take your hands out of your pockets, now." The officer with the gun commanded. People in the terminal started running away, which the police officer thought was good.

The hander called out to his dog. "Rafer, come."

Ra'b hadn't turned the power on to the radio transmitter or cell phone as a safety measure. With one hand out to his side, he started to unzip his coat.

"Stop. Both hands out where I can see them."

Kassab wasn't going to obey. His hand reached the butt of the Czech make Skorpion vz 61 pistol with a 20-round magazine. The fully automatic Skorpion could spit out .32 caliber bullets at 850 rounds a minute. When the butt of the pistol was visible, the officers shouted "gun" and fired double taps from where they stood 20 feet away.

All four rounds entered Kassab's chest as he staggered back dying. His finger closed on the Skorpion's trigger as he fell spraying the ceiling with all 20 bullets.

The bomb squad cleared the Rotunda and needed 30 minutes to disarm the backpack. Then, it took another tense 15 to figure out how to disarm the first suitcase. The second, which had a similar detonating mechanism took less than five.

CHAPTER 22

THE MORE THINGS CHANGE, THE MORE THEY STAY THE SAME

In Muslim Pakistan, Christmas Day was just another day. In 2016, the Christian holiday was Sunday, the first day of a new workweek. If Fatimah had watched the morning news before, she left for the airport, the commentator said Merry Christmas to all the station's Christian viewers.

Because she spent so much time in London, Fatimah was more aware of the day and its significance. For her, because the European and American banks and exchanges would be closed on Monday, this Sunday was the ideal day to travel.

Fatimah was grateful for the choice of cities. Almost hourly flights from Karachi to Gandara International Airport served both Rawalpindi and the nation's capital of Islamabad. Rawalpindi was in Punjab, and Islamabad was in the ICT or Islamabad Capital Territory, Pakistan's equivalent of Washington D.C.

Her administrative assistant had a car waiting for her at the airport to take her to the Hotel Pearl Intercontinental, which Fatimah thought was an interesting choice for this meeting. The hotel was one location in a small Pakistani-owned chain of luxury hotels in the country's major cities. When Fatimah stopped at the concierge desk a little after 11:48 a.m., she was told that a small conference room had been reserved where, if she wished, Fatima could wait there until her host arrived.

The hotel provided a tray of tea, a bowl of spicy chickpeas known as chana masala, and bhalla, a fragrant and often spicy mix of deep-fried green bean paste garnished with dried ginger and tamarind sauce. The pleasant aroma filled the room, and even though it made her hungry, Fatimah only sampled the food, waiting to eat with Sameer.

After plugging her laptop's charger into a wall outlet, Fatimah took a green folder from her soft-sided briefcase placed next to the wall by the plug. For the umpteenth time, she touched the CD in the folder. Now all Fatimah had to do was wait.

Before Sameer arrived, a waiter knocked on the door and asked permission to set the table. Fatimah shifted to the far end of the long table to allow him to do his work. When he finished, the waiter left a copy of the menu next to each place setting.

Sameer was, as usual, late. Fatimah wasn't sure if it was habitual, or a way of demonstrating power or giving his men additional time to see if there was a trap or, what she thought was the most likely reason, tardiness was a way of showing his disdain for her because she was a mere woman. Whatever the reason, Fatimah didn't care and never let his tardiness bother her. This was, after all, her last meeting with him, and somehow, she would not become irritated by being made to wait. Fatimah wanted to get on with her new life as Haversham Private Bank's CEO and her life serving Lord Haversham.

Sameer's presence was announced when the door to the small conference room opened, and a bodyguard dressed in a business suit strode in. Fatimah acknowledged his presence with a nod. After searching the room, he motioned for her to stand.

A woman wearing a dark gray burqa entered and the guard stepped outside. When the woman finished her search of Fatimah, she left, and the guard re-entered, followed by Sameer, who said nothing. He just waved her to a seat next to him.

Sameer put the menu off to one side. "What is so urgent that we need to meet?"

Fatimah had scripted many versions of the conversation in her mind. She wanted to be terse, concise, and firm. There was, in her mind, no going back. "I am leaving Talwar, and the bank's remaining shareholders want to terminate the bank's relationship with you."

"You can't do that! We put you in place!"

"Yes, I can. If you remember, I found the bank and arranged the financing, and you were only one of the investors. All my investors, including you, have been paid back with an eighteen percent return on their investment. I now own the shares free and clear and have sold them to the original owners."

"Where are you going?"

"Sameer, I'd rather not say. The important point is that I am not going to a competitor."

"How do we get access to our money?"

Fatimah slid the CD across the highly polished table to Sameer. "In here are all the documents, passwords, usernames, and accounts where your money is kept. The CD has detailed instructions for you to follow to access your funds."

He kept his hands folded with his forearms resting on the table. His eyes focused on the CD as if the disc was some type of device from outer space.

Fatimah spun the folder around so that Sameer could see the documents. "In here are the necessary letters to the legal firms that represent the corporations I set up and that own the bank accounts. My letters of resignation as an officer from these corporations are here as well. I've prepared all the forms and signed them where needed to transfer my responsibilities to you. They've all been properly attested. I suggest you do the same and courier them to the law firms. They already know that I am no longer involved."

Sameer examined the first two sheets and then let the pages go as if they were contaminated. He glared at her. "Are you getting married?"

"No." *But I am sure I will soon be.*

"Are you moving to London?"

"No."

Fatimah saw a flicker in his eyes, suggested he suspected she was lying.

"So, there is no possibility of changing your mind." Sameer was making more of a statement than asking a question.

"Correct. Just so you know, if I should die an untimely or suspicious death, these documents and a copy of the CD will be released to the authorities."

"Is that a threat or a warning?"

"Neither. It is a statement of fact. I suggest you take it as a reminder that I was your banker, not one of your assets who wants to become a martyr. So, let's leave it that way. I am sure other private banks may want your account."

"Fatimah, you do know you are not perfectly innocent. There is the murder of your partner Saad Nazari who, I believe, you said was poking his nose into places he shouldn't."

"Don't go there. Nazari had the audit responsibility for the bank. I didn't do anything illegal. I merely told you he was poking his nose where he shouldn't. You took it upon yourself to have him killed. And, if you go to the authorities, I suspect you have much more to lose than I do."

The Saudi national was clearly not happy. Fatimah suspected the man had several identities and made a face. One was the successful accountant he was playing now in the conference room of Rawalpindi's top hotel. His behavior reminded Fatimah of her father.

Sameer put the CD in his coat pocket, closed the folder, and headed for the door. Just before he left, Sameer turned and said, "Enjoy your lunch."

TUESDAY, DECEMBER 27ᵀᴴ, 2016, 6:30 P.M. LOCAL TIME, CAMELOT

After the debriefing at the local FBI offices, the employees of Camelot International were told to go home to their families, and on Tuesday, Derek would hold a conference call to discuss what was left to be done.

Eileen and he had just finished lighting the candles on the Menorah on the first day of Hanukkah. They let the phone ring while they finished the blessing.

"Hello…."

"Derek, its Jacob."

"Hi. Happy Hanukkah."

"Happy first day of Hanukkah…." Jacob let a few seconds pass before he changed the subject. "Did you see the president's press conference a few minutes ago?"

"No. Why?"

"He flatly stated that there was no evidence of a coordinated attack. He also tossed the CIA under the bus."

"I'm not surprised. Why aren't you out with some sweet young thing or taking some time off."

"Don't worry, I've got a date. But I just got off the phone with Ed DeCosta and the head of SOCOM, who just got off a conference call with the heads of the CIA, DIA, and NSA. They told him that they wanted to know how to hire Camelot International. So, next week, Ed, Don, you, and I need to get our heads together to figure out how to answer the question."

Derek didn't want to say, "What if I want out of this business?" to his close friend. That was a question for a later day and time. Instead, he said OK and told Jacob to go out and have a good time.

WEDNESDAY, DECEMBER 28TH, 2016, 10:00 A.M. LOCAL TIME, MOSCOW

Citizen Serik Saliemenov stood behind the table next to his defense attorney. He was no longer a colonel in the Russian Army. Once he was charged and had agreed to a sentence, he was stripped of his rank and lost his pension.

Unlike the show trials of the thirties and the secret KGB trials of his youth, he was allowed to choose his defense attorney. He was given the option of negotiating a lighter sentence. In return for appearing as a witness and telling all he knew about his relationship with Novokov and the man he identified as Fadani, Saliemenov agreed to a five-year sentence. At the end of which, if he wanted, emigration to a foreign country of his choice would be approved. Even when he was being tortured, Saliemenov never told the FSB about his Swiss bank accounts. Saliemenov resolved to die first, and knowing the money was growing every year, he looked forward to living modestly but comfortably outside Russia.

FRIDAY, DECEMBER 30TH, 2016, 1:47 P.M. LOCAL TIME, MOSCOW

The man known as Omid Dadiani looked down at his ringing mobile phone. He didn't recognize the number and debated if he should answer. Omid usually didn't answer calls from numbers he didn't recognize, so he let the phone ring.

Dadiani stepped to the curb on Bolshaya Dorogomilovskaya near the Kiyevsky train station in Moscow and looked in both directions as he waited for traffic to clear before he crossed the street. He'd just emerged from the Moscow Metro and was headed toward the Moscow River, where he planned to walk along the bank and make a few phone calls. Only a few hardy souls were walking in the bitter cold on the riverside paths, which made spotting surveillance much easier.

Before he could step onto the street, a black van screeched to a stop in front of him. The sliding door opened, two men wearing ski masks grabbed him by the shoulders and pulled him into the vehicle. While he was being held, a man pulled a dark hood down over his head, and Dadiani heard the door slam shut. He didn't like the process, but this was not the first time he had been carried off to a meeting in this manner.

"Are you Omid Fadani?"

"Could be."

"Or are you Andrei Dadiani?"

"Could be. Who wants to know?"

He was shoved sprawling on the floor and expertly patted down. His Makarov pistol and spare magazines were pulled from their holsters. They even found the Fairbairn fighting knife strapped to his leg.

His wallet was pulled from the back pocket of his jeans along with his Syrian passport with visas that allowed him to enter and leave Russia, Iran, and several other countries in the Middle East.

Dadiani was yanked to his knees, and his arms pulled behind his back. Through the hood, the kidnappers heard a grunt. "Dadiani, if that is your name. The passport says your last name is Boulos, but the face in the picture is yours. You're a well-traveled man. What kind of business are you in?"

"Are you looking for money? I can pay a ransom."

"No, we're not looking for money. We're looking to send a message."

The speaker saw the driver hold up three fingers. He took Fadani's Makarov, pointed at the back of Dadiani's head, and pulled the trigger. Everyone felt the concussion from the shot, and the noise reverberated around the van. The shooter stuffed Fadani's wallet and passport into his back pocket. A folded-up letter went into his jacket pocket that was zipped up.

As the van skidded to a stop, the driver shouted now. "Now."

The van door opened, and the shooter and his helper shoved Dadiani's body onto the street. The corpse slid to a stop at the entrance to the Syrian embassy. The embassy guards quickly found the note handed to the embassy's head of security. It said,

> The next time you want to buy arms for your terrorist friends, go through the proper channels, or their supplies will be cut off.

SATURDAY, DECEMBER 31ST, 2016, 12:26 P.M. LOCAL TIME, LONDON

As she sipped a glass of an Australian Shiraz, Fatimah was surprised that Alain Ducasse's restaurant at the Dorchester Hotel was not crowded. She was swirling the half-filled glass around to enjoy the rich, fruity aroma when Lord Haversham approached the table.

She stood to greet her guest. "Fatimah, you look spectacular."

Fatimah smiled at the compliment. Ever since she walked out of the offices of Talwar yesterday, she felt free despite the chastity belt circling her waist and the leather harness strapped tightly to her body. Every day she'd been in Pakistan, on Lord Haversham's order, she called a number. Maid Daphne answered and gave her instructions on which harness and collar she was supposed to wear, which of the selection of plugs was supposed to be inserted in her vagina and anus, and when. At night, the cuffs around her legs were to be connected by the chrome chains and clips given to her by Lord Haversham.

When Fatimah boarded Haversham's Gulfstream V in Karachi, she felt free and in control. She was almost giddy when she went through immigration at Farnborough Airport, confident she would never return to Pakistan or the Arab world. For the past two weeks, she'd been living out of a suitcase in a hotel in Karachi because her belongings were packed and now air cargo someplace between Karachi and London.

When she finished packing her apartment, Fatimah was surprised at how little she owned other than an investment portfolio worth about 25 million pounds sterling. That, she thought, would continue to get bigger. Material things she could always buy.

"What are you drinking?"

"Shiraz…"

Haversham turned to the waiter. "Laphroaig. Double neat."

The waiter nodded and moved off.

"So, are you ready to get started?"

Fatimah smiled as she bobbed her head vigorously. "Yes, absolutely. My flat in London goes on the market next week."

"Wonderful. I'll pick you up at your flat later, about four. I have a few things to finish up, and then we can fly out to Basingstoke."

"That sounds great." Fatimah took a sip of her wine. "I need to tell you something that is very, very confidential. It won't take long."

Lord Haversham leaned over. "I am listening."

"One of Talwar's clients that I used to manage was a group of not very nice people…" Fatimah told him about Sameer and who she knew they were.

When she finished, Lord Haversham thought for a few seconds. "Your background check came up squeaky clean, and the Financial Services Authority has nothing. You received high marks from your former employers and clients. Have you thought about going to the authorities?"

"I can't because doing so would violate my confidentiality agreements. My role as a banker was not to make judgments on what my clients do for a living or with their money."

"I see. So, what is the favor?"

"I will give you an envelope containing instructions, documents, and a CD. There are only four copies. One is at my law firm in London, one was given to the client, one sits in my bank safe deposit box at Coutts, and the fourth is one I'd like to give you. If I meet an untimely death or die under mysterious circumstances, please work with my law firm and turn the material over to the British government and the Americans."

"I can do that."

Fatimah handed Lord Haversham an envelope with several documents and a CD. He pulled out the top sheet, a letter Fatimah and her attorney signed. "Thank you."

Fatimah leaned over and kissed Lord Haversham on the cheek. She paused to let her breath caress his ear and whispered. "I can't wait to discover what you have planned for me this weekend."

Lord Haversham smiled and took a card from his coat pocket that he placed on the table. "After we finish lunch, go to this address where you have a two-thirty appointment. This store is owned by Victoria House. There, they will take your measurements and fit you with a new body harness that you will wear unless instructed otherwise. You will also be given clothes and instructions on the devices you will bring back. They will arrange for a car to bring you to the heliport where you will wait for me."

Fatimah bowed her head slowly and whispered. "Yes, Lord Marston. As you wish." Her groin stirred with anticipation of what her life was about to become.

THE SAME DAY, 9:30 A.M. LOCAL TIME, ALEXANDRIA, VA

When Adnan Maalouf was ushered into the United States District Court for the Eastern District of Virginia courtroom, he noticed two armed guards by the main door to the courtroom. He could count the other people in the courtroom on one hand. His father was sitting on a bench behind Adnan and his attorney. The prosecutor was at his table, and the court recorder sat at a small desk next to what he presumed was the empty jury box.

He no sooner sat down when the bailiff entered and said in a loud, firm voice, "All rise."

The judge, a white-haired man wearing glasses, entered, and looked around the courtroom. Once he sat down and was comfortable, he banged the gavel and announced that the court was now in session. The court recorder's hands came up, ready to record, when the judge commanded, "Adnan Maalouf, please rise."

Adnan did as he was ordered. "You have been charged with fifteen counts of espionage and aiding and abetting terrorists. Has your attorney discussed the seriousness of these charges in detail with you?"

"Yes, sir, he has."

"And has he reviewed the plea bargain agreement reached with the prosecutor with you?"

"Yes, sir, he has."

"And you are willing to accept a life sentence without any chance of parole until you turn seventy-five in return for agreeing to a debrief in which you tell the U.S. Government everything—contacts, tradecraft, material, and information given, etc. Nothing is to be left out."

"Yes, sir, I am prepared to answer any and all of the government's questions to the best of my ability."

"And, you have not been coerced, bribed, or offered any other inducements?"

"No sir, I have not."

"So, in conclusion, you agree with and are willing to accept the plea bargain agreement?"

"Yes, sir, I am."

The judge paused for a few seconds. "Then, I hereby sentence you to life in Federal prison until age seventy-five without any chance of parole. You will begin your sentence and debriefing immediately. The plea bargain will be entered into the court record." He banged the gavel.

Adnan turned to look at his father, but he was gone. He left the room in tears.

FRIDAY, JANUARY 6TH, 2017, 8:14 A.M. LOCAL TIME, WASHINGTON, D.C.

At his daily press conference, the president's press secretary was inundated with questions about the raids the week before Christmas, their impact on gas and heating oil prices, and the firing of a small surface-to-air missile at an airliner. At first, the press secretary tried to downplay the significance, but even the network reporters who were friendly to the president wouldn't let him off the hook. A new, frightening acronym had entered the reporters' vocabulary—MANPADS.

Frustrated, the press secretary held his hand up as if to say, stop.

"Look, if the president thought the threat from the missiles was that significant, he would have acted much sooner. Again, the president and I have stated that the country is safe." He almost added the word' now.'

He paused, and reporters' hands were already up. The press secretary gripped the podium, trying to control his anger and angst. There was nothing he could say or do that would placate the reporters. What he planned to say sounded just as lame as the words that came out of his mouth when he wrote them. "This is not to say there are not terrorists out there who may have MANPADS. However, some networks like Fox News need to ensure they have all the facts before accusing the president of neglecting his duties to the American people. That is all I am going to say on the matter."

MONDAY, JANUARY 9TH, 2017, 2:38 P.M. LOCAL TIME, BASINGSTOKE

The English winter was in full swing outside the brick and stone walls of what used to be the manor house of Haversham estates. Signs of moisture—rain or dew—were everywhere. And, while the temperature hadn't dipped below freezing, the damp cold penetrated everything. As usual in England during the winter, the sky was gray— the sun hadn't been seen for days.

But Fatimah didn't care. There was a lot to be done. Work was now mixed with intense sexual pleasure. As she cautioned Lord Haversham when he offered her this job, just because one has a license for a private bank, the document doesn't mean you have one. She created a detailed work plan that was approved by Lord Haversham. It had a list of tasks in sequence in which they needed to be done. One of the critical items was a list of people that needed to be found, interviewed, and hired.

The goal was to have Haversham Private Bank fully operational by July 1st, 2017. By offering lucrative compensation packages and the headquarters located in Basingstoke with a satellite office in London, she recruited some of the top bank operations people with extensive private and investment banking experience. Fatimah was surprised that half of the initial cadre of 24 employees agreed to move out to Basingstoke.

The better part of her job was what Lord Haversham did to her physically when she was not in the office. In the house, Fatimah wore a simple smock, either a shade of gray or black. Underneath, based on Lord Haversham's pleasure, she wore a tight-fitting leather harness or a stiff leather corset that came up to her chin, which prevented her from turning her head. Chrome steel chains connected her wrists and ankles and restricted her movement.

When they went out as a couple, she wore the chastity belt and leather harnesses selected by her master. At night, they shared a bed in which Lord Haversham catered to every one of her fantasies. And then, some.

TUESDAY, JANUARY 31ST, 2017, 12:07 P.M. LOCAL TIME, DUBAI, U.A.E

At Dubai International Airport, Sameer Rahal slid his passport through the slot to the immigration officer. The officer took his passport and fanned through the pages noting that the man on the other side had been to India, Syria, Egypt, and Iran and had a long-stay visa for Pakistan since the passport was issued five years before. These were not unusual, but nonetheless, the man triggered the camera.

"Mr. Rahal, why did you come to the United Arab Emirates?"

"I have a business meeting."

The immigration officer for the Emirate of Dubai, one of the seven emirates or kingdoms that make up the United Arab Emirates, nodded. "How long are you planning to stay?"

"Three days."

"Welcome to the U.A.E. Enjoy your stay."

Outside the terminal, Sameer took a cab to the Radisson Hotel in Dubai and, on the way, debated as to if he should call his father. When he left Aramco to join al-Qaeda in 1999, he was the head of financial planning and analysis. Since his departure from Afghanistan many years before, Sameer had not spoken to his father, who was in his sixties when he left, was still alive.

At the hotel, the nagging thought dragged him toward the telephone. He started to pick up the phone and just couldn't. Too many angry words were said, and opposing positions taken. There was no room for compromise, and Sameer's hand fell into his lap. He just couldn't make the call and re-open old wounds.

Standing in front of the large window in his room on the west side of the creek, he could see the British embassy and the U.S. consulate. From his tenth-floor room, he watched a large yacht, guessing the boat was at least 30 meters long, move down the river toward one of the marinas. He'd forgotten how wealthy the U.A.E. had become, and the wealth was no longer from oil. The country was now a transportation hub and the financial center for the Arabian Gulf.

To Sameer, Dubai had become very Westernized making it another London or New York in Arab clothing. The moderate Arab government would, he believed, must be taken down after those in the West.

Walking along the small river called Dubai Creek gave him a chance to see if he was being followed. If he was, he couldn't tell.

Qusay Jabbor apologized for being late, saying he'd taken some project work from KPMG since he returned from the U.S. Sameer asked a few questions to see if he was still committed to the cause. Satisfied that he was, Sameer shifted to the purpose of the lunch meeting.

"What is left of the infrastructure that you set up?"

Jabbor was prepared for the question. He took a sheet of paper from his briefcase and handed the document to Sameer. "This is a list of the bank accounts that were not used by Morcos or me to write checks. They are all still active, and you see the funds still in them. Every month, I log in and check the balances to make sure the money is still there. We still have some assets in place we pay them from these accounts."

Sameer put the sheet down on the table in a spot he was sure was dry. "This is good, very good."

The younger man, eager to please, added, "The lease on the warehouse near Portland, Maine expires in June, along with the one for the slip for *Mary Beth*. We need to either renew or let them go."

"What's there?"

"I don't know, but Abbas Salib would."

"Where is he?"

"Still in the U.S. He still has his crew, and before I left, I called him and told them to lay low. Their bank account gets an automatic deposit every other week of five thousand U.S. dollars. The transfers are not reported to the U.S. government if we stay under ten thousand dollars. They also have valid credit cards, and the bills are emailed to me so I can pay them from the funds in the accounts on the list I gave you. Every week, they take the boat out for a short cruise and pay for the fuel with a credit card. We have enough money in these accounts for another year."

"Where are the leases?"

"I have scanned copies on a thumb drive. The originals are in a safe deposit box in a bank in Portland."

Sameer thought about the young man's answers. "Where are you working now?"

"First Gulf Bank. I'm on a project in their Treasury and Global Markets Group."

"How much do you know about international banking rules and regulations?"

"I'm not an expert. Why?"

"Learn as much as you can. We need someone familiar with international banking rules and regulations who knows how to move money without the authorities knowing the purpose of the fund transfer."

"I can do that."

"Excellent."

Qusay looked up as the waiter put their meals on the table. "One more question. Can you go back to America?"

"To be safe, I would need a new identity because I set up the accounts for Morcos. So, yes, I could go back because I don't think I am known to the American C.I.A. or F.B.I."

Sameer smiled. "Excellent. In the future, we will have much more work for you."

MONDAY, MARCH 13ᵀᴴ, 2017, 2:22 P.M. LOCAL TIME, BONHAM

Rather than use the same contract vehicle as it did before through Logistics Support Corporation, the Special Operations Command issued a new contract directly to Camelot International. The new commercial relationship allowed the CIA, DIA, or NSA to task Camelot International with the approval of SOCOM. The command would hold his employee's clearances, and the new contract specified that the missions would be assigned and funded as needed. Active duty and/ or reserve personnel would be officially assigned if appropriate. The agreement also stipulated that Camelot International maintain a secure place for business and operations. It could bill the SOCOM for that facility every month at its actual cost-plus five percent for overhead.

The message to Derek and the others who worked at Camelot International. The fight with al-Qaeda and other terrorists was not over. It was akin to combating a hydra. When you cut off the head of one tentacle, another pops up. In other words, the counterterrorism war would continue.

MEET THE AUTHOR

F*ailure to Fire* is the second in Marc's Derek Almer Counterterrorism series. Each of plots in the series are based on threats that the U.S. Government is reluctant to discuss but are real to this country. They all take place in the 21st Century.

The first novel – *Flight of the Pawnee* - was an Amazon #1 Best Seller when it was released in January 2020 and then re-released in June 2023. The hero in the series is Derek Almer, a Naval Aviator and helicopter pilot.

At the time this second edition of *Failure to Fire* is released in August 2023, Marc will have published novels in three different series. The Josh Haman series —*Cherubs 2, Big Mother 40, Render Harmless, Forgotten, Inner Look, Moscow Airlift, and The Simushir Island Incident* – follows the career of a young Naval Officer and Naval Aviator from when he arrives in Vietnam in 1970 until he retires after an incident off the coast of South Korea in 1996.

Big Mother 40 was selected as one of the Top 100 War Novels of All Time by Amazon. *Forgotten* has won two national awards— Historical Fiction Finalist in the 2017 Indie Next Generation Book Awards and Finalist in Fiction in the 2017 Literary Excellence.

He is writing an Age of Sail series, the first three of which have been published: *Raider of the Scottish Coast, Carronade*, and *Death of a Lady. Raider of the Scottish Coast* became an Amazon #1 Best Seller. The novels follow the life and careers of Jaco Jacinto, Continental Navy, and Darren Smythe, Royal Navy, as their careers progress and often intersect.

Marc is a retired Navy Captain, Naval Aviator, and combat veteran of Vietnam, the Tanker Wars of the 1980s, and Desert Shield/Storm. is a frequent contributor to military publications and a professional speaker on leadership, military history, and business development.